*Who knoweth whether
thou art come to the kingdom
for such a time as this?*

Contemporary Fiction by Susan McGeown:

Recipe for Disaster

Rules for Survival

A Well Behaved Woman's Life

The Butler Did It

Joining The Club

Embracing The Truth

The Best Secret

Historical Fiction by Susan McGeown:

A Garden Walled Around Trilogy:
Call Me Bear
Call Me Elle
Call Me Survivor

Rosamund's Bower

No Darkness So Great

Nonfiction by Susan McGeown:

Biblical Women and Who They Hooked Up With

Biblical Warrior Women and Their Weapons

Jerusalem Times:
JT: The Jesus of Nazareth Edition
JT: The Twelve Apostles Edition

God's Phoenix Woman

The Rise of the Mighty (A Study of Acts)

What We Believe

C.S. Lewis & Me

Old Testament 101

The Parables of Jesus

Prayer & Me

Windermere Plantation

By Susan McGeown

Faith Inspired Books

www.susanmcgeown.com

Published by Faith Inspired Books

3 Kathleen Place, Bridgewater, New Jersey 08807

www.FaithInspiredBooks.com

This is a work of fiction.

Names, characters, places and incidents

either are the products of the author's imagination.

Any resemblances to actual persons, living or dead,

events or locales, are entirely coincidental.

Footnotes and bibliographic credit appears at the end of this
work.

Magnificent cover art painting

"Cows at the Old Windmill"

by Jill Tattersall Used by permission.

www.Jilltattersall.com

To God's Warrior Women

who despite the trials, tribulations, chaos and calamity of life
still strive daily to:

overcome the past and embrace the future,

obey God's still small voice,

depend on God's promises, and

commit to following God's call.

For God has not given us a spirit of fear and timidity, but of power, love, and self-discipline. 2 Timothy 1:7

Table of Contents

Cast of Characters

The Great House

- Mena Westwood - Plantation teacher
- Mrs. Moira Wagner - Head housekeeper
- Mr. Walter Wagner – Butler
- Jessie Lynn - First floor head maid
- Mary Jean - Second floor head maid, sister to Silent Joe
- Dahlia – Head cook
- John Paul – Kitchen helper
- Peach – Kitchen peeler
- Fancy May – Kitchen pastry girl

Field Workers

- Graham Rhyder - Plantation Manager
- Isaac & Rachel Freeman Family:
    - Isaac Freeman – Plantation foreman
    - Rachel - Isaac's wife, field worker
  6 children, listed oldest to youngest
    - Elizabeth
    - Abigail
    - Rebecca
    - Deborah
    - Ruth
    - Little Mary
- Big Mary – Plantation worker
- Billy – Worker in the mill
- Karl Jakeman - Stable master
- Elijah Hayden - Head gardener
- Old Maisy – Old black woman
- Silent Joe – Young black man who does not speak, brother to Mary Jean
- Winston – Experienced field worker, Isaac's brother
- Willie – Plantation striker
- Simon – Plantation worker

- Ebony – Field worker
- Ivy - Young woman dismissed from Windermere when Mr. Topher was first employed as solicitor about ten years ago.

Mena's "Harvest Children"
- Crybaby James
- Mae
- Angeline
- Stinky Celia
- Biter Joe
- Whiny Louise,
- Wanderin' Sammie
- Will
- Li'l Winston – Son of Winston

Additional Barbados Personalities
- Mr. Nelson Topher, Esq. - Plantation solicitor
- Audrey Topher - Mr. Topher's second wife
- Lord Phillip Walcott - Owner of the 627 acre Forster Hall Plantation
- Lady Maureen Walcott – Fourth wife of Lord Phillip Walcott
- Phillip Elias Walcott - Infant son of Lord Phillip and Lady Maureen
- Sir Alan Russell – Owner of 125 acre Foursquare Plantation

The Windermere Family
(Resides primarily in London)

- Lord Windermere - Alexander Malcolm St. James, Marquis of Windermere, Earl of Lindsay
- Lady Windermere - Lucinda, Marchioness of Windermere
- Lord Gabriel Martin Windermere – Eldest child and only son of Lord Alexander Malcolm Windermere.

- Lady Wilhelmina Constance Westwood Windermere – Only daughter of Lord & Lady Windermere

England:

- Lady Evangeline Kipling – Mena's friend

Graham Rhyder Family

- Dancer – Graham's horse
- Bridget – Graham's dead mother
- Fiona – Graham's dead wife

Friendship Townspeople

- Reverend Samuels – Friendship's minister
- Doctor Thomas Franklin – Friendship's doctor
- Widow Pamela Smitton - Townsperson

Quakers

- Friend Nathaniel – aka Nate
- Friend Sylvia
- Friend William
- Friend Thomas

"One day," she said with a voice filled with such longing it threatened to consume her, "I'll leave all this and become a completely different person."

"But where would you go?" her imaginary friend asked.

"Anywhere but here," she answered in a voice choked with tears.

Da longer yuh live, da more yuh hear.

Chapter One

"Where the hell have you been, Isaac?" Graham shouted. "I know I'm a miracle worker here on this plantation but I certainly can't be in two places at once. There's been machine trouble at the mill that's had me sweating and cursing for the past hour, and God knows what's going on out in the fields with no supervision. You're as much help as Big Mary is at harvest time."

"I's just got back from da dock, Boss, an' came as soon as I could."

"What fool errand did that witch send you on this time? I swear it makes no sense that you're supposed to drop everything and run and do the House's bidding when it's *our labor* that keeps them in the style they so firmly believe they deserve."

"I's sent ta pick up da new teacher – Miss Mena. She's mighty fine, Boss. Yuh's gonna like her fo' sure."

Graham glanced at Isaac and saw the wide grin splitting his coal black face. "Is that so, Isaac? Since when have I taken an interest in any female since I've been here?" *All four years, five months, and twenty five days...*

Isaac was not deterred. "Yuh's just choosy, Boss. I's not fooled. Yuh knows dat qual-it-ee is worth da wait. And dat's what yuh been doin' … waitin'." Graham shook his head as he adjusted the straps of Dancer's saddle, and Isaac continued baiting him, "Rachel, she says yuh needs a fem-ee-nine touch in yuhr life. I got a feelin' dat dis Miss Mena is gonna be it."

That brought Graham to a halt. "And what brought Rachel to her conclusion?"

Isaac attempted not to laugh, but failed. "I's believe it has somethin' ta do with da fancy bit of stitchin' yuh did on yuhr pants da other day, Boss. Even I cud see dat was some sorry work."

Swinging easily up into the saddle, Graham glared down at his still grinning foreman's face. "It would seem that if Rachel has enough time to examine the quality of my sewing skills and make comments on them, then perhaps she has too much free time on her hands. You'd think between dealing with you, five wild little girls and one on the way, not to mention working full time in the field, she'd have no time to check out my needlework." He looked pointedly at Isaac. "Say, is she interested in darning some socks for me? If she doesn't like my fine needle work she'd be horrified with my darning abilities."

"Ah, Boss, yuh knows Rachel would be happy ta take care of yuhr needs. She may be my wife but she does love yuh somethin' fierce jus' da same." Isaac spoke the truth and the irony of it wasn't lost on either man.

"How's she feeling, Isaac? I swear, seeing her out in the fields with her enormous belly …"

"She's right fine, Boss. Keeps me an' da girls in line wit' jus' a look."

"I've got to learn her secret. She's got to have a big switch somewhere close by that she uses to keep all of you behaving."

Isaac smiled. "When yuh loves someone, yuh's quick ta do what needs ta be done."

Adjusting his hat to shield his eyes from the bright morning sun, Graham chose to ignore that comment but Isaac continued, "And speakin' of love, boss, dat new teacher – Miss Mena Westwood ..."

Graham interrupted brusquely, "You're better at the mechanics than I am, Isaac. Check over what I did to get things moving again – I'm sure you'll see what I've tinkered with. Good thing we decided to do some test runs what with harvest time breathing heavy down our necks."

Both men were silent for a moment, lost in thought. Harvest Time four nonstop, back-breaking months – came in February and ended in May. It was an endless grind of work during which every able bodied individual – man, woman, and child – worked to harvest the almighty sugar cane. Harvest Time was followed by Hard Times, the remaining eight months of the year when work was scarce and threatened everything else necessary to survive. During Hard Times – especially now during late December - Harvest Time couldn't come soon enough for most folks. Starvation or death by labor ... sometimes there was little distinction as to which was worse.

"Ask Billy if you need any clarification about what I did," Graham told Isaac. "He hovered over me like a terrified mother hen the moment he realized I was going to start fiddling with his precious machinery rather than you."

"I's get right on dat, Boss. An' yuh's to stop at da House befo' yuh head to da fields." Isaac had saved that lousy piece of news for last, knowing full well the reaction it would bring.

"What the–, Dammit! For what good reason?! First your time is wasted with a fool's errand, and now mine. I've not been in the fields yet this morning! I don't have time for this."

"Cook's made a fresh batch o' apple cakes ta take da edge off. Maybe dat will help. An' yuh maybe can catch a glimpse of dat pretty new gal dat just came – 'member her name is Miss Mena. Maybe, Boss, if yuh didn't rile Missus Wagner as much as yuh see fit ta do she wouldn't see fit ta lord it over yuh as much as she does. My Rachel says–,"

Isaac's ramblings were left to the wind as Graham galloped off towards the house in a spray of dust and rocks. The day he bowed to that stuck up, self-righteous, pig-headed witch of a woman was the day they could put him in the box and bury him. There was a constant battle between the two of them over who had the superior hand on Windermere Plantation. Had Lord Windermere been in residence for even part of the year, the hierarchy – those groups he and Mrs. Wagner represented - could report directly to him and be firmly in place. But Lord Windermere was busy making his new fortune in the Americas and Graham had never even laid eyes on the man. Hired by Lord Windermere's solicitor, Mr. Nelson Topher, Graham had been charged with running the entire farming and production aspect of the plantation – the *money-making part* of the plantation, Graham always felt compelled to point out. He met monthly with Mr. Topher to provide his report, receive any specific instructions, and collect his pay. Unfortunately, Mrs. Wagner was held to a similar reporting structure with her own significant list of responsibilities, which included the overseeing of the Great House and all accounts. For those who lived on Windermere plantation, it was Mrs. Wagner who wielded the power over living conditions, food, clothing, and, aside from Graham, wages. No one in their right mind, besides Graham of course, had the temerity to cross the woman with anything but the utmost respect and caution. *Money is king.*

Only once had Graham questioned the Windermere Plantation's hierarchical structure which, he had pointed out, caused such a divisive power struggle. "Lord Windermere has always been a cautious businessman," Mr. Topher had intoned as he'd peered pointedly at Graham over his spectacles. "He believes that division of power is essential to ensure honesty and integrity amongst employees. He is a wise man who trusts no one: not family, not friends, not employees. Because of that, he is wealthy *and* powerful." The implication was that should Graham have issues with the way the plantation was being run, it was a glaring black mark against his honesty and integrity. And, having arrived with a significant black mark before he'd even had a chance to prove himself simply by the fact of who he was and where he'd come from, Graham knew that wisdom favored his silence and capitulation.

His horse, Dancer, skidded to a halt and had his head in the water trough before Graham had made it to the front door. Striding through the front vestibule over the polished mahogany floors, Graham initiated power struggle number one. He was supposed to enter the house only through the back kitchen servant's entrance. The sharp staccato of his boot heels sounded like small explosions as he tramped through the long main hallway towards the back of the house where Mrs. Wagner's small office was located. Without bothering to knock (power struggle number two), Graham pushed open the door. "Just what the hell do you need to speak to me about that is more important than me seeing to my duties in the field?"

The startled female gasp Graham heard was the first clue that Mrs. Wagner was not alone. Mrs. Wagner didn't gasp. Hell, she didn't cry, didn't raise her voice … Graham seriously doubted whether the woman even had a beating heart. And she would never give him the satisfaction of reacting to his confrontational behavior. "Ah, here he is, Miss Westbrook. We will maintain proper etiquette even if he is unable to, shall we not? Ms. Mena Westbrook, may I introduce to you our field overseer, Mr. Graham Rhyder?" Her brief glance acknowledged to Graham her counter attack; his proper title was Manager, not merely a field overseer.

The young woman stood and hesitantly extended her white gloved hand, seemingly oblivious to the tension swirling around her. "Mr. Rhyder, sir. How do you do?"

Belatedly, Graham removed his hat, casting a piercing glance at Mrs. Wagner, who was not the intended recipient of this sudden flash of manners. The young woman was surprisingly tall, almost looking him directly in the eye with brown hair, carefully styled, and a flawless, fair complexion that looked to have never felt direct sunlight. He bowed his head briefly, "Miss Westbrook. Welcome to Windermere Plantation." He glanced at her extended hand and then up into her bright, green eyes. What was she expecting? Was he supposed to shake it like a man or kiss it like they were at some fancy ball? He chose to do neither and watched as she quickly lowered her hand.

"Mr. Rhyder," she gave him a shy, tentative smile, "thank you for your welcome."

Done with the niceties, Graham turned to Mrs. Wagner. "Why am I here?" he asked bluntly. "I've got things to do." *And well you know it.*

Mrs. Wagner adjusted papers on her desk, straightened the cuffs of her blouse, stood, smoothed her skirt, and walked around her desk before making eye contact with Graham. "Miss Westbrook has been hired to begin a school here on the plantation and would like to discuss her needs with you."

"And it had to be discussed *now?*" Graham glanced quickly at Miss Westbrook's puzzled expression before he turned to glare at Mrs. Wagner.

"I ju-" Miss Westbrook stammered, but Mrs. Wagner's cool, commanding voice overrode her.

"Miss Westbrook's time is no less valuable than yours, Mr. Rhyder." Counter attack number two as this was patently untrue. "She needs to begin making preparations so that she can see to her responsibilities as soon as possible. I was well aware that you spent your entire morning away from the fields and as such saw no reason not to take advantage of your close proximity."

She managed to make it sound like he'd been sitting under a palm all morning drinking rum and playing cards rather than sweating, straining and knee deep in muck trying to repair one of the main presses. Dialogue between he and Moira Wagner was a challenge within a challenge that danced along the edges of propriety with their repeated attempts to push the other over the edge of sanity and reason. The ultimate goal was to cause the other to say or do something that would cost him or her their employment. Breathing deeply to calm himself, he carefully placed his hat on his head and turned to the young woman standing mutely between two obvious adversaries. "Miss Westbrook, I know you must have numerous things to do in order to get settled seeing as this is your first day here at Windermere. As I have demanding responsibilities that need to be seen to immediately, would it be possible for us to have this conversation at dinner this evening? I don't know if Mrs. Wagner has explained her required eating arrangements here at Windermere."

Miss Westbrook nodded and recited, "The head staff dresses for dinner at six and eats together."

"Dresses for dinner?" Graham shook his head in disgust and gave Mrs. Wagner a pointed look before responding. "So would it be convenient to discuss your needs at that time?"

"Oh, er, um, yes, yes that would be fine. I still have all my unpacking to do and Mr. Topher wishes to meet with me as well."

"Fine. Until six then." He was gone before Mrs. Wagner could launch counter attack number three.

⟡⟡⟡⟡⟡⟡⟡⟡⟡

Mr. Nelson Topher, the plantation's solicitor, took his job very seriously. Commandeering the library, he meticulously set up shop with quills and inkwells, file folders and ledger books. Mena fought a smile as she sat across from him as he shuffled through his papers preparing to meet with her; he looked a lot like how she had imagined Bob Cratchit to have looked in Charles Dickens wonderful story *A Christmas Carol.*

"Now, Miss … Westwood, we will begin with the ordinary constraints of your employment here at Windermere. You are expected to put in a full day, meaning from 8 a.m. until 5 p.m., with an hour allowed for lunch Monday through Saturday. Sunday is your day, although your mornings will be taken up with church attendance. Your wages of £70 a year are more than generous as they include both room and board. You will be expected to dress suitably; however. No uniforms will be provided." Mr. Topher removed his glasses and massaged the bridge of his nose. Once his glasses were back in place, he took a moment to study her from across the small table upon which all of his papers were carefully laid out. "You should understand that your salary is commensurate on *progress,* Miss Westwood. This position is *not a handout.*"

"Why, I'm not requesting one, Sir," Mena felt compelled to respond. "I have every intention of working diligently to educate young and old alike. I've come well prepared and see no reason why I should fail."

"Miss Westwood," Mr. Topher sighed, speaking to her almost as if she were learning impaired, "you are stepping into a situation that has many, many volatile situations to which you are ill prepared to recognize or even avoid. This beautiful land of Barbados has been a world unto itself for well over 250 years, and despite your evident education and breeding in England I fear you are unprepared for the reality of life here."

"I don't understand what you are trying to tell me, Mr. Topher. Could I encourage you to speak plainly?"

"The society of Windermere is very much like every plantation society here on the island and this society is further reflected in the small towns and large cities. There is a hierarcy, so to speak, that the education you are proposing will severely disrupt."

"Sir, the slaves have been free for almost twenty years now. Surely everyone understands *this reality* and must recognize that education not only helps the individual but society as a whole."

Mr. Topher gave Mena a wan smile; her ignorance apparently amusing him slightly. "Surely you must know *true reality* is not that simple nor is it so cut and dried! Twenty years compared to two hundred means very little to families of both the slave and the master, Miss Westwood. Freedom is an illusion that no one enjoys. If you do not recognize that now, you will very shortly during your time here. Freed blacks are worse off now with their precious freedom than they were as slaves to say nothing of the poor bakros who -"

"Poor bakros?"

"Hierarchy, Miss Westwood, societal hierarchy," Mr. Topher enunciated crisply. "Obviously book learning only goes so far and I'm not paid to explain the nuances of life at the very bottom rung of society. What you need to understand, however, because you will face this *immediately* in your quest to improve society here in Barbados and in particular here at Windermere, is that the freed slaves' struggle now is worse than ever. They live a hand-to-mouth existence no longer cared for by masters who used to provide food, clothing, housing, and medical care. The wages they earn, should they manage to find work, keep them teetering literally on the edge of life and death; so minimal that within a family every single member, from the moment they can walk and understand orders, are required to work to help keep the family alive. The elite, the plantocracy, have not ceded defeat in this battle of societal stratification, oh no! They have merely renamed the game and added a few more rules to ensure that they maintain their wealth, their superiority, and their place at the top of society.

"Suddenly you arrive; the why and how cloaked in some mystery." At Mena's start, he nodded. "Do not fret, Miss Westwood, all your papers are in order and you come with a fine recommendation from," he looked down and tapped the paper in front of him, "Lady Evangeline Kipling, from a most prestigious family in London, I note. But I am not an ignorant man, Miss Westwood. It makes no sense to me that out of the blue a teacher has been employed to come here to Windermere to set up a school with a private account specifically designated from which I am to draw and pay out your salary." He shook his head and looked piercingly at her. "It's most unusual indeed."

Mena swallowed, her mouth suddenly dry. "What are you accusing me of, sir?" His silent, judgmental perusal reminded her of Father and she felt the old anger spark to life. "Perhaps I am a thief, desperate to become wealthy and powerful on my abundant salary of £6.25 a month! Or perhaps you fear I am some righteous zealot here to encourage insurgence and take over the island with my army of freed, educated blacks?"

He was completely unruffled by her outburst. "Your letter comes *without* any authorization from Lord Windermere or his London solicitor, and it would be terribly remiss of me to overlook that omission. My lord's absence from this property does not mean that procedures are not followed with utmost care, nor suitable caution waived." He tapped Lady Kipling's letter again, "merely by speaking the name of a family highly respected by Polite Society. I must account for my job performance just as everyone else does, Miss Westwood, which is why I will provide full disclosure regarding your presence here in my next report to Lord Windermere along with all the information – that we have and that we lack – regarding your employment. Lord Windermere would expect nothing less of me.

"As the plantation's solicitor, I make every effort to visit here once a month, usually during the final week. I meet with Mrs. Wagner who reports on the house accounts and Mr. Rhyder who reports on the field accounts. In addition, until further instructions from Lord Windermere or his London solicitor, I will meet with you. In order to receive your pay, you will provide me with a written report of your progress. In your report you should include your successes as well as your failures as well as a list of any required necessities." Mr. Topher began to gather up his papers, carefully placing everything in a small leather bound trunk, summarily ending their meeting. Suddenly he stopped and added, "In addition, I will ask you to provide observations regarding both Mrs. Wagner's and Mr. Rhyder's performance."

"To what end?" Mena asked. "Why would you be interested in my observations regarding the plantation's housekeeper and manager?"

He shrugged, his glance revealing a shrewd intelligence her initial impression had completely overlooked. "There's a saying on the island that I've always liked and have subscribed to with great success. *Mo' eyes, bettah sight.* Why wouldn't I want your observation? If you are honest and thorough, my knowledge of the plantation – and my continued effectiveness in my capacity as legal overseer of Windermere - can only benefit."

Her friend's snort of derision was abrupt and loud; something that would never be heard in Polite Society. "Listen carefully as you'll never meet another person more honest and plain spoken than I. There is no such thing as the freedom you're dreaming of! Look around you. Can you find one person that is honestly free to do whatever he or she wishes with no obligations? The freedom that you're longing for is a fabricated illusion; a trick of the mind, and the sooner you understand that, the sooner you can move forward with your life.

"What you need to do is to decide to whom you are going to give your allegiance. A wise decision brings a personal independence you haven't even considered! I chose to give my allegiance to God and trust that He will care for me in all things. I found that once you have made that decision, then finding your direction in life becomes purposeful and empowered. I'm not free; I'm chosen. I'm not frightened, I'm invincible. I'm not broken, I'm transformed."

Ev'ry disappointment is a blessing.

Chapter Two

Her room was larger than she had expected, with a bed, dresser, small desk, bookshelf and wash stand. After opening one of the two windows, a fresh, strong ocean breeze swept into the room providing Mena with a welcome relief to the heat and stuffiness.

Mrs. Wagner's behavior had been disappointing and Mr. Topher's meeting was worse than anything she had dreaded. The last thing Mena needed was to draw undue attention to herself by becoming involved with conflict and drama here at Windermere. Why couldn't she just be allowed to perform her duties? She'd traveled thousands of miles and had been determined to remain separate and apart from anything resembling trouble. Yet within her first day of arriving she'd somehow become embroiled in the power struggle between the manager and the housekeeper. Despite working diligently to not engage in Mrs. Wagner's pointed jabs prior to Mr. Rhyder's arrival, she had nonetheless been forced to listen to a steady litany of derogatory innuendoes regarding everything from the man's job performance to the accident of his apparently ignominious birth. His abrupt appearance and departure had done nothing to improve Mrs. Wagner's opinion of him.

Stepping out of her office at the conclusion of their first meeting, Mrs. Wagner had unhooked the ring of keys from her belt and carefully locked her office door. She had an ageless quality about her: her behavior made her seem elderly to the point of stodgy, while her appearance was that of a much younger woman. "Windermere Plantation has a rich, vibrant history that *most* of us are proud to be a part of. Wagners have been proudly serving at Windermere for almost one hundred and fifty years and are as much a part of this place as Lord and Lady Windermere."

"Is that so?" Mena had asked politely.

Walking briskly down the hall, Mrs. Wagner nodded. "Absolutely. As his Lordship and her Ladyship have not set foot on Bajan land for almost twenty years, Mr. Wagner and I have taken upon ourselves to treat this beautiful place as if it were ours. We *take great pride* in its reputation, the fine history it claims, and the success of its harvests, and we are actively engaged in continuing this great legacy. Mr. Wagner and I do not tolerate insubordination, slacking, or disrespect of any kind. *Appearance is everything* and under no circumstances will anything but the best be expected or accepted from each and every employee." Mrs. Wagner had stopped and looked at Mena pointedly. "That includes *you*, Miss Westwood. Your behavior and your performance will reflect directly upon Windermere.

"Which brings us back to the topic of Mr. Rhyder. He continues to be employed here at Windermere because no one, as of yet, has taken the time to examine the *true character* of the man. As you have already seen, he is irreverent, confrontational and disrespectful of his betters, and you would do well to remember to keep a distance from that man, Miss Westwood. Reputations are hard to establish but easy to lose, and you certainly do <u>not</u> want his soiled history to sully yours." Mena was puzzled by this lengthy speech. What did the woman think? That she was going to somehow throw her lot in with this man? Was Mrs. Wagner implying that Mena's dedication to her job extended only until she could find herself a husband? Little did Mrs. Wagner know that had she wanted to marry, she never would have left home.

As for Mr. Rhyder, without even opening her mouth Mena had incurred the man's impatience. It had been purely Mrs. Wagner's decision to request his immediate assistance in getting her school started and at her first opportunity this evening, Mena planned to release him from any responsibilities. His barely controlled disdain towards even the most basic of civilities made the prospect of working with him nothing she wished to even consider.

Mena was still reeling from those encounters. Mr. Topher's lecture had managed to outline not only her ignorance of Barbados' history and society but her idiocy of attempting to bring help and hope to an area so obviously in need. Surprisingly, Mena had been unfazed with the questioning of her intellectual abilities; it was a cross all educated women regularly bore in silence. (The silence rooted in the wisdom of knowing when to keep one's mouth shut.)

No, it was the challenging of her integrity…and his accurate judgment of the situation that had terrified her. It had not occurred to her as she had done all her preparation and planning to come to Barbados that the thoroughness of one determined individual could undermine everything so quickly.

She bit her lip, recalling the moment she had decided to travel to Barbados and become a teacher. Evangeline had suggested Windermere … *insisted* on it actually. Now that she was here, there was no doubt in her mind that God had directed her to this very spot. There would have been no one in her circle of family who would have applauded or encouraged her – had she told anyone what she was planning to do. Evangeline had been the only person to whom she could trust. How incredible that her opportunity for escape had been provided by the very arena from which she sought to flee? How terrifying that all her carefully laid plans would most probably be destroyed in a matter of months by one thorough solicitor determined to 'do his job with the utmost care and caution'? Mena sighed. Mere months instead of an open, expansive future were not what she had imagined for her time in Barbados.

Mena sighed. Well, she would do what she found the utmost joy and peace in: focus positively on the future, trust that God was in control, and put one foot firmly in front of the other. Her entire life had been a lesson in survival and she should expect nothing less here in Barbados. Whether she was ill prepared or not, she would continue along this course that she felt called to before she was dragged … kicking and screaming … back to the life her parents were determined to force on her. For there was no doubt in her mind that when and if Lord Windermere learned of her presence at the plantation, that was exactly what would happen.

Dinner – at six sharp - was the oddest experience Mena had ever had. Seated around the large formal dining table, Mrs. Wagner at the head and Mr. Wagner (the house's butler) at the foot were herself, Mr. Topher, Jessie Lynn (the first floor head maid), Mary Jean (the second floor head maid), Karl (the stable master), Elijah (the head gardener) and one empty chair. While only Mr. and Mrs. Wagner, Mr. Topher and Mena had managed to formally dress for dinner, most of the others had made significant efforts to appear presentable. Jessie Lynn and Mary Jean had put on fresh, clean, starched aprons and caps while Karl and Elijah sported wet cuffs and collars (as well as meticulously combed hair) from their obvious attempts to wash hands and face.

Although not being a full day present at Windermere, Mena waited with baited breath for Mr. Rhyder's arrival, knowing that his presence would alter the entire mood of the meal. He did not disappoint. He arrived six minutes late (pointed out immediately by Mrs. Wagner), hands and face clean and his black hair wet and tousled from an obvious dip in the horse trough. Refusing to apologize for his lateness, he hung his hat on the back of his chair, declined to bow his head for grace, and refrained from any of the awkward conversation which Mrs. Wagner presided over as he methodically worked through the food on his plate.

Mena cast sidelong glances at him as he sat directly across from her and had to admit, all things considered, that he had acceptable table manners once seated. On one occasion, he caught her glancing at him and ever so slightly inclined his head; she was sure she blushed. Most of Mrs. Wagner's questions focused around Mena. As the meal progressed, she entertained them with a detailed description of her voyage, describing the beauty and grandeur of the wild Atlantic ocean, and had them all chuckling at some of the rather colorful characters – both passengers and ship employees – whom she had encountered along the way.

Eventually, conversation veered to Mena's needs. Mrs. Wagner repeatedly tried to circumvent Mr. Rhyder by asking questions of other staff members around the table, but it was always Mr. Rhyder who gave the final, albeit brief, response. Karl, the stable master, was uncertain as to whether the main trail out to the fields would be suitable for a horse-and-buggy tour of the plantation that Mrs. Wagner wished Isaac to provide to Mena. Per Mr. Rhyder, it most definitely was not. Elijah, the head gardener, was unable to predict the exact day for the start of the sugar cane harvest. Per Mr. Rhyder, it would commence in early February *just as it did every year.* Miss Westwood was an accomplished horsewoman, and Karl was asked if there was a suitable horse for her to use during her time with them. Per Mr. Rhyder, once harvest time commenced there would be absolutely no horses to spare for casual use. Even Mr. Topher, when asked about the number of young children presently residing on the plantation, pointed out that Mr. Rhyder would be better prepared to give an accurate answer. Time and again as the meal progressed, conversation would stop for a brief moment as Mr. Rhyder paused to finish whatever mouthful he was working on to pointedly look at Mrs. Wagner, and provide a brief one or two word answer.

As conversation at the table unfolded, Mena observed a very interesting dynamic: while making every effort to be respectful to Mrs. Wagner, most people around the table clearly recognized Mr. Rhyder as their superior. Mena was certain that while everyone most assuredly knew the answer to every question, in almost every case they skillfully deferred the final answer to Mr. Rhyder. Mena was certain that Mrs. Wagner knew this as well.

Mena suspected that it was a game played regularly in which a majority of those seated were unwilling, captive participants. Observing Mr. Topher as he worked his way through a dinner of roast beef, sweet potatoes and green beans soaked in gravy, he on a number of occasions seemed to purposely ask questions that reinitiated the odd dynamic.

Jessie Lynn and Mary Jean were not unaffected by Mr. Rhyder's presence at the table. They made numerous ineffectual attempts to draw him into conversation and, when that failed, deigned to smile prettily and invitingly whenever he should happen to glance their way, which he patently and completely ignored.

Only Mr. Wagner seemed completely oblivious to the dynamics around the table, wordlessly working through his meal. Oddly, even Mrs. Wagner seemed disinclined to speak with her husband or attempt to draw him into conversation.

As dessert was cleared, Mr. Rhyder wiped his mouth on his linen napkin, folded it beside his plate, and addressed Mena directly for the first time. "Would it be convenient to discuss your specific needs at this time, Miss Westwood?" Both Jessie Lynn and Mary Jean turned to Mena, mouths open in wordless shock. At last, it would seem the game of dinner had made a new, shocking twist that even they had never witnessed heretofore.

Folding her napkin and making every effort to appear calm and self-assured (which she most assuredly was not) Mena answered politely, "Yes, thank you, Mr. Rhyder, now would be most convenient."

Mena could feel the stares boring into her back, through Mr. Rhyder who followed silently behind her as they proceeded out of the dining room. When Mena hesitated, Mr. Rhyder gestured to her left, indicating that she should proceed out the front door. "The evening breeze is always refreshing at this time of night, Miss Westwood," he explained, and pulling a thin cheroot from his breast pocket, he said with not a little bit of humor, "and I would enjoy my one vice without having to listen to Mrs. Wagner's lectures on the horrors of cigar smoke in the house."

Light from the interior spilled out onto the porch, and once again Mr. Rhyder indicated two large chairs to their left. "Do you mind?" He held the cheroot in his mouth and a match in his hand.

When she shook her head, he set about lighting his cigar. Mena closed her eyes as the sweet smell of the tobacco elicited memories of Father and her home so far away. On its own, the smell was rather pleasant, although had it been coupled with alcohol she would have run screaming into the night. It was not the first time memories overwhelmed her, nor would it be the last. Some would haunt her forever, while others were forcibly set aside by sheer force of will. She had made herself come to terms with the reality of her existence on the long ocean voyage, and knew she would need to continue to remind herself to not look back but instead gaze with gritty determination into the future. She had no people she truly missed – and a few whose absence finally allowed her to sleep in peace. Home had never been a place of promise, and for many years had been nothing more than a prison. Whether she was too weak to face her future responsibilities or too strong-willed to respect the decisions of those in authority over her (both criticisms leveled out her different times by her parents), Mena had left all she knew to travel here to Barbados and was determined to make the most of it.

"You're awfully silent for a woman. Now that's a pleasant surprise," Mr. Rhyder observed as he puffed away contentedly, staring off into the dark night. The breeze stirred the towering mahogany trees above them and rattled the leaves of the sugar cane off in the distance.

"Is it an unconscious behavior that makes you offend at every opportunity or do you intentionally work at it?" She shocked herself with the bold, confrontational question.

He chuckled, not at all put off by her rudeness. "Ah, there we go. I've primed the pump so to speak. Knew you had a tongue in your head." He turned to study her in the dim light. "And, just maybe, a brain in your head as well."

Whatever game he was attempting to play with her Mena would have none of it. "Please let us get to the business at hand. I've been employed to teach any and all who are interested to read and write: young and old. I require a building as well as a set time, preferably five to six days a week, in which to do this. In addition, I'd like your support and encouragement as I try to enlist those in need to take advantage of this opportunity. Other than these few things, I release you from any obligations Mrs.

Wagner seemed to imply you have towards me and my position here."

He gave her a pointed look. "I take it you've had this identical conversation with Mrs. Wagner this afternoon."

"Ah, not yet. But I will, Mr. Rhyder, rest assured. The house employees will be just as welcome as the field employees to the benefits of an education."

"And you're confident you will be successful in both arenas." His tone told her that he did not share in this belief.

Mena turned to look at him. She respected a man who was brave enough to speak his mind and converse with a woman as an equal – a rare and refreshing occurrence. Nothing annoyed her more than to have to battle false politeness and barely veiled innuendoes.

"I'd appreciate honesty, sir. Feel free to speak plainly."

He smiled a slow, easy smile and then looked out into the night. Stretching out, he crossed his long legs, and took a deep draw on his cigar. Smoke curled round them as he drawled, "So, you want to teach the niggahs and such, is that it? All the poor unfortunates: young and old, black or white? Come all the way across the ocean, at the risk of life and limb, to impart your wisdom, education, and cultured expertise on these poor, ignorant savages. You plannin' on savin' their souls, too?" He'd continued to puff away on his cigar, never once looking in her direction.

It was her turn to chuckle. He had no idea that his insulting insinuations were nothing compared to her family's. Or anyone else in the world from which she'd come. It was so much easier to deal with this immediately rather than having to beat around the bush endlessly. "You've stated my situation crudely but, I suppose, accurately."

He turned then to look her directly in the eye. "Why?"

Ah, the question of her life. The one question that, despite numerous attempts, she had never been able to get anyone to comprehend. She had many answers.

Because I need to do this to avoid sinking forever into the darkness of despair.

Because I have always felt a call to teach, and it is the one place in my life where I consistently find joy.

Because nothing else presents the greatest challenge and offers the ultimate satisfaction of victory.

Because it is the one thing I can do that I know I can do well.

Because I believe God wants me to.

Each of these answers had never brought understanding and in the case of her family had only brought derision. Oh to be able to erase their caustic comments from her mind... She could not stand to hear Mr. Rhyder's cutting comments and add them to her memory. She. Could. Not. She was starting fresh here in Barbados. A clean slate.

He was waiting for an answer patiently staring directly at her while she sifted through her thoughts. She enunciated her response clearly and concisely, buoyed by the unexplainable feeling that he was perhaps honestly interested in a sincere answer. Empowered by the reality that *she was here in Barbados, free, finally, at last*, she said, "Because I want to and there is no longer anything to stop me."

Mr. Rhyder snorted a loud, rude sound that echoed across the porch. "Oh no! A crusader! God help us all!" He clutched his heart in dramatic fashion. "God save me from women who think they can change the world. Or even one sorry, hopeless individual for that matter! Well then, Miss Westwood, you're more naïve than I feared you to be." He leaned in, the smell of hard working man and smooth cigar smoke filling Mena's nostrils. *"Wantin' don' mean gettin', child,"* he said in perfect black lingo.

Before she could respond, he continued. "You think that all the poor unfortunates here on Barbados are just going to fall at your feet in tremendous gratitude for your selfless commitment to their betterment?" Mena fought the urge to clap her hands over her ears and close her eyes tight to shut him out. "You think everyone's going to be thanking you and dancing a happy jig because you've finally arrived to save their sorry souls? Maybe you hope to fill their hungry bellies with fancy words and carefully formed letters. Maybe you think that getting them to speak the proper Queen's English will help people forget the color of their skin and the circumstances of their birth? Do you really think that you can give hope back when it was beaten out of them more than a hundred years ago? Do you think the Mrs. Wagners of this world are going to pat you on the back and say, 'Oh what a noble cause, how can I help you?' Who do you think you are," he ground out, "God?"

Mena, forgetting propriety and manners, hissed back, "I'm not here at Mrs. Wagner's pleasure, nor, for that matter, am I here for yours. I've been hired to do a job, and despite your fear at my naïveté I assure you that I am well aware of the daunting nature of my task. You can laugh at me, ridicule me, and even condemn me for my ignorance, but *I'm not quitting.*"

Not at all fazed by her outburst, he chuckled and shook his head. "That's what you say. I'll talk to you in a bit. Life here in," he paused to look away, but Mena caught a bleakness in his eyes that he was not quick enough to hide, "the paradise of Barbados has a way of beating down even the most passionate and committed souls."

Her back snapped straighter and her chin jutted out in defiance. "I am far stronger than I appear, Mr. Rhyder, and I pray earnestly that will not be the case with me. My hopes and my dreams are really all I have left."

He stood, ground his cigar out carefully on the bottom of his boot and tucked it back in his front shirt pocket. Looking down at her, he muttered in frustration, "Did *no one* in authority over you try to get you to see reason in the midst of this insanity?"

Mena stood so that she could look him almost eye to eye. One thing she'd learned was there was nothing a man hated more than when a woman who had the temerity to look him eye to eye in an argument. *Mind your manners, Mena! Know your place! Remember your breeding! Women are supposed to be demure, polite and soft spoken. You'll never catch a man when you insist on trying to best one in a verbal exchange. Men don't want a woman who thinks! Men want women who are quiet, submissive, and docile.* She took a step into Mr. Rhyder's space, and even in the dim light she could see his eyebrows arch in surprise. Good. She was already making a point before she'd even opened her mouth. She spoke with a confidence that had begun to slip a bit over this chaotic first day, but she was rapidly recovering. "Authority is who you recognize as your superior, Mr. Rhyder. I'm very selective with that, although it hasn't stopped people from trying to control me. Every person I know back home tried to get me to see reason in the midst of this insanity, Mr. Rhyder. And so far all failed miserably. If you think you've got the tenacity to match my determination, I invite you to get in line, but I'll warn you: it's a lengthy one. Don't make the mistake of underestimating me or my commitment.

"I'm tired of people making assumptions about me because I'm 'just a woman.' I'm fed up with people telling me what I must and mustn't do simply because it's 'the way it's always done.' And, I'm sick to death of having people tell me I can't do something simply because in their opinion it's impossible. I've travelled thousands of miles, willing to forsake everything I've ever known to have a fresh start here. I'll succeed or I'll fail, but I'm determined to do it in my own way." Turning on her heel, she marched back into the house and up the two long flights to her room before the tears began.

*The low male laughter outside frightened him, and his whimpers brought
Momma to the side of his pallet.*

*Sitting beside him on the floor, she brushed his hair out of his eyes and took
his tiny hand in hers. "Hush now. Ye should be sleepin'. Would that I
could find a way to get ye away from all o' this, me sweet boy. I'd do
anyting to help ye escape this life. Here. Have a big drink of me magic
water. You know how it always helps. It'll take yer hunger an' yer hurts
away, give ye sweet dreams, an' make ye forget for a time what lies just
outside da door that we must face tomorrow."*

*"If I drink it Momma, will ye stay home wit me tonight? I get scared
stayin' all by meself in the dark."*

*"Ah sure, o' course I will, darlin'. I'll stay cuddlin' with ye until the sun
rises," she lied just like she always did.*

Fair words don' prevent wrong doin'.

Chapter Three

"Mornin' Miss Mena. Missus Wagner sent me ta tell yuh dat breakfas' is serve yuhself tween six an' seven. Mah name is 'Lizbeth."

Mena struggled to consciousness and turned to find a beautiful young woman – no more than twelve or thirteen - smiling hesitantly at her. She wore the 'uniform' of a house maid with a crisp white cap and apron covering her plain dress. With her heart shaped face, flawless light brown skin and dark eyes, she was perhaps one of the loveliest looking young women Mena had ever had the fortune to meet. "Well good morning, Elizabeth! What time is it now?"

"Jus' half pass six."

Mena couldn't remember the last time she'd slept so soundly. "Thank goodness you've come to rouse me. I'd have slept the day away."

"Wan me ta check on yuh each mornin' 'bout 6? I gots ta come up an' rouse ev'ry one else. Missus Wagner don' tolerate lateness."

Mena gave her a smile. "I'd appreciate that. Who rouses you in the morning, Elizabeth?"

Elizabeth rolled her eyes. "I got lots a little sisters, Miss Mena: five all tol'. Little Mary don' let no body eva' be lazy in bed an' Ruth starts prayin' 'fore the sun comes up." She sighed loudly in exasperation. "Out loud fo' all ta hear."

"I see. Well, I'd be much obliged if you'd check on me each morning although I can't promise how alert I'll be in these first moments."

The dining room buffet was covered with a collection of dishes, giving off an aroma that reminded Mena she had eaten little at dinner last night. She sat blessedly alone at the vast dining room table listening to the sounds both inside and outside the Great House. Animated chatter was heard in the kitchen with occasional bursts of laughter, assuring Mena that Mrs. Wagner was most certainly nowhere near. Despite it being December, outside the sun blazed warm and bright and all the windows were thrown open wide to take advantage of the still cool morning air. The unmistakable smell of ocean, warm earth, and jungle foliage battled with the smells of bacon, eggs, biscuits and hot coffee. Yum.

Mena gave herself a good, stern talking to as she worked through her meal. So, she had allowed Father to bully and terrorize her for a time. She could not prevent the brief moment as her mind remembered his voice ... *the secrets* ... *the threats*. And Mother's relentless criticisms had been fed to Mena almost from birth, causing her to doubt herself and her abilities. For a time, societal and familial pressures may have caused her to bend in unwanted directions. Mena shook her head, closed her eyes and took a deep breath of the aromatic island air. But. She. Had. Not. Broken.

Almost, but not quite.

No more.

Life, if nothing else, had taught Mena to be a realist, to depend on no one but herself, and to remain committed to the direction in which she felt compelled to head *regardless of what anyone else had to say.* Barbados was going to be easy compared to London! One stuffy, domineering housekeeper was not going to slow her forward motion, nor was one sarcastic, irreverent plantation manager. As for Mr. Topher, well, he alone had the power to destroy everything, but she'd cross that bridge only when she was forced to come to it.

Mena smiled and took a deep breath. She was here, at last, on this beautiful island. Hope and excitement and promises yet to be fulfilled were as potent as the sea air. She'd done extensive reading about the British Colony and had particularly enjoyed *A True and Exact History of the Island of Barbados* by Richard Ligon, which had been written almost 200 years ago in 1657. Of course, Mena had worked hard to understand the colony in a more modern light. Obtaining copies of Father's newspapers were her best hope, and her determined attempts to get her hands on them had rivaled clandestine espionage at times. She'd read every single copy of Father's *The Agricultural Reporter* and had even managed to obtain a few copies of *The Times* ("nigger trash" according to Father) and *The Barbados People & Windward Island Gazette* ("radical insanity"). None, she suspected, gave an accurate picture of actual life in Barbados, but by reading none exclusively, Mena believed she had a more rounded view. As a result, by the time she'd disembarked from the ship, she felt confident and capable. She must remain focused, stay committed, and not let anyone dull her enthusiasm. *For God hath not given us the spirit of fear; but of power, and of love, and of a sound mind.*[2]

Before Mrs. Wagner appeared and commandeered her time, Mena rose from the table, unsure what she should do with her dishes, and braved the kitchen staff. The moment that she touched the door all conversation and laughter ceased and Mena entered a kitchen filled with industrious workers. There were two small girls peeling potatoes, a young boy working the butter churn, two older girls industriously rolling out pastry, and one statuesque woman at the stove. None looked her way until she spoke. "Excuse me; I was uncertain what you'd like me to do with my dirty dishes."

"Ain't yuh a novelty der, bringing in yuh dirty plates. Thank yuh so. Missy here checks da dining room every now an' den to see if der are plates need clearnin' so yuh can leave yuhr bits der in da future."

"My name is Mena Westwood. I've been hired to be the new teacher here at the plantation. I certainly hope I'll get the opportunity to teach some of you."

All five pairs of eyes turned to look at the cook who looked at Mena with a carefully blank expression. "Miss Mena, I be Dahlia, da head cook here at Windermere." She looked at her audience. "Let me see, dis boy here sittin' like a bump on a log be John Paul. My two peelers today are Ab'gail an' Peach. My two pastry girls, who all's I'll say are doin' more gigglin' an' talkin' than work are Fancy May an' 'Lizbeth, who yuh already met dis mornin'."

"How do you do?" Mena asked and all five dark faces broke into broad grins.

"Fine thanks yuh," 'Lizbeth murmured shyly and Mena nodded approvingly and smiled.

"As fer schoolin', Miss Mena, I wouldn' know bout dat. Missus Wagner keeps us all busy here in da house, an' findin' time to fit in learnin' might be hard."

"Surely the youngest ones have time."

"*Can' make money wit jus good looks,* Miss Mena. Even da littlest ones here can help a po' family put food on da table.

John Paul here will take home a small share of butta for his work an he et breakfast an' lunch here, too. Da girls here are day workers, an' lucky dey are ta have dem jobs, too."

"What's a 'day worker'?"

"A day worker," came the cultured voice of Mrs. Wagner from behind Mena, "is a worker who's paid a wage for a *full day* of labor as opposed to a *task worker* who is assigned a task, and is paid when the task is done, regardless of how long or how short it takes to be finished." There was a flurry of activity by every person as Mrs. Wagner stepped into the kitchen. "Task workers tend to work quickly and efficiently because when they are done they can leave and receive full pay, even if it's the middle of the day. Day workers, however, need to be *constantly supervised* because they know they get paid whether work gets done *or not*. As a result have a tendency to be lazy, shifty, and unreliable, which, I might add, is exactly what I've found here in this kitchen this morning."

"Please, Mrs. Wagner, this is entirely my fault. I've just finished my breakfast and interrupted things when I brought my dishes in," Mena hastened to explain.

"Which further proves my point, Miss Westwood, and what I will deal with now. Had things been running here properly and had people been seeing to their *assigned responsibilities* as they should have, someone would have informed you of the correct etiquette *before* you finished your breakfast. I'm sure you have responsibilities, Miss Westwood," Mrs. Wagner said firmly, dismissing her. "Please, see to them."

Escaping out the front door and standing in the shade of the wide front porch, Mena felt a coward when relief coursed through her. Nervously she looked back towards the house, uncertain what to do. Staying and trying to defend Dahlia and the rest would probably only cause more repercussions; her one attempt certainly hadn't done any good.

The magnitude of what she wanted to do versus what she faced was only beginning to dawn on her. "Please, don't let everyone be right," she prayed into the wind.

&c&c&c&c&c&c

"So, you going to sign up for school, Isaac?" asked Graham. The two of them were out in the fields supervising the back-breaking work of fertilizing the plant canes. If only the island's elite realized what substance was so essential to their financial success… The irony was not lost on Graham. Truckloads of fertilizer – human and animal - were carted out to the field and loaded into baskets that the women worked to distribute around the tender new shoots called 'plant canes'. With any luck, these new plants would be reaped successfully in two years.

"Wat foolishness yuh talkin' bout, Boss?"

Graham kept a carefully neutral voice as he stared out into the fields, waiting for the next manure truck to pull up. "The new teacher – Miss Mena Westwood – wants to teach anyone who's interested how to read, write, and cipher – even adults. I was wondering if you were going to sign up."

Isaac, a master of expressions, gave Graham a priceless look of incredulity. "I goin' to do dat in my sleep? Maybe she can follow me aroun' in da dark once I git home an' try ta work my own farm."

"How's the garden coming?"

Isaac shrugged. Life, if nothing else, had taught him to be fatalistic. "Same as usual: taters, yams, corn … If'n da good Lord sees fit we have 'nough ta feed us during da Hard Times. Rachel, she's always hopeful we'll have 'nough ta sell at da market. One o' dese days dat might happen."

At the mention of Rachel's name, Graham sought her form working out in the fields. "She's too far along to be working, Isaac."

Again Graham was graced with one of Isaac's looks, "Yuh go right ahead, Boss. I'll stand here while yuh try ta tell my girl she's not fit ta do work. Don' yuh worry none, I'll come an' drag yuh back ta one o' da carts ta take yuh back home should she knock yuh senseless." At Graham's chuckle, Isaac said with not a little bit of pride, "We's a team, dat girl an' me. We watch out fo' each other; yuh have no worry 'bout dat. 'Sides, Rachel says hard work now makes easy work later once it's time for da baby ta come." If it were only that easy, Graham thought to himself.

"When is she due?" Moments passed as a manure truck pulled up and Isaac and Graham worked to unlock the bed and tip the load out onto the ground. As the truck pulled away to travel back for reloading, the two began to pitchfork mounds of steaming, stinking manure into the waiting, empty baskets.

Isaac sighed and shook his head. "Jus' at da end o' Hard Times. Rachel, she worried she'll go over like da others an' den reapin' time will start. Dat," he gave Graham a pointed look, "we fightin' about. I tol' her no child o' mine goin' ta be born *in* a cane field. Bad 'nough he goin' ta spend his whole life workin' in one."

"I'll speak to Mrs. Wagner. Tell her I want Rachel to work in the Great House for the month of January." *That should go over well.*

"Oh, den Rachel will be out ta kill yuh for sure, Boss. Da stories dat 'Lizbeth an' Ab'gail come home wit' about workin' in da house has Rachel certain she wants no part of workin' dere. She says at least da cane can' boss her 'round."

"Elizabeth and Abigail aren't happy at the house?" Securing Isaac's twelve-year-old daughter Elizabeth as a day worker and nine-year-old daughter Abigail as an occasional peeler under Dahlia in the kitchen had involved negotiations and surreptitious deals the likes of which Graham never wanted to deal with again. Had Mrs. Wagner known he was behind it all, the girls would never have gotten the job.

"Ab'gail, she jus' happy to be wit' her sister. An 'Lizbeth is all right at da house. Truth is Rachel an' me wud prob'ly hear jus' as much complain' from 'Lizbeth if she was in da fields *plus* she'd be moanin' 'bout her hands an' her skin an' her hair …" Isaac shook his head and blew out a frustrated breath. "Dat oldes' girl o' mine already causin' me worry an' she still jus' a chile! I thought she'd be happy workin' in da big house rather den da fields but she seems mo' miserable den ever. Lately, she even fussin' with Rachel."

Graham nudged him with his shoulder. "You got five daughters, Isaac. Don't let the first one wear you out too much or the rest of them will take over."

"Don' I know it, Boss. Don' I know it. Me against seven women. I nevah had a chance truth be tol'. God bettah see fit ta give me a son dis time 'round."

"Will you let the girls go to Miss Westwood's school?"

Isaac shrugged. "Won' be fo' lack a wantin' dats fo' sure. But don' know how we can swing dat. Ev'ry penny dat comes in counts. Even littlest Mary will be helpin' pick up da trash fodder for da animals dis Harvest Time. I know as soon as 'Lizbeth hears 'bout da school she'll want ta go. And den Ab'gail will want ta go, too." He sighed in defeat. "And den 'Becca, Deb'rah, an' Ruth, too. And Lord help me, but little Mary can be da loudest of da bunch when it comes ta wantin'." He turned soulful eyes to Graham who worked hard not to laugh, having had similar conversations with his foreman. "An' yuh know what? At some point, Rachel's goin' ta look at me an' say, 'YOU brought dat woman from da boat!' an' somehow it will all end up bein' my fault dat ev'ry woman in my house is cryin'."

Graham could only chuckle and continue to shovel manure. What had possessed this foolishly idealistic woman to travel thousands of miles to offer a service nobody wanted? Lord knew, based on their conversation last evening, it wasn't for lack of audacity. Graham sighed deeply as he shoveled basket after basket of the steaming, stinking manure. Wasn't it just the irony? Wasn't fate just laughing its damn head off with the games it was playing once again with his life? Nothing appealed to him more than a person with convictions who refused to back down despite overwhelming evidence to the contrary. And if that person was a woman … well, God help him. Make her a tall, opinionated, feisty woman … He sighed and shook his head in an effort to shake the thoughts from his mind. Hadn't his mother, even with all her demons, survived every moment of her miserable life because of her fierce determination? Wasn't he the man he was because of that? And hadn't his beloved Fiona had so much of that persistent quality that it literally killed her?

Miss Westwood's words last night kept running through his head, *If you think you've got the tenacity to match my determination, I invite you to get in line, but I'll warn you: it's a lengthy one.* She'd stepped right into his face, so close that her skirts had brushed against his thighs and her subtle perfume had filled his lungs. Even now, knee deep in offal, he could still remember its lilac fragrance. Her green eyes in the dim light had been almost black, and while he hadn't looked he was certain both hands were tight fists. He'd wanted to shake her, slap her, and kiss her all at once. It was Fiona all over again; filled with passionate commitment and reality be damned. Isaac was right – quality was indeed worth the wait. All this made Graham absolutely certain of two things: he had to make sure he stayed far, far away from Miss Mena Westwood while at the same time do everything in his power to make sure she didn't get herself killed. He was uncertain which option was more impossible.

Rachel, Isaac's immensely pregnant wife, waddled toward him to get her manure basket refilled. Graham purposely slowed down his shoveling so that she had a moment to catch her breath. Wiping sweat from her brow, she glared at him over the dipper of water she drank, knowing full well what he was up to. Miss Mena Westwood had never shoveled offal out in a field – she'd probably never even smelled it. She was from wealth, he was certain of it. While outward appearances didn't necessarily communicate it and her employment as a teacher contradicted it, her demeanor screamed it. From the tip of her aristocratic nose, to the pale white 'never labored a day in the sun' skin, to her smooth, uncalloused hands, right down to her tiny little handmade silk slippers, Miss Mena Westwood was from money – big money – or he was Isaac's blood brother. Formal dinner last night had not intimidated her in the slightest; she was as comfortable there as he was on the back of Dancer. Graham would venture that she hadn't even noticed that the majority of the poor unfortunates who were stuck enduring the "Formal Dinner of Plantation Employees" each night were completely frozen with fear should they misuse the wrong damn fork or put food on the wrong damn plate.

Mrs. Wagner's formal dinner farce was something in which he'd initially refused to participate, only to discover that others had been refused their evening meal as a result. Mary Jean, Jessie Lynn and Elijah had commissioned Karl to speak with him after the third night and explain how his behavior had directly affected them. Karl had carefully explained that while no one enjoyed the formal dinners, part of their pay involved receiving a meal. Could Graham possibly bow to Mrs. Wagner's wishes only for their sakes? It had been Graham's first serious clash with Mrs. Wagner and his first lesson in how diabolically cruel she could be. After Karl's talk he'd shown up for every meal, always a tad bit late, and never having changed work clothes. Despite Mrs. Wagner's endless correction and instruction to others at the table, he had consistently eaten slowly, politely, and carefully using *only one fork, one knife, one plate, and one glass.* Maybe he'd show up to dinner tonight in his manure covered clothes with the stench still powerful enough you could find him with your eyes closed.

But what had truly convinced Graham that Miss Westwood was from enormous wealth was his private conversation with her last night; Little Miss "Because I Want To and There Is No Longer Anything To Stop Me." Only the very wealthy, those of greatest privilege, could be so naïve, and so clueless about the reality of life. Did she actually believe all it took to change a person's circumstances was *merely wanting something enough?* Did she honestly think that Isaac and Rachel wanted to participate in their slave labor existence? (And, yes, despite emancipation almost twenty years ago, Isaac and Rachel were *not* free.) Did she honestly think that Graham wanted this kind of life so that he could end up alone with a few meager pennies to his name and a square of dirt to call his own? Too bad he couldn't introduce her to his mother, Bridget, who'd never known a minute of freedom her whole miserable life and whose only escape had been her beloved bottle of rum. Too bad he couldn't let Fiona explain the reality of loving someone so much it could kill you.

"Because I want to and there is no longer anything to stop me." Oh, Miss Mena Westwood was from money all right. Filled with her ridiculous ideals and idiotic determination, she had no idea what real life had in store for her. She was running full tilt right toward an oncoming cliff. Graham would bet she'd never had to struggle, never had to go to bed hungry, never had experienced grief or despair once in her privileged little life.

God help the woman if she didn't wise up fast and begin to grasp the dynamics in play around her. Could he even explain it to her? Should he try? Graham grunted at the impossibility and Isaac gave him a brief glance. What would he say that would sound any different than what he said last night? Another load of manure was released from a truck and he and Isaac grimly shoveled it.

Maybe it would be better to let her experience the cruelty of life on her own, although that hadn't worked for Fiona, who had never lost her willful spirit; she'd had it until her last dying breath. Little Miss Mena Westwood needed to come to her senses. Of course a few months here would help significantly. Maybe she wasn't as committed as she first appeared. Maybe after a few months of discouragement, disappointment and failure she'd pack her bags and run back to where she'd come from. Or maybe Mrs. Wagner would suck all the determination right out of her. The old witch certainly had a gift when it came to sensing opportunities to destroy others.

Or he could simply tell her the hard truth: welcome to Windermere Plantation, Miss Mena Westwood. Welcome to hell.

"God does not intend for you to save them all, Nathaniel. Surely you realize that. Even when I was with the Friends I understood that reality."

"What ye say tis true, but we must save the ones He sends us! That's why I've come to see you and seek your assistance. Ye may not live amongst us anymore but I have faith that ye still embrace that important fact."

Tomorrow is another day.

Chapter Four

"Tell us, Miss Westwood," Mrs. Wagner said from the head of the table, "how go your plans for the school?"

"Well, I'm pleased to say that all of my supplies survived the voyage. Only one slate was cracked and my two large slates were not damaged at all!"

"Now if you could just find a location," Mrs. Wagner pointed out unnecessarily.

Mena concentrated on cutting her roast chicken into a precise portion and then putting it into her mouth. It had only taken her one or two meals to figure out that these formal evening meals were a study in control, decorum, and negotiation. Say too much and you risked getting yourself and others in undeserved trouble. Say too little and you risked igniting suspicions and unwanted scrutiny. "I've been quite busy cataloging everything. Next on my list is finding a place to hold class – even if it will be just temporary. I'd like to get a few weeks of lessons in before Harvest Time."

"Has Mr. Rhyder provided satisfactory assistance?"

Mena glanced across the table at Graham Rhyder, who sat silently chewing his food as he watched her with a carefully neutral expression. Thus far, for this meal, he had managed to not utter a word.

"We spoke briefly my first evening here. He was quite ... in awe ... with my lofty goals. In fact, if I remember correctly, he used words like 'tremendous gratitude' and 'selfless commitment' as we discussed my intended plans." Graham arched an eyebrow at her temerity but maintained his silence.

"Is that so, Mr. Rhyder? Well, well," Mrs. Wagner put her knife and fork down and folded her hands above her plate. "I'm truly stunned. This might be the first time that I've known you to express a positive sentiment about ... well, about *anything*. I'm so very glad that I put you in charge of helping Miss Westwood find a location to conduct her school. Let me hear what ideas you have come up with."

"Miss Westwood and I need to have another serious discussion before any final decisions are made."

"Yes, but surely I can hear your list of suggestions thus far. Why, Miss Westwood has been here almost a week."

The young woman in question stared across the table at Graham. That's right, he thought, looking into her concerned eyes, this is how dangerous it can be when you attempt to dance with the devil. "Perhaps you have some suggestions, Mrs. Wagner," Graham said smoothly. "Your interest implies time spent considering the subject. Perhaps the front verandah? Out on the back patio? Maybe a few of the many empty bedrooms here in the Great House? And, of course, the library would be just perfect."

Mrs. Wagner sat at the end of the table staring silently at Graham as he smiled insincerely and took another bite of roast chicken. Their mutual dislike for each other was its own presence at the table. "Obviously," she said with disdain to Graham, "you've offered the woman no options as of yet, which is really no surprise at all." Turning to Mena, Mrs. Wagner said,

"I certainly hope you have been able to find something constructive to do with yourself during your first days here, Miss Westwood. Failure to do one's job is a most serious concern. I've had this discussion with you on our very first meeting. Surely you haven't forgotten it already."

"I assure you," came Mena's firm reply, "that I remember *everything* you tell me, Mrs. Wagner. You need not be concerned with my work ethic."

"*On the contrary, Miss Westwood,*" Mrs. Wagner responded, "I am concerned *all the time* with regard to Windermere, its employees, and their performance. *That* is *my* job."

Escaping from the Great House, back to his hut, Graham contemplated that the woman had not even been here a full week and yet every aspect of his world seemed shaken. Usually a day of hard work shoveling manure was enough to wipe every other thought from his mind, but not tonight. After sitting through tonight's farce of a dinner he had been more bad-mannered than ever, having shoveled in his meal and excusing himself with less finesse then even he usually found acceptable. Now sitting on the front porch of his hut – he'd never called it home – Graham had already smoked through one of his precious cigars and was hankering for a second, this one with a good dose of rum.

Not good. Not good at all.

He worked hard and Windermere got more than its money's worth with him as manager. All that he was paid for was to sit on his horse and make sure everyone did just enough back-breaking work so as to not kill themselves. Dead workers couldn't come back the next day. But right from the start he'd discovered that sitting on Dancer's back for hours at a time wasn't enough to keep him mindless or exhaust him enough to sleep at night. So whenever the opportunity afforded itself, he joined in with the labor … to the utter shock of the men and women he was to supervise.

It had not been his intention to ingratiate himself with workers who a mere fifteen years ago were worth slightly less than his horse and cared for even less. Nor had it been his intention to get to know them or to earn their respect or even their friendship. He'd simply wanted to keep himself mindless with exhausting labor; too tired to think, too tired to stay awake, and too tired to find himself a bottle.

That was all.

But Isaac's ready wit and Rachel's giving nature had been tough to ignore. Within two months of starting as manager at Windermere, Graham had promoted Isaac to foreman – the first black man to have the role. It had been a common sense decision and nothing more. Graham wasn't a freed slave activist and had no agenda regarding their quality of life. Not that he had lost much sleep over the plight of the poor 'old plantocracy elite' either, who cried about their financial woes while sitting comfortably in their twenty-two room Great Houses on hundreds of acres of land.

No, elevating Isaac to foreman had been purely a wise business decision; Isaac was hardworking, honest, and dedicated. Plus he had a wife and growing family that he was committed to. So there was no chance that the man was going to up and run off to dig the damn Panama Canal in an attempt to make his fortune like so many other freed blacks had done. But that one sound business decision had cemented two things permanently whether he wanted it or not: Mrs. Wagner's permanent hatred for him and the blacks' tentative respect and trust towards him.

Prior to that, his relationship with Mrs. Wagner had been difficult, but he hadn't felt a committed purpose in place to destroy him or anyone he had found favor with. She had just hated him pure and simple because of what she knew he was.

But by promoting Isaac and putting him in a position that Moira Wagner deemed above his station – a situation that she could do nothing about – Graham had firmly established a pact of war between them.

In all honesty, had he known then what he knew now – how deep seated Moira's hatred and bigotry could extend – he might have thought twice about putting Isaac and his family in her sights. *Lookin' back don' get yuh forward.* After the fact, he'd learned quickly to not show the slightest kindness or friendship to anyone within Moira Wagner's presence. She couldn't fire him or discipline him or control him financially but she did have influence on just about everyone else. And didn't hesitate to use it. She was like a spider lying in wait for the innocent and clueless fly.

Hell with it, he was going to have another cigar. He'd earned it today having dealt with manure, Mena, and Moira. Sitting on his porch, he tried to let the calming habit roll over him: the aroma of the smoke, the red glow of the tip in the darkness, the hiss of the burn as he inhaled, the exhalation of smoke and tension as he blew out. His left hand clutched, itching for a glass … just a finger or two. Or three. Or five. Or a bottle. Cursing, he stubbed out the cigar and got up, the quandary of his situation refusing to be pushed aside, impossible to make disappear. There would be no sleep tonight. There would be no peace. He'd walk the cliffs and maybe take the path down to the water. Life threatening danger sometimes was the only thing to shake his need for the bottle.

What was it about Mena Westwood that caused him to feel so off kilter? No woman had even managed a glance from him in the past decade. First, because he'd had eyes only for Fiona, whether it was the three brief years they were married or the almost seven years since she'd been dead. Perhaps it was the woman's height. Yes, Miss Westwood's height did remind him of Fiona's … plus her feisty spirit. He'd never been one for a simpering, weak, guileless female. Oh no. Give him one who stood on her own two feet, had a quick, ready wit, forged ahead determinedly into the future, with some innate inner quality that he was practically helpless to resist. He'd been known to be foolish enough to fall in love and marry. Once. But oh to have been loved by a woman like that … It was almost as intoxicating as rum…

A vision of Fiona, laughing as she walked ahead of him, knowing he would follow her like a panting dog, filled his mind. Fiona, one hand on her hip and the other pointing directly at him, reading him the riot act over something she needed him to understand. Fiona, reaching out to touch his cheek, with the look of love bright in her eyes. She'd managed to break through all of his bitter, angry layers, pry back all his messed up life's scars and love him without reserve. How glorious it had been to be in love and to be loved like that. Once tasted, never forgotten.

He knew what love was, knew what magic it could do if you had it, and knew what unmitigated agony it was to lose. Why the gaping hole in his chest where his heart used to be was as raw as the first night. Maybe even worse because regret was a constant irritant he could not escape.

Stalking out to the cliffs that edged the property surrounding his hut, Graham remembered the way Miss Westwood looked at him on the porch: right in the eye, not flinching at his caustic comments and actually stepping in closer, invading his space to make her point and knock him down a few pegs. In his mind's eye, Miss Westwood's brown hair morphed into auburn and her green eyes changed to blue. Graham could almost hear Fiona's laughter on the wind and closed his eyes at the agony of it all as his mind continued to display pictures he couldn't shut off.

Fiona lying in a pool of blood, cold and lifeless.

Fiona's coffin being lowered into its grave.

Their newborn child's small coffin buried beside it.

Him alone.

Him responsible.

Fiona: seven years gone and still haunting him.

The all-consuming desire for a drink dropped him to his knees as he buried his face in his hands. If he couldn't find relief in a bottle, perhaps he could be brave enough to embrace the final freedom by stepping off a cliff.

✺✺✺✺✺✺✺✺✺✺

Not a full week in Barbados and she was already scuttling around like a frightened rabbit trying to avoid Mrs. Wagner and Mr. Rhyder with equal determination. How quickly one fell back into old, bad habits: afraid to speak, afraid to act, afraid to trust.

Enough. She must remember what the Lord promises: *For I know the thoughts that I think toward you, saith the LORD, thoughts of peace, and not of evil, to give you a future and a hope.* She must stop this trembling and worry and remember Who she trusted and Who was going before her and Who was in control.

This was *not* what she had envisioned for herself here in Barbados and, despite Mr. Rhyder's incredulity regarding her rationale, she truly *did not* have anything here to stop her in her forward momentum – except her own insecurities. Well, until Mr. Topher followed through on his threat and traced her references.

Enough hesitation. Which was precisely why she was standing outside the kitchen door, adjusting her wide brimmed straw hat and slipping on her gloves, determined to explore the plantation by herself and search for an appropriate location for her school. *By herself.* Forget Mr. Graham Rhyder. Ignore Mrs. Moira Wagner. From her third floor bedroom window and even standing on the back patio, buildings of every shape and size were visible in every direction; surely one would be available to meet her needs. Polite inquiries had been met with hesitation and deflection by every individual she'd spoken with. If no one would help her she would progress by her own determination.

Just as always.

Beyond the vast kitchen garden were the chicken house and smoke house. To her right was the well, the bathhouse and the five-seater outhouse, and in the distance she could see what had to be the stables and the paddock. Trees obscured much of what was to the left, which piqued her curiosity. Mena headed in that direction.

She realized the error of her ways almost immediately as she approached the first collection of buildings. The heat bore down on Mena like a living thing, even though it was barely mid-morning. With each step she took, the sum total of her attire weighed down on her until she felt she could barely breathe. Chemise, pantaloons, stockings, petticoats (three), corset, and long sleeved muslin gown might be the appropriate clothing for a cultured woman as she went about her normal daily responsibilities, but definitely unsuitable for walking about out of doors at Windermere Plantation. Already her satin slippers, what she had deemed most fitting for a casual walk, were ruined due to the uneven and, at times, muddy terrain. And the heat! Taking a moment to catch her breath under the shade of a huge mahogany tree, the realization that *it was the winter season* brought a level of panic she could barely contain. It was painfully obvious that her entire wardrobe – aside from her hat – was completely inappropriate for functioning anywhere but inside the great house.

To make matters worse, Mena had the distinct feeling that she was being watched. On at least three occasions she had turned and scanned the dense foliage surrounding the path, only but saw nothing. Still the tingling sensation that someone was out there persisted, making her hurry despite the oppressive heat.

"Yuh looks like yuh's about ta melt. Come sit a spell." In the shade of the trees near the closest building sat a woman perched on a small three-legged stool. "Don' worry, I don' bite. At leas' not since I los' my las' toot'." She was still chuckling at her own joke as Mena approached. "Log's not as com'fa'able as my stool but it's all's I got ta offer." As Mena lowered herself down, the old woman reached down into a bucket at her side and pulled out a dripping tin cup of water.

"I'm much obliged," Mena said and greedily gulped the entire cup.

"Ab'gail gits me a fresh bucket o' water each mornin' an' sits it right here by mah stool. I'm happy ta share."

"My name is Mena Westwood. I'm the new teacher here at Windermere."

"I knows who yuh are. Mah name's Maisy." While she examined Mena, Mena examined her. She was the oldest woman Mena had ever seen, her face a mass of wrinkles, her sparse grey hair twisted in tiny knots all over her head. Barefoot, she had a heavy woolen shawl wrapped around her bony shoulders and, unlike Mena's present overheated condition, seemed to be fighting a chill. "It cool winter time now, chile. Yuh's never goin' ta survive da summer wit' all dat foolishness yuh's wearin' if yuh hot now."

Mena chuckled. "I was just thinking that."

"Windermere, bein' it's so close ta da water always gots a nice breeze, but da heat is sometin' fierce all da same once summer comes."

Plucking at her layers, Mena said, "I'll have to speak with Mrs. Wagner. Surely she can advise me on more appropriate dress."

"O, she'll 'advise yuh' all right. Tell yuh what's proper an' what's right an' what's 'spected, then we'll be pickin' yuh up dead on da side o' da path melted away ta nothin' but a puddle."

Mena gestured to her woolen shawl and out of politeness asked, "Well, what do you wear in the summer to stay cool?"

The old woman grinned a wide, toothless smile and said with a twinkle in her eye, "Well, when no one's lookin' I's wears my birfday suit," and threw her head back to laugh long and heartily at her own joke.

"How do you think that would go over if I tried it at the Great House?" Mena asked with a smile.

Still chuckling, the old woman said, "I suspect yuh'd cause a bigger stir dan I wud!" Dipping the cup into the bucket, she offered Mena another drink. "And Silen' Joe wud have a fine look-see if he cud. Here, have another. Yuhr lookin' bettah, but not perfect."

As Mena sipped slowly she asked, "Silent Joe?"

Maisy smiled and tapped the side of her nose. "He's almos' always out der unless dey got him workin' in da fields. Joe? You der? Cum on out now an' say hello ta da new teacher, Missy Mena. Maybe, if yuh gud, she'll teach yuh how ta write yuh name."

Mena froze and felt a wash of fear as the trees began to rustle and out stepped the most enormous young black man she had ever seen. He wore a shirt that was far too small for him and pants that were far too short for him, and he stood quietly on the edge of the foliage looking at Maisy. And Mena.

"Cum ahead, boy," Maisy gestured him to come close. "Yuh scarin' da teacher. Lookit her starin' at yuh lik yuh some monster from da deep. Mind yuh manners an' come say hello."

The young man approached and then when he was almost within reach, gracefully folded himself down to sit in the dirt. Looking at Mena, he blinked slowly and then held out something in his enormous hand.

"I suspect he's brought yuh a gift," Maisy said to Mena. "He's got magik hands, dat Joe does. Can weave jus' about anything from suga' cane an' palm leaves an' such. Ev'ry hat yuh see da workers wearin' Joe's made. Keeps him outta trouble, doesn't it, Joe?"

"Th-Thank you, Joe," Mena said as she took the item and then looked down at it. It was a fan, made from palm leaves intricately woven together in the most amazing fashion. She looked up into Joe's solemn face and then gave him a tentative smile. "A fan! Why thank you, Joe. Did you make this yourself?" After a moment he nodded. "It's most beautiful. I shall use it often!"

"Joe don' talk do yuh, Joe?" Maisy said to him. "Dat's why we call him Silen' Joe. Been quiet for nigh onto his who' life."

Mena looked at Joe and then at Maisy. "Did Joe ever talk?"

"Oh yas! Dat boy neva was quiet an' den one day it all stopped. Shut up tight like a clam our Joe did. His momma, God res' her soul, never knew why. Joe's sistah works up at da big hous – Mary Jean. Joe's otha sistah, Nancy Fae, ran off with Winston's brother bout four years ago, dat right Joe?"

Joe nodded solemnly.

"Will you come and visit me at the school, Joe? I'd love to teach you how to read and write if you can find the time."

Joe looked at Maisy. "Don' look at me boy! I'm not yuhr Momma! If yuh can find da time, den yuh get yuhself up to see Missy Mena an' maybe she can teach yuh a t'ing or two." Joe looked back at Maisy and then nodded his head.

"Joe, you are my first official student!" Mena smiled reassuringly at him as he watched her intently. "You don't have to talk to learn to read and write. Just don't sneak up on me, please. That's scary." Joe blinked solemnly and gave another tiny nod.

Maisy asked, "Where's yuhr home?"

It was a simple enough question but Mena struggled with the answer. She felt the old woman's scrutiny as she searched her mind, and finally her heart, for an answer. "For most of my life I've lived in England …,"

"Yuh dressin' like yuhr home's far away. But yuhr strugglin' with an' answer fo' me, I see. Don' yuh know fo' sure?"

"I…," Mena was surprised to feel the telltale tightening of her throat and the building pressure of tears behind her eyes. Taking a deep breath she said honestly, "I *want* Barbados to be my home."

Maisy nodded sagely. "Don' feel quite homely yet, I s'pect. Dat's a fine way fo' things ta be jus' now. *Home is where yuh hang yuh heart.* Nevah a reason ta rush nothin' 'specially wif da heart."

"I have family in England," Mena offered. "None were happy with my decision to come here. I'm a great disappointment to them."

"Dat so? Well, yuh sure gots plenty a time ta make up fo' dat. Why yuh still gots yuh whole life ahead a yuh." Maisy reached out her old wrinkled hand and took one of Mena's smooth ones. Besides the light and dark contrast, Mena could feel the leathery callouses against her smooth palm. "Yuh trust da Lord, Miss Mena?"

"Oh yes."

Cradling Mena's hand in her surprisingly strong one, Maisy asked, "Yuh belive He got yuh in da palm o' His Hand?"

"Yes."

"He talkin' ta yuh an tellin' yuh ta do things dat you canno' say no to?"

Looking into Maisy's wise old eyes, Mena felt her own tear up. It would seem that it had taken her entire life plus thousands of miles to finally find a person who seemed to understand exactly how she felt. "Yes."

"Well, yuh's listenin' ta a good Voice. Can' argue wit dat. Yuh keep talkin' an listen' and followin'. God did da same ting wit po' ole Abraham and his wife Sarah. Had dem traipse far away from home, too. God likes ta work dat way sometimes." Mena smiled, feeling optimistic for the first time since she'd stepped foot on Barbados. "Wat you doin' paradin' around in yuh finery tryin' ta kill yuhself in da heat?"

"I was out this morning trying to find a good location to conduct my school. I'm so anxious to get started and show everyone how serious I am about all this."

"Ain't getting' much help, I s'pect. Missus Wagner don' want nobody doin' nothin' but her stuff. Mistah Rhyder pro'bly don' know what ta do wit yuh." She chuckled to herself and muttered, "Yuh pro'bly scare dat man ta death!"

Mena stared at Maisy, completely puzzled. "Why would I scare Mr. Rhyder? I think I'm nothing but a nuisance to him. He's already made it patently clear that my mission here is fruitless. He even called me naïve."

"I s'pect yuh don' know much about men so here's a bit o' advice fo' yuh. Don' put too much stock in da words dey say as much as look at da actions dey do. Mr. Rhyder, he's a lot like da dog dat gets kicked an' whipped a bit too much. He don' trust nobody an' so keeps his distance. He might even growl an show his teeth if yuh get close. But soon yuh goin' ta see dat dog wherever yuh go an'," Maisy gave a slow, conspiratorial wink, "dat's cuz he followin' yuh everywhere yuh go." She winked at Joe, who ducked his head but not before Mena caught a smile on his face.

"Following me! I'd hardly think that will be true." But Maisy chuckled and pointed out in the distance. Mena could make out a man on horseback riding purposely through the fields toward the House and frowned in confusion. "What does Mr. Rhyder heading to the House have anything to do with me?"

Maisy smiled and tapped the end of her nose, refusing to respond, and went back to the original topic at hand. "Don' 'spect da workers ta run ta yuhr school. Dey gots ta work e'vry minute dey can. An', o'course, if anybody gots free time an' dey can't be workin' ta make a penny or two den dey's workin' in der own garden ta put food on da table."

"Yes," Mena sighed in defeat, watching Graham Rhyder and his horse disappear from view, "that seems to be the way of it. I'm trying not to get discouraged. I just need a building! I've got books and writing boards and pens and quills…"

"*Yuh got to creep, chile, before yuh kin walk.*" The old woman said, taking the empty tin cup from Mena's hand and helping herself to a drink. At Mena's puzzled silence, she smiled. "I sit's here all day, ev'ry day." She nodded off to the left and tilted her head as if listening for something. "Mos' days I gets visits from all manner o' folks, dependin' on if it's hard times or reapin' times." Suddenly Mena could hear the chatter of little voices growing louder as they came closer. "Dey bring me treats ta eat an' I tells dem stories." She gave Mena a pointed look. "Yuh welcome any day, ta come an' sit an' talk an' listen. Maybe yuh can teach me a ting or two," she smiled as five small children of various ages came skidding to a halt at the sight of Mena sitting beside Maisy, "an' maybe my visitors might learn a bit, too, right Joe?"

Shy at first, within no time two of the smallest children were sitting on Mena's lap and the others were seated at her feet while Maisy spun out a Bible story about David and Goliath. The children had obviously heard the story many times because periodically Maisy would purposely make mistakes in telling the story and the children's voices would rise eager to correct her.

"David don' throw chickens at da giant, Maisy! He t'rowed smooth stones!"

"Da rock didn't hit his knee, Maisy! Da rock hit his for'head an' killed him dead!"

"He didn't gets his hair cut off! Dat was Samson whut dat happened to! He gots his head clean cut off by David wit' his own sword!"

Finally, with the story finished, Maisy asked, "Wat did David say to da doubters?"

"Da LORD who rescued me from da claws of da lion an' da bear will rescue me!" the children shouted at the top of their lungs like a battle cry.

"An' what do *yuh* say to *yuhr* doubters?"

"Da LORD who rescued me from da claws of da lion an' da bear will rescue me!" the children shouted again.

Walking home with renewed vigor in her step and plans swirling in her head about what she might bring along with her when she visited Maisy again, it suddenly occurred to Mena that perhaps Maisy's Bible story hadn't been intended just for the children. As she rounded the final corner and took the path that led to the House, she heard footsteps ahead of her walking swiftly down the path towards her.

She stood and waited, thanks to Maisy, knowing full well who was approaching, and began to gear up for her next confrontation with Mr. Graham Rhyder.

"So you've decided then, I see," he said with a smug smile. "Choice is a wonderful privilege of the free, isn't it? Come here then, girl, and let's see what you have to offer me. If I'm pleased, maybe I'll have a treat or two for you; my girls are always happier because of the baubles I give them. Hurry and get that dress off. I don't have all day."

One door shut, another open.

Chapter Five

Exhaustion weighed heavily on Graham as he rode
Dancer in from the fields, although it was only the noon hour.
It had been another long, sleepless night that he feared would
repeat itself again tonight.

The 'Hard Times', that period of the year between July
and January when there was only limited work to be found, and
then by only a few fortunate workers, didn't mean that his job
was any easier. Money was always the bottom line and although
he wasn't the owner and with Lord Windermere never on the
premises, he was the point man to answer all difficult questions,
and the one who bore complete responsibility for success or
failure. Everything needed to be in order because very shortly,
with the beginning of February, the reaping would begin. For
four endless months every living soul would work themselves
near to death. Work would go from sun-up to sundown and,
should the moon be bright enough and the presses keep
functioning, which was always a concern, work would continue
through the night as well.

For now during these final weeks leading up to harvest
Graham had to make sure the workers were hired and in place
and the mill's equipment was greased and ready. He'd been the
one to push for the modernization and purchase of the steam
engine to run the presses (making the windmills on the

plantation obsolete), and felt the pressure to justify its expense every moment of every day. This second year was almost more important than the first in showing a profit.

Despite his resolve to remain uninvolved and despite the ridiculousness of Miss Westwood's plan, he also suspected that she would not let up in her quest to have a building to conduct her school. And there would be no one but him who would be willing to go against Moira Wagner and assist her. As another sleepless night slowly rolled into the dawn, an idea for a school location had occurred to him. Better to offer her a solution that suited his purposes then have to deal with some other nightmare idea he'd have to tolerate. She was a fighter; he was sure of it. Whether Graham helped or not, she wasn't going to give up. He might as well let her know that he'd at least made an effort to follow through on her request.

Dahlia couldn't provide Graham with Miss Westwood's location. He'd come away from the kitchen with a full stomach and a general direction in which little John Paul had pointed. "I saws her by dem trees, Mistah Graham, when I wus takin' a wee in da bushes." After Graham impressed upon little John Paul about the dangers of 'weeing' on Mrs. Wagner's prized bay leaf tree (and what would happen to him should he get caught), Graham set out in search of the illusive Miss Westwood.

Graham's employment here was always tenuous at best. Oh, his top notch skills, proven track record (every year since he had been hired had shown a greater profit than the year before) and tireless work ethic had been what had kept him in this job, and what had enabled him to secure permission and funds to purchase the steam engine. But he was also well aware that it would take only one mistake, one drunken show, one single year of financial loss to find himself dismissed. It was impossible for him to escape the reality of who and what he was: a *poor bakro*. A worthless piece of Irish trash lower than the least valuable black slave, with a reputation that promised laziness, drunkenness and worthlessness. Any education, any success, would never change the reality of what he was. It was like trying to put a shine on a turd.

Yuh kin tek da man out o' da pig pen, but yuh can' tek da pig pen out o' da man.

There were even times in the darkest, most miserable, paranoid hours of the night that Graham actually feared all of his successes here at Windermere were merely an illusion. Was it possible that there was someone who had arranged for his employment here at Windermere? Were his independence and success mere figments of his imagination? Was this all some twisted, long range plan to bring him back up from the very depths of hell only to bring him crashing down, completely incapable of recovery for one final lesson in despair and misery? Graham knew his sins and couldn't even defend himself, which made him crave a drink all that much more.

He rounded a bend, feeling the urgency to get back to the fields, and would have barreled right into the woman had she not been standing off to the side of the path and therefore avoiding him. Miss Westwood appeared before him looking for all the world like she'd just gone out for a morning stroll on the high streets of London. What in God's name was the woman wearing? Where in God's name did the woman think she was? "Who are you trying to impress in that get-up?"

"I beg your pardon?" She stood there calm as you pleased, her brows arched in disdain.

"You heard me. What are you dressed for? A ball? A presentation to the Queen?" Graham looked behind him and then squinted further down the path. "Have I interrupted an assignation?"

"I was just returning from a visit with Miss Maisy. I heard you barreling down the path and stood aside to avoid a collision." Mena swept her gloved hand. "Please, don't let me keep you. Continue on at your breakneck pace." She then stood there, calmly, watching him, a ridiculous straw hat perched on her head.

"I, well, I was actually looking for you," he managed and the admission was galling to say the least.

"Oh? Have you thought of something else you'd like to tell me regarding my naïve plans?" Mena looked down at her billowing skirt. "Obviously your sarcasm about my appearance is spontaneous, as you seem surprised by it, so that cannot have been your intent. Please, Mr. Rhyder, don't keep me waiting. What exactly were you in such a rush to insult me about this time?"

Graham had the grace to flush. She was right of course. Every time they had encountered each other he'd been rude and abrasive. He took off his hat and ran his fingers through his hair, taking a moment to reset. "I apologize, Miss Westwood. I'm in a rush to get back to the fields and had only come in specifically to speak with you. You see, I've thought of an idea for a school location, although it's rather unconventional. And somewhat small."

The change in her was instantaneous. A smile bloomed across her face, her eyes shone, and the defensiveness in her posture was replaced with enthusiasm. Taking an excited step towards him back onto the path she breathed, "Where?"

"Well, it would take a bit of work to clean and clear up because the area has been used for storage for over a year and a half. But the location is convenient and I don't think there's anyone on the plantation that wouldn't be able to find you if they wanted to. And the building is certainly sound.

"Yes…?"

"The old windmill."

Her smile slipped a bit. "The 'old windmill'?"

Graham replaced his hat and motioned for them to walk the path leading back to the House. "Please, I've got to get back to the fields. Tomorrow if you'd like, someone can take you out to the mill so you can have a look. Since we've gone to steam power, there's no need for the windmills – there's two actually – and they've just been sitting fallow for almost two years." Her silence spoke volumes. "Look, Miss Westwood, I know this isn't what you had in mind. Who would? You should know that while there are many outbuildings on the property, few are empty and none are in as sturdy shape as the windmills. All other possibilities require major structural repair. The windmills are weather tight, solid, and as of now completely unwanted." They'd reached the House and Graham stopped, intending to head back to Dancer and the fields. Her silence communicated her lack of enthusiasm, and a wave of annoyance surfaced. He'd wasted valuable time to seek her out and offer her this solution! "Miss Westwood," he said gruffly, "I'd encourage you to wait until you see them before you say no with certainty. Now, if you'll excuse me, I have responsibilities I must see to."

As Graham turned away, Mena called to him and he was forced to halt, standing stiff and obviously annoyed. At her silence he turned back to find her gracing him with a brilliant smile which lit up her green eyes. "I don't have any intention of saying no with certainty anytime soon, Mr. Rhyder. My silence is a product of my thoughtfulness, nothing else. Please accept my most sincere appreciation for your suggestion. I thank you and will plan on visiting as soon as it is possible. Aside from Maisy's, your assistance is the first I've received since my arrival – and means more to me than you could possibly know."

The smile and words of appreciation took the wind out of his anger, causing him to finally bow slightly and say awkwardly, "Oh. Good. All right then. A good day to you, Miss Westwood."

eeeeeeeeeee

Finally, some progress, and from Mr. Rhyder! Mena wasted no time as she swept into the Great House, delighted with the positive turn of the day thus far. "Mrs. Wagner, might I have a word with you?" With thoughts of David and the Giant still fresh in her head, Mena walked briskly up the main staircase after the housekeeper.

"Yes, Miss Westwood?" She stopped at the top of the staircase and watched Mena negotiate the stairs, petticoats in hand. "How has your morning gone?"

"Quite well, thank you. I've met Miss Maisy and had a brief walk around the grounds. I'd like to speak with you regarding the house staff."

"Surely, Miss Westwood, you're not going to advise me how to do my job."

"No, not at all. But I would like a similar courtesy."

That response certainly surprised Mrs. Wagner. "Excuse me?"

"I've been hired to teach. However, as attending school is not compulsory it will be my responsibility to convince those who would best benefit from this opportunity to consider investing their precious, albeit limited, free time. I do not see how I can accomplish this when I will be forever concerned that by having a conversation with anyone, I might unwittingly secure your displeasure."

Mrs. Wagner said authoritatively, "I will not have you interfering with the workings of this household."

Mena bowed her head briefly. "I understand. What I'm asking is for you to advise me of a time of day when I might freely, without concern, interact with your household staff in an attempt to get to know them and perhaps convince them to attend my school."

"Most household staff, except for Dahlia, answer to me for their time from six a.m. in the morning through eight p.m. in the evening with an hour allowed for lunch time, Monday through Saturday. Sundays are theirs. This is the same work schedule expected for field workers, in case you've not had this adequately explained by Mr. Rhyder."

"And Dahlia?"

Mrs. Wagner shrugged. "Dahlia gets her work done to provide for breakfast, lunch and the formal evening meal as she sees fit."

"So … prior to six a.m. and after eight p.m. and lunch – from noon to one I assume – and dinner from five to six I assume," Mena waited until Mrs. Wagner nodded, "would be the times you would not have issue with should I choose to interact with the household staff?" It was a very reluctant nod that Mena finally received. "Do you have any issue with me taking my noon meal *with* the household staff?"

"No. But I will caution you. Should you wish to have people *look up to you,* than how you utilize your free time is almost as important as how you utilize your work time." It was said with the utmost disdain, as if the very thought of eating with the staff was simply too offensive to even to consider. Mrs. Wagner turned to proceed down the west wing of the House, but Mena spoke up.

"Pardon me, Mrs. Wagner, but I'm not finished." Mena's David courage slipped a bit at the look of impatience she received. "Up until six a.m. and after eight p.m. do you have any issue with me sitting and meeting with household staff in the kitchen at the large work table?"

"For what purpose?"

"You see, I'm thinking that teaching the field staff versus the household staff will need to be done in two different styles as rarely do their schedules coincide. "

"Are you asking me permission to conduct school in the House kitchen?"

"Yes I am."

Mrs. Wagner gave Mena a cool look. "No."

"But, I-"

"I run an organized House, Miss Westwood. I wouldn't allow Karl to service the horses on the front porch nor would I allow Elijah to repot plants in the formal living room any more than I would have sugar cane processing happen in the kitchen. You must find your own place in which to conduct your schooling, and it *will not* under any circumstances occur here in the House."

"All right. But you have no problem with me interacting informally with the staff during the times we've discussed."

"I will not have Dahlia disturbed."

Mena bowed her head. "Absolutely. I will seek Dahlia's full permission for anything I plan to do." Mena bit the inside of her lip to keep from smiling, knowing full well what Mrs. Wagner thought about Dahlia being given such authority.

"Anything else?" Mrs. Wagner, though expressionless, seemed to exude an air of satisfaction at denying Mena her primary request.

"Yes, just one more question. *Outside the House,* am I right in understanding that I must gain Mr. Rhyder's permission for anything else I plan?"

It was a subtle, barely discernible reaction, and had Mena not been looking specifically for it she would have missed it, but it was there nonetheless: a slight narrowing of the eyes and a miniscule pursing of the mouth at the man's name. "Yes, Miss Westwood," Mrs. Wagner said, "anything outside the Great House is Mr. Rhyder's domain."

"Thank you, Mrs. Wagner, for your time."

In her room, Mena twirled around in victory, delighted with the very successful morning. It had never been her intention to conduct school in the kitchen; no one would be able to rest easy enough to concentrate and learn. She'd suspected, however, that giving Mrs. Wagner a small, worthless victory would suit her ultimate goals in the end. It had sometimes worked for her in the past. What she'd wanted – the ability to visit and chat with the staff in order to get to know them without fear of recrimination – had been the only thing she'd been hoping for.

My, my, she was getting quite accustomed to working in a world that didn't want her and still getting exactly what she wanted. Tomorrow, thanks to Mr. Rhyder, Mena would travel out to the old windmills and examine them. But today she would go through her wardrobe and begin the wise process of coming up with suitable outfits for being a teacher here in Barbados. Where could she acquire a sturdy pair of boots? Dahlia would know. Good thing she'd brought her needle and thread because some serious modifications were in order.

"Your plan offers no opportunity for return to this station in life. You realize this of course."

"It's actually part of the appeal. Should I be found out, there will little cause to drag me back. To what end? Who would want me?"

"Be careful, my friend. Be certain God's hand is guiding you to do this and not just your powerful desire to escape your father. Anger and betrayal do strange things to people and cause them to act in the most inexplicable and irrational ways ..."

She could not contain her desperate laugh, "As does bitterness and loss of hope..."

It takes two hands to clap.

Chapter Six

"Mr. Rhyder," Mena said at dinner the following night, "do you have some workers that you could spare to help me clean out the windmill?" She was delighted with the sturdy, albeit unconventional, prospective school location and couldn't wait to get to work.

"Clean out the ... windmill...?" Mrs. Wagner's face frowned in annoyance at the realization that she was ill informed about an event occurring on the plantation. "Whatever are you talking about, Miss Westwood?"

"Mr. Rhyder had the brilliant idea about using one of the unused windmills as the location for my school. I walked up there today and he's right it will take a bit of work to clean it up, but it's sturdy, weather tight and certainly large enough for me to conduct classes for up to ten students." Like two large sentinels, the abandoned windmills sat on a small rise overlooking the cane fields. The actual blades were gone, as were the doors and any other wood that could be salvaged for better use. But Mr. Rhyder had been right; the building was sound and due to the thickness of the stone walls and the shading of the nearby kapok tree, the interior was wonderfully cool. "I'll have to fight the cows that have a tendency to collect there in the shade, but other than that I can find no other reason to not use the site. Why, it's quite ... delightfully unique."

All eyes turned to Graham. He swallowed his roast pork and said, "How many men are we talking about?"

Mena shrugged. "Two? Three? I started to clean the building out today, but there are a substantial number of items in there that are rather heavy. In addition, it would be helpful if whoever you sent would be capable of building a few benches for seating and shelves for supplies."

"Have you secured a list of people willing to attend your school?" Mrs. Wagner asked. "It seems rather presumptuous to pay workers to perform a task if there are no students to make use of the facility being prepared."

Mena bit her lip and frowned. "Well, no one has given me an affirmation that they plan to attend yet. But I'm still trying to spread the word that I'm here."

"My dear Miss Westwood, just like gossip and scandal, news travels fast in small communities, and Windermere is a community. I can assure you that your presence, as well as your mission, has already been fully broadcast." Mena noticed that as Mrs. Wagner spoke, both Jessie Lynn and Mary Jean kept their heads down looking at their plates. One thing Mena knew for certain, there would not be any house servants at her school if Mrs. Wagner had anything to do with it.

With sudden clarity, Mena realized that Mrs. Wagner had no desire for her to succeed. *She wants no one to thrive unless by her permission.* Not only did she not support Mena's efforts, but it would seem that she would also use her power to cause Mena to fail. Apparently, Mena's struggles in life thus far had only been the first act. Here, perhaps, would be the second. "I've met quite a few of the children. I have been visiting Maisy in the mornings and have been slowly but steadily introducing myself to all of the families in the plantation village. I think it is important to put a personal connection alongside whatever has been already spoken about and let people make as informed a decision as possible." Mena looked at Mrs. Wagner. "Are you saying I shouldn't proceed with establishing a school building until I have a roster of students?"

"I am merely encouraging both you and Mr. Rhyder to be diligent with the Windermere's coffers. We would not want Lord Windermere to ever accuse any of us of being careless with his money … or his time."

Mena lifted her chin and took a deep breath. "Nor would I wish to be accused of not doing the job I was hired to do." It was time to put both Mrs. Wagner and Mr. Rhyder on the spot. "As Mrs. Wagner has assured me that issues outside the house are your domain, Mr. Rhyder, I'd appreciate your opinion regarding this."

Mr. Rhyder had finished his meal, laid his napkin by his plate, and leaned back in his chair apparently enjoying the show. He gave Mena a slow smile. "It is most reassuring to me to hear Mrs. Wagner's affirmation of my responsibilities here at Windermere." Mena dared not turn to see Mrs. Wagner's expression as Graham continued, "Yet we all know that *too much o' nutten ent good.* You've no roster of students but you also have no building. It makes perfect sense to me to make use of the windmill as your preliminary school. That's exactly why I suggested it in the first place." Turning to Mrs. Wagner he said, "After all, I was asked to help you secure a location."

"Then *you* apparently would have no trouble helping Miss Westwood improve it to her satisfaction tomorrow, Mr. Rhyder," came Mrs. Wagner's tight response. "The staff *you* insist on keeping employed during the off season could not possibly have time to devote a full day's labor to this issue."

Graham Rhyder graced her with a smile, knowing full well it would only add to her fury. "I'll just have to take stock of *my domain* which includes *my workers* and their responsibilities and make a decision based on what I view to be the best choice, *Moira.*" Jessie Lynn's gasp at his familiar use of her name sounded almost as loud as a scream. "Surely you can find no fault with that."

No one, *no one,* said a word as they waited for Mrs. Wagner's response. With exaggerated calm she dabbed at the corner of her mouth, folded her napkin, pushed her chair back, and excused herself from the table. The remainder of the meal was eaten in complete silence except for Mr. Wagner's subtle burp at the very end of dessert.

Mena was up bright and early the next morning – even before Elizabeth could pop her head in and wake her. She didn't want anyone who had willingly volunteered to help her at the windmill to arrive before her. When Graham Rhyder casually rode into view, her heart sank, assuming after last night's show he'd come to tell her there would be no help coming. Mena stood there watching him approach and made every effort to hold back her despair.

"Enjoying the view?" came his mocking comment as soon as he was within speaking range.

"Just tell me what you've come to tell me and leave me to my business, Mr. Rhyder," she said tersely. That stopped him.

As he dismounted from Dancer, he asked, "Don't you want any help? Are you sending me on my way?"

"YOU'RE my help for today?" Mena said incredulously.

"My, my, I've never felt more welcome." Shaking his head, he led Dancer to some shade and then walked past her into the windmill and stood in the doorway, hands on his hips, taking stock of what needed to be done. "I suppose you've been here long enough to understand that Moira Wagner and I are almost always at odds. What you haven't been here long enough to understand is the extent to which Moira Wagner goes for retribution to those who go against her."

"What do you mean?"

Graham turned and looked at her over his shoulder, his blue eyes shaded by his hat. "Other than myself, anyone who showed up today to help you would, at some point in the near future, feel the bite of Moira Wagner's anger in a most painful way. She has quite a skill at inflicting punishment, and many have felt her anger or know someone who has. Turnover here at Windermere is high – most unusual considering people are desperate to find work and willing to do just about anything to earn a steady wage. Many leave here at the insistence of Moira Wagner, and as it almost always involves a house matter, there is little I can do about it. After last night's little dinner show, I thought it wise to tell both Winston and Billy to stay away, so I've come in their place." He held his hand up when Mena went to speak. "They'll be building the benches you've requested while I do as much of the general clean-up as I can manage in these morning hours." With a mocking glance he muttered, "You don't have my help *for the day;* you've only got it for the morning." Taking off his hat, he hooked it high on a protruding beam and slipped on a pair of leather gloves he had pulled out of his back pocket.

"I had no idea," Mena said quietly.

"Well, now you do. The fear you see in workers' eyes is real and justified. And don't dismiss Walter Wagner; he's quieter but he's certainly no better."

"I've never exchanged anything other than a brief nod with him."

Graham snorted. "I'd advise you to keep it that way. You can't be married to someone for decades and not be of similar mind."

A picture of Mena's parents rose briefly in her mind. "Do you speak from experience, Mr. Rhyder?" she responded jokingly.

It was as if the sun went behind a cloud. "I suspect I'll start with those large pieces of broken equipment. Billy's been saving them for spare parts, so I'll store them in the other windmill." Without another word to Mena he set to work.

Graham Rhyder labored with a singular intense focus that Mena had never witnessed before. Very shortly there was a pile of rubbish taken from both windmills and stacked in the yard. "Someone will be by to haul this away in a day or two," he explained to her in passing. Other items, somehow determined to be of worth, were removed from Mena's windmill and carried to the other windmill. Twice Dancer's strength was needed to help pull large items out from one place to another. Within no time Mena was able to begin to sweep and haul away smaller debris that still remained on the floor.

As the morning wore on, Mena felt compelled to break the silence that had settled between them. "Thank you for doing this, Mr. Rhyder. I know that you are not any more inclined to support my school than Mrs. Wagner." He glared at her as he carried out two large bundles of old, dried cane stalks and was puzzled. "Do you deny what I've just said?" she called to his retreating back.

After tossing the bundles on the rubbish pile, he turned with hands on his hips and spoke in anger, "Do not ever, *ever,* compare me with the likes of Moira Wagner. I speak my mind when I see something that calls for an opinion that could help the situation. I see no reason to interfere or prevent opportunities that will provide assistance or improvement to others in need. I am also quite content to be proved wrong with solid evidence."

"I'm sorry if I've insulted you, Mr. Rhyder. I had assumed, based on our very first conversation, that you had similar opinions regarding my position here at Windermere."

He shrugged, walking past her to stand once again in the windmill doorway to determine what he needed to do next. "You're a crusader," he said, knowing that she stood behind him and wouldn't move until he'd responded. "You see the opportunity to do good and it intrigues you. You have stars in your eyes and dreams in your head with the possibility of changing the way things are at Windermere. It would be a shame to see you discouraged. Life ..." he sighed suddenly as if wishing he'd never opened his mouth, "life crushes people like you."

He couldn't see her face but knew she was frowning as she puzzled over his cryptic comments. "There has been someone before me who tried to do something like I'm trying to do?"

She had no idea what she was asking. None. Graham turned, shook his head, and looked off into the distance. By his calculation, the morning was almost over and he would have to get out to the fields to relieve Isaac very soon. Finally he looked at her. "Tell me again what you are trying to do." His tone wasn't sarcastic, his expression wasn't mocking. He looked tired, drawn, and almost in pain.

For some unaccountable reason, Mena wanted to comfort him, which was both impossible *and* ridiculous. "I'm trying to help people have better lives. I'm trying to open up new possibilities and new opportunities for people. I'm trying to help people realize their own potential. Is that so very bad?"

"The world is littered with broken people who embraced a cause they felt passionate about, Miss Westwood, only to be destroyed by the very same cause. It's not a pretty sight."

Mena, having tried once to defend her position and explain her goals to him, was wise enough to not try again. Instead, she pointed out exactly what she saw. "Yet even though you obviously doubt my ability to succeed, here you are giving me your morning to help me further my plans. Doesn't that imply the same thing about you?"

Graham grabbed another pile of rubbish and brushed past her. "That's me," he finally threw sarcastically over his shoulder, "tender and solicitous to all those in need."

"Why *are* you helping me, Mr. Rhyder? You could do the same as Mrs. Wagner and between the both of you I would be in dire straits indeed."

He stopped then and looked at her, sweat trickling down the side of his face dampening his hair and his shirt. "I've known true kindness once in my life, Miss Westwood. I am compelled to reciprocate when the opportunity arises."

Mr. Rhyder was a most intriguing man; a true dichotomy. "I see," Mena said quietly. "Well, I appreciate you speaking to me and I do apologize for ever having implied that you were of the same mindset as Moira Wagner." He remained silent. "Why is she the way she is?"

Sighing, he ground out, "Moira Wagner is a frustrated bigot. She was born into a station of life she feels is beneath her, forced to work with people she feels vastly superior to, and stuck in a life that she feels fails to recognize her true worth. She's vicious and vindictive, and you would be wise to guard yourself around her at all times."

"Are you saying I'm in danger?"

"All I know is what I have seen in the past. No one lasts long here at Windermere who is in conflict with Moira Wagner. And few people ever find themselves on her good side." Graham snorted.

Mena had the audacity to put her hands on her hips and ask, "How long have you been here?"

"A little over four miserable years," he bit out with impatience, "but we are not discussing me, we are discussing you."

"I see."

"I hope you do, Miss Westwood. I sincerely hope you do. You are ... trusting. You seem to want to only recognize the good in people. I would caution you that there are many people who have no good in them at all."

She was shaking her head even before he finished his sentence. "No, Mr. Rhyder, I cannot believe that. Why, look at the impression I got of you the first day I was here at Windermere! I may be young but I am not foolish. We are all products of our upbringing and our life path. But that does not mean that there is not hope for change for *everyone*. I will not preach to you but I will tell you that God's grace and power knows no bounds."

He surprised her by grinning at her. "I have had this discussion before with the same person who showed me kindness. I *do not* doubt God's might; I doubt man's willingness to accept the opportunity to improve. Some of us are just too far gone to change."

Mena lifted her chin, comfortable with debates that challenged her faith and grinned back at him, enjoying their discussion thoroughly. "You seem to have included yourself in that grouping. I find that odd given this situation and given what you've just told me about true kindness. It seems to me that you have already begun to change."

He grabbed his hat, placed it on his head, removed his gloves, and stuffed them in his back pocket. "If you'll excuse me, I've got to relieve Isaac in the fields." Before Mena could fully process his hasty departure, he was mounted on Dancer, preparing to ride away.

"Oh wait!" she said, rushing over to a tree. "I made lunch for whoever came to help me! It's just sandwiches with last night's roast pork." She handed him a cloth wrapped bundle. "And some of Delilah's apple pie. Please, I made enough for three, so share this with Winston and Billy. Let them know how much I appreciate the building of the school's benches."

Nodding his thanks, he reached down to take the bundle. "When time permits, we'll try to build you a few shelves. I noticed all your books along the one wall."

"As time allows." Mena reached out and touched his leg to keep him from riding away. "I appreciate your help, your honesty, and your caution, Mr. Rhyder. I will not dismiss anything that you've said to me. I promise." Shading her eyes against the sun, she smiled at him. "And any time you'd like to continue this discussion regarding the ability of a person to change, why I am always ready for a good debate."

He said nothing in response as he rode away towards the fields.

ⲈⲤⲈⲤⲈⲤⲈⲤⲈⲤⲈ

Bit by bit his control was slipping. Graham's thoughts should have been filled with the prospect of harvest time beginning in little more than a week's time, but they weren't. The ability to wall off everyone and everything and focus only on what needed to be done had always been his greatest skill. It was the way he had learned to keep his mental ghosts at bay and the furious need for the bottle under control. But with each day his well-ordered existence seemed to be falling further apart.

Squinting into the distance against the setting sun, Graham could see the object of his thoughts, Miss Mena Westwood, walking away from the Windmill School (as everyone had taken to calling it), woven basket in hand. In the past few weeks, there had been a steady stream of people coming to and from the school. He knew from dinner conversation that she had been unable to get any formal classes organized, but that hadn't slowed down her enthusiasm or her drive. Avoiding encounters with her since his help at the windmill had been relatively easy, aside from the accursed dinners. But he'd rapidly realized that out of sight did not necessarily mean out of mind where the woman was concerned.

"Did yuh see Ole Maisy's fine new chair? Sure beats sittin' on dat tiny stool wit' all its fancy soft cloth. Such a fine thing! Miss Mena done foun' it up in da House attic. Ain't seen Maisy so full o' herself since she caught an' married Jeb almos' a lifetime ago! She sits der like da queen bee wit' Miss Mena b'side her, tellin' her Bible stories ta dose dat come visit her each mornin'. An' den once Miss Mena starts teachin' she sits der along wit da little ones practicin' her letters."

"Wuht I singin'? It's da al-fe-bet. Miss Mena's teachin' my littlest, John Paul during lunch at da House, an' he's singin' it mornin', noon, an' night. I swear he singin' it in his sleep! Anyways, I figure I might as well try an' learn a bit myself."

"Miss Mena's eatin' breakfas wit' the house staff almos' e'vry day. Got da okay ta sit an' talk durin' dat time. She not uppity at all an' willin' ta learn as much as she willin' ta teach. Even helps wit' da fixin's and cleanin's."

"You been ta da win'mill school? E'vry day right at lunch hour Miss Mena sits an' teaches anyone who comes. I hear tell dat she even brings treats sometimes, too. Dahlia learnin' her letters an' numbers at night and givin' Miss Mena bakin' lessons at da same time. Dos treats ain't haf' bad!"

Graham was grudgingly forced to admit that in the past three weeks she'd made far more progress than he'd ever thought she would.

The wee hours of the night had become one long, sleepless nightmare of things both past and present, and the need for a drink had become almost all consuming. Behind him was the ghost of Fiona and the role he played in destroying her. Ahead of him was the growing interest in Mena Westwood. Each thought pulled and tugged at the other and was slowing tearing him apart. The need for peace found in unconsciousness seemed to grow with each breath he took. He remembered ... the need, the pull, the incredible desire to find oblivion.

This was dangerous. Very dangerous.

He had learned to confine thoughts of Fiona to very carefully regulated moments when he deemed himself strong enough to withstand the earthquake of emotions that were guaranteed to follow. A brief moment in the morning, if the breeze was just so, when he was riding out on Dancer watching the sunrise. A certain flowery scent on the wind just before spring switched over to full summer heat. Not daily. Never repeatedly. And not to the exclusion of other things he should be focusing on. But recently she had begun visiting his nightly dreams, alternately crying in worry for him or screaming in frustration at him. *Graham, my love...*

Thoughts of Fiona only reminded Graham of what he'd lost. Those thoughts only succeeded in reminding him of how responsible he was for the path of death and destruction that seemed to follow him like a putrid river wherever he went. And once he faced *that* reality, the only thing capable of making him forget was found at the bottom of a bottle.

Sobriety. Quite honestly a quality he'd never thought to achieve in this lifetime. Not even Fiona had been able to calm that demon but had merely dealt with it as best she could. Perhaps if they had known it would be his drinking that would kill her, it would have been enough to make her leave him. Or make him sober up. He felt his control slipping. The chained up demons he so carefully kept contained were rattling precariously. If he wasn't careful, all hell was likely to break loose. He'd almost succeeded in killing himself with drink after Fiona died...

"The evils of drink are something thou must not succumb to, Friend. When was the last time thee had a good meal or cleaned thyself?"

"Who the hell are you? Where's my bottle? Did you take it?"

"Relax, my Friend, I meaneth thee no harm. My name is Friend Nathaniel and I've brought thee home to my house. Here, enjoy a hearty meal with me whilst the Good Lord blesses us with this fresh, cool morning breeze."

"Where am I?"

"Thou wast found unconscious against our meeting house door late last evening. Friend James wast forced to climb out the window to move thee so that the ladies could exit! Twas quite a sight to see! As I wast the only Friend who had arrived in a wagon, we felt it wast the Good Lord's sign as to who should take thee home."

"Thanks. Now I'll be leaving. Hey, where the hell are my clothes?"

"The rags thou wast wearing have been burned. After washing thee, it wast the most prudent thing to do. Friend Sylvia will be bringing thee a new set of clothes sometime soon."

"What? I have to get out of here! I have to go! What am I supposed to do in the meantime?"

"Rest. Eat. Pray. Think. Talk with me."

"Hell no. I need a drink. I need a drink, now."

"Giveth me thy hand, Friend. I will pray that thy tremors will calm and-"

"WHERE THE HELL ARE WE? I don't see another building as far as the eye can see!"

"The Good Lord has graced me with a plot of land quite a distance from town."

"HOW DISTANT?"

"God's green pastures go on for a good twelve miles before-"

"TWELVE MILES!"

"Come back to bed, my Friend, I see that thy tremors are getting worse and I fear thou shalt fall down. Sit. Eat. Let me pray over you. The peace of our Lord Jesus needs to fill thy heart and mind.

Stunningly, Friend Nate's quiet, simple, self-effacing life style was exactly what Graham had needed to achieve a level of peace *and sobriety* he heretofore had never believed possible. Oh, Graham never bought into all the God spiel that Nate was forever spouting, but the sincerity of the man and his Quaker friends just couldn't be denied. They were the first people that Graham had ever known who lived what they believed.

Nate had encouraged Graham to pray, but Graham was certain that God didn't want to listen to his endless litany of complaints and injustices. The truth was even he was sick of the lengthy list of disasters, failures, and unfortunate circumstances that made up the sum total of his life. God couldn't change his past nor could He erase the misery Graham carried in his heart, so why bother talking with Him about it? During his six months with Nate, Graham had learned to put things in mental boxes in his mind. Pack them up, chain them closed and store them so far away that he could almost - *almost* - forget about them.

With Nate's stubborn determination (and a distinct lack of clothing for almost a full week), Graham managed to force his desire for drink, often more powerful than food or sleep, into his first mental box. Sobriety brought clarity and clarity brought common sense. By the time he was strong enough and clothed sufficiently to walk the twelve miles to the nearest town and the nearest bottle, Graham had managed to at least chain the demon of drink into some semblance of control.

"What is the benefit of drink, Friend Graham?"

"It helps me forget my whole miserable life, Nate. There's significant value in that, trust me."

"Forgiveness is far better. With the Good Lord's inner light thy sins are washed away. Thou hast no need to forget what the Good Lord has forgiven."

"Nate, we come from different places. Trust me; there are just some things that cannot be forgiven or forgotten. Now, hang on. I can see you're getting ready to give me one of your lessons. Before you start, let me give you the whole picture: my mother died before I was able to help her and my wife died simply for loving me. To what end, I ask you? You saw the quality of man I am — you washed the filth off me and burned the rags I was wearing. I'm a worthless, thankless, bakro whose greatest contribution to this earth will be the literal death of me."

"Thou believest thyself to be more powerful than God Almighty?"

"Of course not! Haven't you been listening to me?!"

"Thou claimeth to have sins greater than even the Good Lord can forgive and forget. Thou claimeth to be a man so low that even the Good Lord cannot redeem. Most importantly, thou claimeth a life that even the Good Lord cannot make right."

Eventually his mother, Bridget, from whom he'd gotten his doomed bakro heritage, his blue eyes and auburn hair, and his passionate, unquenchable love for the bottle was relegated to a mental box. In that box he shoved all the responsibility he carried for never being able to save his mother and the suppressed anger and frustration for her part in his doomed heritage. Despite the fact that she'd given him the opportunity to overcome his miserable, drunken existence, there was little to show for her sacrifice.

"Bakro. Explain to me thy understanding of the meaning."

"An Irish slave; first slaves here on the island, actually, even before the blacks. We're lower than the blacks, actually, 'cause we have that problem with … drink. Some claim bakros are lazy and shifty and arrogant. Hey, you know where the term 'bakro' comes from? It's because in church the whites sit toward the front and the blacks are always required to sit in the back. But if you're an Irish slave —even worse than a black slave — then the <u>back row</u> is relegated to you."

"What mattereth whether thou be black, white, male, female, rich or poor? The Truth is that all persons are capable of being filled with God's inner light. Whether thou be rich or poor, man or woman, slave or free, the Truth is there be no person on this earth who is of greater worth to the Father than the next."

"I guess if I lived here the rest of my life, twelve miles out from the nearest human being and associated only with others of like opinions, then it wouldn't matter."

"Thou thinketh that I have not known my own share of sorrow and grief, Friend Graham? I stand before thee the only surviving member of my family. Friends have been persecuted <u>specifically for their beliefs</u> almost since the first moment they began to speaketh the Lord's Truth. Almost every faith hath hated us; almost every country hath banished us all because we simply wisheth to live as we believe the Good Lord hath called us to live. Take heed, Friend Graham, that thou remember to see the world with wise eyes and an open heart."

Fiona was finally stored away during his time with Nate, too. Her love and belief in him had been the only good thing in his past, but Graham had gradually realized that it was those very two things that fed his tremendous guilt. She'd foolishly cast her lot with him, stepping forward with him into the future, never looking back, confident that nothing could stop them. And he'd led her right to her death in a matter of only a few years. The topic of Fiona was not something that Graham could speak of, even with Nate.

Closed off from everyone and everything, Graham spent weeks just sitting and doing nothing but staring off into the horizon, eating when Nate handed him a meal and sleeping when Nate told him to go to bed.

"Friend Graham, what wilst thou do with thyself now that thee is strong and sober? What are thy skills?"

"I know how to drink, Nate."

"I'll miss thy humor once thee is gone, Friend Graham. Methinks thee lies. You may battle with the demon drink but thou hast intelligence and skills aplenty."

"All I know besides drinking is sugar cane. Was born in the midst of it. Grew up working it. Was finely educated thanks to it. For a short time before the bottle claimed me, I made a living for a while as a result of it. Lately, I've enjoyed the drunk I could gain from the rum produced by it. I suppose I could try to get work on one of the plantations. For a very brief time I managed one of the larger plantations down on the south end of the island. Someone who doesn't necessarily know my full history might be willing to hire me in one capacity or another."

"There is no rush, Friend Graham. God's time is not man's time."

One day Nate had ridden home with a letter requesting Graham to come for an interview at the end of the week for manager of the Windermere Plantation, three miles due north of the town of Friendship in the parish of St. Lucy. Friend Sylvia had provided two more changes of clothing. Friend William had provided Graham with a fine young mare that fairly danced with energy. Friend Thomas had provided Graham with a fine new wide brimmed hat. And Friend Nate had smiled but remained silent in the face of Graham's numerous questions.

"Go with God, Friend Graham. I will not concern myself with thee for God is with thee whether thou believeth it or not. All I ask of thee is that thou dost not give up on God and that when the opportunity arises that thou wouldst show the same kindness to others as we have shown to you."

For over four years Graham had managed to keep himself separate and apart from everyone and everything while he worked as Manager here at Windermere Plantation. Diligently, he worked to keep all of his boxed demons chained and controlled. *Care for no one but oneself. Focus on no one but oneself.* Utilizing this formula, he had managed to keep the demon desire for drink controlled, the guilt and anger of his mother at bay, and the grief of Fiona's death from driving him insane.

Until now.

Little Miss Mena Westwood had waltzed into his life with her plans and her dreams and had managed to rattle every aspect of Graham's existence so that there was nowhere to go for peace. In one short month she'd managed to shake up every aspect of Windermere plantation as effectively as a hurricane. God help him, he'd become so familiar with thinking of her that he no longer thought of her as "Miss Westwood" but instead regularly thought of her as "Mena."

He needed to get back to the place that had enabled him to embrace sobriety and remain in the land of the living and the functioning. He must focus solely on himself and no one else – alive or dead. He must not become interested in someone, grow to care for someone, or allow himself to love again. As lonely and dismal as his life was now, it was far more preferable than how he'd been when he'd lost Fiona and the babe. If it came to that, he'd either begin to drink again or finally force himself to walk off that cliff.

The man swirled the amber liquid casually in his glass as he observed the angry young boy before him. "Is it your plan to fight the entire world then?"

The hatred almost choked him, making it difficult to speak. "Aye, if I have to."

"Best rethink that strategy. If you win, you'll only succeed in being more alone and more helpless than you already are."

Da more yuh watch, da less yuh see.

Chapter Seven

"Da baby's comin', Miss Maisy! Mama says I need ta fetch yuh quick!" Deborah arrived in a breathless rush.

"All right, chil', jus' take a breaf. Dat baby comin' all in his own time an' nothin' we can do much about dat. Lord knows Rachel's done it enuf times dat she don' really need me." Maisy stood as quickly as she could (which was quite slow), grabbed her walking stick and instructed Mena as she made her way down the path to the other homes. "Miss Mena, inside by my bed, is a sack tied up tight. Run an' fetch it an' bring it ta Rachel an' Isaac's place."

Mena had stood at Deborah's breathless arrival and stared at Maisy's retreating back with horror. "M-me?"

Maisy didn't bother to turn around. "Why sure, Miss Mena. Know how yuh say yuh always wan' ta learn new things? Now's da chance ta lern how ta birth a baby."

The house was distinguishable only by the small collection of children standing outside trying to peer into the dark interior. Otherwise the eighteen small homes, barely larger than shacks, that made up the plantation village all had the same sun-bleached, weathered look of wood structures that had been baked in the sun for endless years. The front door was open to provide some ventilation, Mena assumed, and inside around

Rachel's bed were all five daughters wide-eyed and silent as their mother writhed in agony.

"Wash dem hands a yuhrs, Miss Mena, an' roll up dem sleeves o' yours. You sit up by Rachel's head and wipe her brow an' keep tellin' her wut a good job she doin'. Can' hear dat too much when you pushin'." Maisy fired off orders and soon each and every one was busy doing this or running to get that.

"Da little ones gone?" Rachel gasped at the first lull in the commotion. "Doan want dem here if it can be helped."

"Yessiree. Sent Little Mary, Ruth, and Da'brah off to da fields to find yuhr man. I s'pect at da rate yuh goin' dat baby will be here by da time dey come back wif him. Ra'becca is fetchin' water, Ab'gail is fetchin' kindlin' and Eliz'bet is here right beside me. She old enough for da full show."

"I'm early."

"Not surprisin'. Babies come quicker an' quicker da more yuh have. Little Mary was a week early."

"Been bleeding fo' past week."

"Hm. Dat must be yuhr secret since I not caught a whisper of dat at all. Anyt'ing else I should know?"

"Der might be two."

Maisy ran a practiced hand over Rachel's distended stomach. "Only feel one movin'," she murmured almost to herself.

"Up until da last month or so … I was sure…"

"All right den," Maisy said wrapping an apron around her waist and tying it at her stooped back. "Le's get dis done den. Elizabeth, help me spread dis cloth…"

Graham found Mena sitting on the front porch step as the sun set, with tears streaming down her face. He'd come as soon as he could, but wanted to finish Isaac's work so his foreman could still collect a full day despite leaving early to attend Rachel. He approached slowly, with great dread. Nothing dismayed Graham more than crying women. And nothing terrified him more than childbirth. "Miss Westwood?"

When she didn't answer him but just continued to sniff and stare off into the distance, Graham cautiously sat down next to her and removed his hat. "Miss Westwood? Is the news bad?" Graham realized as he sat beside her that she didn't stand out so much anymore. She was wearing a practical pair of sturdy boots, a serviceable skirt and a plain white blouse with the sleeves rolled up past her elbows. No longer was she the London fashion plate. One month of living at Windermere plantation had changed her significantly.

"There were two babies," and she spoke so quietly that Graham was forced to lean in, "a little boy and a little girl. Only the little girl survived." A sob caught in her throat and she used a crushed linen handkerchief to blow her nose and wipe her eyes.

"Rachel?"

Mena nodded. "Fine as far as I know. I stepped out after both of the babies were born and Isaac arrived." She wrapped her arms around her waist and seemed to rock herself.

"Are all the girls in there?"

Mena nodded. "Maisy left a bit ago. Rachel knows I'm out here. I wanted to give them privacy but thought I'd stay in case I could do something."

"We'll both wait for a bit, then."

They sat there watching the sun gradually set. Eventually Isaac came out to stand with them, holding a small blanket wrapped bundle. Graham stood. "I'll help." Isaac nodded once briefly, stepped off the stairs and walked briskly down the path.

Scrambling to standing, Mena asked, "Where-?"

"To dig the grave," Graham said grimly. Glancing into the cabin he said, "Will you stay until we get back?" At Mena's nod, he trudged after his foreman.

Thank goodness for Dahlia's beginning lessons in the kitchen! As quietly as possible, Mena set to stoking the fire in their small stove and warming up the stew that sat in a large pot. All five girls lay huddled in their bed while Rachel lay in an exhausted sleep with the newest baby close to her breast.

"Yuh don' cook," came a muffled voice down near Mena's knees. "Yuh teach." It was Little Mary sucking her thumb and twirling a bit of her hair.

Mena chuckled in spite of herself. "You're exactly right, Mary. But I think I can manage to heat up what's already made. Are you hungry?" Little Mary nodded. "Can you get me out the bowls and spoons like a big girl?" Another nod. "I'd be much obliged to have such a good helper."

Little Mary put the bowls around the small table. Slowly the other girls began to help, each performing what Mena assumed to be their assigned job: spoons were placed by the bowls, cups were filled with water from the dipper bucket, a bit of bread was unwrapped from a cloth on the shelf, and then quietly went to the wash stand to wash her hands and face.

"Let's leave your Momma and the new baby to sleep, shall we?" Mena asked as the five sat silently on the benches.

"Her's ta be called R'becca," volunteered Ruth as Mena found a spot on the end of bench near Abigail.

"Pray," little Mary commanded Mena around her thumb.

"Why don't one of you girls pray?" Mena said rather desperately. Why was she so uncomfortable praying aloud in front of five children, she wondered?

Little Mary shook her head and again commanded, "Pray!"

Elizabeth managed a tiny grin. "Little Mary's job is ta pick who says da dinner prayer."

"I's pick who says da bedtime one," Ruth said proudly.

"I see. Do you ever get to say the bedtime prayer, Ruth, or do you only get to pick?" Mena asked, fascinated by the intricate protocol she was witnessing.

"Oh, she prays," Elizabeth said with an exaggerated eye roll reminiscent of father's animated expressions, "sumtimes we can' get her ta hush!" Ruth was unaffected by this bit of information and simply closed her eyes, bowed her head and folded her hands.

Everyone immediately began to copy Ruth, including Mena. "Dear Lord, we thank you so very much for sending us Rebecca," Mena began and couldn't help peeking at the five dark heads all bent in prayer, "and we thank you that Momma is well. Please help her to have a good rest so she can feel stronger tomorrow.

"We're sorry that ...," and Mena hesitated, horrified to realize she did not know the baby boy's name. Her mind scrambled with how to refer to him.

"Jacob," Rachel said quietly from the bed.

Mena felt the rush of tears building behind her eyes and threatening to close her throat, "We're sorry that You've taken

Jacob back to be with You so soon. We would have enjoyed getting to know him and I'm sure he would have loved having so many smart, pretty, helpful big sisters. But we know and trust that Your way is best, Lord. Please help us to feel Your loving arms around us when we miss Jacob for we know that when You are close to us, we are close to Jacob also. Amen."

"Amen," said five voices in unison.

"Amen," came Rachel's tear soaked voice from the bed.

⌾⌾⌾⌾⌾⌾⌾⌾

All six of Isaac's girls were crowded around Mena on the front porch steps. "Now Abigail, Nabal's wife, was a beautiful, sensible, and wise young woman who trusted God in all things. Everyone ran to her in a panic. 'What should we do, Abigail?' they all cried certain that David and his angry soldiers would come back and kill them all. 'What should we do?!' Abigail wasted no time gathering together what she knew every hardworking group of men could not resist: a delicious dinner. She got together bread, wine, and cooked up some delicious lamb – enough for four hundred men! - and then loaded it all on donkeys and set off down into the valley directly towards the angry army that everyone was afraid of."

"Was der sweet cakes?" Little Mary asked around her thumb, sitting perched on her sister Elizabeth's lap.

"Probably," Mena nodded and Graham could see that she fought a smile. "So, when David and his very angry soldiers came rushing up to her, Abigail got down off her donkey and bowed low to the ground. 'Please accept my apology for my husband,' Abigail said to David, 'I will take full responsibility for his terrible manners.'"

Mena looked around at her rapt audience and Graham saw her start when she finally noticed him. "What do you think David did?"

"He et dinner!" Deborah said with a smile. "Poppa always says when he comes home dat he's hungry enough to et a horse an' Momma always says, 'Dats not whut I'm servin' tonight' but Poppa always ets whut ever Momma gives him."

Mena smiled and nodded. "That's right, Deborah. Those angry soldiers were hungry soldiers, too. So they took everything that Abigail had brought them and went peacefully back to their camp. And that's how Abigail saved the day against an army with just a picnic basket!"

Everyone clapped, and though it was dark Graham was certain she blushed.

"Time fo' bed," came Isaac's voice, and there was a mad scramble to get into the house. To Mena and Graham he said simply, "I thank yuh."

Standing, Mena said quietly, "If it's allright, Isaac, the girls have asked me to come back tomorrow evening to tell another story. I'd enjoy that and I suspect it would give Rachel a bit more time to rest."

Isaac nodded. "Thank yuh. Dat wud be a help."

Graham and Mena walked home side by side by in the moonlight, both quiet for a time. Finally Graham chuckled. "Fighting an army with just a picnic basket. Now that's a technique I was unaware of until tonight."

Mena grinned at him. "Don't forget that she was wise, sensible, and beautiful despite her ignorant, ill-mannered husband."

"Don't recall hearing him described as 'ignorant'."

She grinned at him again. "You came late then. We talked quite a long time about how bad manners were a sign of ignorance."

"Abigail was certainly sitting tall hearing all about her namesake."

"I was worried about her more than the others. She was so quiet and sad and never said a word throughout dinner. "

"Bet Little Mary didn't concern you in that way."

For the first time Graham heard the sound of her laughter. "Isn't that the truth! I suspect she runs that household."

"That's how Isaac describes it." After a few moments of silence Graham volunteered, "It was good of you to stay and kind of you to offer to come by tomorrow evening, too. You did well with them."

His praise obviously made her uncomfortable. "It's not anything you wouldn't have done."

He snorted in the darkness beside her. "Hardly."

She glanced at him with an expression Graham supposed her students saw often. It was one of impatience at his apparent ignorance and her determination to enlighten him. "You seem to regularly sell yourself short, and I'll have none of that. You work hard to present a hard, grumpy, tough-talking individual, but that's not the true you. I may have been here only a little over a month, but it is clear that you are well thought of, dependable and trustworthy."

Graham snorted again. "I *am* a hard, grumpy, tough-talking individual. Were you not a proper lady, I'd share with you a few other descriptive words that would apply." The woman had no idea what she was talking about.

"One thing life has taught me thus far, Mr. Rhyder, is that we are all called to do *something good*. Each of us can choose to do this good thing or not, but I regularly see you doing good things. Oh, I know you're probably laughing to yourself once again at my naiveté," she turned and gave him a glare, "and you can go right ahead. A person does not need vast experience or years of living to have intelligent and discerning perceptions."

"Oh? What *does* a person need?" he asked as they walked side by side down the dark path to the Great House. It was fun pushing her, getting her to turn feisty and opinionated.

She was silent for a moment or two as if debating how to answer and then said quietly, *"Be not thou envious against evil men, neither desire to be with them. For their heart studieth destruction, and their lips talk of mischief. Through wisdom is a house builded; and by understanding it is established: And by knowledge shall the chambers be filled with all precious and pleasant riches.* That's from the book of Proverbs, chapter 24, verses one through four."

Nodding, Graham observed quietly, "So, your goal then is riches," thoroughly enjoying baiting her.

"No!" Mena exploded, "that's not the point of that verse at all!" Taking a deep breath to calm herself, she said carefully, "And you know that, too. It means that evil men focus on destruction and their lips talk of mischief. My point being that what I've seen here at Windermere since my arrival is nothing but *construction* and *productivity* from *you*. Don't you think that is a wise way to discern if someone is good or not?"

This was getting far too personal for Graham. "Why, Miss Westwood, are you becoming my champion? Will you next be going to Mrs. Wagner to sing my praises and press for her to reevaluate her opinion of me? Maybe I can entreat you to speak to Mr. Topher about a wage increase."

"Why is hearing good things about yourself so hard for you to accept, Mr. Rhyder? Why are you embarrassed about the good you do? We can ignore the call to do good or follow through with it. In my brief experience, I know for a fact that listening to the call brings joy and peace. Surely you know what I am talking about! Sitting with Isaac and Rachel's girls tonight brought me that joy and peace. Once it's touched you, it's hard to forget." She sighed. "You get … hungry … for it. Desperate almost. You find yourself searching for it, determined to find it again no matter what." She briefly met Graham's eyes again. "You find yourself doing crazy things like running away from home and traveling thousands of miles to a small island in the Caribbean Sea hoping for more opportunities to find it."

They walked for a time in silence, both lost in thought. "Please don't misunderstand me. It wasn't my drastic move that brought me this joy and peace." She chuckled. "That brought quite a bit of terror and self-doubt, actually. But sometimes, *sometimes* you have to find a place where you can *hear* the call rather than the shouts of endless criticism. The opportunity to sit on the steps in the quiet of the evening and comfort a small child … The opportunity to wipe a tear from a grieving woman, to say an encouraging word to a struggling friend, or to teach an eighty-two year old woman how to write her name… I've found that all those chances are my opportunities to find joy and peace in this world. It's listening to the call and obeying."

Mena stopped and touched Graham's arm, making him stop and look at her as she made her final point. "It's being with a friend when he's burying his child. It's finishing a man's day of work so he'll receive full pay even though the man has left early to attend to his wife. It's watching out for his workers because he knows no one else will."

Graham looked at her, unable to accept what she was trying to give him. "You make more out of my behavior than you should. I've got a reason for everything I do and it's never to serve anyone but myself, whether I'm helping you muck out the windmill or working in the fields doing Isaac's job. You'd do well to remember that. *If yuh head bad, yuh whole body bad.*"

She shook her head at him, smiled and then resumed walking. "The people here think highly of you, Mr. Rhyder, and that's significant praise. The shadow you cast is significantly different than the shadow Mrs. Wagner casts. You may have felt you needed to correct me about comparing you to Mrs. Wagner, but no one else needs that instruction."

Graham had no response and chose to fall back into the familiar habit of remaining silent, which kept Mena talking. "And while we're listing your good deeds, it's kind of you to walk me home. I know your home is still quite a distance and it's been a long day for you."

It's not a home. Just a shed. But Graham kept those words to himself. "I don't sleep much, so it's no trouble."

Mena shook her head and smiled. "Well, since I've come here, I've gotten the best sleep of my life! I'm asleep almost before my head hits the pillow, and if Elizabeth didn't knock on my door first thing in the morning and talk to me for a bit to make sure I'm conscious and functioning, I'm afraid I'd sleep right through until lunch." She turned to look at him walking beside her. "But I used to have terrible trouble sleeping. Worry's an awful bedfellow. So is fear and despair."

"What about misery?" It was out before he could stop himself.

She chuckled, thinking he was joking. "Misery? What causes you to be so miserable, Mr. Rhyder? You've got a good job, you're well liked," she had the audacity to wink at him, "except for Mrs. Wagner, of course, and you live on the beautiful island of Barbados. It sounds to me like you're living the dream."

He stopped, the Great House within sight now, and she stopped and turned to continue talking with him in the moonlight. She sighed a sound of peaceful contentment. "Do you know that I've never had the freedom that I have here? Why," he's certain she blushed but couldn't actually be sure in the light, "I've never even walked or talked with a man unescorted until Barbados." She waggled her finger at him in jest, "That's not what a proper, privileged lady should do, you know. Appearance is everything. Decorum is key. Reputation can be gone," she snapped her fingers, "just like that and before you know it your family doesn't know what to do with you. Opportunities for marriage dry up, coveted invitations cease to come, and before you know it-," suddenly she was no longer smiling, perhaps realizing what she was revealing about herself.

"And?" he prompted watching her inner light shutter and grow dark.

All smiles, laughter and teasing were gone. In their place was a haunted sorrow in her eyes so profound Graham could almost feel it. Mena managed a quick breath and a polite smile. After moments of silence she said quietly, "I should go in. Thank you for the escort home, Mr. Rhyder."

Graham gave her a small bow. "I apologize."

"For?"

"It would seem that in conversing with me you've lost that joy and peace you find so precious here in Barbados. I have that effect on some. I would suspect that I've also robbed you of your good night's sleep," he murmured and then turned and walked away.

"I thought it only fair to tell you that I'm going to be your wife one day," she said with a mischievous twinkle in her eye.

"Has no one told you that it's the man's job to do the chasin' and the courtin' and, finally, the proposin'?"

"No one tells me what to do, Gray! Not my Da, not my governess, and certainly not you. I am a modern woman and I go after what I want." She stamped her foot trying to drive home her point and only succeeded in reminding him how very young she was.

"Look around you, me girl. There are crowds of young men just begging for a smile from ya. Why would you want me? There's no accounting for your taste, lass."

"You let me be the judge of that."

Don' ask me weh uh gine, ask me weh uh went.

Chapter Eight

Graham trudged away into the gathering dark with almost a full rum bottle clutched in his hand. Great, just great. Willie, the highest paid employee on the plantation second only to him, had better pull himself together. Of course everyone knew that Willie had them between a rock and a hard place. The day before Harvest Time started Graham wasn't about to fire his one and only striker and hope to find another one at this late date. Strikers, those highly skilled in boiling and refining the cane juice down to the perfect consistency needed to make the sugar, were practically worth their weight in gold. Once a plantation found a good striker, they held on to him with promises, bribes, and salaries other plantation workers could only dream about. Although Willie was good, he wasn't great; but he was the best one Windermere could afford for now.

"Jus' celebratin' da end o' hard times, my ass," Graham grumbled. He stood taking in all the sights, sounds and smells of the night. The cane, ripe and ready, swished and clacked in the night breeze, which also brought in the scents of further celebration over by the worker's huts. Were he to walk over there, he'd find many a man and woman doing exactly what Willie had been doing – enjoying the last night of 'freedom'. Huts were filled to bursting with seasonal workers ready to begin work bright and early tomorrow while makeshift camping spots dotted the outlying perimeter. Celebrating was customary before the first day of harvest; who cared how you felt that first morning when all you had to look forward to was four endless, backbreaking months of labor?

He remembered. Dear God, he remembered. His first serious drunk had happened when he was no more than six or seven on a night such as this right alongside his dear mother. From as early as he could remember, he'd labored right along with the others doing whatever job he could physically manage to help put money in his mother's always-empty pocket. When he'd been taken from that life, cleaned up and forced into another life in which he didn't belong, Harvest Time was always four months of guilt that he couldn't escape while his mother and the others toiled relentlessly to keep him in the life he was supposed to have become accustomed. Memories rattled and clanked, trying to escape their confines and destroy the last vestiges of his desperately held onto peace.

He could smell the rum in the bottle even over the ocean breeze and the smell of the campfires. Gripped tightly in his hand, the bottle felt as familiar as the boots on his feet. Graham lifted the bottle to his nose and deeply inhaled. Ahh, yes, there it was - that aroma so strong that you could almost taste it in the back of the throat. He felt his teeth ache and his mouth water with the need for a taste. Just one taste.

What could it hurt, really? He had less than a full bottle. Back in the day when Fiona was still alive, he could polish off a full one and still keep most from even knowing what he was up to. Except Fiona, of course. She always knew. Sometimes she seemed to know even before he'd go on one of his bad drunks which would last for a day or two. Or five. "Stay with me, Gray," she'd whisper in his ear as he was on his way out on some false excuse, desperate to find a bottle. During those times even the feel of her arms around his neck and the promising allure of her body couldn't compete with his desperate need to have a drink. Nothing could. He'd give her a hug and kiss and make a promise they both knew he'd never keep about coming home right away. Fiona's voice whispered on the wind as Graham stood there clutching the bottle, "Gray, don't leave me …" But he had and she was dead, and so was their child, all because of him.

If he'd only ignored the call just once. *Just once.* Had he stayed home just that one night Fiona would have lived as would their child. But no, he'd found himself a bottle which had led to another and then another and when he'd finally dragged himself back two days later he'd found his wife and newborn son dead on the floor. When they had needed him most he'd not been there, and nothing anyone could say would ever change that.

Now Miss Mena Westwood was looking at him with stars in her eyes and praise on her lips like he was some mythical hero of old who spent his days rescuing the needy, and his nights on his knees praying for the suffering. The next time she started to tell him what a wonderful man he was, maybe he should tell her about the lovely Fiona who was dead within four years of their first meeting, and the innocent babe who never lived long enough to draw a single breath. All because his need for the bottle was more important to him than anything else on the face of the earth.

These memories were killing him, bit by bit, slowly tearing him apart. That's why the drink had been so important and why it was still so powerfully alluring; it helped him forget everything that he'd done wrong, everything he'd failed at, everyone he'd destroyed. But over four years he'd been able to keep that demon chained.

Graham looked down at the bottle in his hand. *Hell.* He put the bottle to his lips and drank, rejoicing in the burn that poured down his throat and the fragrance that filled his nose. Ahhh, at last. He closed his eyes to focus all his senses on the ecstasy of the alcohol burning up his stomach and slowly seeping into his blood. Quickly, please, quickly let it seep into his brain so his memories would fade into oblivion.

There was an expectant feeling in the air that no one could miss. It was all attributed to Harvest Time which began tomorrow at sunrise: a time that everyone seemed to dread and anticipate with equal measure. Even the Wagners seemed affected by the charged atmosphere. Today, Mr. Wagner, the most unemotional, unresponsive human being that Mena had ever met, had actually smiled at Mena and wished her a good day. It was the first time the man had even acknowledged her existence, let alone spoken to her. Then, not moments later, Mrs. Wagner had surprised Mena with the announcement that formal dinner would not be held that evening. Furthermore, it was to be suspended for the foreseeable future. Meals for those privileged to partake of them at the Great House, would now be served buffet style any time during the six o'clock hour. Had Mena not known any better, it would almost seem as if Mrs. Wagner was addled. But after a little over a month here at Windermere, it seemed a proven fact that nothing addled Moira Wagner.

There had been little time for grief over the death of baby Jacob, with baby Rebecca's demands joining that of her six sisters. For the past two weeks, Mena had faithfully spent the evening hours with Isaac and Rachel's girls, giving their parents time to grieve, and had been escorted home faithfully back to the Great House each night by Silent Joe. The family had welcomed Mena with a gracious appreciation and warmth, inviting her to join them for dinner (she often brought a basket of goodies supplied by Dahlia) and quickly incorporated her into their evening routines. Watching Isaac and Rachel interact with their girls and with each other, as well as their neighbors and friends, provided an insight that no book reading could have provided. Time with the family had allowed her an opportunity to see many of the workers from a different perspective as she sat on the front porch giggling with the girls. It had also allowed the people to see her as something other than just "da new lady teacher." With each visit, the community's familiarity with her had grown, and now she was warmly greeted and even teased on occasion.

"Good day to yuh, Miss Mena! John Paul an' I were practicin' our al-fee-bet taday!"

"Da moon's full, Miss Mena. Yuh best be bringin' a par'sol ta keep dat fair skin o' yuhr's from gettin' crispy."

"I hear Dahlia was givin' yuh cookin' lessons, Miss Mena. Ole Yancey says fer one o' yuhr smiles he's willin' ta teach yuh how to gut an' skin catfish if yuhr in'trested."

"Heard tell yuhr sewin' sum new skirts wit' Jessie Lynn's help. Yuh should ask Big Mary for sum o' her hand-me-downs. Yuh could fix yuhself up jus' fine fo' da whole year wit' jus' one dress o' hers!"

"Need an escort home, Miss Mena? I do believe dat Willie's in'trested an' even took a bath in da river so he'd smell sweet!"

"I see dat Silen' Joe is waitin' to bring yuh back ta da Big House! He's becomin' yuhr shadow!

Tonight Mena walked home from the workers' village amidst a revelry she'd never witnessed; the sounds of celebration still ringing in her ears. She would miss her time with Rachel and Isaac's family and hoped, once Harvest Time was over, that she could resume her visits. Cabins were filled to bursting with workers drawn by the promise of coins for their pockets. Children danced with expectation of more food appearing on the dinner table. For Mena, Harvest Time only brought a sense of dread. Four months of endless work for almost everyone old enough to walk and perform a task. What would she do during this time? If people had found it difficult to find time to attend her classes during the Hard Times when there was little work to be found, what chance did she have once everyone was caught up in the fevered pitch of Harvest Time?

What exactly was she expected to do with herself for these four months in which even Little Mary would be out in the fields performing a job? The pressure to have something productive to show for her time weighed heavily upon her, especially given her expected monthly reports for Mr. Topher. He'd been extremely businesslike and not at all inclined to discuss anything in depth during her first report meeting just last week. Yet there was no doubt in Mena's mind that once Mr. Topher had received a response from Lord Windermere regarding her presence on the plantation, his demeanor would change substantially.

Self-doubt had always been her greatest enemy and it reared its ugly head as she trudged back to the Great House. Had Mrs. Wagner and even Mr. Rhyder been merely humoring her attempts to start a school knowing full well the impossibility of her success? Certainly neither individual had ever been overly supportive or encouraging.

"My, my, aren't you lost in thought."

Lounging in the shadows against an enormous kapok tree was Graham Rhyder, looking more relaxed than Mena had ever seen him. "Why, Mr. Rhyder! I see that you are taking advantage of your last evening of freedom before harvest begins." She peered into the shadowed gloom. "Why, I don't ever recall seeing you just sitting doing nothing."

"Oh I'm doing something allright."

She enjoyed speaking with him, she realized. Unlike other men, he seemed quite interested in what response – biting or not – she would deliver. He sat, seeming completely at ease, one leg drawn up with his arm resting on his knee. "Well, you must admit I've never see you so at ease."

Suddenly he rose and walked toward her, his approach so purposeful that Mena took a step back. He stopped close enough that she could see the day's growth of reddish beard dusting his face. Gazing down at her, he sighed. "Yes," he murmured, looking into her eyes, "at this moment you're right. I am *more at ease* than I will be tomorrow in more ways than you can imagine."

Mena didn't know what to say. Something was clearly different, and yet she was at a loss as to what exactly it was. To her utter shock, he slowly reached up and touched the long, heavy braid of hair that lay across her shoulder. She'd taken to wearing her hair as practically as possible, rather than any of her more elaborate hair styles. For a brief moment, Mother's sharp criticism over the general state of her appearance invaded Mena's thoughts, but she forcefully pushed the painful words aside. Without a comment he deftly retied the ribbon that had loosened and threatened to slip. "Mr. Rhyder, I-"

"I would like to end these formalities. Call me Graham. And I shall call you Mena. I'm not your boss, I'm your equal."

"I-I couldn't," Mena stammered. "It w-wouldn't be proper."

He laughed briefly. "Oh, it's a lot more proper than some other things I'm considering," he muttered almost to himself. "Only the Wagners insist on such ridiculous formalities. I'm tired of it." He gave her a pointed look. "Say my name." He took a deep breath and had the temerity to roll his eyes before muttering, "Please."

Her natural urge to resist an order roared to life. "But Mr. Rhyder -"

"Do you call the stable master 'Mr. Jakeman'?" He asked, hands fisted at his hips.

"No, I-"

"Do you call the head gardener 'Mr. Hayden'?"

"No, I-"

"Do you call Isaac and Rachel 'Mr. and Mrs. Freeman?'"

"Mr. and Mrs. Freeman?" Mena said in a puzzled tone, "no, I-"

Graham shocked her by suddenly grabbing her hand and pulling her along with him as he walked with purpose back towards the workers' huts. "Come with me. I'd like to see if you speak with anyone else with such formality at the village celebrations. And we might as well enjoy the celebrations while we can."

"Mr. Rhyder! Stop this behavior at once!" Mena tried in vain to tug her hand free.

He turned his face lit by the moonlight, and grinned at her. "I'm not going to listen to you unless you call me Graham. It's my new rule."

That's when she caught the subtle aroma that evoked memories of Father and his friends clustered together in the library smoking their after dinner cigars and drinking Father's rum. It was a smell that caused her insides to roil and her heart to begin to pound. She frantically tried to dig her feet in but failed. "You've been drinking ...!" she gasped.

"Knew you were a smart gal," he threw over his shoulder, shocking her further with a wink, as he continued to drag her along.

Heart pounding, Mena struggled desperately to gain her freedom so she could run. She took a deep breath to calm herself and made herself remember where she was and whom she was with. "Please," she said when she managed to find her voice, *"Graham, stop. You're scaring me."*

He immediately halted, turned, and released her. "That was not my intention," he said with utmost sincerity. "However," his face suddenly lit with triumph, "I did get you to say my name. That wasn't so hard, now was it … *Mena?"*

Working hard to control her pounding heart, Mena reminded herself that this was Graham Rhyder. She was in the tropical island of Barbados. She was *not* in England. He was *not* … Taking a deep breath, Mena allowed herself a moment to look at the man standing before her. She suddenly felt an unexplainable need to keep Graham from the workers and their celebrating. "I don't want to go to the workers' village … Graham. You have proved your point and gained your objective." She gestured to the Great House. "I was on my way back to my room. It's been a long day and I'm exhausted." She pulled on her hand which he still held fast. "Come, Graham," Mena said quietly, "walk me back just like you've so kindly done before."

He allowed her to lead him back along the path, the way they'd just come. "Tell me," Mena tried to speak as casually as possible as she walked alone with a man hand-in-hand in the moonlight, "do you know anything of the stars and the constellations here? They're different than they are in England and I'd like to know more. I plan to do a course in astronomy for my older students and don't want to make any mistakes."

Silent at first, Graham sighed, a sound that seemed to be pulled deep from his soul. Finally, he acknowledged, "Yes, I know the stars." He walked them both to a clearing and then drew her to stand in front of him, turning her just so, his big, warm hands on her shoulders. "Can you see those five bright stars that make a distinctive **W**?" Silent as she searched intently, he finally leaned in closer and raised her arm to direct her where he wanted her to look. Slowly he traced the shape once. Twice. "Do you see it yet?" he asked quietly. Suddenly it was vividly clear and she nodded excitedly. "That's Cassiopeia, named after that vain queen from Greek mythology who boasted about her unrivaled beauty," he murmured. His arm crept around her waist to hold her against him while he positioned her arm with his and traced another shape slowly while saying, "Andromeda, Cassiopeia's daughter who was served up as dinner to the sea monster Cetus," and then, "Perseus, Andromeda's rescuer" and then, "Cetus, the sea monster Perseus slew." By the time Graham got to the final constellation, even their cheeks were touching as he whispered and traced, "Cephesu, Cassiopeia's husband and Andromeda's father." They stood there like that under the stars for long moments saying nothing, and Mena was unsure whether she wanted him to release her or hold her like that for the rest of her life. Putting a small bit of distance between them, Graham finally rested both his hands warmly on her hips and murmured, "Now it's my chance to test the teacher," and Mena heard the teasing in his voice. "Show them again to me without my help."

With his hands on her hips and his looming presence behind her, Mena's heart had yet to take a calm beat. In fact, she was quite certain she could barely remember her own name. Never had star gazing had been so difficult to focus on. She found Cassiopeia easily enough, pointing it out with a shaky finger, and then Andromeda, but needed assistance with the others. With her back to him and his hands still holding her, she finally braved an observation. "You are quite a dichotomy, Mr. Rhy-, er, Graham. You work like a laborer and yet you speak and act – when it suits you, of course – like an educated gentleman."

His hands tensed at her waist as he breathed deeply and then exhaled. The aroma of rum surrounded them both, but before Mena could tense he released her and took two steps back. "Never mistake me for an educated gentleman, Mena," and when she turned to face him he reiterated, "*Never*. The next time you're inclined to sing my praises and try to convince yourself that I'm always eager to do something good, remember *tonight* for that is the farthest thing from my mind right now."

"*The last thing I'd ever want you to be is an educated gentleman,*" Mena whispered to his retreating back, "*that is the essence of my nightmares...*" And then she was alone with her thoughts and the stars.

"Oh, how I shall miss you! I will remember you in my prayers daily. I earnestly hope that my assistance in your ... endeavor ... will bring the results you wish for your life. Out of concern for your safety, I've only been willing to give you a recommendation for Windermere. I cannot allow you to simply disappear off into the horizon with no knowledge of where you shall end up. I pray you will not hold this against me.

"You are a strong woman, never doubt that. I admire your courage, your determination, and your perseverance despite all odds. You are the essence of what transforming faith can do for a person and I rejoice in having known you. Don't forget your promise to write to me and tell me of your adventures.

"I have one request of you before you go: you must promise me that you will not give up on love. I know that life has seen fit thus far to be miserly to you in that regard but you must not shut that door completely. I tell you that love in this world exists! And you shall find it in the most unexpected places! Look at me! Remember me and my story! Certainly I am vivid proof of God's love and mercy! Who would have thought that someone such as me – with nothing of any merit to offer anyone – would end up such as I have? I am loved, cherished, and well cared for – more than my wildest dreams.

"Wherever you end up in this world, whatever you end up doing, you must not give up hope in this regard, my dearest friend. You have chosen to give God your allegiance, so you must never doubt the incredible miracles He is capable of performing."

Drunk or sober, mind yuh business.

Chapter Nine

Tossing and turning in the early morning hours before the sun rose, Mena knew she was in trouble and it was all Graham Rhyder's fault. He'd ruined her. She had not had a good night's sleep since her conversation with Graham when she'd foolishly revealed a bit too much about her life in England.

Conversing with him was always dangerous because she enjoyed it so much, whether he was being blatantly provocative or politely attentive. He spoke with her – not as a simpering, fragile, ignorant female but as a person with an equal intellectual awareness. But what had she been thinking, prattling along about opportunities for marriage drying up and invitations ceasing to come, and what madness had she participated in standing alone with him under the stars?

At first her lack of sleep had stemmed from thinking about her tenuous situation here at Windermere, imagining letters flying back and forth across the Atlantic between Mr. Topher and Lord Windermere. Full disclosure would destroy her. She had burned all her bridges in London, there was now nothing there for her. Were this opportunity here in Barbados to disappear, the life she had run from would most certainly not be waiting patiently for her to return nor would anyone welcome her back with open arms. What would she do with herself then? Where would she go?

But last night Graham had touched her and called her Mena in a way that no one else had ever spoken her name. *Mena.* Now she simply could not stop thinking about the feel of his warmth surrounding her last night: around her waist, against her back, along her arm, against her cheek... Now there was a whole other topic that was invading her sleep.

She did not *need* a man. God above knew she did not *want* a man. Men could not be trusted, for they wanted women for only one specific purpose. Romantic love was an illusion. Marriage was merely a business negotiation between powerful families in which she had refused to participate. And yet what was she doing? She was lying in bed mooning over a man who'd merely taken the time to show her the stars. She was behaving like some idiotic school girl and it galled her.

But he was impossible to ignore. His bold presence was something that had dominated every aspect of her time at Windermere, almost from the first morning he'd burst into Mrs. Wagner's office. Originally, she'd merely found him refreshing as he was unlike any man she had ever encountered - alternatingly confrontational, shockingly blunt, dependable, helpful and insightful. Yet it had been highly appealing to find someone equally dismissive of the very things that had stifled her in England and had sought to drag Mena down like suffocating quicksand. He challenged her opinions and made her think past her assumptions. Surely that was the only reason she found him so intriguing...

So why did she continually think of his blue eyes or his illusive smile? And now she knew the sound of her name when he said it in just a certain way ... *Mena.* And the way his arms felt wrapped around her waist... With a groan, she rolled over for the thousandth time.

"Mornin' Miss Mena. Are yuh well? I heard yuh groanin' b'for I even opened da door. Yuh got to be sick 'cause yuh never awake b'fore I cum up here."

Sitting up, Mena said, "Good morning to you. No, Elizabeth, I'm fine. Just have a lot on my mind, that's all." She gave the young woman a brief smile and pushed thoughts of stars and mythical stories and mocking blue eyes to the back of her mind.

"Missus Wagner says yuh ta clear out o' yuh room an' stay out fo' pro'bly two days. She says yuh can sleep in da blue room on da second floor til yuhr room's done." Elizabeth stood in the doorway, a single candle lighting the darkness.

"Must I pack up all my belongings?"

Elizabeth shook her head, her brief smile and her crisp white cap flashing in the dim dawn lighting. "Yuhs to jus' take whut yuh will need fo' today an' tomorrow."

Mena sighed. "All right then, Elizabeth." She couldn't stop a yawn and hastily covered her mouth. "How are you this morning? Everyone at home off for the start of harvest?" They always exchanged brief pleasantries, and sometimes Elizabeth shared an interesting tidbit or two.

Elizabeth nodded. "All 'cept me an' Ab'gail. Only Lil' Mary seems excited 'bout it all, tho'. Thinkin' she's a big girl now since she old 'nough ta pick da fodder. I 'spect she'll be singin' a different tune by dis afta'noon." Elizabeth looked over her shoulder and then stepped further into Mena's room. Every time Mena spoke with the girl she was overcome with how lovely she was. "Will yuh be close by t'day, Miss Mena?" she whispered. "here in da Big House?"

Mena frowned, her suspicions raised. "Well, I'm not sure yet. For some reason, Mrs. Wagner has told me to stay away from the harvesting and as of yet I've nothing much to do with myself, what with everyone fully involved with harvest or house cleaning. Is there something you need me to do?"

Shaking her head vigorously, Elizabeth said, "Oh no, Miss Mena. I's jus' wond'rin' dat's all." Again she peered out into the dark hallway. "Jus' wond'rin' who's ta be in da house an' such. Dat's all."

Mena misunderstood. "Well, it's hard to tell who will show up if at all. With formal dinner suspended."

Elizabeth bit her lip. "Dat ain't been ever don b'fore."

Now that was odd. Mena had assumed that the suspension of a formal evening meal was standard practice at this time of the year. "I had no idea…" Perhaps the girls weren't being fed as they should be. "Are you receiving your proper meal rations? You and Abigail? If you're not I'll speak to-"

Elizabeth's eyes grew wide with panic. "On no, no Miss Mena! Ev'ryting is jus' fine! Please don' go sayin' nothin' ta Missus Wagner or …," she swallowed and looked back again. "I's gots ta go."

As she dressed, Mena made a mental note to speak with Dahlia about the girls.

Harvest Time began like a blast from a cannon, and it was as if the entire world was turned on its head. Not so much because Mena was aware of the work going on in the fields, but Mrs. Wagner, apparently unwilling to be outdone, took it upon herself to launch the most ambitious of yearly cleanings at the same time. Rooms were stripped to the walls; what could be washed was washed and what could be painted was painted. Rugs were lugged outside to be beaten, mattresses were aired and flipped, and windows were cleaned inside and out. The project was a yearly event dreaded by every member of the household staff. Eventually, even the several outbuildings also under Mrs. Wagner's control, would receive similar attention. Dahlia whispered to Mena that this year wasn't as bad as others; some years the entire outhouse (a massive five-holer) was completely dismantled and moved to another location. "Dems da years I come down wif a powerful case o' sick," she confided with a completely straight face. "Nobody gonna see Dahlia diggin' no poop hole at dis time o' her life."

All meals for those who ate at the Great House were now served buffet style so that all could come and go as their responsibilities allowed. Casual conversation with Dahlia over breakfast (Mena ate every morning with the kitchen staff at 5:30 a.m.) revealed no concern regarding Elizabeth's and Abigail's meal rations, although Dahlia was so frazzled by the cleaning chaos Mena wondered how accurate her observations could be.

Everywhere she looked people seemed to be hurrying to the next chore. Except Mena. Even Old Maisy had been enlisted to stir the gigantic cleaning kettles which were in full use at the Great House from sun up to sun down. "Dey's payin' me ta sit an' stir, how can I pass dat up?" she'd confided to Mena with a toothless grin.

Mena was at a loss with nowhere to go and nothing to do. The prospect of being in this situation for *four months* filled her with total dismay that bordered on outright panic. How ironic that despite all her struggles it seemed she was destined to fail after all. What could she report to Mr. Topher? How could she possibly justify her presence here for the next four months? By the time the harvest was finished, Mr. Topher would most assuredly have heard from Lord Windermere and once that happened...

By the afternoon of the first day of Harvest Time, Mena abandoned the chaos of the Great House. The third floor, including her room, was in the midst of being painted, and the fumes from the paint made her head ache something fierce.

Elizabeth and Abigail were alternately pounding rugs, carting laundry, or rushing off to do one of the many other chores ordered by Mrs. Wagner. Even Dahlia was frazzled and short tempered as all her usual help had been enlisted by others. "Don say it, Miss Mena," Dahlia'd puffed as she worked the butter churn, "yuh's not a house worker. Yuh's da teacher. Missus Wagner'd have mah head should she come in a see yuh peelin' taters or kneadin' da bread. Off wit' yuh; I don' have da time or da breath ta tell yuh twice."

With no other options and despite Mrs. Wagner's firm admonition to stay away from the fields (and Graham's surprising agreement), Mena decided to visit her Windmill School. As she walked, she reasoned that the Windmill School was *by* the fields, not necessarily *at* the fields. A fact that would hardly pacify Mrs. Wagner should she choose to take exception to Mena's rationale. Since things at the school had been hastily put together, perhaps she could busy herself at least for a few days with rearranging and organizing things a bit.

Mena was forced to admit that the school wasn't much to look at as it came into view in the distance. Stepping inside would reveal three rows of sturdy benches, her two large and precious slates, and the books and small slates stacked against one wall (no shelves as of yet) so that one would perhaps understand that they were indeed looking at a school room. As she crested the rise where the windmills sat she could see a large portion of the plantation. She stopped abruptly and stood in stunned amazement at what was laid out before her: Harvest Time in all its chaotic glory.

❧❧❧❧❧❧❧❧❧

"Isaac!" Graham shouted from the back of Dancer, "Talk to that first row man you've got on the fifth gang! His timing is off! Tell him to get those cutters and headers in synch or I'll have his damn head for dinner!"

"Yes, Boss!" Isaac shouted and galloped off down the specified rows.

"Jims! Once you get to the mill and finish unloading, get Karl to take a look at your horse's front right leg. He's favoring it, and I'd rather spend a few minutes getting that checked out than lose a whole damn horse the first week!"

"Yas, Mistah Graham!"

As he rode slowly down the edge of the field Graham called out, "Darci! If you and Willie are so interested in each other, perhaps you'd like to step aside and let someone do your job with more focus? I've got six willing workers who showed up at my cabin door this morning before sunup hoping I could give them work, and I'll bet they'll still be sitting there when I get back tonight."

Everywhere he looked it seemed as if something needed his attention. "Josiah! You sharpen that bills of yours tonight instead of drinking yourself into a stupor or I'll get someone else to be my cutter on gang two tomorrow. What sense does it make to work with a dull blade? Are you trying to make things harder for yourself, man?"

"Isaac! One of the headers in first gang is stacking the cane wrong in the cart. Every time she leaves a bundle it needs to be adjusted. What's wrong with her? Can't she follow instructions? Tell her if she can't handle being a header, then she can join the older women and men and start clearing and weeding the drainage ditches, but she better expect to see a difference in her wage!"

"Yes, Boss!"

"Winston! The next time you drop your load off at the mill, you make sure that Billy has enough wood and dried cane to keep the fires burning. Remind him that he's the one who's got to let me know – with plenty of advanced warning – when he needs me to send him people to bring in more fuel. Unless he says something, I've got them working in the drainage ditches."

"Yas, Mistah Graham!"

Ripping his hat off his head, Graham used his sleeve to wipe the sweat dripping in his face. Dear God, was it only the first day? Yes, he reminded himself, it was the first day. That's why everything was so difficult. By the end of the first week, and definitely by the second week, in they'd all be running like a well-oiled machine, which was exactly when the machinery would start to act up. As he rode Dancer to a small crest, he squinted his eyes against the bright sun and surveyed the five gangs that were harvesting today. When an odd fluttering caught his eye, he turned to see Mena standing near her Windmill School watching the chaos. Thinking of her and his incredible idiocy of last night was certainly something he didn't need now, and he turned abruptly away.

Cursing aloud, he wheeled Dancer around and galloped out to the fifth gang. If he wasn't mistaken, someone had just lost a hand...

ⓔⓔⓔⓔⓔⓔ

Bare-chested men wielded huge, dangerous looking blades that glinted in the sun as they swung and slashed, swung and slashed. Before them stretched an endless forest of ripe sugar cane and behind them stretched the chaos of production. Close behind the shirtless, sweat gleaming cutters were men and women who gathered the cut cane, quickly wrapped it together and carried it balanced atop their heads down the length of the

row to the waiting carts. Horse drawn carts in various stages
either waited patiently to be filled or were rushing to and from
the processing mill which stood nearby to Mena's Windmill
School in full, steam billowing production. With utter
fascination she sat down on the crest of the hill and watched the
scene that was spread out before her.

On first glance it looked like utter chaos, but as Mena
continued to watch, a distinct pattern began to emerge. No one
group, no one cart was at the same point; like a tightly organized
dance, each team was slightly ahead or slightly behind another.
Carts departed and arrived in almost military precision, timed
almost to perfection. There was no waiting; no wasted time or
motion. In addition to the cutting and transporting, there was a
second group of individuals that seemed to consist of older
children and older men and women. This group stayed away
from the intense action of the actual harvesting, busily collecting
odd bits of cane in baskets or weeding and clearing the irrigation
trenches with shovels. Mena thought she recognized a number
of the children in this group from her times in the workers'
village and the Windmill School.

A cart arrived with two barrels, and she recognized, due
to his enormous size, Silent Joe simply as he lifted the barrels
one after another and carried them off to the side. He retrieved
two other barrels that were obviously empty and left. Mena saw
Isaac and Rachel's Ruth carefully walk and fill buckets at the
edge of each group from the newly arrived containers, which
were obviously for drinking. Once that chore was done, Ruth
wandered over to the far edge of the field and filled a final
bucket. It was then that Mena saw a number of very young
children clustered in the shade of a tree. Shielding her eyes from
the sun's glare, Mena stood in an attempt to see better and
caught Ruth's attention, causing her to wave. To Mena's
amazement, soon more than sixteen very young children around

Ruth were all waving enthusiastically at Mena up on the hill from their spot in the shade.

❧❧❧❧❧❧❧❧❧

He saw her heading down the hill, skirts billowing in the breeze like a damn flag. He knew where she was headed, knew what she'd find, and could guess what she would do once she discovered what was there: infants in makeshift baskets and children as young as three whiling away their day while their parents worked to make enough money to hopefully keep them alive through the Hard Times. Mena would never realize he knew exactly what those children experienced because *he'd lived it;* she was getting a vivid picture of his own miserable childhood. The callouses on his hands had formed when he was a young child, the body's wise protection from the razor sharp edges of the cane plant's leaves. Nothing stung more than the salt of your own sweat burning into the myriad of cuts along your hands and arms after an exhausting day in the fields. He still remembered crying over the pain until his mother had shut him up with a glass of her precious rum and a slap. *Share yuh food, I love yuh. Share yuh drink, yuh love me.*

Harvest Time. The irony was not lost on him that he was one of the only people on the plantation who knew what the experience was like from both sides. There was the endless back-breaking labor under the boiling sun. There was being at the mercy of others who literally had the power of life or death over you. There was living a life that held no hope for change and no expectation of escape. Just get up, put one foot in front of another until someone says you can stop and collapse until it was time to get up and start all over again. He supposed it was the essence of real survival: the desire to stay alive only for being alive's sake since there was no other reason, no other reward, and no other purpose imaginable.

Of course, his mother's primary goal was always to make it to the next drink, God rest her drunken soul, and she did anything necessary to accomplish that. Sell her possessions? Yes. Sell her body? Yes. Sell her son? Yes. In the early years her body had served her well to acquire her precious rum when coin was not available. Graham had grown up with the knowledge that Mama liked rum, men, and him in that specific order. Her beauty was something that even hard living, alcohol, and the scorching sun had taken decades to finally destroy. When sober – a state few people truly ever witnessed - she was quiet, almost shy. Filled with rum she was opinionated, feisty, sensual, and impossible to ignore. Graham had heard her described as a temptress, an enchantress, and a siren by men who had wanted to kill her out of jealousy and rage.

She claimed she'd caught the eye of Graham's father as she worked in his fields when she was barely fifteen. According to her, and she had every reason to lie, she'd seduced the honorable Lord Phillip Walcott, owner of the six hundred and twenty seven acre Forster Hall Plantation, as he rode by with the overseer to peruse his sugar cane holdings. Lord Walcott had taken one look at the dark haired, blue eyed beauty standing proudly amidst his slaves and had fallen head over heels in lust. Mama liked to remember of that first meeting and say those few months were the best Harvest Time she ever worked. Like many landholders of the time, Lord Walcott had many properties in numerous locations around the globe (tea in India, tobacco in America, and vineyards in France), so it wasn't until Graham was nearly eleven that his mother had the opportunity to press and prove the case of his paternity.

Even Mama had had no way of knowing that Lord Walcott, at the ripe old age of fifty-two, had been unable to sire an heir with any of his wives (three) or former mistresses (too many to count). Merely looking for an extra bit of coin to feed her constant need for drink (she was unaware that Graham had been helping himself to her supply for years), she'd been overjoyed to discover her son's valuable claim as the sole heir – bastard or not.

But by eleven, Graham had assumed much of his taciturn personality, not to mention his patent mistrust of every human being on the planet. Working in the sugar cane fields made men out of boys, and being a white slave – a detestable backro – had made him tougher than most. Muscular and tall for his age, life had done little to calm Graham's hot Irish temper, and as a result he was already a skilled brawler. Standing before Lord Walcott and being scrutinized from head to toe like a prized hog ready for the slaughter did little to make the first meeting between father and son positive.

Graham had never held much stock in the fact or fiction of his paternity. *Ask no questions, yuh hear no lies.* A lifetime with his mother had taught him that truth was not a skill Bridget Rhyder possessed. Surely this man of education and means would not be as stupid as all the other men who had fallen – albeit briefly – under her spell.

"You know who I am," Lord Walcott had finally murmured as he lounged in his fancy upholstered chair in front of a massive desk in a room with walls covered in books. Graham had been required to remove his shirt, bear his teeth, and turn slowly not once but twice for close examination.

"Yuhr my master," Graham had said. He stood straight and tall, hands fisted at his side with one foot forward and one foot back, his best fighting stance. He depended on himself and no other and was always prepared for a fight.

"Your mother claims I am also your father."

Graham had shrugged, caring little for a piece of information that had done nothing for him thus far.

"That birthmark on your back, above your right shoulder blade … it's known as the Walcott mark. I have it, my father had it, and his father before him. In fact, every Walcott male has had it for the past two hundred years."

"So?"

"What's your mother ever said about it?"

Graham thought about this question before he answered it. In truth, his mother used to call it her "rum money mark." Not something he suspected Lord Walcott would necessarily wish to hear at the moment. He shrugged again.

"Have you always had it?"

"How wud I know? I ain't never looked at my back."

Lord Walcott looked impatient. "Did your mother put it there?"

So the man wasn't as stupid as Graham had originally suspected, and knew what type of woman Bridget Rhyder was and what lengths she would go to get what she wanted. "Me mum's always called it her 'rum money mark' fer as long as I can remember. Dat's all I have ta say."

That night three men arrived and informed Graham and his mother that Graham would no longer be living, working or even associating with any of the slaves of Forster Hall Plantation. It was Lord Walcott's intention to take responsibility for Graham as his bastard son in the form of education and care. Perhaps, with extensive training and significant polishing, he could be turned into something of worth. Graham was to gather his belongings and depart with them immediately. Although his mother's lack of enthusiasm was assuaged by a large purse of coins and the promise of more in the future, it had taken all three men to subdue Graham and finally drag him, bound and gagged, away into the night.

A fury at everyone and everything was born that night. Perhaps it had always been simmering just below the surface, but it ignited in full as they'd stripped him, scrubbed him and tied him down while they'd trimmed his hair, cut his fingernails and measured his feet for his first pair of shoes. He was a wild animal that refused to be tamed. He'd spit in the doctor's face who'd come to examine him, and his strong right hook had knocked the tailor unconscious. Lord Walcott – Graham would never think of him as his father – had remained a silent observer throughout. Finally he'd said tersely to his trembling and bleeding staff, "Leave us."

Once they were alone, he'd walked up to stand before Graham and said, "Enough of this." At Graham's mutinous glare, he'd said, "Do you care about your mother?" and then waited a beat for Graham to consider the implications of the question. "Surely, you have some of your mother's intelligence. She may be a drunk and a whore," he stared at Graham but there was no use denying the truth, "but she knows what will get her what she wants most in life: rum first and a better life for her son second."

As Graham had stood there silent as a stone, Lord Walcott had turned and walked to the windows, gazing out into his lush sugar cane fields. "Use your head, boy. Stay with me and make the most of what you can grab. Take advantage of this opportunity that most people would kill for. Your mother … well, your mother will be cared for …"

"If yuh give her coin, she'll jus' drink herself ta death."

Lord Walcott turned and stared at him. "Is that why you're fighting all this?" At Graham's stubborn silence he finally asked, "How long have you been caring for her?"

Graham stood tall. *"Forever."*

The older man nodded. "Then why not make the most of this opportunity as quickly as you can? Maybe you'll be able to care for your mother better than you ever dreamed? I'll send foodstuffs and other provisions besides just coin. But we both know that if she doesn't get coin for her drink, she'll still manage. The reality is there's only so much that can be done, boy, and well you know it."

Recognizing the truth of Lord Walcott's words, Graham redirected his energies towards consuming everything that was offered to him as fast as it could be taught. He learned math, reading, writing, literature, foreign languages, sciences and history, believing that education was the key to escaping. He adopted etiquette and dress that enabled him to associate with the upper echelon of Barbados' society, and tolerated the condescending intolerance of people who feared Lord Walcott's power but detested the reality of Graham's birth.

Bridget Rhyder lived eight more years, just in time to be granted her freedom with the Slavery Emancipation Act of 1838, and drank herself to death in celebration at the ripe old age of thirty-four. Graham's transformation from lowly Irish slave boy to educated bastard son was completed at almost the same time, just as Lord Walcott's fourth wife gave birth to a healthy, strapping legitimate baby boy.

Graham had been promptly turned out for the worthless piece of trash he'd always known he was into a world which no longer held any place for him.

"We shall live happily ever after," she said as she threw her arms around him and kissed him. "Now tell me how much you love me."

Every time he looked at her he could not believe that she was truly his. Young and privileged, she had no concept of the cruel lessons life could teach a person. He had never been so happy in all his life. And, consequently, never been more terrified. "I love you, lass, with every fiber of my being," he whispered fervently into her hair.

His vow felt like a challenge to the fates to come and do their worst.

Da longest day does bring home night.

Chapter Ten

She quickly counted and there were twenty-two children in the shade of a small group of trees off to the side of the vast sugar cane field in the process of being harvested. They ranged in age from infancy to toddlers: some were fast asleep, others sitting and staring at her, and at least three in various stages of crying. Adding further to Mena's dismay, Little Mary appeared to be one of the senior members of the group.

"Dat's Crybaby James," she pointed to the chubby toddler sitting in the dirt who had obviously been wailing for quite a while as his face was awash in tears and snot. "He cries lots," Little Mary stated matter of factly, not at all bothered by his sobs.

"Would it help if I picked him up, Mary?" Mena asked as she stood, overwhelmed at what she was looking at.

Little Mary shrugged. "He jus' wants his Ma an' she's busy." Two other toddlers, both girls, were not at all happy with Mena's arrival, and tears trailed silently down their cheeks as they both sucked furiously on their thumbs.

"Little Mary," Mena said as she sat down amidst the children, "come sit on my lap and introduce me to everyone." Little Mary happily complied, giving a vivid description of each child as only she was capable of doing. "Dat's Stinky Celia, dat's

Biter Joe, dat's Whiny Louise, dat's Wanderin' Sammie, dem's da babies dat we can't touch no matter if dey are sleepin' or if dey are screamin', dat's Will – he eats anything yuh give him even bugs an' rocks, dat's Li'l Winston – he's mah cousin …"

By the end of the introductions, Crybaby James had subsided to noisy sniffles and the two crying toddler girls (Mae and Winnie) were quietly twirling their hair and studying Mena and Little Mary with open curiosity. "Well, Mary," Mena finally wondered aloud, "shall we sing a song or tell a story?"

"Tell dat story you told da other night 'bout da baby in da basket," Little Mary said, and then turned around to Mena and said, "but first yuh gots ta change Stinky Celia's nappy b'fore she makes da rest o' us cry wit her smell."

Over the course of that first day, Mena gradually encountered each of the parents who came occasionally to check on their children as labor permitted. Many knew of her, either from her windmill school or through her time spent at Rachel and Isaac's home in the past weeks after baby Jacob's death. With each one, Mena spoke politely and asked them about their children. Was it alright for her to care for them while they worked? Was there anything special she should know about them? Would they reassure their child that Mena was a friend and would help them if they needed something?

Rachel came at lunch time, baby Rebecca tucked in a sling at her breast. She smiled tiredly at Mena, while she nursed the baby and ate with Mary. "Wut yuh doin' here Miss Mena?"

Mena smiled. "I'm not quite sure. I saw the children from the school and wandered down to say hello." She nodded to Little Mary. "I'm not even sure I'm needed; Mary seems to have everything well under control."

Rachel gave a small smile. "Dat so, Li'l Mary? Yuh not bein' too bossy, I hope."

Little Mary finished her bite of biscuit and then said, "I jus tell wut needs ta be said, Momma."

Rachel nodded. "I s'pect dat's true. Jus' mind who is da boss."

"Ruth says it's God. Dat who yuh mean, Momma?"

Rachel gave Mena a look that seemed to say, 'This is what *really* makes me tired!' "God made mo' bosses fo' all of us, li'l girl, an' well yuh know it."

Little Mary gave her mother a practiced shrug that Mena was rapidly coming to know was her way of dismissing what she didn't necessarily wish to acknowledge. "I certainly hope that Mary will be willing to help me with the younger children tomorrow," Mena said.

"Yuh gonna do dis ev'ry day, Miss Mena?" Rachel said in surprise.

"Well, I came to the school this morning because I had nothing else to do. I'm being paid to be the plantation teacher and there doesn't seem to be much opportunity to do that, with everyone busy working both here in the fields and up in the Great House. Why not?"

A cloud seemed to pass across Rachel's expression. "Yuh see 'Lizabeth and Ab'gail today?"

"Your Elizabeth is the only thing that keeps me from deep trouble each morning," Mena offered. "She rouses me from my bed each morning."

"Sumpins wrong with dat oldest girl o' mine but I can't get ta da bottom o' it," Rachel murmured to herself as she moved the baby to her shoulder and gently began to pat her back. "Got all quiet an' full o' secrets all o' a sudden. When I try ta talk ta her she clams up an' won' even look me in da eye."

Mena thought about this morning when Elizabeth had asked about where she was going to be over the course of the day. Would telling Rachel about that conversation only make her more concerned? She certainly had no helpful information to give her. "I'll try to speak with her the next time I see her."

Rachel looked concerned. "Missus Wagner don' like da girls ta talk. It slows down der work."

"I'll be careful, Rachel, don't worry. I wouldn't want to get either of the girls in trouble."

❦❦❦❦❦❦

The last of the workers were gone, trudging off tiredly in the direction of the worker's village, some with their children in tow. God help him, but Graham could almost hear Mena already making plans about how to entertain the children and formulate arrangements as to how she could care for all the youngest children by herself for the next four months. Surprisingly, it had been one of the few topics he and Moira Wagner had agreed on: that Mena Westwood was to stay away from the fields during Harvest Time. The woman had the makings of a protester; she seemed to enjoy a fight and welcome a cause. All the woman needed to see was the grim reality of work on a plantation and heaven only knew what would develop.

The oldest children in the group – those like Little Mary – could eventually help pick up the scraps left behind to feed the plantation animals, but at this early stage of the harvest there was just too much chaos and danger to have the littlest children wandering around so closely. Once an entire section was cleared – maybe by the end of the week – then the little ones would get their collection baskets and be left to their own devices while their parents slaved – correction - worked to harvest the next section over. Some of the parents were angry that Graham hadn't allowed the youngest to begin collecting the fodder immediately and therefore begin earning their precious pennies. But hell, it was bad enough that he had to deal with Simon's carelessness today and Ebony's stupidity which had resulted in the loss of her hand. He could barely justify the injury between two consenting and experienced adults. How could he rationalize that type of injury or worse with a child who couldn't comprehend the first thing about safety and danger?

Graham sighed. At least he'd slept the last night and he had no doubt he'd sleep fine tonight as well, although now he was haunted in his dreams by Mena's subtle scent and the feel of her in his arms from the night they'd watched the stars. He lifted up a half full container of drinking water high over his head and let the lukewarm liquid drench him. As he shook the water out of his eyes, he caught movement under the trees.

He could no longer deny it; he was attracted to Mena Westwood. Not that anything would ever come of it, but there was no reason he couldn't enjoy the give and take of feisty conversation with a woman who seemed quite willing to speak her mind. Nothing infuriated him more than nonsensical societal small talk with its hidden innuendoes and veiled truths. Graham knew that reality was hard, painful and inescapable, and he had always refused to play the denial game with anyone. Cleaning him up, educating him well and force feeding etiquette down his throat was never going to make him forget what true life was really like.

Mena sat in an exhausted heap after the last of the children had been collected. She didn't move to turn his way until his shadow fell across her. "Bit off more than you could chew?"

She was obviously too tired to spar with him. "Tomorrow I'll be more prepared."

"Tomorrow?"

Mena forced herself to stand and a wave of dizziness swept through her. Even though she tried to hide it, Graham watched her lean against the tree for support. Instantly, Graham dismounted and was beside her. "Have you been drinking water all day?"

"Yes," she hissed at him just like a belligerent child, "I've been drinking water all day."

"And what have you eaten?"

When she hesitated, he knew he had her. "I'd not anticipated spending the full day here so I didn't think to pack a lunch. Some of the workers offered to share their meals, but I didn't feel right knowing what little they have." She shrugged.

Muttering under his breath, he went over to his horse's saddle bags, pulled out a wrapped cloth and stalked back to her. "Here. Eat this. It's not much but it's nutritious and salty – two things essential for survival down here in the heat."

Mena unwrapped it and looked down at the hard stick of … meat. "What is this?"

"Salted, dried fish." As she took a bite Graham continued. "You've got to eat and drink out here in the heat, Mena. You think you're sitting in the shade, but the heat will sap you of your strength and before you know it you'll be unconscious with heat stroke." He gave her a quick glance. "At least you're dressing more sensibly than that first time I saw you."

"Are you trying to pick a fight with me?" she asked around a mouthful of the salty, yet tasty fish.

Graham grinned at her. "Why not? I quite enjoy provoking you. It's one of the few pleasures I find in a day.

Especially since you're the only one, besides Mrs. Wagner, who has the guts to talk back to me."

"So that's the way to catch your eye." Mena seemed to realize how provocative her comment sounded and to hide her embarrassment, she reached down and helped herself to a dipper full of water.

He didn't miss the comment, though. He rarely missed anything. "Are you interested in catching my eye, Mena?"

She stood, wiped her mouth on her sleeve as delicately as she could and meeting his stare directly, said clearly and succinctly, "No."

Despite his obvious exhaustion from a long, brutal day in the fields, Graham grinned a big, wide wolfish smile. "Methinks thee lies," he said in his best Friend Nate Quaker speak.

Graham watched her chin go up, her back bone stiffen, and her eyes spark. "I don't l-," but the words seemed to get stuck in her throat.

Like a predator bird swooping in on its prey, Graham stepped in closer. He was drenched from head to foot, having poured one of the water buckets over his head. She smelled of sunshine and lavender. "Hmmmm, you were going to claim you don't lie but caught yourself." He narrowed his eyes. "Interesting. Very interesting. Are you lying about this or something else?" He tilted his head slowly as he pondered the possibilities. "Mena, Mena you can't seem to help yourself; you become more interesting by the minute."

She went to brush past him but stumbled as her skirts and snagged on the tangle of tree roots at her feet, and he caught her before she fell. Obviously too tired to spar with him with words, Mena stood there mutely while he looked at her for long moments. Finally, still holding her upper arm, he said, "If you can stand a dirty, hot, sweaty man and a dirty, hot, sweaty horse, Dancer and I can give you a ride back to the House. You seem barely able to make it up the hill to your school, let alone the long walk all the way back." He glanced at the sun. "I'm heading back there for a meal anyway."

She looked him up and down. "You forgot 'wet'."

He smiled. "That I did."

"And tired."

He nodded. "And by the time we make it to the Great House you'll be as dirty, hot, sweaty, and wet as Dancer and I. I suspect you're already as tired."

Graham watched her weigh the pros and cons of his offer. Mrs. Wagner's fury would already be high, for he knew that Mena had specifically gone against her admonition to stay away from the fields during Harvest. Factor in her showing up *with* Graham Rhyder on the back of his horse and Graham couldn't quite comprehend what level of rage she would soon have to face. "There will be ... talk," she finally said.

"Darlin', don't you realize," Graham Rhyder said to her in a mock southern drawl as he bent down and cupped his hand to boost her into the saddle, "they were talkin' about us before we'd even spoken a word."

Originally sitting stiffly in front of him - Graham suspected due equally to propriety as well as his less than fresh condition - by the time they came in view of the House she was slumped against him fast asleep.

"Mena," he murmured softly against the top of her head. He brushed his hand against her cheek and tucked a strand of hair behind her ear. "Mena, we're in sight of the House." He felt her start awake and then could feel her struggling to get her bearings. "I thought that perhaps, if you were up to it, you could walk the rest of the way to the house while I take Dancer to the stables." He didn't care about appearances, but he knew she did. She turned to look at him, blinking owlishly, and he had a sudden, overwhelming urge to kiss her. "Unless you'd rather stay in my arms. I can think of a number of other things far more appealing we could do than suffer through a stiff necked dinner."

That got through to her. With a gasp, she sat bolt upright, causing Dancer to shift nervously. "Easy now both of you, or someone's going to end up on their back in the dirt." He made a point to make eye contact with her and waited, with not a little bit of amusement, for the innuendo to seep into her exhausted mind. At the point where it did, and, he suspected, at the point where he was just shy of getting slapped, he slid her down unceremoniously to the ground. She stood there practically spitting sparks while he grinned down at her. Tipping his hat, Graham smiled and said, "The ride was my pleasure, Mena. Looking forward to seeing you at dinner," and rode away before she could come up with a sharp response.

Peering down his nose, gazing through his glasses, the solicitor carefully read through the documents before him. At last he made eye contact. "I take my responsibilities very seriously."

What was he expected to say to that? Clearing his throat, he offered, "I would expect nothing less, Sir."

"You come with satisfactory references and your experience as a foreman on a plantation larger than this carries significant weight. What do I need to know about you that these papers do not tell me?"

He swallowed determined to keep his deepest, darkest secrets buried where no man would ever learn of them. "I'm determined to make the most of this opportunity or die trying," he finally managed.

The solicitor smiled and nodded. "I'll hold you to that. It's a deal then."

Today is a funny night.

Chapter Eleven

Mena sat before Mr. Nelson Topher waiting for him to finish reading her monthly report. She had agonized over this second report. On one hand she'd desperately wanted to make what she had been doing over the past month sound as educational as possible, more than simply telling Bible stories, singing songs, changing nappies, and wiping noses. But with twenty-two little ones almost all under the age of three, that was impossible. Mr. Topher had already shown that he was an astute business man and would quickly recognize any attempt at subterfuge. So, in the end, she'd been brutally honest, recording the impossibility of conducting any sort of formal schooling with anyone over the age of three due to the intense harvest schedule as well as the extensive cleaning program currently being conducted in the Great House. That did not stop her from making every effort to highlight the absolute necessity of what she was doing. She'd outlined the challenges (twenty-two against one, meager supplies, the less than optimal setting) as well as the victories (positive feedback from parents, better care and supervision for the children, and visible progress with her twenty-two charges including verbal, emotional, and physical advancements). In the end she was quite satisfied with the report but doubted Mr. Topher would be. Mena sat tense and ready, anticipating battle.

Windermere's solicitor finally looked up, removed his glasses and looked across his carefully laid out supplies. "Tell me about the children."

That was a surprise. She'd purposely kept her report businesslike, referring to her "students" rather than Crybaby James or Stinky Celia or Wandering Sammie, names that had stuck in her head and had proved to be incredibly accurate descriptions. In fact, she had two healing marks on her left arm from Biter Joe before she'd learned to move more quickly around him.

She couldn't prevent the smile from blooming on her face. "Each of them has a distinct personality and it's been a delight to get to know both the children as well as the parents. Most days the parents eat their noon meal with us, so I find it enlightening to watch the interactions between them and their children. Mary, Isaac and Rachel's girl, is the self-assigned leader of the group and she's proved to be remarkably helpful. She's exceptionally verbal as well as insightful, and more often than not has accurate perceptions.

"The first week was the hardest. As my report states, I began to work with the children on the first day of harvest when no real routine had been set anywhere. I tried immediately to put one in place, which helped the children acclimate to me as well as to the situation."

"Your report says you start with prayer?"

Mena smiled. "Well, I don't necessarily say the prayer. Mary's sister, Ruth, is also one of the water girls and she," Mena bit back a chuckle, "well, she's already quite dynamic at praying. Ruth brings us our first bucket of water and usually opens our day with a rousing prayer which is always unique and heartfelt.

"James is one of the most … emotional … of my charges and is often upset. Mornings are the hardest for him after having been just left by his mother. We've all found that if we sing loudly he eventually begins to sing along, too."

Mr. Topher looked down at Mena's report. "That would be your hymn-sing time."

Mena nodded. "We usually take advantage of the coolest part of the day and go for a walk once we have James calmed down. We don't go far, of course, because while all but four are walking or crawling we can't manage a very far distance."

"Adventure time," Mr. Topher murmured.

"Exactly. Before any of the children arrive, I always put something new and different up in my windmill school. A shoe. A new story book to read. A flower. You get the idea. Before we go up I give them hints such as, 'It's smaller than Louise's foot', or 'it's in a basket covered with a red cloth', or 'yesterday Winston mentioned it.' It gets them thinking a bit – at least the older ones anyway, and then we make our way up to the windmill."

"How do you transport the small ones that can't manage the distance?"

"Mr. Rhyder provided me with a small wheelbarrow that the little ones ride in and the rest of us push up the hill." Mena paused, "At one point I was going to just care for all the children up at the school, but I worried that the walk up the hill would be too much for the working parents. It's easier for the children and I to make the trek in the morning and then come back down in time for lunch.

"After lunch is story time. Many of the little ones fall fast asleep during this time. It's the hottest time of the day so we all just stay under the shade of the trees. I usually tell a story and then often one of the older ones will tell one, too."

"What type of stories?"

"Oh, almost all Bible stories. Gideon and the fleece, David and the giant, Abigail and the picnic basket, Deborah and her army …," Mena blushed, "I'm not certain the local reverend would be happy with my childlike interpretations of the scripture but I make every effort to make sure that the true lesson of the story is preserved.

"Late afternoon is the hardest. By then the children are anxious to be reunited with their parents. Willie and Joe are always hungry. I've taken to bringing some small treats for the afternoon but …" Mena stopped talking suddenly. She'd forgotten herself; become too complacent in her enthusiasm over talking about her charges.

"But…?"

Mena shook her head. "I don't wish to cause trouble or tell tales, Mr. Topher."

Mr. Topher frowned. "Miss Westwood, your report is thorough and complete except for one area: your needs. It would seem that this would perhaps fall under that category."

Mena took a deep breath. "It would be helpful, Mr. Topher, if I could bring a small collection of treats with me each afternoon to serve as a light snack for the children. Nothing fancy, mind you. Maybe some biscuits or a bit of bread. It could simply be leftovers from the previous day's meal at the Great House."

"You feel that this is a reasonable request?"

"Yes, sir."

"Have you posed this request to Mrs. Wagner."

"Yes, sir."

"I see. And, I would assume, this was not met with a favorable response." At Mena's silence, Mr. Topher sighed and nodded. "I see."

"I would be willing, sir, to forfeit my evening dessert or work an additional hour to compensate for financial expense this would incur."

"It would seem to me, Miss Westwood, that you are already working additional hours as your lunch time is certainly not free of responsibilities."

"No, sir."

Mr. Topher picked up a collection of papers. "Are you aware that Mr. Rhyder made reference to you in his monthly report?"

Mena started in surprise. "No, sir!"

Placing his glasses on the tip of his nose, Mr. Topher said, "Let me read to you what he's reported. 'The assistance of Miss Mena Westwood with the smallest members of the Windermere community has proven to be invaluable this harvest season. I find without question that workers are better focused on their responsibilities with the presence of Windermere Plantation's capable teacher overseeing the care and safety of their children while they work. Any support that can be provided to assist her in this continued endeavor can only benefit Windermere.'"

Mena was speechless with shock. "You are aware," Mr. Topher said as he removed his glasses, "that both Mrs. Wagner and Mr. Rhyder are required to submit written reports each month as you do." Mena nodded. "Why are you so surprised at Mr. Rhyder's praise?"

"I ... well, I regularly feel that I am somewhat of an annoyance to both Mr. Rhyder and Mrs. Wagner, as I seem to unintentionally upset their way of doing things on a regular basis."

"Miss Westwood, people fight change. Status quo is always the preferred method of doing anything. It takes a truly gifted person to be able to make a significant change while at the same time pleasing those who are experiencing the change. You seem to be managing to accomplish exactly that here at Windermere."

Mena couldn't help herself. "I suspect you have not heard similar good things regarding my work here from Mrs. Wagner," she said with a discouraged sigh.

"My dear Miss Westwood, I do not know whether you can comprehend what I am about to tell you or not, but I shall try. Mrs. Wagner's behavior will never, ever be a surprise. Mr. Rhyder's comments, on the other hand, are truly miraculous. That carries more weight than you can possibly imagine."

"Why ... why is that?"

"You are a Christian woman who believes Christ's great commission to go out into the world and tell others about Him. Am I right, Miss Westwood?"

"Yes, sir, you are correct. But I fail to see-,"

Mr. Topher raised his voice slightly and continued on. "Each of us, by God's great design, is called to a purpose. Those of us who are obedient to Him spend our lives working to fulfill the call He has put before us." Mena sat silently. "Your purpose is obvious to me with your God-given gift of teaching. I suspect, however, that you are unaware at how of much your gift can influence others.

"Mr. Rhyder is a man who has seen much misery in his life. He blames himself for it all. He arrived here a broken man with nothing to live for, nothing to gain, and nothing to hope for. He was incapable of seeing any goodness in this world because he honestly did not believe it existed. His comments regarding you seem to indicate otherwise now.

"I don't understand what you're telling me, Mr. Topher."

He managed a small smile and murmured, "Which is all part of your charm, Miss Westwood."

"How do you know so much about Mr. Rhyder, sir? He has not impressed me as someone who is forthcoming about the difficult, private, sorrows of his life, to you or anyone else for that matter."

Mr. Topher stopped his careful packaging of all his work-related items. Very precisely, he tapped the side of his nose and said, "Never, *ever*, Miss Westwood, doubt the ability of God to accomplish what He needs to accomplish."

"You're an ignorant fool!" she hissed, her eyes blazing with fury. "Once again you're going to create a complication that puts everything at risk! I am sick and tired of having to clean up your messes."

He shrugged, unconcerned with her vehemence. "You and I have never agreed on what was important and what was not."

"And yet," she spat with hatred, "without me you would be nothing."

A cunning smile bloomed across his face as he turned to look at her. "As you would be without me, my dear wife. Never, _ever_ forget that. The stain of who you are is just as black as the stain of what I chose to be."

Chapter Twelve

Graham stood looking toward his hut, unsure what to do. Overwhelmed with delight to see such an unexpected visitor, he was equally horrified by his reaction. He stood there for so long that the object of his intense focus finally stood hesitantly and began to walk toward him. "What are you doing here?" he finally asked gruffly, and then winced at the unwelcoming tone.

"Well, I can see why you don't get many visitors based on that greeting," Mena said. She stood about ten feet away from him, and the strong ocean breeze tugged at her skirts, her brown hair and her Sunday best hat, causing her to eventually remove it and hold it firmly in her gloved hands.

"God's going to be annoyed at you for skipping church. As is the good Reverend Samuels."

"We had a talk already this morning, God and I, and it was at His encouragement that I finally decided to pay you a visit," was her quick reply. "As for Reverend Samuels, I understand he's been trying to get you to church since you came to Windermere – with no success." Mena grinned at him. "Maybe he's enlisted my aid."

Trying to get hold of himself, Graham stalked past her towards his hut. "Well, you have the distinction of being the first person God – and Reverend Samuels - have ever sent to call on me," he threw over his shoulder.

Mena fell into step behind him. "I've been waiting for a while. Where did you come from? You just seemed to appear over by the cliffs."

He stood by the porch and ran his fingers through his hair, which he assumed was sticking up all over his head. He needed to get it cut but Rachel had been busy with the new baby and he hadn't wanted to bother her. The desire to take stock of his appearance – comb his hair and straighten his shirt – made this morning's foul mood reassert itself. "Sunday mornings I always walk the cliffs. There's a path that leads down. Sometimes, if I'm in the right mood, I take it all the way down to the water's edge."

"What kind of mood were you in today?" she asked with a conversational smile.

"The same mood I'm always in: the mood to die," he answered curtly and walked into the hut, hoping Mena would take the hint and leave, but knowing full well she wouldn't. He emerged with two tin cups brimming with water. "Here, you're probably thirsty. It's quite a walk here from the Great House."

She took the cup but didn't drink from it. Looking at him seriously she finally said, "You've said things to me – sometimes harsh, shocking things – that I have always assumed were joking comments." Mena tilted her head to the right. "But you never really joke, do you?"

He remembered his manners and gestured to the front step. As she sat down, Graham joined her. As he had only one chair it made any other option rather awkward. "Mena, please believe me when I say that I don't have a joking bone in my body."

"I see," she said after a brief hesitation. He wasn't sure she did, but he'd be damned if he'd say anything else. He took a big drink of his water and tried to ignore the feel of her pressed against his right side. Belatedly, he realized they should have probably stayed standing. "It's lovely here. Do you get this breeze all the time?"

Ah, jeeze, she was still going to try polite conversation. "Most days."

"How is the harvest going?"

"We're finally in the right rhythm with the workers. Now it's time for the machines to start to give us trouble."

"Is machinery malfunction a problem that you face every year?"

Graham looked at her. "Mena, you didn't come here to talk about harvest or machinery performance. Why are you here?"

She blushed a bit, which Graham thought was rather intriguing. Taking a deep breath she said, "Yesterday, Mr. Topher read me what you wrote in your monthly report. I came to thank you."

Scoffing, he said, "I spoke the truth. There is no need to thank me."

"I disagree," Mena said crisply, and Graham fought a smile as she did that pointy thing with her chin and sat up straighter as if she were getting ready for a fight. "We both can guess what Mrs. Wagner is saying about me in her reports. You know full well that mentioning my performance in a positive light would carry significant weight regarding Mr. Topher's evaluation of my presence here." She looked at him and narrowed her eyes. "And I'll have you admit it, too."

Graham had to put a stop to this. Leaning in, he said in his best smarmy voice, *"I could admit a lot of things to you, Mena Westwood, although I doubt you'd want to hear them all."*

"You don't frighten me, Graham Rhyder," she said, and had she stuck her tongue out at him her bravado would have been no less effective.

Graham kissed her then, leaning in closer so that their lips touched. Before she could pull back in shock as any proper lady would, he brought his hand up to gently hold the back of her head and keep her exactly where he wanted her. The kiss lasted long enough for him to feel her shock, sense her struggle with outrage and then, just as he felt her begin to lose her grip on reality, he stopped and sat back from her. "Do I frighten you now?" he murmured.

Nothing she did was as he expected and, God help him, it was another thing about her that he liked. She didn't slap him nor did she gasp in outrage and stomp away in a huff. No, Mena Westwood slowly opened her big green eyes to study him as she gently lifted her gloved hand to touch her lips. "Why did you do that?" she finally asked him.

Graham snorted and shook his head, drinking the last of his water. The kiss had unsettled him more than he'd thought it would. He stared off toward the cliffs and thought seriously again about taking the perilous trek down to the ocean, this time blindfolded and running. Maybe this time his luck would fail him and he'd finally be free at last. And then, God help him, she began to talk.

"I have always been a great disappointment. Mother hoped for a glamorous, confident daughter; someone of *beauté et l'équilibre inégalé* – unparalleled beauty and poise," Graham felt her shrug and turned to see her staring off at the ocean. "Instead she got me: bookish, terrified, spiritual, uninterested in fashion or fetes. Someone whose social consciousness focused on those in desperate need rather than those in the acceptable circles. As for … F-Father, well he simply never should have had a daughter. They both thought that they could force me into becoming something I was not." She was silent for a moment and then said firmly. "They were wrong.

"I cannot bear that they must hold the title of Father and Mother … but I refused long ago to claim them as 'mine'. It was a small, personal victory that I held close to my heart during some of the worst times. I'm sure," Mena sighed, "they have similar opinions of me."

Intrigued, Graham asked, "What do they think of you being here?"

Turning to look at him, Mena said, "They do not know."

"Are you telling me that you, what, ran away?"

"Yes, that's exactly what I'm telling you. Rather than face a future that was not of my choosing in a life that offered no opportunity for joy, I left. I had a small amount of money left to me by my great aunt; it was mine and mine alone. I quietly made arrangements and, with the help of a friend in London, traveled here to Windermere to do what I have always wanted to do."

"Are you telling me that you are *paying yourself to work here?*"

There went the chin and the back again. Mena nodded, regal as a queen. "That's exactly what I'm telling you."

"What "future" did they expect you to face?"

"I don't wish to discuss it," Mena said primly as she straightened her skirts and took a sip of her water, suddenly intently focused on the cloud formation to her left.

"Why? You've told me this much already." Graham leaned in towards her and said, "I could kiss you again. Look how much information I got with the first kiss."

She turned. "I thought you said you didn't have a joking bone in your body!"

"I don't." And he kissed her again, this time with a bit more finesse, digging deep into the recesses of time and memory. When this kiss ended, she touched his lips with her gloved hands. He couldn't help his slight smile. "You've never had a man kiss you, have you?"

"Surprisingly, no. Truth be told, I have never been kissed by anyone ever." She stood and walked to the edge of the shade cast by his hut.

Graham frowned trying to put all the pieces together. "Why Windermere?"

"Why not?" she said with a casual shrug, back to him. "I made use of connections I was aware of due to my father's business dealings. Mr. Topher has suspicions which he voiced in our first meeting." She turned. "That's why your positive report of what I've been doing meant so much to me and why I felt I needed to thank you. Initially, Mr. Topher seemed to have some suspicions regarding my being here, but in our last meeting, thanks to you, he seemed much more positively inclined."

"Glad to be of service." When she turned, he tipped an imaginary hat and bowed slightly.

"You may not joke, but sarcasm seems to always be readily available." Graham stood, staring at her. "It was Mr. Topher who helped me understand the error of my ways regarding your sense of humor ... or lack thereof. He implied that..." She stopped and bit her lip, belatedly realizing that perhaps she was revealing more than she should.

He stepped closer. "Implied what?"

"He implied that it was significant that you went out of your way to speak in support of me."

"So."

"Well, just as it was unique for you to do such a thing, it was unique for me to have someone do something like that for me. It meant a lot to me, more than I suspected you knew, which is why I felt compelled to come out and thank you."

"You can come out and thank me as you've done," Graham waited until he was certain she'd gotten his provocative innuendo, "anytime."

Mena took steps toward him but stopped just out of reach. "Do you remember the first night we spoke and I asked you if it was an unconscious behavior that made you offend at every opportunity or if you intentionally worked at it?" Her question didn't really require an answer and she continued. "I believe you do it intentionally; it keeps people at a distance. I have always been a good judge of character, Graham Rhyder, and so far everything I've learned about you says that you are a good man, despite your propensity to provoke whenever possible." Here a slight blush bloomed across her cheeks but she continued. "I think those that you deem worthy of your care and attention are privileged whether they are friend, colleague, or worker under your authority. Despite the sorrows of life, you are a still a good man and still walk on the side of right," Mena smiled at him, seemingly pleased with her little speech.

There she went again, singing his illusionary praises and it infuriated him. "You do not know me at all, and what you think you know is absolutely wrong."

Mena tilted her head, her expression as serious as his. "Then enlighten me. Why is the real person who is Moira Wagner, so readily evident and without any contradictions? Who is the real Graham Rhyder? I'm not foolish enough to think that you are some paragon of virtue who has led an exemplary life! I don't for one minute believe that you don't have things in your past that you wish you could erase and forget." Mena smiled at him and sighed. "Graham, my life has been privileged – but it has not kept me from experiencing cruel, awful things. Whatever is in your past, I can see that it haunts you still today. It drags you down and colors every aspect of the man that you are. But do you know that there are people in this world who are responsible for cruel, awful things that are untouched by the damage they have done? They wake up every morning, dress in their fine clothes, look at themselves in the mirror and say, 'I am a great person. I am powerful. I deserve all the privileges I enjoy because I am better and smarter than anyone else.' They sleep well at night and have not a care in the world. They bear no concern for the tragedies they have caused and only look forward to a future full of more of the same. I *know of* such people, Graham." She paused, stepping closer so she could place her hand on his chest. Looking at him intently she murmured, "Do you understand what I'm saying?"

Graham stared into her serious green eyes, trying to ignore the warmth of her hand on his chest. "I'm 'good' because I know I'm bad?" A vision of Fiona and the babe rose in his mind, a vivid reminder of just how bad he truly was.

Mena smiled. "I prefer 'better than many' because you at least recognize your faults. There are many who can't even distinguish between good and bad."

"Be careful, Mena. I've told you before that I'm not the paragon of virtue you seem to believe, nor am I someone you should deem worthy of rescue or redemption. Don't let a few kisses steal your heart."

Surprising him yet again, she laughed out loud. "Are you afraid that in my naiveté I will be swayed by a few kisses and that I'll fall hopelessly in love with you?" She grinned at him and shook her head. "Rest easy on that! You may think that I am innocent in many areas of life, but on *that* subject I know the truth."

Graham finally reached up to capture and hold her hand against his chest. "Oh? And what's the truth you know about love, Miss Westwood? Do enlighten me on that subject."

Tilting her head to one side, Mena searched his eyes. "Why, love is … an illusion. It's not real. Except, of course, related to God…" She seemed to wait for his affirmative response as they stood in the shade with her hand clasped in his. At his continued silence, she swallowed. "You have nothing to say on that subject?"

Leaning down, he kissed the side of her face and quietly whispered, "You are absolutely right that my life has been anything but exemplary, and the mistakes I have made haunt me with every breath I take. But it is not something that I ever wish to forget because you see, despite all the misery, I *have experienced true love.* And of this fact I am absolutely certain: love is the only thing in the world worth living for."

The memory haunted her at her very lowest points and seemed to suck all confidence from her, leaving her trembling and terrified. It still visited her in the dark of night when dreams could change to nightmares and nothing could keep the remembered sights, sounds, and smells at bay.

"Hanwell Asylum is an impressive facility isn't it, daughter? I am privileged to sit on the board that governs this place; I was one of the significant financial benefactors that enabled it to be built.

"It's the first purpose-built asylum for paupers and lunatics in England and Wales right here in West London. Come, I've brought you here specifically to give you a tour... As you can see, there are "airing courts" which allow patients to have fresh air and exercise albeit bound by walls. Those who are capable labor in the various areas such as the laundry, bakery, carpentry; the facility strives to be as self-sufficient as possible. Once here, very few ever leave, for these maladies are most certainly lifetime afflictions. Those that die here can be claimed by friends or relatives for burial, but many are sold to a licensed anatomy school; I understand they're always looking for bodies..."

"Ah, here is the women's wing; notice that there seems to be all manner of conditions represented here. Some are obviously physically and mentally challenged like that poor wreck over there in the corner. I wonder what has become of her clothes? Others, well, others are here for vaguer but nonetheless just as serious maladies: the inability to be obedient, the failure to be discreet, the disappointment of expectations not met... One must always be conscious of ones obligations and responsibilities, daughter, as I'm sure you are well aware."

Head ent mek fuh hat alone.

Chapter Thirteen

"Love is the only thing in the world worth living for." Graham's words resonated in Mena's head. She tossed and turned, hearing his words whether she was awake or asleep. How could a man of such angry, moody countenance believe in the existence of love? It made no sense to Mena. No sense at all. And who, a quiet voice whispered in her head, had loved him so? And why, the voice persisted, did Mena wish to know the answer so desperately? She groaned and rolled over in her bed once again.

"Miss Mena? 'Liz'beth says I'm ta wake yuh in da mornin'."

"Abigail?" Mena struggled to get her wits together just as she did every morning. Standing in her doorway with the requisite candle was Abigail, looking uncertain and nervous. "Where is Elizabeth? Is she unwell?"

Abigail pursed her lips and her eyes darted left and then right in the early morning dimness. Not as lovely as Elizabeth, Abigail had a tiny, fairy-like quality to her. Everything was small: her nose, her ears, her hands… "Liz'beth … she's not workin' in da house no more. She's gonna join Momma an' Poppa in da fields."

Fully alert now, Mena turned to Abigail. "Why?"

Abigail said hesitantly, "Missus Wagner, she said Liz'beth was done workin' in da house. I don' know why."

Mena began dressing hurriedly. "When did this occur?"

Like a sudden break of a dam, information flowed out of Abigail almost faster than Mena could process it. "Liz'beth come home yes't'day an tol' Momm an' Poppa dat she couldn' work at da big house no more. Said Missus Wagner done wit her an' she was ta stay away. Momma tried ta get Liz'beth ta tell wha' happened but Liz'beth's mouth's shut tighter den a frightened clam. Momma been houndin' Liz'beth somethin' fierce lately tryin' ta get her to tell wha's botherin' her, but her lips ha' been sealed. Even Momma's shoutin' hasn' done no good. Poppa's gonna speak wif Mr. Rhyder an' see if she can work da fields doing God knows wha', cause she sure can't sit home doin' her hair an nails." Abigail glanced nervously behind her. "I gots ta go 'fore I gets da boot, too." In a flash, Abigail was gone.

Nearly three months into harvest season and over four months present at Windermere, Mena was now a seasoned resident at the Big House. She knew that just a look could communicate a full message of caution, and that an innocuous statement could mean something entirely different than what appeared to be said. Mena also knew that Dahlia knew more about the goings on in the Great House than Mrs. Wagner ever would. If anyone knew about the circumstances surrounding Elizabeth and her dismissal from the Great House, Dahlia would. Mena's problem was that the skill of finding the right time and *asking* Dahlia in the right way was still something she hadn't yet fully mastered. Rarely did her questions gain any response except a pointed look, a shrug of the shoulders, and a clever saying which sometimes took her days (if ever) to understand, such as *"Trouble tree don' bear no blossom"* or *"It ent fuh want of a tongue dat a horse won' talk."*

It would be somewhat easier to get information from Graham, another person at Windermere who knew more about things than people gave him credit for. Of course visiting him at his place was out of the question based on her one experience there. She saw him regularly – usually from a distance thank God – although sometimes he was close enough to give her a smirk and a wink. Twice he'd offered her a ride back to the Great House at the end of a long day of harvesting, but she had declined simply because she was dismayed at how much she had wanted to say yes.

As expected, there was no opportunity to talk with Dahlia about Elizabeth. Since Mena's conversation with Mr. Topher, each morning Dahlia always had a large basket packed with treats – some fresh, some not – meant for Mena to share with whomever she liked over the course of her day. With the Great House cleaning finally finished, Maisy had resumed her spot in the shade. As a result Mena's first stop on the way to the fields was always to say good morning and share a treat from her basket. Walking purposefully, Mena headed to another person experience had shown was far more astute than many gave her credit for, determined to get some answers.

ᘓᘓᘓᘓᘓᘓ

Graham was tense and he shouldn't be.

The days were slightly easier now that a firm routine had been established, and all the workers knew what was expected of them. So far, the machines had functioned without a hiccup, Willie had been managing to stay sober enough to perform his striker duties to everyone's satisfaction, and aside from the loss of Ebony's hand, no other injuries had yet to be sustained. It was the smoothest harvest season he'd had in the five years he'd been a part of at Windermere.

But the addition of Elizabeth to the group of older men and women who collected the fodder and weeded the tilled fields was disturbing. Not so much because she was now in the fields and no longer at the Great House; personnel was always changing or shifting for any number of reasons. No, what was disturbing was the feeling of imminent disaster, like that subtle shift in the wind that hints of something coming far more destructive than a summer rainstorm, even though the sun is still shining and the birds are still singing.

Of course, Isaac was tense, too, as was Rachel with the unexplained dismissal of Elizabeth from the Great House and their daughter's tight lipped response to their questions. No one was talking about anything: not about Elizabeth's sudden appearance in the fields, not about what had happened at the Great House ... Even Moira Wagner hadn't weighed in with her outrage at his hiring an employee that she had dismissed.

Straightening up from dunking his head in the last of the day's drinking water, some things suddenly became crystal clear for Graham. *Moira Wagner hadn't objected... That's* what was making him tense. Never in the past would she have tolerated him employing a worker that she had dismissed. Never. In fact, it was an unspoken rule between the two of them not to interfere with how they chose to run their portion of the plantation. Only last year he'd been forced by Mr. Topher to dismiss four field hands at the height of the harvest because Mrs. Wagner had caught one of the house maids stealing; a problem that she regularly seemed to have to contend with. As the perpetrator and the four field hands had been from the same family, all were required to be discharged. In fact, as he thought further about it, in his time as manager there had been at least three other instances where because of dismissals at the Big House, workers in the fields had been let go as well.

Graham's mind whirled as he wiped the water from his nose and mouth. Why had Elizabeth been dismissed? That had been the terminology used by Isaac, "Mis Wagner says 'Lizbeth no longer welcome in da Big House. She's bin *dismissed.* Can we find a place in da fields fo' her?" Why *had* Moira Wagner operated differently this time? *Why hadn't* Mrs. Wagner tried to have Isaac fired? She'd never approved of hiring a darkie as foreman … this would have been a perfect opportunity to get rid of the entire family. And were Isaac and Rachel so tense because they feared for their jobs?

The idea of approaching Moira Wagner to discuss the situation was unthinkable. Mounting Dancer, Graham turned his horse to head towards Isaac and Rachel's, only to catch a glimpse of Mena's distant form, empty basket in hand, trudging back to the Great House. She lived in the Great House. Maybe she could provide some insight…

Despite a number of offers, Mena had declined evening rides back to the Great House. Of course, he'd mucked things up pretty well during her one visit to his hut, effectively making any and all interactions between them tense and awkward. Which had been his intention all along, of course. He didn't need the woman showing up at his hut whenever the mood struck, as if they were friends or something… Which was also why he'd continued to be a bit in her face whenever the opportunity presented itself.

But a sudden whim had him turning Dancer and heading in Mena's direction rather than towards Isaac and Rachel's. "Interested in a ride back to the House today?" he called to her. "I wouldn't blame you. This week's been the hottest yet."

Not slowing her step, she threw over her shoulder, "You're nothing if not persistent, Mr. Rhyder. No thank you."

"What's this? Back to formalities? I had no idea that a few stolen kisses would set us back this far." Graham swung down from Dancer and fell into step beside Mena, who did her best to continue to ignore him. They walked in silence for long moments. Finally, with nothing better to say he managed, "I'm sorry."

With a sigh she stopped and turned to look at him directly. "Why?"

"I've … offended you … obviously ….," Graham stuttered while searching her blank expression in an attempt to gain some insight. "I took … liberties … with the kisses, and then, perpetuated such liberties with further behavior designed to make you uncomfortable around me." For long moments Graham stood in the dappled shade of the trees watching her fascinating mind work to order her thoughts. Smiling or - God forbid - laughing at her would only make matters worse. He bit the inside of his lip.

Looking off into the distance, Mena began speaking, "I was sincere with my intentions when I came to see you at your home, Mr. Rhyder. I recognize the importance you place with your privacy and thought it was the best way to approach you with an honest word of thanks for your unsolicited support to Mr. Topher. I had no ulterior motives other than to do exactly that." Graham opened his mouth to respond, but she had the temerity to wave her finger at him. "You will be silent and let me have my say, for I have been practicing this speech – for my own peace and sanity – for weeks, and will say it in full." Only after Graham clapped his mouth shut, did she continue. "I have never represented to be anything other than what I am: a determined woman who wishes to make a difference in this world. I have come to this island to find a place for myself where I will, hopefully, find some joy, peace, and satisfaction. I have always been quiet, thoughtful, studious, and determined. Not necessarily the best qualities in a young woman whose family had higher hopes and plans, but there you have it. *I have left everything behind* to gain the life of my choice. And *by God's Grace I will succeed.*"

Graham watched her back straighten and her chin jut out as she once again looked him square in the eye. "I don't know how to interpret your kisses, or your winks or the familiar looks you give me. You have even spoken with me of believing in love and how it was the only thing in the world worth living for! How am I to take all these things? I have no use for romance or," here she made a face of disdain, "love. The moment I left my life in England I forever acknowledged the end of that ... farce." She took a deep, calming breath and then said fiercely, "I failed miserably in my season with Polite Society, unwilling to play the games that most young women apparently excel at almost naturally." Mena sighed. "Mother was right that I could have made more of an effort. Father was right that I would have been far more content with life had I been born a man.

"I did not ... anticipate a man such as you, Mr. Rhyder. Much to my dismay I find you ... equally disturbing and intriguing. I enjoy speaking with you, even disagreeing with you, because you seem to welcome sincere, honest thought. You are *the first man* I have ever encountered who seemed to view me not as anything other than an intelligent human being with whom we share thoughts, ideas, and observations. It is refreshing." Breaking eye contact with him, she looked down at her hands clasping her empty basket, and almost to herself she whispered, "It is *nice.*

"Here at Windermere I've worked hard to find my place. I feel useful and necessary. I like being in control of my life and the direction it is taking. But you are a ... a... confusion to me, Graham. Whereas at one point I thought I understood where we stood with each other – we are colleagues as well as intelligent, opinionated human beings - now I find myself ...," again she sighed and this time looked over at Dancer happily cropping away at the shady green grass, "now I find myself utterly confused and unsure." She glared at him briefly. "I *hate* that feeling." She suddenly seemed completely deflated.

"Have you finished your speech?" At her silence, Graham sighed and tentatively took her arm, leading her over to a large fallen tree where they could sit. He took her empty basket, and placed it on the ground at their feet. "I don't know what to say to you, Mena, other than offer you my apology."

"I have found that honesty always serves best in the end," she said grimly. "'Mena, you have always been a profound disappointment.' 'Mena *keep silent*.' 'Mena, you are never going to succeed in Polite Society if you continue this behavior.' 'Mena, remember your obligations and responsibilities.' 'Mena, no man will ever have you if you continue to talk like that.' 'Mena, you have the appeal of a boil.' 'Mena, you-'" She stuttered to a stop when Graham took her chin in his hand and turned her to face him.

"You know, I am inclined to tell you that when you go on like this I only want to kiss you again. It seems the quickest and easiest way to make you be quiet." He'd meant to shock her into silence, but was dismayed to see her eyes fill up with tears. Before he examined his sudden pressing need to comfort her, he gently pulled her into a careful embrace. "Ah, now here you aren't even riding on Dancer with me and you are going to end up dirty, wet, and sweaty once again all because of me and my fine sense of gallantry." She stayed in his arms only long enough to gather herself together. Straightening beside him, he let her sniffle and make use of the fancy embroidered handkerchief she pulled from her skirt pocket without comment.

She was in such danger from him and she had no idea. His need to care and protect as he had done for Fiona grew each time he conversed with her and she revealed more and more about herself. Fiona had been the same kind of woman; determined to be unique, committed to pursuing only what she deemed worthy, and, God rest her soul, loyal to him to death. He would close his eyes to stop the images he recalled, but they were burned into his soul.

Mena wanted honesty? He'd give her honesty. "Don't try to convince me I'm a good man, Mena Westwood. You *will not* succeed. The truth of what I am is almost more than I can bear to think of, let alone voice out loud, so you will just have to take my word for it. I am a man and you *must never* forget that. I find you quite intriguing, and since you are encouraging such honesty here, I'll tell you that you're lovely to look at, even when you're not wearing all your fancy London finery. I, too, enjoy having intelligent conversation with you. In particular, I enjoy trying to rattle your carefully thought-out ideas and perceptions, because when I do, you seem to be readily able to hold your own with a response." He leaned in to press his point. "You *do not* want my attention; it will only bring you grief." It was his turn to sigh and turn off into the distance. "You make me think and that's refreshing and intriguing for a man who has forsaken …" He caught himself before he went too far.

Of course she wouldn't let that go unnoticed. Touching his arm, she said, "Forsaken what?"

Shrugging, Graham muttered, "Life, I suppose. I've forsaken everything I used to hold dear. Forsaken everything I once was and everything that was ever of importance. I cannot forget the mistakes I've made, Mena. They will haunt me until my dying day, and nothing I've tried has helped erase them."

She studied her hands clasped in her lap and took a few moments to think. "Like when you walk your dangerous cliff path?"

He nodded. What was he doing sitting here having this conversation with her? "And my most favorite - liquor. And before you get going talking about God, I'll stop you. Another fellow, and he was far more determined than you, had me in his clutches for nigh onto six months and failed in that regard as well."

They were both silent for a moment lost in thought. Quietly she said, "Life is impossible, Graham. I suppose the only thing of value we really have is the ability to make choices each day in the hopes of improving our circumstances. There is a Bible verse I love that says, *And we know that all things work together for good to them that love God, to them who are called according to his purpose.*[3] I like how it's a promise about all things – not just the good things, or the important things – *all things.* I have to believe in this promise; otherwise I'd not be able to get out of bed in the morning." Graham felt her turn and study his profile. "Why *do you* get out of your bed in the morning if you've forsaken … everything?"

"Find me enough liquor and I'd stay in bed."

She had the audacity to give him a tentative smile and a shake of her head. "That's not true. You could secure enough liquor right now and do exactly that, but you haven't. Try again."

Graham bent down and pulled up a blade of grass that he then methodically began to tear apart. "I almost succeeded in killing myself with liquor. Once." Murky visions of trying to drink himself into final oblivion danced along the edges of his mind … and the sad part was that the idea still held an appeal.

Mena leaned into him. "Your six months with that very determined God fellow I'd bet is part of this story. And also, quite possibly why you're still here today."

She was too astute for her own good. Graham stood, retrieved her basket, and offered Mena his hand. "I'm done with stories for today, Miss Mena Westwood. Come, let me help you up onto Dancer or we will miss our only opportunity for a meal, which would probably delight Mrs. Wagner. And, as you know, more than anything I try to never, *ever* delight Mrs. Wagner." With just a brief hesitation, she placed her hand in his and then allowed him to boost her up into the saddle. Mounting behind her and determined to keep her from making any more of her perceptive observations, Graham wrapped his arm tightly around Mena's waist and then whispered in her ear, "Hang on!" as he urged Dancer into a gallop.

"Dahlia, she da one to go to if yuh have a question or need sum help but she can only help yuh so much an' afta' dat yuh on yuh own. She knows a lot but she don' know everyting dat happens in da Big House. Miss Mena is nice but she don' know nothin' an' if'n she tinks yuh need help dat can jus' make a biggah mess dan der already is. Missus Wagner knows <u>everyting</u> but dat fo' sure does not make her yuh friend; she's no one's friend but herself. Be sure to 'member dat.

Don' nevah back talk or even look like yuh thinkin' a back talkin' 'cause dey can always tell wha' yuh thinkin'. Keep yuh head down an' yuh mouth shut. Yuh doin' good if'n no one knows 'bout yuh 'cept Dahlia but dat's mighty tough to do.

Dey likes ta hear 'yas ma'am' an' 'yas sir' a lot so if'n you have to speak ta anyone says it as of'ten as yuh can.

Jobs dat keep yuh in da kitchen wit Dahlia an' such is bettah dan jobs dat take yuh upstairs on yuh own even if dey are jobs like cleanin' da privy or pluckin' chickens or scrubbin' da floors. Upstairs jobs seem bettah <u>but dey are not.</u>

Keep yuh ears sharp jus' like Momma does wit' us. Ain't nobody der ta help yuh but yuhself if'n yuh end up alone ..."

Don' trouble trouble till trouble trouble you.

Chapter Fourteen

"I would like to talk with you later about something that's concerning me, but you had best hurry in and get dressed for dinner before anyone's the wiser," Graham encouraged Mena as Dancer skidded to a halt in front of the Great House.

"Hurrying," came the annoyed voice of Mrs. Wagner from the front porch, "would be a wasted effort in regard to keeping your dirty little secret, although it might allow enough time to still consume a meal. Since formal meals resumed last week I believe that either one or both of you have been late. *Consistently.* This ... exhibition ... further confirms the poor expectations I have of you, Mr. Rhyder. Miss Westwood, it would seem that you have little care for the company you keep or the reputation you are creating. Based on the truth that *appearance is everything,* it is obvious exactly whose company you have chosen to keep."

Graham hastily dismounted and assisted Mena down. Knowing nothing he could say that would help, he remounted and rode Dancer to the stables without speaking, although he did give Mena a quick wink.

Moira Wagner was still on a tear as Graham made his way into the dining room minutes later. "... as I'm sure you will agree, horrible manners are indicative of a poor upbringing. Ah, here he is now. Graham Rhyder, may I introduce you to Lord Gabriel Martin Windermere – eldest son of our very own Lord Alexander Malcolm Windermere." A tall, thin man stood at Graham's entrance. He was impeccably presented in comparison to Graham's hastily donned clean shirt, sweat-stained trousers, and hair still wet from the horse trough.

"Mr. Rhyder," the man inclined his head like a prince greeting one of his subjects.

"Lord Gabriel," Graham responded as politely as possible, knowing full well the dangers of biting the hand that fed you, no matter how hungry one might be. "Please forgive my late arrival at dinner."

Lord Gabriel gave a curt nod, resumed his seat and gestured for Graham to take the only unoccupied seat at the table across from him, "Sit. Eat." Moira and Walter Wagner, along with Mena who sat beside Lord Gabriel, were the only others in attendance. It would seem that Jessie Lynn, Mary Jean, Karl and Elijah had only conditional privileges when it came to formal dinner times – depending on who else was in attendance. "I'm anxious to hear how the harvest season is going, Mr. Rhyder. I have already heard an extensive report by Mrs. Wagner and Miss …," he hesitated and gave Mena a long, studied look, "… Westwood was just giving me a report of her progress so far with her goal to educate the workers. Please, *Miss Westwood,* continue."

As Graham claimed his seat he glanced briefly at Mena only to stop and look at her fully. She was flushed and wide-eyed, obviously extremely disturbed. Suddenly, all his senses were on high alert as he began to fill his plate from the dishes set before him.

Mena cleared her throat. "As I was saying, I've found everyone I've approached eager to learn. Managing a time that works for all involved has been tricky." Mena swallowed and glanced towards a silent Mrs. Wagner. "During the harvest season it is impossible to have a set time for anyone – young or old – to sit down for formal lessons, so I've been helping to care for and entertain the smallest of the plantation's residents."

"What does that entail?" Lord Gabriel asked as he took a sip of his wine.

"It means that she trudges out to the fields like a common laborer every morning, abides out in the dirt and the bugs all day, and then returns home late in the evening smelling and looking nothing like a lady," came Mrs. Wagner's terse reply.

"I answer to no one but myself and Mr. Topher," Mena said carefully with a jut of her chin and a glance of defiance toward Moira Wagner. "Thus far, Mr. Topher, *the Marquis of Windermere's chosen solicitor,* has been fully informed of my actions and, as of yet, has had no objections." Graham hid a smile as he took a bite of beef. Mena was obviously not bothered by Moira; it was the important guest that had disturbed her.

"Indeed. And how do you do to fill your day with your charges?"

Graham listened to the dialogue between the two and took the time to observe Lord Gabriel. He was young, not yet thirty by Graham's calculations, and had the smug, entitled air that most wealthy, and privileged young men seemed to specialize in. Graham had the uncomfortable experience of having been both at their mercy and, for a brief time, in their company. Neither had been enjoyable.

Finally, it seemed to be Graham's turn. "How goes the harvest so far?" Lord Gabriel turned his cool green eyes towards him as the supper dishes were being cleared and a dessert of pears in honey was served.

"It's the best season we've had so far concerning injuries and equipment performance. I can't believe that we've actually got the end in sight – just a couple weeks now – and everything has gone so smoothly." Graham gave the standard report he would give anyone in authority, relaying the progress thus far, the difficulties to date, and the expectations of future headway. "If you can wait until Sunday – we still harvest but mornings are lighter – I'd be happy to give you a full tour of your family's holdings."

"No, that won't be necessary." Turning to Mena, he had the audacity to look her up and down before he said, "I'm sure … Miss Westwood … can manage to find time to give me a tour well before Sunday." He gave Mena a benign smile. "Isn't that so?"

Frowning, Graham turned to watch Mena work to swallow a pear, wipe her mouth with her serviette and then try to find her voice. "Gra-, er, Mr. Rhyder is much more familiar with the grounds than I am. I've only been here a little over five months."

"You can ride, I assume, can you not?"

Mena bit her bottom lip. "Yes, I can ride."

"Well then," Lord Gabriel said with finality, "we shall plan to explore the property *together* since it would seem that both of us need to gain some understanding of Windermere Plantation and its holdings. I have no desire to wait until Mr. Rhyder can find the time to play tour guide, and surely your young charges can fall back on old habits while you perform this service. Between the two of us we should be able to find our way around without getting lost. I'm sure we have much more to discuss, and this will give us ample opportunity." He gave Mena a tolerant smile as he issued his order. "I look forward to your company tomorrow."

"Absolutely," Moira answered from the head of the table with a nod of deference. "Miss Westwood will be happy to accompany you as she is like any employee at Windermere: here, at your service. Lord Gabriel, how long will we benefit from your company?"

"I've not decided as of yet," was the man's response.

"Might you be here long enough to enjoy the celebrations that traditionally mark the end of harvest time? We could send word out to the surrounding plantations and have a more formal celebration than usual here at Windermere." She gave a rare smile. "It's been far too long since Windermere has hosted a celebration that draws the entire island's notice."

"I like that idea," Lord Gabriel enthused. "A formal ball that reminds all – neighbors as well as employees – that Windermere is a place of note: in culture, in style, and in class. Let us both speak later, Mrs. Wagner, and put your exceptional idea into formal motion." As Mrs. Wagner preened under Lord Gabriel's praise he turned to Graham. "Your improvements here at Windermere have not gone unnoticed. Nor has the progress in sugar cane production – you've shown an increase of almost 15%! Father and I are intrigued with your steam powered extracting success and wish to discuss with you the feasibility of constructing a rum production facility to complement the current molasses business. Are you familiar with any aspects of that?"

"Want to make Kill Devil, is that it?"

Lord Gabriel frowned. "Kill Devil?"

"What the natives used to call early versions of rum. Yes, I'm familiar with the process. My prior place of employment grew cane and produced molasses as well as rum." He glanced at Moira Wagner sitting stoically at the head of the table listening to what must assuredly be an unwelcome discussion of future responsibilities for Graham. "I've mentioned improvement ideas to Mr. Topher, as well as the financial and logistical ramifications." Actually, he'd done more than mention an idea to Mr. Topher; after his first successful year at the plantation he'd carefully prepared financials, projections and plans for the exact thing that Lord Gabriel was now considering. Mr. Topher at the time had been so against the idea that he had refused to include Graham's suggestions in his monthly report packet. Those meticulously prepared papers were currently collecting dust somewhere in his hut.

Lord Gabriel frowned and asked pointedly, "What sort of ramifications?"

Graham shrugged. "Well, workers for one thing. It would require a whole new way of thinking regarding employees. Windermere keeps only a bare-bones staff for most of the year; almost all harvest workers are seasonal and disappear come May. Rum making takes skill, manpower, and time. It's financially top heavy with significant investments necessary in the beginning, and the eventual payout sometimes years in the making. Not every plantation is willing – or forward-thinking enough – to take the risk."

Lord Gabriel motioned for his dishes to be cleared and stood. "Perhaps we could retire to the study and discuss this further." He nodded to Maura Wagner and her ever silent husband. To Mena he said, "I look forward to our adventure tomorrow, *Miss Westwood*. Let us plan to depart immediately after we break our fast."

After drinks (which Graham declined) and cigars (which he happily accepted), Graham was immediately forced to face the reality of Lord Gabriel. Just like many others like him that Graham had unfortunately had to deal with in the past, he was young, smug, entitled and woefully ignorant. Particularly dangerous, Lord Gabriel considered himself to be an astute business man and had fired question after question at Graham. The reality, however, was instead of showing a clear understanding of business in general *and* rum making in particular, he'd proven just the opposite. Lord Gabriel was a vivid example of the fact that simply being part of a family that already *owned* a rum distillery *did not* qualify one to run one. Graham knew that a majority of the molasses that Windermere Plantation produced was shipped to the American state of Rhode Island where the family owned and operated a rum distillery.

"Why the bother?" Graham had finally asked him. "Why go to the expense to build something you already have?"

Lord Gabriel had winked at him. "Those Americans; they enjoy the fight too much. They've already battled us, the bloody French, the Mexicans, the savages, and now it would seem they have no one left. You mark my words, Rhyder, they've run out of others to battle so now they're going to fight each other." He'd puffed on his cigar and taken a drink of his rum. "It makes no sense to gamble with our livelihood by relying on the Americans' tenuous ability to control themselves. We're not going to *close* any business; we're merely going to *build another.*" He'd shown significant interest in Graham's ideas regarding expansion here at Windermere and was hopeful that Graham could find the plans Mr. Topher had so quickly dismissed.

Standing out enjoying one last evening cigar under the trees, Graham sensed Mena before he even heard the rustle of her skirts, and then puzzled over how that could be possible. His spirits lifted at the prospect of a conversation with her, which made him sigh. It was time he faced reality; he wanted-

Mena's quiet voice interrupted his thoughts. "That's quite a sigh. Is Lord Gabriel the cause?"

Graham turned to look at her. Moonlight or sunlight, dressed like royalty or looking like a common worker, she was lovely to look at. "Partly."

She came to stand beside him. "I came out to find you because you mentioned you had something you wished to discuss with me, and I wanted to share my concern over Elizabeth's dismissal from the Great House. Was that what you wished to talk about?" At his nod, Mena sighed and said, "I've just had a very disturbing conversation with Mrs. Wagner."

Reaching into the pocket of her skirt she pulled out a lace handkerchief which, when she unwrapped it, contained an exquisite silver hair clip. "While you were having drinks and cigars with Lord Gabriel, Moira Wagner informed me that this was found in Elizabeth's possessions when they searched her room. I confirmed it was mine but said that I gave it to Elizabeth as a gift." She sighed. "I lied, though, Graham. I don't know how Elizabeth came to be in possession of my hairclip, but I didn't give it to her."

He took a draw from his cigar while he thought. Finally he asked, "Do you think she stole it?"

"No." Mena said it immediately. "That's why I lied. There *has* to be a better explanation than she stole it."

"Can you think of the real reason why she was dismissed from the Great House?"

"No," Mena sighed, "can you?"

Graham shook his head. "As far as I know Isaac and Rachel don't know either because Elizabeth's not talking." Graham shared his concern with her and the inconsistencies he'd thought of out in the field earlier that day.

Standing beside him in the light of the moon, Mena turned to look at him and said, "Whether you like it or not I consider us friends, Graham. You are the only one I can honestly talk with here. I value your opinion and I trust your judgment." Graham's cigar tip glowed. "I don't know who else to speak with and I'm very worried about Elizabeth."

"You should be," was his response. "And, since we're such good friends, *I'll* tell *you* that you're the other person I'm worried about and the reason I'm standing out here sighing in the moonlight." He almost smiled as he anticipated the show to come.

"Me?" She looked suitably shocked. "Why ever would you be standing out here under the stars worrying about *me?*"

"I'll tell you why so we can hopefully get the argument over quickly; I'm tired and I'd like to try to get some sleep." He couldn't help his grin as he watched her stiffen and prepare for battle. "I'll not have you spending any time alone with Lord Gabriel."

She stared at him for long moments, and Graham suspected she was frustrated by the fact that with his back to the moon and his hat on, she probably was only able to distinguish the flash of his teeth when he grinned at her again. *"You'll not have me...,"* she finally muttered under her breath. She squinted her eyes at him, "and *why*, may I ask, do you feel compelled to make this ridiculous – and inappropriate edict?"

He shrugged. "Don't trust him. He's a snake, title or no."

"I see. And the fact that he's my *employer* and he's specifically requested that I do this service and I have already agreed to escort him around Windermere tomorrow...?"

"Shouldn't matter. Fall ill. Have an attack of the vapors. Women do it all the time." He drew deeply on his cigar to hide his smile; she was just so fun to rile.

Ah, and there went the hands on the hips. "Not this woman!" Mena hissed furiously. "Why, I've never missed a day of work or failed to meet a responsibility due to illness in my life!"

Graham shrugged again and blew a stream of cigar smoke into the night. "Well, here's to first times. If I had a glass, I'd make a toast."

"What are you afraid he'll do? *Take liberties* with me?" He watched her glare at him, and although he couldn't quite be certain given the dimness, he suspected she was blushing at the memory of their kisses and the liberties *he'd* already taken with her. "Take advantage of my naiveté?" It was her turn to shrug – as she turned and strolled a bit down the path. "At least I'm more experienced with such things now – *thanks to you*." She was now obviously trying to bait him.

Which was exactly what he was afraid of; that she would be foolish enough to think that one or two stolen kisses would give her the mistaken belief that she knew all she needed to know about what went on between a man and a woman. Throwing the stub of his cigar to the ground and crushing it under his boot, he took two long strides until he was close enough to grip her shoulders. "You listen to me, Mena, *you are as inexperienced as they come.* I do not like the way the man looked at you; you're not as knowledgeable as you think you are and … men of … a certain ilk … believe that it is their right and privilege … to behave inappropriately with women they view as their … subordinates." He gave her a little shake. "I *forbid* you to go out alone with the man, Mena."

Reaching up, Mena wrapped her warm hands around his wrists but did not push him away. She searched his eyes in the dimness. "You really are concerned…," she said with wonder. He stayed silent, but his hands tightened. Up went the chin. *Dear God, help him.* Quietly, she cajoled, "Try again, Graham…"

What did she want from him? Declarations of love? A passionate embrace? No, he suddenly remembered she'd said the greatest thing she treasured was that he spoke to her like an intelligent, *equal*, human being. Graham took a deep breath. "I don't know exactly why, except to say that I have a sense about the man, and I don't like or trust him. So I'm *asking you*, Mena, *please*, do not go *anywhere* unattended with him. For your safety." Through gritted teeth he added, "And my own peace of mind."

"All right," she said quietly. "I'll make sure to take a groom with us when we ride out tomorrow." She smiled at him. "There. That wasn't too hard, was it?"

Dropping his hands from her shoulders, she released his wrists and he turned his back to her. It was either that or kiss her again, and Lord knew that wouldn't help the situation. He felt her hand on his back, warm but firm through his shirt. "Thank you, Graham Rhyder," she said softly. "You are the first man I have ever known who has ever had an honest concern for my health and well-being. It means more to me than I can adequately put into words."

He felt the warmth of her hand against his back long after she'd disappeared into the house.

"Don't stand there looking at your feet, you little fool. You know why you've been summoned and it's not to brush my jacket or straighten my shoes. Come close and let me have a look at you. Let's see if you're as cooperative and as wonderfully silent as your sister."

"Yas, sir."

Even if da devil bring it, God sen' it.

Chapter Fifteen

"So ... Miss Westwood, how long did you say you've been residing here at Windermere?"

"A little over five months." Mena rode beside Lord Gabriel, uncomfortable in her formal riding habit, gloves, boots, and hat. She'd forgotten how miserably uncomfortable corsets, stays and petticoats could be and longed for her serviceable skirt, blouse and functional shoes. They had traveled as far as the north border, near Graham's home near the cliffs, through the workers' village where Mena had delighted in introducing Lord Gabriel to Maisy, through much of the undeveloped western border where they had passed Silent Joe on one of his many water runs, and now they were headed to see the actual harvest in progress. It had taken all morning. The promised groom trailed at an appropriate distance behind them. Unfortunately, while Graham was right to worry about Lord Gabriel, a groom wasn't going to help Mena in the slightest.

"Five months, you say. That's quite an adventure for a young woman to undertake, traveling unescorted thousands of miles to a distant locale. Surely your family must be ... concerned." When Mena remained stoically silent, Lord Gabriel sighed and asked, "What is your opinion of Windermere plantation here on Barbados?"

Mena shrugged. "From what I see it is well run. The people I have met, on the whole, are kind, honest, and hardworking. But I have little experience adequately evaluating a plantation's effectiveness. Mr. Topher is the one who would give you the report you are seeking. I understand that he has been employed as the plantation's solicitor for many years. Mrs. Wagner, Mr. Rhyder and I are required to submit written reports to him as well as meet in person with him on a monthly basis."

"I agree with you that you are ill equipped to properly evaluate the plantation from a business perspective. Such topics are not suitable for a lady, and we will, of course, afford you that courtesy title. However, I can't help but notice that you said 'on the whole,' which implies that you have seen certain improprieties or, at the very least know of someone who is *not* kind, honest or hardworking. Are there some here who do not qualify for your otherwise glowing description? Perhaps it's the manager, Graham Rhyder? The man has got obvious issues with drink, as he refused my finest rum last evening, and yet was happy to enjoy one of my best cigars. I find it hard to trust a man that I cannot relax and converse with over a drink or two. Was he who you were referring to?"

Mena refused to rise to the bait. "From what I have seen, the workers respect him and he's dedicated to his responsibilities."

"Well, then, to whom might you be alluding? Come now, Miss Westwood, should you have any concerns, who but me should you voice them to?"

Anyone but you, was Mena's first thought. Disseminating, Mena said, "I merely meant that I have not met *all* employees here at Windermere and, therefore, cannot provide an accurate evaluation."

"Well, let's take Moira and Walter Wagner. You have met them. Wagners have been a part of this plantation longer than I have been alive. Do the workers respect them? Would you say that they are both dedicated to their responsibilities?"

Finally turning to make eye contact with Lord Gabriel, she found him smiling benignly at her. "It is not my place, Lord Gabriel, to speak of my superiors. While I do not report to Mrs. Wagner as such, she still holds a position of authority here at Windermere, and this line of questioning is inappropriate. What you ask would be better answered by Mr. Topher. When do you expect him?"

Lord Gabriel ignored her question and smiled briefly. "I think that you're regretting your honestly spoken opinion, Miss Westwood. One must always be careful with the truth; it is not always the best policy. But I understand. As I said before, discussing business is clearly not something meant for a woman. So let us focus, instead, on you. The Windermere family owns holdings in America, India, Spain, and here in Barbados. What brought you to this particular location?"

"Barbados had the greatest appeal and was the place where I thought I could do the greatest good."

"Ah, the need to serve; such a noble goal," yet the man's tone spoke otherwise. As they made their way towards the harvest fields Lord Gabriel murmured, "I wonder what you would envision as your ultimate triumph? Is it your arrival here after safely navigating such a dangerous ocean voyage all on your own? Or is it the future goal of educating the black masses here at Windermere so that this plantation will be able to claim the highest educated working class on the island?" Mena kept her eyes straight ahead, refusing to look at Lord Gabriel as he continued to muse out loud. "Perhaps, it's the opportunity to begin a new life; fresh and uninhibited by the past which is riddled by mistakes and scandal." Leaning towards her he whispered, "Are you running from something, Miss Westwood?

An angry husband? A jilted lover? Are the authorities printing wanted posters with your likeness?"

The current field being harvested came into view and Mena could see Graham on Dancer riding amidst the controlled chaos. The sudden desire to fling herself from her horse and run headlong down the hill to seek his protection was so unexpected that it caused her to jerk the reins and make her mount start. Apparently, Graham had been watching for them because he immediately halted and stared in their direction. Mena didn't need to be able to see him to know the grim expression that would be on his face. *He's a snake, title or no.* As she struggled to calm her horse, she turned to Lord Gabriel and said through gritted teeth, "I seek to make God smile, Lord Gabriel, and am determined to use the abilities He has given me to do that. *My* ultimate triumph isn't the purpose of my life."

Lord Gabriel stared unemotionally at Mena for long moments and then turned to stare out into the fields. "Is Graham Rhyder enjoying any of your God-given abilities, Miss Westwood?"

The innuendo was foul and offensive, and Mena remained silent. Life had already taught her well that men who thought and spoke that way were not worth her breath. At her silence, Lord Gabriel urged his horse closer to hers. Before Mena could think, he took her hand and lifted it to his lips. "Think Mr. Rhyder's eyesight is good enough to see me do this … Miss Westwood?" he whispered against her hand. She tried to pull her hand away but he held on firmly. When he did finally release her hand, he reached up to touch her face. Before Mena could consider the ramifications, she slapped his hand away. Lord Gabriel chuckled, not at all bothered by her behavior, and turned to look back to Graham. "Ah yes, he can see us," he murmured with a delighted smile, "and he already reveals more about himself than I had even hoped." He grinned at Mena.

"Perhaps he hasn't enjoyed your God-given abilities *yet*, but he wants to make sure that no one else does either."

Mena turned to see Graham riding purposefully toward them through the fields. Although she waved, trying to signal him that she was all right, he still continued toward them. "Now," Lord Gabriel said, "we shall see just what you wish your Mr. Rhyder to know," he winked at her, "and what you wish to keep secret."

Rich, privileged men had a way of thinking of themselves that caused a weakness, and Graham had every intention of capitalizing on it. Lord Gabriel Windermere believed that he was superior to all: in cleverness, in skill, and in wisdom. Having always been underestimated and misjudged, Graham had learned to exploit such opinions to his benefit on numerous occasions. The problem was whether Mena would be astute enough to realize this. Or not.

"Lord Gabriel," Graham said respectfully when he was within ear shot, "Miss Westwood. I trust your tour of the plantation is going well." The brief flash of disappointment that flitted across Lord Gabriel's face confirmed all Graham needed to know; the show of affection towards Mena had been purely for Graham's benefit.

"Why, yes," Lord Gabriel recovered quickly but continued to attempt to push Graham's buttons, "it has been a lovely morning thus far. Miss Westwood is an *excellent* riding companion and I hope to enjoy her company *as often as possible* while I'm here."

Graham nodded briefly to Mena, her face a careful blank mask, although two spots of color in her cheeks confirmed that she was upset. "I'm glad to hear that. I thought that perhaps you'd like to ride down and meet my foreman, Isaac, as well as some of the other workers. Harvest is for only one more month, and then many will disappear off to parts unknown. If you wish to begin immediately on your plans for a distillery, I've got my eye on a number of workers that I know would be perfect for some of the upcoming positions."

Laughing, Lord Gabriel said condescendingly, "Surely we don't need to hire skilled workers for the distillery until the distillery *is actually built*, Mr. Rhyder."

Graham cleared his throat and took time to use his kerchief to wipe his face and the back of his neck. "I was referring to workers that I know have experience in *construction*, Lord Gabriel," he said quietly. "As these men work from sun up to sundown, and some labor even later, the opportunity for you to meet with any of them is rather limited."

"Ah, I see."

"If you resided here full time, you would already be familiar with many of these individuals. As you were so eager to see all aspects of your holdings, I thought you'd be pleased with this opportunity. Your arrival is perfectly timed as they'll be taking their lunch soon."

"Miss Westwood-"

Graham interrupted. "And you have no need to be concerned about Miss Westwood. Her charges will be delighted to see her, and I'm sure she'll be happy to check in on them." He turned and winked at Mena so that only she could see, and then turned back to Lord Gabriel. Not giving Lord Gabriel an opportunity to decline, Graham wheeled Dancer around and shouted over his shoulder, "Why, you could meet the children as well! Come! Mena will show you where to tie your horse."

Mena watched Graham and Lord Gabriel from the shade surrounded by 'her' children, who had degenerated – apparently immediately – to their "pre-Mena" existence in the one brief morning of her absence. Little Mary informed Mena immediately that Will had eaten four beetles and two rocks, Stinky Celia was as ripe as ever, and Crybaby James was so upset with her absence that he was still hiccupping and sniffling even after sitting on her lap for almost fifteen minutes. "Little Mary, where is Biter Joe?" Despite her best intentions, many of the nicknames had hung on.

"He wit Wanderin' Sammie."

"Oh dear. What direction did they head?" Mena carefully set Crybaby James down and stood, which caused him to immediately grip her skirts and begin to cry again. She stroked James' head as she shading her eyes to look for Joe and Sammie,. "It's all right, James. I'm here now. How about I tell a story? But first, let's sing your favorite song. Can you get us started?" It was a song Mena had made up that taught colors, and James was developing a lovely voice when he wasn't howling.

In time, Sammie and Joe were eventually returned by Winston who had found the two – as well as his son Li'l Winston - playing in "mud" which actually was a manure collection point. He grinned at Mena, and joked, "I'ma guessin' dat Stinky Celia might git a run fo' her money dis day!"

Mena, in the midst of telling the story of Hannah, joked back, "I'm going to pray for an extra bucket of water so that I can clean these four up a bit!" Water was only used for drinking until the very end of the day.

Once everyone was settled Mena finished her story. "Hannah prayed for a son and was blessed with the great prophet Samuel. She believed in the power of prayer and knew that God was always listening to her when she spoke to Him.

"Ruthie prays," Little Mary said around her thumb, "all da time."

"Yes, she does," Mena agreed. "She's a champion pray-er, isn't she? What are some things she prays for, Little Mary?"

Little Mary hesitated and then said in a whisper, "Well, right now Ruthie prayin' dat 'Lizbet has a baby boy."

Mena felt the smile slip from her face as the ramifications of Little Mary's words made full impact. *Ruthie prayin' dat 'Lizbet has a baby boy.* Trying to be casual, she asked, "Is Elizabeth going to have a baby?"

Little Mary pulled her thumb out of her mouth to hold a finger in front of her mouth and say, "Shhhhhh! Don' tell, Missa Mena! Ab'gail says it's a hush!"

"Oh dear," Mena said just as Biter Joe leaned over and took a bite out of Whiny Louise.

⌘⌘⌘⌘⌘⌘⌘⌘⌘

Something was terribly wrong.

The smiling, optimistic, opinionated young woman that Graham was finally forced to acknowledge he was attracted to appeared to have completely disappeared in the space of one day. Pale, silent and distracted, when he finally escorted Lord Gabriel over to the spot where Mena cared for the little ones she hadn't even spared him a glance. As she mounted her horse to head back towards the Great House a wave of such concern for her swept over Graham that he almost called Mena back so he could speak with her. But that wouldn't have done either of their positions at Windermere any good, especially under Lord Gabriel's watchful presence. Standing and watching their departure as the groom followed dutifully behind them, Graham puzzled over what could have upset Mena so profoundly and how he could manage some private time to speak with her.

He stood there so long watching their departure that, Isaac finally had come to fetch him. "Gots yuhrself sum com-pee-tition der Boss wit' dat Lord Ga'brl. I tol' yuh dat Miss Mena was sumpin' special. What's yuh gonna do 'bout it?" Graham turned and was greeted by Isaac's delighted grin. "I tol' yuh, Boss dat yuh needed ta step up yuhr game. Now yuh's gonna hafta scramble fo' sure. *Da early bird get da sweetest flower.*"

"Shut up, Isaac."

Isaac held up his hands and grinned even wider. "Now don' go gettin' testy wit me jus' cause I bin speakin' da trut'. Yuh should know dat Maisy says dat Miss Menas got an eye fo' yuh, too, so I don' think yuh need to worry too much."

Suddenly Graham had an idea that would kill two birds with one stone, so to speak. "You think I could come by after dinner to speak with you and Rachel, Isaac?"

Isaac studied Graham for a moment, growing serious. "Why sure, Boss. Yuh haven' been by in ages. Since b'fore Harvest Time. Der somethin' in pa'ticular yuh needin' ta talk 'bout?"

Graham nodded. "You should know what Mrs. Wagner accused Elizabeth of. Miss Westwood had a conversation the other night with the witch and shared her concern with me. We should probably both talk with you."

The grin was long gone from Isaac's face now. "How yuh gonna git Miss Mena ta come? Yuh need me ta send one a da girls ta fetch her?"

It was a tempting solution, but Graham was loath to put Isaac's family at any further risk. He shook his head. "No, I'll manage something." Clapping his foreman on the shoulder he said, "Come on. Let's get to the end of this day."

Dinner was hell listening to Lord Gabriel continue his veiled attempts to upset Mena, while having to endure the usual nightmare of Mrs. Wagner hosting over 'formal evening supper.' In addition, having a formal celebratory event at the end of harvest – in less than two weeks! - was now in full planning mode. Already Moira was attempting to draft some of Graham's workers for her insipid purposes, and a battle of great significance was gearing up, especially with Lord Gabriel supporting Moira's 'inspired plans.' Mena, quiet and withdrawn, seemed either unwilling or unable to do anything more than drift through dinner like a leaf in a storm. By meal's end, Graham's fear had reached almost epic proportions. He was concerned that somehow Lord Gabriel had done something to Mena despite the groom's presence on their morning ride. When she excused herself from the table after dessert to go to her room, he could barely contain a groan of frustration. How was he supposed to communicate with her? The irony did not escape him that for weeks Graham had worked to avoid her and now his need to talk with her was almost as desperate as his need for his next breath.

Unable to decline Lord Gabriel's offer for after dinner cigars, the two men spent well over an hour reviewing Graham's proposal notes which he had thankfully found. Despite Lord Gabriel's provocative agenda with Mena, it would seem that he was committed to pursuing expansion plans at Windermere, and Graham was going to play a significant role. Under different circumstances he might almost to be … excited about life.

Making his way out the front door and down the pathway to stand in the spot where he usually enjoyed his evening cigar, Graham agonized over how to proceed with his concern over Mena. Did he dare ask Dahlia to send a message to her? It was either that or sneaking up the back servant stairs himself to her room, which was worse.

"Graham? We need to talk."

He whirled to see her standing silently in the shadows. "Mena!" He walked quickly to her, and unable to help himself pulled her into his arms. Holding her tightly, he murmured against her hair, "Are you all right?! Something's wrong! I can tell…"

She didn't fight his embrace but instead gripped the front of his shirt tightly in her fists. "It's Elizabeth, Graham. I know what's wrong." She lifted tear-filled eyes to his. "She's pregnant."

Mena winced at the curse Graham muttered under his breath. "How do you know? Did she speak with you?"

She shook her head. "Little Mary and Ruth are praying that she'll have a boy. It's a 'hush'. I'm not to tell anyone." A sob caught in her throat. "What are we going to do?"

"Well, first we're going to visit Rachel and Isaac. Can you come with me now?"

Nodding she said, "Of course. My time is my own now."

"But first I need to know something and you must be honest with me *please*," he said in a low voice, reaching to tilt her face up so he could see it as clearly as possible in the darkness. He searched her eyes using his thumb to brush away the tracks of tears that were barely visible on her cheeks. "Did he hurt you today? Touch you? Cause you any grief? For if he did, Lord or no, I'll have to kill him. I *need* to know the truth, Mena."

"Oh, Graham," she sighed, an expression of tenderness softening the worry on her face. She wrapped her arms around his waist and rested her face against his chest. How long had it been since he'd been touched with tenderness and affection? A wave of delight swept through him and he reciprocated the embrace, holding her tightly against him. After a time Mena sighed and said quietly, "No, Lord Gabriel did not touch me." She held him for long moments and then picked her head up to look at him. "Your concern for me means more than I can ever put into words." When Graham started to speak, she reached up and gently put her fingers against his lips. "I am so worried about Elizabeth. Can we please go to her?" She caressed his cheek and smiled. "I think the time has come where even you must agree that we must truly talk. No more games and no more secrets."

Leaning forward, he rested his forehead against hers. "I-, I don't know if I can do that. I'm not good at this, Mena."

"Neither am I," she answered honestly. "I've always been solitary, Graham. If I couldn't accomplish it myself then I chose a different path. But ... Barbados is more than I expected; it has made me care about too many people, and yet never have I felt so necessary. It's a job bigger than I can do by myself." Mena looked up at him. "I ... need you. Your friendship. Your concern. Your advice. Your strength. I'm afraid that it's not what you want to hear from me and I'm truly sorry for that. I know you've worked hard to keep me at a distance and, quite frankly, I've tried the same." She sighed and reached up to cup his cheek. "But the truth is, whether you like it or not you've become important to me."

Graham didn't have anything to say to that so he simply leaned in and gave her a soft, brief kiss. Then grasping Mena's hand tightly in his, he led them off in the direction of the worker's village.

Mr. Nelson Topher
Windermere Plantation

Mr. Topher:

I am in receipt of your communication regarding the presence of one Mena Westwood who is currently holding the position of teacher at Windermere.

If he has not arrived already, you should expect my son, Lord Gabriel Windermere shortly, who I am charging with the handling of this situation. Kindly provide my son with the enclosed, confidential missive in which I communicate my directives.

Regards,

Wha' yuh believe in, yuh boun' to die in.

Chapter Sixteen

Elizabeth sat before her mother, her father, Graham and Mena and refused to utter a word. By the light of the flickering candle, her lovely face, awash with silent tears, looked from one adult to the next and then down at her tightly clasped hands.

"We're just trying to help you," Mena said gently, although a quick glance at Isaac and Graham communicated that they were more inclined to commit murder if only they could find the culprit. "How long have you known about the baby, Elizabeth? Can you tell us who the father is? Is it someone from the village?" The clenching of Elizabeth's hands was the only evidence that she'd even heard Mena's questions.

"How 'bout yuh two leave us be fo' a bit?" Rachel finally said to Graham and Isaac. "We maybe need ta have sum girl talk." Once the men had gone to stand on the front porch, Rachel put her arm around her daughter and drew her close. "Sumbody hurt yuh, chile, I kin tell," she whispered as she kissed the top of Elizabeth's bent head. "If dis baby was from love, yuh wud be willing ta tell us who da daddy is, but yuh bin actin' strange for a while. An' yuh ain't never given no man in da village a second look even if dey can't seem ta keep der eyes offa yuh. Why cain't yuh tell us who hurt yuh, baby?"

Mena's head was suddenly filled with the roaring of the past rushing up to bombard her. "Because she's still afraid," Mena said tightly, gazing at Elizabeth's bent head. Mena's hands, just like Elizabeth's, were tightly clasped in her lap as she suddenly and clearly understood what the situation was. "Sometimes silence is the only thing a person can do when she is so frightened she doesn't know what else to do." Rachel looked pointedly at Mena, her eyes searching. "It's a fear that makes you feel small and lost and helpless," Mena whispered, suddenly lost in the terrible memories, "and worried about the tiniest shadows and the smallest of sounds. You feel like you are the only person alive in the whole world and believe that no one can ever keep you safe or rescue you." Now Elizabeth was looking at Mena, too. Mena breathed a shaky sigh and didn't stop the tears that slowly tracked down her face. "I know of that fear, Elizabeth. It's partly what brought me here to Barbados on my own; to escape the shadows and the sounds and to stop feeling so helpless and alone. It is the most awful feeling of helplessness in the world, and I was about your age when the fear first started for me."

Mena leaned over and extended her hands palm up, and after a brief hesitation Elizabeth placed her hands in Mena's. "I'm going to ask you some questions," Mena said quietly, "and you *must* make yourself answer them. I am only going to ask you questions about *you* so that those of us who love and care for you can help you as best we can. All right?" Tentatively, Elizabeth nodded.

"Do you feel safe here at home with your mother and father and sisters?" A small nod yes. "Is there any other place you'd rather be where you'd feel safer?" No. "Are you in physical pain? Is there some way you are hurt that needs to be tended?" No. "Can you walk here in this village without fear for the most part?" Yes.

Mena nodded. "All right. That helps us. Now have you felt the baby move yet?" Yes. "Has there been any bleeding or spotting?" No. "Can you tell me how many months it's been since you last had your menses?" Elizabeth carefully held up three fingers. "All right. You're doing a wonderful job answering questions for me, Elizabeth. Thank you. These things you are telling us will help the baby. Now, I don't need you to tell me any names, but is there anyone in the fields when you are working that you are frightened of?" No. "So you are content working in the fields right now?" Yes.

Mena smiled and squeezed Elizabeth's hands. "You are doing so well, Elizabeth. Thank you for answering all my questions. It is helping those of us who love and care for you to understand how we can help you feel safe."

Without letting go of Elizabeth's hand, Mena said, "Now I must talk with you about something, because you have been accused of an action that I can't believe to be true. Did you take anything that didn't belong to you while you were working at the Great House?" A vigorous nod no. "Did you find anything while you were working there and accidently forgot and left it in a pocket of your apron or in your room?" No. "All right. That is exactly what I believed to be the case. Now I am going to ask just one more question. Did anyone *give* you a gift while you were at the Great House? Perhaps it was a present that you did not wish to have but did not know how to refuse?" The silence returned and Mena sighed. "I see. Well, I will take that as a 'yes', but we need not talk about it any further."

Mena squeezed Elizabeth's hand. "Elizabeth, listen to me carefully. Look at me and see how serious I am." When Elizabeth lifted sorrowful brown eyes to look at her, Mena continued. "*Nothing* that has happened to you is your fault. We all know that if you could have done anything in your power to stop this you would have. Am I right?" Looking away, Elizabeth slowly nodded her head yes. "So even though it is very, very hard to do, you must work to not blame yourself. Your family and your friends care for you no matter what – nothing will ever change that." Quietly, Mena said, "I know what I am talking about, Elizabeth, but it took me far too long a time to believe these things. I had no one to reassure me or comfort me and I spent a long time worrying about what I should have done differently. But you must look at me now, Elizabeth, and believe me when I tell you that the woman that I am now is because I came to believe in God's love, grace, strength and guidance. I learned that when doubts assailed me, to say something over and over to myself that helped me remember that I was *never* alone. It is the truth of the universe; something that gave me strength and reassurance: *Fear thou not; for I am with thee: be not dismayed; for I am thy God: I will strengthen thee; yea, I will help thee; yea, I will uphold thee with the right hand of my righteousness.*" Mena lowered herself to her knees before Elizabeth, and still gripping the girl's hands, she used her sleeve to wipe the tears she didn't remember crying. "Can you remember that when you think you are all alone, Elizabeth?" she whispered. "Write it on your heart and let it become your battle cry just as I did." Mena stood, reached out and touched Elizabeth's cheek. "Anytime you wish to talk, I am always willing. I'm going to go now and give you some time alone with your wonderful mother and father who love you so very much. Is there anything you'd like to ask me before I go?"

Elizabeth looked at Mena and swallowed. "When will da bad dreams stop?"

Mena leaned in and embraced the girl. "Eventually, but not soon enough. But remember, God is always ready to listen no matter what the time it is. I have spent many hours late in the night talking to God about my fears and my worries."

Mena wanted to get into a hot bath and scrub herself raw.

She felt dirty and tainted with memories that she had hoped she would never have to dredge up. Yet sitting there in Rachel and Elizabeth's small home she had recognized herself in the girl's posture and agonizing silence, and not sharing was suddenly impossible. Never had it occurred to Mena that there was *anything* she had to be thankful for regarding that horrible dark time of her life, but now she knew that there was at least one thing: she had never conceived.

What had never occurred to Mena was that *because* of her past she would actually be able to provide some comfort to another person. Why it was ... remarkable.

One night during her voyage to Barbados, she had stood looking out at the dark ocean and the night sky filled with stars and just let all the fear, anger, and shame finally drift away and made a promise to herself to *never think about those feelings again.* Barbados offered her not only a chance to teach and do what she felt called by the Lord to do, but also a chance to start fresh. Lord Gabriel's comment - *perhaps, it's the opportunity to begin a new life; fresh and uninhibited by the past which is riddled by mistakes and scandal* - held more truth than she cared to admit.

However, just moments ago she had willingly resurrected those awful times from her past and had been able to *help* someone. It was ... incredibly empowering. Like scrubbing out the last dark stain that you had never thought to eradicate and feeling ... victorious.

"Who?" was the first word Graham spoke as they made their way back from the village. Mena was so immersed in her raw thoughts, she had almost forgotten his presence.

"Elizabeth didn't tell Rachel and I anything more than-"

"I'm not talking about Elizabeth," came Graham's gritted reply.

Mena stopped and turned. He carried a lantern to light their way and his facial features flickered in stark, angry relief. "You ... heard ...?"

Setting the lantern down at their feet, Graham gripped Mena's shoulders and gave her a small shake. "WHO?"

She thrust her chin out. "He stole many years of my life, Graham, but no more. He is no longer important; I refuse to give him any more of my life."

"I-, I wish...," Graham's face twisted with frustration, and then with a muttered curse he turned and stepped away, his hands fisted on his hips.

"Graham Rhyder, you will look at me and you will listen." It took him a number of deep breaths but he finally turned, his hands hanging loosely at his side. "We are all a product of our past, and life is hard whether we are born slave or free, privileged or poor. I spoke of this once before to you, but I suspect you dismissed my words as the ramblings of a naive, spoiled, little rich girl.

"Though the past cannot be changed, *I* chose to change. I could have remained a frightened, broken, insecure mess, but instead I chose to be the woman you see before you. I am strong through God's help, I am purposeful through God's guidance, and I am determined through God's encouragement." She stepped in as close as possible without touching him and looked into his eyes. "And I am no longer broken and bleeding through God's love, grace and peace."

Mena looked down at her tightly clasped hands. "I *thought* that God was sending me to Barbados to get away, start fresh, and never, ever think of ... certain times in my past ... that I wished had never happened. Up until now, I have felt exactly that way: refreshed and renewed, and it is one of the many blessings I have received since coming here. And yet tonight, something truly amazing has happened to me that I am only just beginning to comprehend." She looked up at his angry countenance. "Graham, just now because of my dark, awful past I was able to *help* a person in some small way! Elizabeth now knows that she is not alone and that she has someone nearby who understands some of what she is feeling."

She shrugged and sighed. "I never intended to let *anyone* know of that part of my past. It is something that I forever planned to wrap up and hide away, never to see the light of day. But now Rachel and Elizabeth know. And you know. And it's not so horrible after all – and maybe it will produce even a tiny bit of good." Mena reached up to touch Graham's cheek briefly. "*Perhaps,* Mr. Graham Rhyder, you can begin to understand why your kindnesses have been so wonderful, whether it is championing me in your monthly reports or showing concern over my safety or welcoming my outspoken and oft-times blunt observations. I have never had … someone … do that for me. Ever."

"Your ability to find a goodness in *everything…*" Graham shook his head in wonder as he retrieved the lantern. Mena fell into step beside him as they resumed their walk back to the Great House.

"I have a friend. Back in England," Mena explained. "We met during our debut season when we were only sixteen. She was born of privilege just as I, but was the only person I knew who thought as I did – that wealth *did not* immediately qualify someone to be right or worthy or … special. She was fortunate enough to meet a young man during that first season and plans were made for them to wed. She had such expectations for the future! However, it became public knowledge that her father had gambled away all of the family's money and holdings and incurred debts so massive he faced debtors' prison. Once her family's financial woes became public the man withdrew his suit as was his right. Disgraced, with no hope of ever marrying, she sought a position as a governess. When my parents learned of this they forbade me to have any contact with her after that." Mena smiled at Graham. "You can probably guess that I defied my parents. Evangeline was my one and only true friend, and I cared little whether she was a woman of privileged wealth or a scullery maid. We would meet in the park when she was out with her two young charges and talk of many things.

"Evangeline gave me the gift of my faith, Graham. She fairly glowed with her trust in God and her belief that He would care for her in all things. It was easy to roll your eyes at her spiritual passion when she was dressed in emeralds and silks and betrothed to marry a handsome, rich young man and live happily ever after. It was impossible to ignore her faith when she still shone just as brightly as a penniless young woman with no hopes for the future. She made me face the truth about both my blessings *and* my burdens and helped me understand who was worth trusting my life to ... and who was not.

"Today, Evangeline is *Lady* Evangeline Kipling, happily married with two foster children and two of her own. She and her husband live comfortably and quietly on the outskirts of London, away from the insipid London society. It was Evangeline who helped me arrange things so that I could come to Barbados, and who is the only one who knows of my whereabouts. I owe her my life."

Graham stopped and turned to her. "How old are you?"

Mena smiled. "I turned twenty-four just two weeks ago."

"And yet you have never known love nor do you believe in it," he said studying her face intently by the flickering lamplight.

Her smile faltered a bit. "God's love abounds ...," she said hesitantly. "It flows to us through the kindness of friends and the blessing we receive..."

Reaching up, Graham hung the lantern on a low hanging branch. "I am thirty-three years old, Mena. My life is a study in broken promises, endless poor choices, and the abject cruelties of life. And yet the one shining light has been the presence of love in my life: from my mother, from my wife, and from a friend. It is because of this love that I am standing here alive, upright, and functioning." Graham took Mena's hand, kissed it and then held it against his chest. "It would seem that we each have something we need to teach the other. You need to teach me how to see the joy in this miserable existence and I need to teach you about the realities of true love."

"I think-,"

But Graham didn't give her a chance to argue. With his one hand still holding hers against his heart, he reached up and drew her into an embrace and kissed her. Just as he'd been dreaming of doing since their stolen kisses at his hut. "Maybe that's your problem," he murmured against her lips, "you think too much. You should know that love doesn't always make sense, Mena. It rarely happens at a good time and usually causes far more complications. But when the *feeling* happens, you just can't ignore it."

Mena whispered back against his mouth, "Love is patient and kind. It rejoices in truth. It beareth all things, believeth all things, hopeth all things, endureth all things ... it never fails."

Graham searched her face lit by the glow of the lantern. "For someone who doesn't believe in love you've got an awfully thorough definition of it."

She smiled. "It's from the Bible. It's the reason I can't believe in earthly love. Not only have I never experienced it, I couldn't possibly imagine ever being the recipient of a love such as that."

Kissing her once more because he couldn't help himself, he took her hand, retrieved the lantern, and they resumed walking back to the Great House. "Tell me again what you just said love is," Graham said quietly. After Mena had repeated it he sighed deeply. "So I will tell you my awful secret, Mena, so that we're even. My wife, Fiona, loved me with the kind of love you just described. She was patient and kind and never stopped believing in me." They walked in silence for a time. Graham felt her glance his way at least twice but he couldn't bring himself to look at her. "Fiona loved me despite my drinking and endured my inability to control it. She always hoped, each time I disappeared for a binge – sometimes for days – that somehow I'd manage to learn how to control it." When the awful memories and emotions began to build, he tried to take his hand away but Mena wouldn't let him. "Her love never failed," Graham muttered in despair, "even though it eventually killed her. I left her alone when she was far along in her pregnancy, to have just one more bit of the drink before the babe arrived. I was gone for three days. *Three days!* When I managed to get myself back to the cabin, she and the babe … were dead."

"Oh, Graham!" Mena tried to embrace him but he stood hard and unyielding, just like a tree. "What sorrow you carry with you," she whispered against his neck. She placed her cool hand against his cheek and made him turn to look into her eyes. "Do you still love her, Graham?" she asked gently.

He nodded. "I do. It's one of the only good things I've still got left."

She placed her hand on his heart. "And it would seem that her love is still with you, Graham. That patient belief and hope that you'll accomplish the things that Fiona believed you to be capable of is still alive and enduring. *That's* why you get up in the morning and *that's* why you are fair with your workers and *that's* why you're so intolerable of Mrs. Wagner's cruel behavior." She leaned in and kissed him softly on the mouth. "You describe a love that I once dreamed of, but that life thus far had convinced me didn't exist. Evangeline tried to help me to believe. Tried to help me to be patient. Tried to get me to trust. But the unfulfilled longing … it was too much to bear. It was easier for me to stop believing."

"I don't want to love again, Mena," Graham said through gritted teeth as he touched his forehead to hers and closed his eyes at the remembered agony. "I'm not sure I'd survive it."

"What a pair we are," she whispered, and Graham could hear the smile in her voice. "You're alive only because of the love you've known, but also supremely broken by the loss of it. And I'm alive only because of the endless search for a love that I've never experienced, but want more than my next breath."

"I've spoiled you, daughter; I'll take the full blame for that. The loss of your mother just about did me in and were it not for the blessing of you I don't think I would have ever been able to survive. But even while I've spoiled you, I've dedicated my entire life to keeping you safe and healthy. What you're asking is too much for even this permissive, dedicated father to accept."

"Da, I love him! He's my heart and my soul and all the stars in between."

"He's a tortured man; he's already filled with the tragedies of life. I see it in the way he looks at everyone he encounters."

"Not with me, Da. Not with me."

"You two remind me of your mother and me; love at first sight and refusing to believe there was anything but rainbows and butterflies in our future. But it's not just love that you need to get you through this life, daughter. You need patience and understanding, loyalty and forgiveness. And, most of all, when the sorrows hit, and they most surely will, you must believe that there is Someone else far greater than anyone you could ever comprehend Who's holding you in the palm of His hand."

If yuh head bad, yuh whole body bad.

Chapter Seventeen

To Mena, the final weeks of harvest, if possible, seemed to be busier than the first. Mrs. Wagner was completely consumed with the planning of the Crop Over Fete, a celebration that seemed to grow in scope and complexity with each passing day. There was a guest list to compile, invitations to deliver, food to order, rooms to be arrange, dishes to be prepared, musicians to be secured, and temporary staff to be hired and trained.

In addition, Lord Gabriel's presence ensured that everyone was tense with the need to be seen in a favorable light, whether a house maid, a groom, or a gardener. The construction of a distillery was scheduled to begin at the end of harvest, which meant that workers needed to be hired, plans to be formally drawn, materials to be ordered, and machines to be purchased and shipped.

At any given time, Mena saw people coming and going from the Great House – almost always at a run and with an air of utmost urgency. She wondered if Graham slept, as he was either overseeing harvest matters, battling with Mrs. Wagner over the use of workers, or planning with Lord Gabriel behind closed study doors. At the formal evening meals – when he showed up – he looked exhausted and preoccupied and had dark circles under his eyes.

Aside from her usual duties with her young charges, and in an effort to stay away from both Mrs. Wagner *and* Lord Gabriel, Mena had taken to once again visiting the Freemans after the evening meal. She often took a small package, courtesy of Dahlia, and found great peace in sitting on the front porch chatting with Rachel, visiting with Elizabeth, or telling Bible stories to the younger girls. For Mena, it was the first glimpse of what she felt a *real* family ought to be: loving and supportive.

"Yuh goin' to da party at da big house, Miss Mena?" Rachel asked one evening. Isaac often supervised bedtime preparations for the girls, giving Rachel her one and only break after a very long day.

Mena shrugged unenthusiastically. "I suppose. I don't really think I have a right to refuse. Mrs. Wagner has informed all house staff that they will be expected to be on duty throughout the night. I don't suppose I'll be teaching, but I'm sure she will expect my presence."

"Yuh not much fo' parties an' such?" Rachel asked as she leaned against the porch post and sipped a cup of water.

Mena shook her head. "No, I've never been the type that enjoyed all that." She smiled. "I do enjoy dancing though." Elizabeth came out just then. "Come, Elizabeth," Mena stood and extended her hand and bowed. "Let me show you how to do the waltz. It was quite the rage in London Society. I'll even hum my favorite Chopin Waltz. It's quite easy; I'm sure you'll have no trouble learning it. Let me show you the main steps – you need to think of a box…" To Elizabeth's delight, and with Mena humming along, the two were soon twirling around the hard packed dirt in front of their home in the gathering dark. When Isaac finally appeared, Elizabeth took her father's hand

and Mena took Rachel's and soon there were two grinning couples twirling to Mena's humming.

"What fun dat was!" Rachel chuckled once they were all seated again on the steps of the front porch.

"I have a music box," Mena said, "that plays the tune much better than I can hum it. Next time I visit I'll bring it along."

"Yuh got a dress ta wear to da party?" Elizabeth asked. Since the revelation of what she had endured had come to light, Rachel had confided to Mena that though Elizabeth was still quieter than she used to be, her interactions with family members had improved.

"Oh my. I hadn't thought of that. I only brought serviceable things with me when I came to Barbados, and to almost all of those outfits I've made additional alterations so that I'm comfortable here in this climate." Mena tapped her lip. "I've got one that with a little reconfiguring would probably suffice." She smiled at Elizabeth. "I'll have to get busy with my needle and thread. It's a good thing you said something Elizabeth, or I'd be showing up in my old brown skirt and the boots that Dahlia got for me in town!"

"Ders a shop in town dats got sum pretty things," Rachel said. "Dahlia wud know."

Mena stood. "If I can catch Dahlia with a free moment I'll ask her. I best head back. Thank you for being such excellent dance partners."

"Yuh cum anytime, Miss Mena," Isaac smiled. "Yuh always bring us a bit a' sunshine." He looked into the darkness. "You have your friendly shadow waiting for you?" Mena's heart skipped a beat thinking Isaac meant Graham, who was hardly her shadow. Isaac chuckled. "I've seen more of Silent Joe around since you've been visiting."

Oh. "He often appears somewhere along the way on my trip home, but not always." Sometimes Graham surprised her instead and Mena felt herself blushing. How much did Joe know and see? "I sing sometimes on the way home and I think he likes to listen, although I'd never win any prizes with my limited ability."

Walking back to the Great House and to keep herself from thinking too much of the dark, Mena continued to hum her favorite Chopin waltz. She twirled in the dark and smiled to herself. The simple pleasures in life here in Barbados brought her more joy than all the finery and riches that she had had back in England. *Please,* she prayed, *keep me headed in the direction where You need me to be. Let me recognize the good and overcome the bad. Let me make You smile in all I do.*

"Can I have this dance?"

"Graham!" Mena gasped. "You've almost scared me to death!"

He frowned and stepped into her space. "Why are you walking in the dark? On full moon nights it's understandable, but on nights such as this you need a lantern." He took Mena's hand and wrapped his arm around her waist. "Dance with me, Miss Westwood," and before she could say a thing he twirled her expertly.

"You can dance?" she said in surprise.

"I've got all kinds of tricks up my sleeve that you don't know about," was his response as he pulled her close and hummed another of Chopin's waltz tunes in her ear. They danced for long moments in the darkness of the night. *Simple pleasures,* Mena thought and looked up towards heaven and added, *Thank you for these joys, Lord.* Eventually, Graham kissed her nose, took her hand and they began to walk.

"Were you spying on me?" she teased.

He looked offended. "I was missing you and came to find you. We haven't spoken in days, and I only get to see you sitting next to that buffoon across the table at Moira's accursed dinners. I wanted to make sure all was well with you. When I found you dancing and laughing, I didn't want to interrupt. I haven't seen Isaac, Rachel, and Elizabeth smiling and happy – simultaneously ...," Graham paused, "well *ever*, Mena. After you left the Freemans', it was fun walking behind you for a bit watching you sing and dance... So I *was* watching, but *not* spying. There's a difference.

"Are you well? Has Lord Gabriel been suitably busy to stay out of your business? Have you been able to fend off Moira? I know what you've been doing – coming here every night and escaping the madness known as the Great House. Moira has reached a new level of insanity, expecting me to give up necessary field hands to ride across the blasted island to hand-deliver invitations to this absurd Crop Over Fete. And when I'm not battling her, I'm dealing with his lordship who doesn't know much of anything about anything, but because he has "Lord" in his name I'm supposed to bow and scrape and try to find politely careful ways to tell him he's an imbecile. He doesn't know a damn thing about constructing a distillery - let alone running one."

She laughed out loud. "Oh please. Stop holding back. Tell me how you *really* feel."

Graham looked at her smiling face and couldn't help but shake his head in frustration. "Did you know that Winston was part of the construction of not one but two distilleries here on the island? He's got the ability to draw plans, too, and has almost a photographic memory when it comes to numbers and measures. But can we use what he knows? *Of course not.*" Here Graham switched over to a stuffy British accent. "I say! He's a bloody ignorant field hand! What could he possibly know? Have you noticed that his skin is *black*? I'm a Cambridge educated gentlemen! I have shiny riding boots, a top hat, and at least fifteen different colored ascots! My daddy is a Marquis and an Earl, and that means everyone who looks at me should bow and acknowledge my inbred intelligence."

Mena was laughing so hard that she finally had to stop and catch her breath. She looked at Graham with shining eyes. "I don't know what I enjoy more about this conversation: that our opinions are identical or that you are happily conversing and sharing with me." Wiping her eyes, she sobered. "Thank you. You give me wonderful gifts almost every time I speak with you. You'd best watch out; if you're not careful you'll never be able to get rid of me."

Graham stepped in close. "Who says I ever want to get rid of you? I find you quite entertaining myself. Didn't know you dance… You'll have to save me a space on your dance card for this ridiculous party next weekend."

"You're coming?" The prospect of having to attend the Fete suddenly became much more appealing.

Graham groaned. "Oh yes, I've been ordered to attend. I've got to meet some other ignorant Lord something or other that Gabriel has invited to the party who wants to discuss the distillery construction. I tried to explain that the venue was less than optimal for a business conversation, but the idiot will hear none of it."

"And you want to dance with me?"

Graham stopped and looked at her. "Damn straight I want to dance with you. And furthermore, I'd be quite happy if you dance with no one else but me."

"There will be talk, you know."

He leaned in to her. "You've said that before. How did I answer?"

She smirked at him. "If I remember correctly, you said, "'Darlin', don't you realize they were talkin' about us before we'd even spoken a word.' I can't mimic your excellent accent, though."

The Great House was just around the corner. Graham looked carefully around before he took Mena into his arms. "I'm going to ask you a question and I expect you to give me an honest answer. All right?" Mena nodded. "Do you *care* if you're seen with me? Do you *care* if people begin to talk because of what *they see* rather than merely *what they're guessing?*" He put his finger against her lips. "Don't make any rash responses, now, Darlin'. Make sure you're certain of your answer because I intend to hold you to it."

It was the look in Graham's eyes as he stood there in the dim evening light that made Mena's heart stutter and flip. It was suddenly, vividly clear to her that *this was what it felt like to be loved.* And by the joy she felt in her heart and in her soul, she knew she could love him too. She kissed him before she answered. A slow, sensual kiss that he'd taught her. Against his lips she whispered, "No, I don't care who sees me with you, Graham Rhyder. In fact, I'd be content to let the whole world know."

Two days before the fete, an air of excitement filled the Great House, and evidence of the upcoming party was visible, from the whitewashing of the outside privies to the construction of the outdoor dancing pavilion to the new uniforms for every house employee. Delicious aromas wafted from the kitchen both day and night, and guests were expected to begin arriving from the most distant parts of the island beginning tomorrow.

Mena stepped out the front door on her way to the Freemans' only to smell the aroma of cigar. With a bright smile on her face she turned to find Lord Gabriel lounging on one of the verandah chairs. "Oh…," she managed as the smile slipped abruptly from her face.

"Miss Westwood," Lord Gabriel stood and extended his hand toward the complementary chair beside him. "I've been waiting for you. Won't you join me?" Once Mena was seated he murmured, "If I didn't know better, I would suspect that you have been purposefully avoiding me."

"I have no reason to avoid you, Lord Gabriel. I simply have no business to discuss with you."

"But I am your employer, am I not? Shouldn't you be seeking me out and attempting to leave favorable lasting impressions on me?" At her stony silence, he sighed and drew deeply on his cigar. As he exhaled he said, "Are you ready for the grand celebration? Have you a dress hidden up in your room to make you look like Cinderella? Perhaps you might even find yourself a Prince Charming?"

"Yes, I have a dress."

"Are you looking forward to the fete?"

"No. I care little for festivities such as this."

"And why not? You are an attractive young woman. I'm sure that any number of young men would be more than pleased to have you on their arm." When Mena did not respond, Lord Gabriel asked, "Can I look forward to a dance with you?"

"It would be unseemly for you to dance with me, Lord Gabriel, and well you know it."

"Now, now," Lord Gabriel said in an annoyingly placating tone. "Things are *much* more casual here in Barbados. Why, don't I sit down to dinner every night with a housekeeper, a butler, a manager and a teacher?" He chuckled at the ridiculousness of it all. "If I have to tolerate *that*," he muttered, "then I should at least be able to enjoy the benefits of dancing with whom I choose." He turned to her. "Of course, I wouldn't want to cause any problems between you and Mr. Rhyder. The last thing I need to is be called out and have to kill someone in a duel." He sighed and took a long draw from his cigar. "Mr. Rhyder *is* replaceable, but it would be such an inconvenience given our construction plans."

"What do you want from me?" Mena asked in a tired voice.

He waved his hand. "Oh, nothing at this moment. I must admit I've quite enjoyed watching the two of you scuttle around in the dark of night when you think no one is the wiser. I'm quite amazed, Miss Westwood. Stolen kisses and gropings in the dark seem to appeal to you far more than I thought they would." Mena went to stand and he gripped her arm. "Mr. Topher has just arrived and delivered a private missive to me from father. Would you be surprised to know its primary topic involves you?"

Mena forced herself to remain outwardly calm and silent.

Lord Gabriel tsked and shook his head. "I can only imagine Lord Windermere's shock. He was completely unaware that a teacher had been hired to educate his workers!" Mena felt Lord Gabriel turn to look at her but refused to look at him. "But then you knew that, of course." The chair creaked as he leaned in closer. "Would you like to guess what he has decided to do?" He reached out to tuck a strand of hair behind her ear and whispered, "He's so very relieved that you're safe, *Wilhelmina.*"

The gorge rose in Mena's throat and she abruptly stood. The shaking could no longer be contained and Mena grasped her trembling hands in front of her. Turning, she closed her eyes and remembered her battle cry. *Fear thou not; for I am with thee: be not dismayed; for I am thy God: I will strengthen thee; yea, I will help thee;*

yea, I will uphold thee with the right hand of my righteousness. "I care not what you have been instructed to do, as Lord Windermere holds no power over me aside from my teaching position here. Have you been instructed to relieve me of those responsibilities? If that is so then I will pack my bags and depart immediately." *Oh dear Lord, guide me.*

Lord Gabriel came to stand beside Mena at the bannister and went to place a calming hand on her shoulder, but she stepped away. "Why not at all, Miss Westwood! Not at all! Mr. Topher's reports of your performance have been glowing. Why would he wish to dismiss you? What His Lordship has decided to do is to *make preparations to visit.* It's been far too long since he has seen the beauty of this island and *enjoyed all its delights.* I'm sure he looks forward to experiencing *all* the exciting opportunities that Barbados has to offer."

CROP OVER FETE

The Company of

M_____

is requested at Windermere Plantation, on

Saturday, 28th of May, 1853, at 4 o'clock P.M.

Managers,
M. WAGNER
W. WAGNER

It takes one finger ta feel a louse, but two ta take it out.

Chapter Eighteen

The changes Mena felt within herself made it feel far longer than five months since she had first arrived in Barbados – more like a lifetime. As she stood in her room with butterflies in her stomach regarding tonight's party, she fussed over her hair and her dress - something she had *never* concerned herself with in the past. Peering at herself in the mirror, she acknowledged that she looked somewhat different, but couldn't quite identify what exactly it was. Did she look more peaceful? Happier? Perhaps it was a stronger self-confidence, for even with Lord Gabriel's threat of visitors coming from England Mena felt relatively calm.

Relatively being the key word. There were so many unknowns about tonight's festivities: Lord Gabriel, Mrs. Wagner, the numerous Bajan natives she had never formally met... And of course there was Graham and their ... friendship. That final thought caused her to place her hand against her stomach and take a deep, calming breath.

As Mena stepped out of her room to head to the festivities she couldn't help but feel that for some reason, tonight felt like it was going to be far more than just the end of harvest celebration. *Keep me on the right path, Lord. Guide my words, my thoughts, and my actions.*

Windermere's Great House was already bustling with numerous guests having arrived the day before. "Oh, there you are," came Mrs. Wagner's imperious voice. Mena turned to greet her and couldn't help but stare in surprise. Wearing a lovely gown of forest green instead of her formal housekeeper's attire, Mrs. Wagner looked almost … pretty. With her hair swept up in an intricate style and emeralds winking at her ears and at her throat, the dour, vicious, unfeeling Mrs. Wagner looked rather young and carefree. But then she began to speak and Mena was reminded that *Jus' cause da apple is shiny don' mean it's good ta eat.* "I need you to assume the responsibility of greeting the guests as they arrive. You are to collect the women's wraps and the men's hats and canes and put them in the study. I've set aside two serving girls, Joelene and Amanda, to assist you and help you keep everything organized. Then direct the guests to the outside venue." She gave Mena a once-over. "Can you come up with something welcoming to say or shall I coach you? Something like, "Please follow the music to our outside celebration" or "Kindly make your way through to the festivities in the outside garden.""

"I will be happy to. When those responsibilities have been seen to, what else would you like me to do?"

Mrs. Wagner studied Mena's face. "Need I remind you that I expect you to be on your very best behavior? You have a disturbing habit of speaking before being spoken to and offering opinions when they have not been sought. Not to mention what you apparently do during your *off hours* in the dark of night. Remember your place here, Miss Westwood. You might be dressed as a young woman of society, but you are nothing more than a paid servant and here at the pleasure of those whom you work for."

Enough. Mena picked up her skirts and began to step away but Mrs. Wagner gripped her arm, stopping her. "Have you studied the guest list, Miss Westwood? I've provided you,

Mr. Rhyder, and Mr. Topher with copies so that you could familiarize yourself with our visitors."

Mena looked down at Mrs. Wagner's hand gripping her arm and then up into Mrs. Wagner's cold eyes. Had she only moments ago thought the woman looked young and pretty? Only when Mrs. Wagner had removed her hand from Mena's arm did she respond, "Yes, just as you asked, Mrs. Wagner."

Mrs. Wagner smiled, looking very pleased with something. "I'm so looking forward to the arrival of Lady Maureen Walcott. It is an absolute honor that she has deigned to attend. She has only just come out of her year of mourning after the death of Lord Phillip." Mrs. Wagner tsked, all the while watching Mena closely. "Please make sure that Mr. Rhyder knows when she arrives. They have a *history,* so to speak, and it would be appropriate for him to express his condolences at the death of her beloved husband."

"Is that all?"

Patting her hair, Mrs. Wagner turned to look towards the kitchen and then back to Mena. "That's it for now. I expect you, Miss Westwood, to remain available at all times should I have need of you. No disappearing off into areas you have no reason to be with persons you have no business spending time with. Appearance is everything." Mrs. Wagner arched her eyebrows at Mena's carefully neutral expression. "Need I be more specific?"

"By all means," Mena said quietly as she turned and walked away without a backward glance.

"Mr. Rhyder."

"Mr. Topher," Graham inclined his head respectfully to the plantation's bespeckled solicitor. "I see your wife is enjoying the musicians. I take it dancing isn't your forte?"

"Given my unique upbringing, I never was much for the pastime. Audrey loves to dance, however, and forgives me my lack of skill."

Graham turned to Mr. Topher. "Unique upbringing?"

"Yes, Mr. Rhyder," Mr. Topher elaborated, "for a major portion of my life I was part of the Religious Society of Friends. Dancing, although not forbidden, is rarely done, hence my lack of ability. I left the Society some fifteen years ago." Graham allowed one eyebrow to rise but otherwise remained silent. He wasn't sure, but he *thought* he saw Mr. Topher suppress a smile as he looked out onto the dance floor to watch his wife. "I can just imagine your thoughts at this very moment," he said carefully, "and yet I know how much you value privacy, and you will not ask, so I will tell you. Friend Nathaniel was my brother-in-law. Long ago I was married to his sister." When he saw Graham glance at Audrey he added, "Audrey is my second wife. We have been wed happily these past ten years."

"I see," although it was patently clear to both men that he was lying.

"In all the time you have known me, Mr. Rhyder, I do not think I have ever given you – or anyone else for that matter – the impression that I have anything but the very best for Windermere Plantation as my goal. So before you begin to question – either aloud or merely in your heart – whether your position here was earned in any way other than legitimately, let me disabuse you of that. When Friend Nathaniel approached me about you, the only favor that was granted was the opportunity for you to interview with me. What you have earned thus far in position and reputation is all your own doing and nothing else."

"So you know some of my ... history," Graham murmured.

"Friend Nathaniel was not forthcoming with your secrets, if that is what you are thinking. Rather, the death of my first wife caused me great sorrow and despair such that I could not continue to abide my life and I ran from it. Away from my family, my friends, and my faith. Were I a stronger man I may have killed myself." He turned to look directly at Graham. "And were I a drinking man I may have decided to do it that way." At Graham's silence, he added gently, "You provided references, Mr. Rhyder, and I am a thorough man. I spoke with each person that you listed. Some people," he sighed deeply, "will tell everything regardless of whether the information is wanted or not."

"I see."

"And here returns my beautiful wife," Mr. Topher smiled as his wife came to stand at his side. "Audrey, may I present to you Windermere's Overseer, Mr. Graham Rhyder?"

"How do you do, sir?" Audrey Topher smiled up at Graham, who inclined his head respectfully. "Are you as unskilled at dancing as my husband?"

"On the contrary," Graham said, "I quite enjoy a dance when I can find a willing partner. And as I have been fortunate enough to have been promised a dance, I was hoping to claim it. If you will both excuse me, I have been searching for the young woman for quite a while now." He extended his hand to Mr. Topher. "It has been a pleasure speaking with you, Sir. It would seem that I owe you my gratitude in even more ways than I was aware."

The last time Graham had seen Mena was at the receiving line collecting wraps from the arriving guests. But with the party in full swing she was no longer in the main hallway.

He'd just searched the dance floor. Perhaps she was in the dining room sampling the buffet.

"Why, if it isn't Graham Rhyder," came a smooth, cultured voice to his right as he stepped into the dining room. "Looking quite debonair, too, in his shiny boots and suit. If I recall, you used to hate shiny boots and suits. I believe my tailor still bears a scar or two as a result of that hatred."

"And I still do," Graham turned to face the incredibly beautiful woman standing to his right, "but all my work clothes were dirty so I had no other choice. What's your excuse for ditching your mourning clothes, Maureen? Oh, that's right. You never could stand to miss a party."

"Still with a quick come back, I see. For your information, the death of *my husband* was over a year ago and my period of mourning ended three weeks ago. This is the first event that I've had the desire to attend. I'm just beginning to face the prospect of my remaining years as a lonely widow." She turned to watch intently as Lord Gabriel helped himself to a selection of delicacies from the buffet table.

Graham snorted. "I'm sure your widowhood won't last long. What was Lord Phillip for you? Husband number two or three? I'm sure there are plenty of rich single men you will be able to find and attach yourself to. Don't dismay."

"I made Lord Phillip happy enough," she hissed, "since he finally got his precious heir. It took him four wives, but it finally happened *thanks to me.*"

"Ah yes, the precious heir, young Phillip. Your crowning achievement, I'm sure."

Sensing a presence beside him, Graham looked into Mena's searching green eyes. His welcome smile encouraged her to speak. "It seems we have been running around in circles looking for each other. I was just looking for you outside only to learn from Mr. Topher that you were searching for me. Is everything all right?"

"Just wanted to claim my dance is all," Graham murmured.

Maureen wasted no time. "Graham, where are your manners? Introduce us."

Taking Mena's elbow, Graham turned. "Mena Westwood, may I introduce Lady Maureen Walcott, wife of the late Lord Phillip Walcott of Forster Hall Plantation?" Turning to Lady Walcott, Graham continued, "Lady Walcott, I'm pleased to introduce you to Mena Westwood, Windermere's teacher."

"A teacher," Lady Walcott said, "how quaint. I was unaware that there was a sufficient population of children here at Windermere to justify employing a teacher."

"Oh, I don't teach just children – although there are plenty," Mena smiled, "I teach adults as well. My services are open to anyone who can find the time and has the interest."

Looking suitably puzzled, Lady Walcott asked, "Has the Windermere family suddenly made plans to travel to and reside in Barbados? I was unaware of any of the family present aside the charming Lord Gabriel, of course." She tittered, looking pointedly at Graham's hand still at Mena's elbow. "And I'm certain Lord Gabriel wouldn't be at all interested in making use of your services, Miss Westwood."

Graham felt Mena stiffen. "Mena has been teaching *anyone* who has shown an interest," Graham supplied, "including field and house workers. Why, she's done a marvelous job throughout this harvest caring for the smallest of Windermere's children. It's been the smoothest harvest season we've ever had."

"You teach *the darkies?*" Lady Walcott said as if it was the most amazing thing she had ever heard. She looked back and forth between Mena and Graham, who stood in united silence. "Well," she smirked at last, "at least here at Windermere you don't have bakros. They're a vicious, ungrateful lot, and any attempt at schooling is always met with ignorant derision. Just leave them to their gambling and drinking and anything else they can manage to find to escape their responsibilities. They have no desire to rise above their station unless it's to try to steal from their betters." She turned to Graham and put her hand to her throat. "Oh, pardon my mistake! What am I talking about? Windermere *does* have a bakro! How could I have forgotten, Graham?" With a slight incline of her head, she turned and made a regal exit.

It was Graham's turn to stiffen, and he felt Mena turn to look at him in concern. Putting a hand gently on his arm, she whispered, "Graham? Are you all right? Mrs. Wagner had wanted me to let you know that Lady Maureen Walcott would be in attendance. That fact put me on high alert and I have been looking for you to warn you. It seems, however, I am too late." She turned and watched the woman disappear outside towards the dancing pavilion. "Who *is* that awful woman?"

After taking a deep breath he turned and said in a voice filled with deep regret, "That, Miss Westwood, I am very sorry to say, is my stepmother."

"Now that I have provided Lord Phillip with a healthy, legitimate *son your position here is highly questionable. What I am saying is that Forster* Hall no longer needs *an illegitimate, bastard, slave-get son roaming around the halls pretending to be something he most surely is not. You must be able to appreciate that the stench of that embarrassment is best cleared out as soon as possible! We all know you have never been able to hide your discontent here.*

"Why, now is your chance to find a place for which you are much more amply suited; something back in the fields. Perhaps not like in your past, but maybe a step or two up. Plantations would most assuredly be able to make use of someone with such well-rounded *skills as yours. Might as well put all these past years of schooling and* previous labor experience *to work, no? I'm sure someone would welcome a manager or an overseer who knows firsthand what the work responsibilities are and who can read, write and cipher. Who knows? Your experience from* both sides *of the fence might enable you to actually … accomplish something of some small merit.*

"If you wish, I shall have Lord Phillip speak to his overseer, Mr. Blackman. Perhaps there is a position he can find for you. You remember, Mr. Blackman. Wasn't he an intimate friend *of your mother's?"*

Wha' yuh do in da dark does come out in da light.

Chapter Nineteen

"Your father is the late Lord Phillip Walcott of Forster Hall Plantation." It was said by Mena as a statement of acceptance as Graham steered them away from the food and the dancing and the party in general out into the privacy of darkness. He held Mena's hand firmly in the crook of his elbow, refusing to let her pull away.

"And my mother was a fifteen-year-old Irish slave girl who caught his eye one harvest season almost thirty-four years ago. She liked to reminisce that spending that season on her back was the easiest harvest she had ever worked," he bit out. "After slaves were freed in '35 she worked as a whore for a time. Drank herself to death by '39." He swallowed. This woman knew just about every one of his dark secrets.

"Do you think any of this matters to me, Graham?" Her words and the firm grip *she* had on *his* arm gradually worked their way through his roiling emotions. "My existence certainly is living proof that ancestry and title and place in society mean little when it comes to determining the quality of an individual." She made a loud, unladylike snort. "And Lady Maureen Walcott has merely provided further proof of this."

He wanted to shake her. *"It should matter, Mena. We are all the products of our past. We may try to run and hide from it, but the reality is that our past is the essence of what forms us. We can't escape it because it's who we are."*

"So who are you, Graham Rhyder?" Mena stopped and turned her serious green eyes to him, reaching up to cup the side of his face. "Tell me. *I want to know.* And then I'll tell you who I am."

"I'm a lousy, good-for-nothing bakro. I'm an angry, bitter drunk. I'm a man who never wants to love or care about anyone ever again because it only leads to such a pain and misery that you want to die. I want to stay alone and distant for the rest of my lousy life; far away from those who are bad because I'm just so damn similar it makes me sick, and even further away from those who are good because I've seen how easily I can destroy them."

She was shaking her head almost before he finished the first sentence. By the end of his little speech, she had stepped in close and wrapped her arms around his waist. As Graham fisted his hands against his sides refusing to let himself return the embrace, she whispered against his shoulder, "That can't all be true, Graham. How could it? You've taught too many good things like integrity, loyalty and fairness..." Picking her head up she looked at him with tears in her eyes, "...and the best of all: the existence of love." He glimpsed her tender smile before he closed his eyes and muttered a curse. *She could fall in love with this man.* The thought came to Mena in a sparkling burst of clarity that shook her with the profound rightness of the emotion. "I will always see you as a good man, Graham Rhyder, no matter what you try to do to convince me otherwise. You're the first man I've ever been able to say that to. Whatever becomes of us, you have given me the most precious gift and I shall ever be grateful. I am a better woman for having known you."

He kissed her then. A desperate kiss filled with hope and fear, frustration and longing. After a time they stood locked in a tight embrace, and in the silence the music of the party drifted to them. "Dance with me," he murmured against her hair, and in the dark privacy of a kapok tree they finally waltzed.

For the first time since Mena had been in Barbados no one woke her for breakfast. Of course that probably had something to do with the fact that just about everyone had made it to bed just before the sun rose. She stirred in her bed due to the fierce beam of sunlight that shone in her face. "Oh my," she squinted at the offending light and then, realizing how high the sun was in the sky, sat bolt upright and gasped, "OH MY!" It had to be far past noon for the sun to shine into her west facing window.

Only Dahlia was present in the kitchen when Mena entered. "Good morning, Dahlia."

"I 'spect yuh mean good afta'noon, Miss Mena," Dahlia said as she bent over to pull hot rolls from the oven. "Hep yuhself," she added as she set the hot tray on the work table.

"Where is everyone?" Mena asked as politely as she could with a mouth full of hot roll.

"Der are still sum guests, so Missus Wagner has organized a show a sorts."

"A show?"

Dahlia gave Mena a look. "Sum a da men are meetin' wit' Lord Gab'rl 'bout makin' da kill da'vl here an' da ladies need en-ter-tain-ment. So Missus Wagner showin' off wut da darkies at Windermere can do. I believe Ole' Yancy an' Willie are supposed ta play da banjo, 'sept Willie mus' surely be feelin' da worse for drink so I don' know how dat goin' to go. Ab'gail, 'Lizabet, an' Deb'ra supposed to sing a tune or two, an' I heard, but can't truly believe it, dat Maisy goin' to do a story tellin' or sum such thing."

Mena stopped eating her second roll. "Elizabeth is coming up here to sing?"

Dahlia gave her the eye. "Dat's wut I heard."

Standing up, Mena went over to stand close to Dahlia. "I've been trying to find a time to talk to you about Elizabeth," she said in a low voice. "I'd like you to tell me what you know."

"Why Miss Mena, tellin' yuh wut I know would take mos' da res' a yuhr life," Dahlia said.

"Tell me a lie, I listen wit' jus' one ear. Tell me da truth an' I'll listen wit two."

Dahlia threw her head back and laughed. "Ain't nevah heard dat one befo'," she said.

Mena smiled. "That's because I just made it up." Crossing her arms, she leaned against Dahlia's work table as she began to chop up carrots. "Look me in the eye, Dahlia, and tell me that you don't know about the personal secret I shared with Rachel and Elizabeth." Dahlia turned and looked directly into Mena's eyes but kept patently silent. "I see." Sighing, she thought for a moment. "The only reason to keep a secret such as this is because of fear." Dahlia went back to chopping as Mena mused out loud. "It's one thing for Elizabeth to be afraid, but it's quite another for *you* to be afraid, Dahlia."

"Sum fears don' eva' leave yuh. We all gots secrets. Sum a us more dan others, I 'spect," Dahlia muttered, barely loud enough for Mena to hear. "Don' yuh gots places dat still don' let yuh sleep, Miss Mena? Have yuh fears all gone?"

"Why can't you give me a name?" Mena whispered back.

"Yuh wan' ta give me da name dat goes wit yuhr secret, Miss Mena?" Dahlia shot back. She looked up at Mena and waited a long time to give Mena time to think. "An' why not? Why yuh lips held tight shut?" The two women stared at each other, suddenly identical in their misery despite one being old and black and one being young and white. "It all 'bout power. Yuh know dat, Miss Mena. Da haves and da havenots. How small kin yuh make a'nother body feel? How big kin yuh make yuhself feel at da same time? It ain't jus' a name an' well yuh know it."

"Are you saying that there is nothing to be done? We are to just sit here and let it happen again?"

"Dats da way a things here at da Big House. *I wus born here.*" She glanced quickly at Mena as she said, *"Growed up here."* She shrugged as she added the chopped carrots to a large pot on the stove. "Saw freedom cum mah way but it didn't git me much but a few sorry pennies in mah pocket an' longer work hours if dat be possible. Life here bin da same fo' years an' years. *A'pearance is everyt'ing,* yuh know."

Mena stared at Dahlia. *"Appearance is everything ....,"* she murmured with a frown. Dahlia began chopping celery and suddenly refused to make eye contact. "Mrs. Wagner likes to say that: 'appearance is everything'. She has impressed that on me since the first day I arrived. I remember it particularly because it was something that ... Mother and Father ... used to say regularly to me. And I hated it." Dahlia didn't look up. "It's Mr. Wagner, isn't it, Dahlia." But Dahlia just turned and stirred the large pot on the stove.

"Father stole all my power and made me feel small and terrified," Mena said on a sigh.

"I guessed as such," Dahlia said, her back still to Mena.

"I was sure for years that my mother was unaware …," Mena mused suddenly, lost in miserable thoughts, "but now that I'm older and … wiser, I'm not so sure. She's … hated me for such a long time: never a good word to say, always critical, and determined to be rid of me as soon as I became of age. Since I … since he …" Mena shook her head as if it would shake the bad thoughts away. "In my memory I lost both of them at about the same time. It was like one morning I woke up and I was a different person to both Father and Mother. I tried for many years to be invisible to Father and yet be brilliantly perfect for Mother. I failed miserably in both areas."

Dahlia turned. "It ain't nothin' yuh cud do, chile. Didn't cum from yuh so it ain't somethin' yuh could fix. Ain't a rabbit's fault da hunter afta it; da hunter jus' like da taste a rabbit."

"What can be done, Dahlia? I think about Abigail working up here in the Great House now, and all the other servants that are in and out of here at all hours of the day and night. *What can be done?*"

Dahlia waved a finger at Mena. "Don' be quick ta tell now wut yuh jus' learned, Miss Mena. You gots ta think dis all through from start ta finish. It ain't a simple secret dat will get better once it's told. How yuh think Isaac goin' ta act once he knows da trut'? How wud Rachel care fo dat family of *seven babies wit one on da way* all by hersef? An' ne'er mind dat. Wut about yuh man, Mister Grah'm? He hates da Wagners sump'in fierce already. He jus' needs one gud reason to kill one or bof' a dem. Den where wud we all be?"

Mena stood staring at Dahlia for long moments with absolutely nothing to offer in response. As her eyes began to fill with frustrated tears, Dahlia nodded, "I'm sorry ta tell yuh dat *now* yuh wit us all right in da same bad spot, Miss Mena. *You can' help yuh ear from hearin' but yuh kin stop yuh mout' from talkin'.*

Wandering outside, Mena found a small group of women, dressed in their day finery seated out in the shade attending Mrs. Wagner's 'show.' Mena had just passed their husbands huddled over the large work table in the study with Graham and Lord Gabriel. Trying her best to stay in the background, she scanned the area for Elizabeth, Abigail, and Deborah, and found them sitting quietly off to the side near Rachel. At Rachel's small smile, Mena relaxed and leaned against a palm tree.

Maisy was deep into the telling of her story, and almost immediately Mena recognized it as one of her favorite Bible stories: Esther the Queen. "Now dat Est'r, she knew dat she was da only one dat could save her people from da evil Haman an' his plans. But she was jus' a girl an' she was scared sumpin' fierce. She cried an' sent a message ta her uncle Mord'cai, 'Da king can kill me jus' for comin' to him without bein' invited! I don' know wut ta do!'" Now Maisy was a master story teller and knew how to draw out the suspense; on more than one occasion Mena had found herself on the edge of her seat as she listened to her weave a story. Today was no exception: young, old, black, and white listened intently as Maisy paused and looked at her audience, making eye contact with each and every one. "Did dat uncle tell her to git he'self safe? Did he say, 'Hide yuhself, girl! Do it quick now!'" Maisy shook her head slowly in resignation. "No siree. Dat uncle Mord'cai sent dis message to Est'r." Slowly Maisy looked at her group until she was gazing directly at Mena as she said, "Who knows if God didn't put yuh in da very spot yuh are right now jus' fo' dis purpose? Maybe, dat da only t'ing dat God intended yuh to do all along? So, yuh can be quiet – an' yuh an' yuh loved ones will surely be hurt – or yuh can open yuh mout' an' let da Lord use yuh like He can." Maisy turned to her audience, a wide, toothless smile lighting up her face.

"Dat lil' girl – she was jus' a mite of a thing – she did as her uncle tol' her. She straighted dat back a hers an' stuck out dat chin a hers an' she walked right into dat king …,"

Who knoweth whether thou art come to the kingdom for such a time as this? The scripture verse repeated itself over and over in Mena's head, getting louder each time. It drowned out the conclusion of Maisy's story, the sigh of the breeze through the trees and the quiet singing of the birds.

Who knoweth whether thou art come to the kingdom for such a time as this?

It was as if the Lord Himself had reached down from heaven and tapped Mena on the shoulder to get her attention. Something had to be done and there was no one else to do anything but …

Who knoweth whether thou art come to the kingdom for such a time as this?

"Here I am, Lord," Mena whispered from the center of her heart, "send me."

"How dare you stand before me making pronouncements about what <u>you</u> want and what <u>you plan</u> to do regarding your future! Your duty has always been first and foremost to this family and all that it represents. I will not have it destroyed on the sudden whim of a spoiled, selfish young woman who refuses to see to her responsibilities.

"You will cease this conversation and do as you are told. I will not listen to this endless nonsense about a longing to serve others and a 'call from God.' These past years of allowing you educational pursuits have obviously done nothing but fill your head with insignificant noise.

"Despite your mother's best efforts your failure in not one, but two seasons to bring in a viable proposal has gotten us absolutely nowhere except that you are now two years older with a cloud of suspicion surrounding your mental capacity. Might I remind you what awaits those who have deficiencies in that area? Were you eleven or twelve when I took you on a tour of Hanwell Asylum…?

"In a month's time you will no longer be my problem. Lord Rowlands has survived two wives and will be better suited to deal with you. As my close and dearest friend he does me this favor, and I will forever be in his debt. You will follow through on the commitments I have made regarding your betrothal. You will be obedient, polite, and <u>silent</u>. I will not have you spread false innuendos. And I will not discuss this topic with you further. Get that fact into your much too educated head once and for all."

Yuh fryin' in yuh own fat.

Chapter Twenty

"I demand that you remove yourself from plantation property forthwith."

"Yas, Missus. We happy ta go as soon as we speak ta Mistah Graham. We here lookin' fo' work."

"Mr. Rhyder should communicate to all involved that showing up at the front door of Windermere Plantation begging for-,"

"I've got it, Moira." Hopeful workers showing up in the morning had become a standard litany these past weeks since Harvest Time had ended and Hard Times had returned. Often they were found in the morning sleeping out on the front yard under a tree. The brave ones had the temerity to knock on the front door, causing Mrs. Wagner to rant. As a result, Graham had stopped eating a sit-down breakfast and now merely piled up whatever was transportable in a cloth in an effort to head off Moira's lengthy dissertation on the proper behavior of the lower classes.

"Mr. Rhyder, I insist that this ... *display* ... be stopped. I *will not* have every morning interrupted-,"

Most mornings Graham tried to do what he did best: ignore Moira Wagner. But this morning he was in a particularly foul mood since meeting with the idiot, otherwise known as Lord Gabriel, regularly caused that effect on him. "What would you have them do, Moira?" he said not with a little bit of impatience. Calling her by her first name was the newest piece of enjoyment he received; it infuriated her. "They need work and we need workers. Until we have an actual construction site established where those in authority can regularly be located, there's not much that can be done beside have them seek me out here first thing in the morning. They must speak with me and, in most cases, first thing I'm meeting in the library with Lord Gabriel discussing and planning. After that, I could be in a hundred other locations all over the property."

Moira Wagner said with disdain, "Oh, I can suggest a few *other* locations where you can be regularly found. And not always alone."

Narrowing his eyes, Graham leaned in and said, "You have something to say, Moira, *say it.* You have something to accuse me of, *do it. Then I will take my turn.* Stop dropping your petty insinuations and just spit it out, otherwise you're nothing more than an annoying hot wind."

Graham chuckled and placed his hat on his head as she stared at him with hatred. As he stepped off the porch steps, he threw over his shoulder, "Always a pleasure, Moira."

Meeting with Lord Gabriel every damn morning was getting old and it had only been a little more than a month. The man seemed to show no signs of departing, and in fact had begun to behave as if Windermere were his permanent residence – God save them all. As none had the authority to formally ask him of his future plans; all were at his mercy. His presence gradually had begun to influence everything from daily work responsibilities (Graham and Moira were now required to report to him each morning to 'plan out the day') to formal dinner arrangements, as only the Wagners, Graham and Mena were welcome at the table at which he now presided as head. Time and again Graham longed to have a quiet meal in the kitchen with those lucky few who had been displaced. If the man knew even half of what he thought he knew, or was willing to listen to even a third of what Graham and Winston *did* know, it wouldn't be so bad. But...

Graham was forced to admit that there was a plus side to Lord Gabriel's complete involvement with the construction of the distillery: he was too busy to harass Mena. This left her to do as she wished, which was organizing her Windmill School in earnest. They both knew, however, that this reprieve would only be for a brief time, and Graham could do little to stem his growing anxiety. While Mena insisted that the man had made no unwanted overtures, Graham wasn't so certain. Mena couldn't hide the fact that Lord Gabriel caused her undue amounts of uneasiness. If it wasn't due to romantic overtures, what else could be the cause?

"You men good with a shovel?" Graham said as he walked past them and they fell into step behind him. "That's all we've got need of right now as we're clearing and leveling the land for construction."

"All mens good wif a shovel, boss," came the reply.

Thinking of Lord Gabriel caused Graham to grunt and mutter, "Not necessarily."

꧁꧂꧁꧂꧁꧂

Six months in Barbados and little more than one month since the end of Harvest Time and Mena could barely recognize herself.

Something was happening to her but Mena couldn't quite put her finger on what it was. It was great. It was big. It was wonderful. It was frightening. She was changing in a significant, exponential way like a butterfly coming out of its cocoon. Did a caterpillar know what its destiny was? Did it spend its early life inching around saying, "Be patient, soon you'll be able to fly" or "Don't be discouraged with your unattractive appearance, soon you will be gloriously beautiful"? Or did the caterpillar one day as Mena had, after fighting and struggling to get itself out of its cocoon, suddenly realize that … this was what it had been all for?

First there was her teaching. Her days started with the sound of children's shrieks of laughter rushing into her Windmill School. Children, initially brought hesitantly by their parents soon arrived enthusiastically on their own. During this time, the most "traditional" type of teaching happened with recitation, singing, maths, and writing practice on the slates.

At lunch time the children returned home, and Mena ate her lunch quietly and … simply waited. The style in which her afternoon unfolded was dictated by her students and was never the same. Because the school was centrally located on the plantation, almost any individual who had a mind to visit her could manage with only a short hike. Without fail Silent Joe appeared every day, and Mena suspected he often sat outside the windmill listening carefully to her formal lesson time if he could manage. Though few knew, Joe was her star pupil, grasping reading and writing with a ferocious intensity that no one came close to matching. Already he had managed to read almost all of the primer books, and she was seriously considering sneaking some books from the Great House library for him to try. He dearly loved writing on her large slates and would practice endlessly all manner of words that she gave him to practice. Many days, beside Joe's silent presence, she was eventually joined for lunch by two, three or more adults who came to chat and ask all manner of questions while they ate with her. Many questions were basic such as "Kin yuh teach me ta write mah name?" while others were more ... interesting. And not all of them was she capable of answering. "Kin yuh tell me da bes' way to git rid a dis sore toot'?" "Is it true dat London has gots buildin's as tall as mountains?" "Why yuh really here wif us?" "My wife says yuh says we shud wash hands all da time. Wut goods dat fo'?"

By afternoon, Mena would travel to the workers' village for what had morphed into a 'lady's time' for want of a better term. There was no woman on the plantation who had the freedom to spend an hour or two at the Windmill School, but they could give a bit of time to come and sit on the front steps of different homes to socialize. Women of all ages would come - some with babies in tow – to laugh, talk and tease. It was during this time that Mena learned more about Bajan life and history as she sat and listened to the women talk. More importantly, she began to make friends.

Gradually, the time had turned into a Bible study of sorts, with Mena often reading directly from her Bible and then the group discussing the passage with passionate abandon. "Wut was Sarah thinkin' givin' dat maid Hagar ta her man?" "Don' think much a dat Lot willin' ta give his baby girls ta dat crowd a men." "Sumbody needed ta give dat Rachel a smack wit all dat whinin' she did." "Dat Rahab sure landed on her feet!" Each meeting ended with prayer when they listed things they were thankful for and things they were worried about.

Only the end of her day ended with some measure of frustration, for she had made no progress in teaching any who worked in the Great House. But her daily success made Mena feel bigger, stronger, and more capable with each passing day. The students, adult as well as children, called her "Teacher," or more shyly, "Missy Mena," and all were always eager, grateful, and gracious. They brought her small tokens such as a piece of sugar cane candy, a shiny rock or a pretty shell, a handpicked bunch of bright yellow shak shak flowers, and once even a pair of clean, carefully mended socks. Early each morning and late each night Mena lay in bed delighting at the miracles unfolding before her in both her students as well as herself. *At last* Mena had found her place in life. *This* was why she had traveled thousands of miles away from everything familiar. *This* was what the driving need she had always felt was all about. *Thank you, dear Lord, for the abundant gifts you send me each day. Show me what You want me to do. Let me make You smile in all I do.*

In the evenings she often visited Isaac and Rachel, who always welcomed her with open arms. Sometimes in the secret recesses of her heart, Mena imagined what it would have been like for her to have grown up in such a home as theirs. Watching Elizabeth quietly heal even as her pregnancy grew visible, or Deborah working to read the books that Mena brought her, or young Ruth with her passion for prayer or little Mary with her penchant for speaking her mind regarding just about anything ... Each child in that poor, cramped one-room home was loved, encouraged and protected. To have had an upbringing such as that ...

And then there was Graham. She saw him less now than she had during Harvest Time as he never stayed for breakfast and rarely showed for dinner now. She found things, though. A flower high up on the peg where he had hung his hat the day he helped clear out the windmill. A detailed drawing on her chalkboard of a school house building which even had a bell tower. Just last night she had found an absolutely perfect shell sitting on her pillow when she'd gone to climb into bed. *That* one she needed to ask how he'd managed...

Mena was not a foolish woman. She knew that her feelings towards Graham were not going to mean that her future was in any way changed ... because she was living a lie. At some

point in the very near future she needed to sit down with
Graham and explain things. It had been a brave but woefully
naive young woman who had boarded a ship in London bound
for Windermere Plantation in Barbados who thought that none
of her secrets need ever be known by anyone but herself. But
her time in Barbados had taught her that secrets were awful
things. They made you live a lie. They forced you to hide the
reality of who and what you were. It was impossible for a
person to accomplish his or her greatest good constrained by
secrets and lies. Mena wanted *all* her secrets gone.

The secret of her abuse had always eaten at her, having
the ability to drag her down and consume her. Keeping it had
been a battle in which she had honestly believed she had no
other option. What good could possibly come from revealing
reveal it? But – amazingly - there *had* been good. For herself,
Mena felt a freedom so profound that she knew now there was
literally nothing that could stop her forward momentum. *There
was no longer any fear or shame.* That was because she had actually
helped someone as a result of this horrible aspect of her life.
Because of this she was stronger and more capable than she'd
ever imagined. Never, ever, in even her most positive moments
had it occurred to her that such a thing would be possible! Yet
each time she experienced Elizabeth's tentative overtures of
friendship or was the recipient of Rachel and Isaac's appreciative
smiles or received Dahlia's deliberate expressions of support, it
was evident. It was a miracle that Mena had never thought to
ask or hope for.

Unfortunately her other secrets: namely the truth of her
identity, who she really was, weighed heavily on her. As her
relationship with Graham blossomed, Mena realized that this
secret had the greatest potential to destroy all she now held
precious and dear. When she'd originally made the decision to
keep her identity a secret … it had been for her own safety and
security. How foolishly naive she had been! What could they

really do? Throw a sack over her head, tie her up and drag her home? To what end? Who would want her? Polite Society had been practically done with her before she'd even left ... dragging her back disgraced and unwilling certainly wouldn't improve anything! Her self-confidence had grown so that now *that fear* was no longer an issue. Should she be found out and dismissed from Windermere, she would merely resettle somewhere in a town here on the island and continue to teach. Her financial state, while not wealthy by any means, was sufficient to keep her solvent; luxurious living had never been her goal anyway.

Speaking directly to Graham and telling him the unvarnished truth was the most likely place to begin, but they rarely had but a few stolen moments and what she needed to tell him would take ... time. *Lots of time.* For the more he revealed about himself, the more Mena feared that once Graham knew the secret about who and what she was ... he would have nothing to do with her.

After much prayer and thoughtful consideration Mena had decided on an alternate route, and it was unlike anything she had ever done before. She had no specific plans. She had rehearsed no formal speech. She wasn't even sure what type of outcome she wished. All she knew was that she *had* to speak to *someone* for advice. Quite frankly, she didn't know if she was *jumpin' out a da pan an' into da fire* or not. But as this was a problem she couldn't seem to solve herself; this was the solution the Lord had sent her.

She stood outside the library door, she smoothed her skirt, patted her hair, took a deep breath, said a quick prayer and then firmly knocked.

"Enter," came the reply and Mena opened the door and stepped in.

Mr. Topher showed little emotion while Mena haltingly explained herself. He also asked no questions, letting her say all she had to say until she was nothing more than an empty, exhausted heap.

"Might you be able to clear your schedule for tomorrow, Miss Westwood?" he finally asked.

"Well, I teach the children every day but Sunday and meet in the village with the women every afternoon. I'd need to send word …"

Mr. Topher nodded. "Do that then immediately. We'll leave after formal dinner," he said as he collected Mena's monthly report and filed it carefully away.

Mena swallowed. "Leave?"

"Yes," he said quite matter-of-factly. "I have a business colleague and friend I'd like you to meet. We'll journey to my home, where you will be able to meet my lovely wife, Audrey. We'll stay the night there and then in the morning the three of us will travel on together. I should have you back here at Windermere by noon on Sunday."

Mena sat, unsure what to say or do, and at last Mr. Topher gave her a small, reassuring smile. "It is clear that you need to know the truth of things so that you can make wise decisions. You've trusted me this far, Miss Westwood. Don't give up now."

"Please don't think me too forward, Sir, but I was curious to know what book you are so avidly reading out here in the bright sunshine. It is such a lovely day."

"Nothing too exciting, I'm afraid. It's An Analysis of the Laws of England[6] *by Sir William Blackstone. Sunshine or no, it is rather dull."*

"Nothing that provides educational enlightenment is a waste. Are you a lawyer, Sir?"

"I'm a practicing Solicitor, which in answer to your question would mean that yes, I am a lawyer. I often refer to Sir Blackstone's writing when I wish to refresh myself in one particular area of the law or another. But I would be remiss not to inquire what engrossing book has brought you out into this lovely day."

"Oh, it's Robinson Crusoe *by Daniel Defoe, but I've read it four times already so it's not that engrossing. I'm an avid reader but my resources are always a bit slim so…"*

"Do you know, I have a client who has an extensive library that is just gathering dust. I wonder if he would be interested in lending some of his books out. Would you like me to inquire?"

Love ent as easy as it seems.

Chapter Twenty-One

The Tophers lived on a small piece of land five miles outside of Friendship in almost the direct center of the parish of St. Lucy. Audrey Topher was a diminutive woman with a ready smile and a welcoming personality, and didn't seem at all ruffled to have her husband appear well after dark with a young woman in tow, only to be told that they would be taking an overnight journey first thing in the morning. "Nelson is always full of surprises," she said as she kissed Mr. Topher on the cheek and then escorted Mena to her room. "Why don't you get yourself settled and then come down and join us for a cup of tea? I made Nelson's favorite tea cakes this afternoon and have been waiting until he arrived home to enjoy ... a few more." She laughed. "I've got a terrible sweet tooth."

As Mena sat in their comfortable living room, she learned that they would be traveling in the morning to Foursquare Plantation to meet the "always enjoyable" Sir Alan Russell. "He's got a lovely place – not anywhere near the size of Windermere or some of the other larger plantations – but lovely just the same. Nelson's been serving as his solicitor for, what is it – three years, dear?"

"Closer to five."

"Has it really been five years, Nelson? My, the time just flies. Anyway, Sir Russell has been a widower for years and all on his own for as long as I've known him." She tsked and shook her head. "Does nothing but see to that plantation. All work and no play makes for a dull life, I always say, so whenever possible I travel with Nelson whenever he makes a trip out to Foursquare to visit with Sir Russell. I make him cakes – although his cook is quite good – and bring him some new books I've enjoyed." She grinned. "And I raid his most excellent library, too! For my birthday just this month past Nelson secured a copy of Mary Shelley's marvelous story *Frankenstein.* Oh my! I didn't sleep for a week after I read that one." She winked at Mena. "Of course, that was probably Nelson's plan all along as I snuggled most closely to him for many nights terrified of the dark."

Mena sipped her tea and cast a quick glance at Mr. Topher, who sat silently beside his wife a contented smile on his face. Never had Mena thought to see the serious Mr. Topher looking so in love.

"Anyway, I've got *Frankenstein, Oliver Twist* by Charles Dickens, and I finished *The Three Musketeers* by Alexandre Dumas just the other day to take to Sir Russell." She looked fondly at Mr. Topher. "Nelson indulges me my passions of reading whenever possible. I don't think he ever comes home empty handed."

Mena couldn't hide her surprise when Mr. Topher gave his wife a meaningful wink. "I've got it."

"*NO. You didn't!*" Audrey exclaimed and immediately put her teacup down.

"Would I let you down? I promised we'd manage to get a copy of it."

"Where is it?!" Audrey said breathlessly looking around as if something might appear out of thin air.

"In my trunk." Audrey stood to walk towards Mr. Topher's familiar trunk which had remained in the hallway. "And, there's an added surprise …," he said to her retreating back.

Audrey turned. "You didn't manage to get …,"

Mr. Topher smiled. "I got you both. *Wuthering Heights* and *Jane Eyre* by the Bronte sisters." Audrey stood in the middle of the room apparently torn between retrieving her books or hugging her husband. "Go ahead and get them. They're right at the top, my dear. But you must promise not to start either tonight. We've got an early start in the morning, and a long day ahead."

After a light breakfast the three of them headed out in Mr. Topher's covered carriage. A tight fit for the three of them, it was preferable as Audrey was not as adept at riding as Mena. "I don't know how you made the entire journey from Windermere to our home riding! Nelson's always saying that he prefers being out in the open air as opposed to the confines of the buggy, but I just can't see the benefit. Plus we at least have a bit of shade from the sun!"

Aside from her trip with Isaac from the dock in Speightstown to Windermere, Mena had seen nothing of the island and said so. This prompted Audrey, and on occasion Mr. Topher, to be excellent tour guides, pointing out plants, birds, trees, and even exceptional rock formations that were indigenous to the island. When Mena complimented Audrey on her extensive knowledge she'd smiled and said, "I've lived here my entire life, and I'm just one of those people who enjoys learning."

Mena shared about her ocean voyage and the latest styles and fashions in London when Audrey asked. They had an enjoyable, uneventful ride and then Foursquare Plantation appeared on the horizon.

Sir Alan Russell, owner of the 125-acre Foursquare Plantation, was a tall, thin, serious looking man with salt and pepper hair, a handlebar mustache and alert blue eyes. He welcomed Mr. Topher with a handshake, greeted Audrey with a genuine smile, and managed a hesitant bow for Mena.

"Miss Westwood is currently employed at *Windermere Plantation* as a teacher," Mr. Topher said in his introductions. At the mention of "Windermere" Sir Russell stared at her for long moments. Mena felt her back stiffen and her chin jut out. Whoever this man was and whatever Mr. Topher had planned, she would not slip back into the meek, naïve young woman she had been only a few months ago. "She's come at my invitation, my friend, to merely speak with you and *nothing more.*"

"I see," Sir Russell said carefully as he continued to look at Mena intently. "And what does she wish to speak with me about?"

"Quite honestly, I don't know what is expected of me, Sir," Mena allowed, meeting Sir Russell's direct stare. "I shared some private information with Mr. Topher yesterday, and as a result he's brought me here with no explanation at all. It would seem that we are both at a loss as to the exact nature of my visit."

Mr. Topher made no attempt to remediate the rather awkward situation Mena and Sir Russell found themselves in, merely suggesting, "While I do my work and Audrey invades your library, I thought that perhaps the two of you might … talk a bit."

Sir Russell sighed and looked at Mena. "Miss Westwood, can I interest you in a walk in my garden? My wife was a passionate horticulturist, and despite her passing many years ago I have attempted to maintain her garden in her memory. It's a lovely, peaceful place with shade and benches."

Mena nodded her head. "It sounds lovely, Sir Russell."

The garden was a work of art - a profusion of colors and scents meticulously maintained and divided into herbs and edible plants, medicinal plants, and plants grown merely for their beauty and scent. They walked for a period of time, and then when they approached a bench Sir Alan Russell took Mena's elbow and encouraged her to sit. When he had settled himself beside her he said quietly, "What would you like me to tell you about Graham Rhyder?"

Mena started and turned shocked eyes to look at Sir Russell. Graham Rhyder was hardly the topic she had assumed she was here to discuss.

Sir Russell nodded and allowed a small smile. "You must understand that Nelson would never reveal a confidence or be put in a position where he could be accused of gossiping. You are wondering why I would assume Graham Rhyder is the subject you wish to discuss, or why I would have information about him. I can see it in your eyes." When Mena nodded hesitantly, he sighed and looked off into the beauty of the garden. "Graham Rhyder, was my son-in-law at one time, Miss Westwood. My only child, Fiona, fell in love with him and they married when he was employed as overseer here. They lived here at Foursquare until her death almost seven years ago."

Fiona. This was her father. Foursquare was her childhood home. Sir Russell's beloved wife was Fiona's mother. Fiona had been the daughter of a wealthy plantation owner and had been someone who had loved Graham enough to throw caution and propriety to the wind and cast her lot with him. Only to die. By Graham's account due to his negligence. *I want to stay alone and distant for the rest of my lousy life; far away from those* who are bad, because I'm just so damn similar it makes me sick, and even further away from those who are good because I've seen how easily I can destroy them.

Fiona. Graham's wife. The mother of his child. The reason why he walked the cliff walk, dreamed of death, and firmly believed he had done nothing good in his past. *I'm a lousy, good for nothing bakro. I'm an angry, bitter drunk. I'm a man who never wants to love or care about anyone ever again because it only leads to a pain and misery so bad you just want to die.*

Fiona. The woman with whom Graham had known true love. *You are absolutely right that my life has been anything but exemplary and the mistakes I have made haunt me with every breath I take. But it is not something that I ever wish to forget because, you see, despite all the misery, I have experienced true love. And of this fact I am absolutely certain: love is the only thing in the world worth living for.*

Mena covered her face with both her hands as the storm of emotions ripped through her. "Miss Westwood?" came Sir Russell's concerned voice. "Shall I fetch you a cold drink? Perhaps I should summon Audrey…"

Sir Russell stood and would have rushed away had Mena not been able to rouse herself. "No, please, Sir Russell. I just need a moment to … process what you have told me." With shaking hands she retrieved a handkerchief from her skirt pocket and dabbed at her eyes and forehead. "I … I spoke with Mr. Topher yesterday to seek advice; he is one of only a few people I felt I could trust with some very private matters. He said I needed to know the truth of things so that I can make wise decisions…" She offered Sir Russell a tentative smile. "I traveled here to Barbados to pursue my own dreams despite the disapproval of all who know me. I … I may look young and alone but I am much stronger than I appear. Please, just give me a moment or two to gather myself together and then I would very much like to continue our discussion."

Sir Russell nodded. "You don't look like my Fiona, but you remind me of her just the same. She was a strong, dynamic, opinionated young woman who didn't let custom or propriety stop her from doing what she wanted. Her mother died at her birth so I raised her with the help of a governess, and always worried that I spoiled her but ...," he chuckled, "I suspect there was no one on the planet who could have altered the woman that my Fiona became." He looked at Mena, and seeming to determine that the worst was over, smiled and patted her hand. "I apologize for my initial cool reception. There have been a rather endless stream of well-meaning friends who have tried to get me to marry again, and I feared that ...," he cleared his throat and looked significantly embarrassed, "you were Audrey's newest attempt."

"She's tried before?"

"Oh, heaven's yes. Audrey is a pure romantic and believes that miracles do happen." He chuckled. "I suppose her and Nelson's marriage *is* a miracle of sorts." He leaned over and bumped Mena's shoulder in a teasing manner. "On the ride home you should get Audrey to tell you the story of how they came to be married. That should fix Nelson for the discomfort and untoward anxiety he's caused both of us in bringing you here without explanation." He paused, then said, "Speaking of romance, what are your feelings about Grey?"

"Grey?"

He nodded. "That was what Fiona called him and we eventually all followed suit."

Mena studied Sir Russell. "You don't seem to ... hate him."

"Grey?" Sir Russell looked horrified. "Why would I hate him? I loved him like a son!"

~ 255 ~

Mena frowned in puzzlement. "He ... well, he's told me he's to blame for Fiona's death. And the babe's."

Sir Russell was shaking his head emphatically before Mena finished. "No. NO. That's absolutely not true! Fiona's death is something we all hold responsibility for, but none more than Fiona herself. Fiona was ... difficult to live with. Oh, she was beautiful and captivating and a joy to be with when she was happy, but ... she was also spoiled, stubborn, and intensely emotional. Right from the start she insisted on not living here in the main house. Wanted very much to have her own place to call home. Felt that Graham would never be comfortable living here with me and that he would always feel out of place. They commandeered a caretaker's cottage on the far side of the property and the both of them worked diligently to make it into a home. For a while it worked quite well, as it was closer to the fields anyway, and easier for Grey.

"If Grey has told you about Fiona and the babe, then you must know that he has ... demons. I don't know his whole history, but unfortunately, his ... stepmother has never been discreet when it comes to Grey regarding his lineage and his upbringing, so I know some. Grey, for all his railing against the rules and mores of society, initially refused to marry Fiona without my blessing, which positively infuriated her." He chuckled again and shook his head. "My daughter never sought anyone's approval but her own *for anything*. Had Grey been willing, I suspect she would have run off with him and never looked back. I liked Grey as a man, as my overseer, and as my son-in-law. And I did my level best to make sure he knew that, too." He gave Mena a sad smile. "When I gave my blessing I did try to warn him about Fiona and what a difficult future he had in store... But there was no holding those two back. Even though I lost my Mary far too early I loved her passionately, and I knew that Grey and Fiona shared that same kind of love. I could not have cared less about his heritage, and told Grey that I would much rather have my daughter marry for love than for status. By the time they married he knew I meant every word.

"He had trouble with the drink. It's a curse that's hard to beat; I watched my father battle it all my life. Fiona was young, but she knew and loved him anyway. He managed to stay sober almost their entire marriage, and I was proud of him for that. In the later months of her pregnancy, Fiona began to have some complications. Everyone was concerned. Grey did the sensible thing and tried to get her to move here to the big house. His responsibilities on the plantation often meant that she was on her own, and he didn't want that. Of course, Fiona refused. Said that their child was going to be born in their home and that was the end of it. Grey was desperate enough that he tried to enlist my help to get her to move to the main house temporarily, but she would have none of it. And she was furious that he'd tried to elicit my assistance."

Sir Russell stood and walked a few steps away from Mena as she sat on the bench. "They fought a lot in Fiona's final weeks. About everything. Drama followed them wherever they went. My daughter had a fine Irish temper and Grey had a lifetime's worth of anger and fury, so the sparks flew. I'm sure they were both afraid of the impending birth – each in his or her own way – and fighting was how the fear came out. It got to be too much for Grey, and one day he apparently saddled his horse and planned to go off for a time. Fiona knew where he was headed – to drink - and told him good riddance. She followed him all the way out to the main road as he rode away, screaming and yelling at him to have a drink or two for her. I was in the stables and heard the whole thing."

Sir Russell shrugged. "I tried to get her to come home with me. I worried about her being alone as Grey did but … she was just so *angry and stubborn*. Grey was gone three days, but during that time she was never alone for long. Everyone on the plantation found reasons to check on her throughout the day and even late into the night. Grey came home that fourth morning and found her ..." He turned to Mena. "He'll always have to carry with him that their final words were filled with anger, and that he let the demon drink take over for a time. *But I've never* blamed Grey for her death."

Walking back to Mena, Sir Russell sat down and took her hand. "I'm a believing man, Miss Westwood. My belief in the Lord and what He has promised me in the next life is what gets me out of bed in the morning and has kept me putting one foot in front of the other throughout these many years I've had to exist without my beloved Mary. Losing my daughter and my grandson caused me untoward grief, but it didn't shake my faith. My soul is well even when my heart is breaking." Looking intently at Mena he said, "Grey ... doesn't have that kind of faith. Do you?"

She nodded. "Yes sir, I do."

Sir Russell smiled at the conviction in her voice. "Good. You are an answer to my prayer, then. Do you care for him?"

Mena swallowed. "Yes. A great deal."

"I've been praying for the past seven years that Grey would find a way to forgive himself for the things he mistakenly believes he's responsible for. When Mr. Topher came to see me years ago to verify Grey's work experience, I was delighted to recommend him, and prayed that his time at Windermere would allow him to do exactly that. Perhaps you are the final step in this."

Mena shook her head sadly. "I doubt that. Yesterday, I decided to speak with Mr. Topher and reveal to him a secret I have been keeping from *everyone* at Windermere since my arrival. Even Graham. I now understand the reason for my visit to speak with you," Mena said quietly, "and based on what you've just told me, I fear how Graham will react once he knows."

"Never keep secrets from those you care about," Sir Russell said quietly, "it creates a distance that only causes distrust and hurt." Sir Russell took Mena's hand in his and she looked up at him. "In this brief encounter, you have not impressed me as a frivolous young woman in any area of your life, Miss Westwood. You have told me that you care for Grey and I would suspect that the feeling is reciprocated. Talk with Grey, my dear. Trust him, but more importantly trust our Lord. There is no coincidence in this life. You are here for a purpose. You have come to care for Grey by God's design. Follow God's lead and remember this: God is love!"

"What are you looking at, boy? Don't tell me you've never seen a dead body before. Put your damn coal bucket down and get over here and help me. Pull that blanket off the bed so we can wrap the body, and here, use this shirt to wipe up the mess.

"This is between you and me, boy, do you hear me? You better make sure you don't say one damn word about this to anyone for the rest of your worthless life or I'll cut that tongue of yours right out of your damn head. If one single word gets out – I'll make sure this same thing happens to your sisters – there are two of them, aren't there? Pretty little things if I recall…

Chapter Twenty-Two

The road that led to Windermere followed some of the furthest fields, so long before the Great House came into view Mena knew that she was on plantation property. Gazing at the now quiet and empty fields as her horse stepped up his pace at the nearness of home, Mena wondered where this time next year would find her. She sighed.

"Was it a mistake to bring you to speak with Sir Russell?" asked Mr. Topher finally. Since dropping off Audrey at home, most of their journey had been in silence.

Mena turned and smiled at him. "Please forgive me! I should have thanked you immediately. No sir, it was exactly right. Not only did Sir Russell give me important insight, he also provided me with spiritual guidance as well. I am most appreciative to you."

Nodding, Mr. Topher explained, "You have not once mentioned Mr. Rhyder in anything but the most professional of tones and yet, I am not an ignorant man, my dear." He chuckled and Mena thought she saw a slight blush. "I read words of praise regarding you and your work from Mr. Rhyder and words to impugn your character from Mrs. Wagner, and I began to put two and two together and wonder … Audrey insists I am more a romantic than she is. As soon as you shared your secret with me, I felt it most important for you to have as much information as possible to help you make a wise decision, and to guide you in how you execute it. I always find that the avenue of truth is the best way to proceed, yet being fully informed of all the circumstances of the journey certainly helps."

He paused and then said. "There is one more piece of information that I would like to impart to you, my dear, although I suspect you may be aware of some if not all of it."

Mena was uncertain she could endure any more of Mr. Topher's information. "What is it, sir?" she said with trepidation.

"In another life, I was a Quaker. Did you know that?"

Mena raised her eyebrows in surprise at the direction of the conversation. "No, sir, I did not."

"Well, although I do not practice the life, I still allow many of the teachings to guide my daily living. Our heritage, the where, when, how and why of who and what we are is not something we can ever truly escape, is it? You are just discovering that critical lesson while I stopped fighting it long ago." Mena waited. "Some people never learn, however. A person's upbringing can be something she spends her entire life trying to hide or escape from. Because she's angry. Or ashamed. Or because she wants things that are otherwise unavailable to her and is determined to get them." Clearly Mr. Topher was no longer speaking of himself.

"A person might do everything in her power to distance herself from who she *really is,* and try at all costs to align herself with someone who will help her achieve what she *really wants.* She could be so determined to get what she wants that she would be willing to lie and cheat and scheme and overlook horrible injustices done to others, all in the name of achieving what she believes she deserves: to be better than most. In living so close to this ... evil ... she gradually loses the ability to distinguish between what is right and what is wrong. She becomes as tainted as those with whom she has chosen to associate herself.

"Whether through greed or evil, this person can become a danger to others not only through her lack of action, but also through her selfish greed. And yet, because she has achieved her goal and is now in a position of power and prestige, she has managed to elevate herself to a place far above those who could bring much needed justice..."

Mena stared silently at Mr. Topher as they rode the final miles that would bring her to the Great House. Finally she said, "How long have you known about Mr. Wagner, sir?"

Mr. Topher shrugged. "There has always been a steady dismissal of young, female servants from the Great House after little more than a year of service for issues regarding theft or laziness or insubordination... One would be a fool to not question the integrity of the accuser eventually ..." He sighed. "One young woman had the temerity to accuse Mr. Wagner almost ten years ago when I was first employed as Windermere's solicitor. Her name was Ivy. I am embarrassed to say that I didn't have the slightest idea as to how to proceed, and then she simply disappeared. I assumed she was put off the plantation."

"What are you hoping I will do with this information, Mr. Topher?" Mena asked through wooden lips.

Reaching into his saddle bag, Mr. Topher removed an envelope and handed it to Mena as she rode beside him. "Enclosed is a copy of a specific item from this month's plantation report that I plan to send Lord Windermere. I wanted you to read it as it addresses this difficult issue we have just discussed, and I have specifically mentioned you as a possible source for a solution. Given all *you* have told me about yourself, I was hopeful that perhaps your father might be persuaded to help in the remediation of this problem ..."

As Windermere's Great House came into view, Mena's bitter burst of laughter turned slowly into silent tears as Mr. Topher's hopeful expression turned to stark confusion.

෬෬෬෬෬෬෬෬

Mrs. Wagner was waiting, hands on hips, as Mena and Mr. Topher rode up to the front of the house. Initially, Mena's trip had met with her stern disapproval of "responsibilities not met," although Mena knew full well her primary issue was simply because she had not been provided any specific details. "At last you have arrived home, Miss Westwood! We need your help upstairs immediately. Since you have already had your day off, the upstairs girls could use your assistance in preparing the main bedrooms." Lord Gabriel strolled out onto the front porch just as Mrs. Wagner finished speaking and leaned nonchalantly against one of the large white pillars. He looked relaxed.

"What's happening?" Mena asked as she dismounted and unhooked her bag from the back of the saddle. She was not inclined to hurry in the least.

"We have had word," Mrs. Wagner said with what Mena assumed to be excitement, "that His Lord and Ladyship shall be arriving here at Windermere, perhaps as soon as tomorrow! They are already on the island, currently doing business and renewing acquaintances in Bridgetown."

"If that be the case," Mr. Topher spoke to Sir Gabriel, "I will make it a point to return on the coming weekend to sit down and discuss plantation business with His Lordship. I've already finished my report for this month, and rather than sending it, I can give it to him directly."

Mrs. Wagner put her hand to her chest as if to still her beating heart, "We've had absolutely *no warning* other than a brief note that was delivered late Friday, and there is *much to do.*"

"That's surprising," Mena said, looking up at Mrs. Wagner as she walked and put her things on the verandah's steps. "Lord Gabriel mentioned something about His Lord and Ladyship intending to visit weeks ago."

Sir Gabriel chuckled. "Surely you must be mistaken, Miss Westwood. Why would I discuss such an important issue with someone such as *you?*"

"Precisely," came Mrs. Wagner's clipped reply.

Mena ignored both of them and strode over to Mr. Topher as he sat silently on his horse gazing down at her. He had said nothing since her bitter laughter and subsequent tears, and seemed at a loss. "Will you come inside, sir, and have some refreshment before you make the journey home?" Mena heard Mrs. Wagner's hiss of disapproval behind her; it was not Mena's place to offer hospitality.

Mr. Topher shook his head. "Thank you but no, my dear. I still have the refreshments that Audrey packed for both of us and I am eager to get home before dark." He glanced briefly up at their silent audience and then into Mena's serious eyes. "I have great confidence in you, Miss Westwood. It is *no coincidence* that you are here at Windermere at this time; *never forget that.* I firmly believe in the comforting fact that God is bigger than our greatest problem."

Mena smiled at this kind gentleman. "It is always a pleasure talking with you, Mr. Topher. Thank you very much for your wise counsel."

Tipping his hat to Lord Gabriel and Mrs. Wagner, he turned his horse and was gone without further word.

Mena assisted the girls as they made beds and shook out curtains and dusted the upstairs bedrooms. Not only did they have to prepare two new rooms. In the end, they had to move Lord Gabriel out of the master suite and resettle him as well. Rather than resenting the assigned work, Mena welcomed the time to pray long and hard about what she needed to do, recognizing that timing was everything.

Never keep secrets from those you care about. Sir Russell's firm admonition rang true to Mena and she decided that, first and foremost, she must somehow manage to speak with Graham *today.*

Graham was not at dinner. Mena knew that often it was the only time for Graham to meet with the workers without Sir Gabriel's presence to give direction and reinforce whose orders were to be followed. In addition, the numerous daily responsibilities needed to be met, whether a new distillery was being built or not.

Excusing herself from the table Mena went directly to her room, but only to obtain a lantern. It was her plan to walk to Graham's place this evening, and with little moonlight, a lantern was an absolute necessity.

Mena had never been afraid of the dark until … Well, until a time in her life when she learned she had sufficient reason to be. Walking the dim path by lantern light, Mena hummed a favorite hymn, trying not to focus on the deep darkness just beyond her lantern's glow. Soon she was singing quietly. *"Joy to the world, the Lord is come! Let earth, receive her King! Let every heart, prepare Him room, and heaven and nature sing! And heaven and nature sing! And heaven, and heaven, and nature sing. Joy to the world! The Saviour reigns! Let men their s-,*[7]*"* Mena stopped mid-song due to the rustle in the bushes that was distinctly different from the sound produced by the wind. "Hello? Is anyone there? Joe? Graham? Is that you?"

A tall, silent apparition appeared before Mena from out of the foliage. "Joe! What a surprise!" Mena took a shaky breath to calm herself. "I'm on my way to Graham's cottage. I'd welcome your company if you're up for the walk." Nodding, Silent Joe fell into step beside Mena, and when she suddenly tripped, he commandeered the lantern with one large hand and carefully held her elbow with the other. "Thank you, Joe; the dark isn't my favorite time." Beside her Silent Joe quietly began to hum the same tune that Mena had been singing, and she grinned up at him in delight. "Silent Joe! Why, you're humming! What a delight! You know the song I was just singing? Well that's good! I'll sing and you hum along and we will serenade the night life together, just us two."

⁋⁋⁋⁋⁋

As they trudged home, the last thing Graham expected to find was Mena and Silent Joe sitting on the front porch of his hut singing and … humming. Exhausted, he'd stopped by the Great House hoping to catch a glimpse of Mena, but all he'd managed was a packaged meal courtesy of Dahlia. Now, standing in the dark watching her, he realized just how much he had missed her. Harvest Time had been hell, but at least he'd seen her almost every day at various times. Lately, he'd only managed to visit places where he anticipated she'd eventually appear.

As expected, Joe heard his arrival long before Mena did. Graham heard her say, "Joe? Why have you stopped humming?" In the dimness he could barely make out Joe pointing in his direction.

Mena stood. "Graham? Is that you?"

"Yes, it's me," Graham said as he approached them. He extended his hand. "My thanks, Joe, for keeping Mena company. Things aren't always as safe as they seem, are they, my friend?"

Joe stood and shook hands with Graham and then looked at Mena. "You needn't worry about Mena getting home safe," Graham said with a smile, "I'll escort her."

"He's such a kind young man," Mena murmured as they stood side by side watching him disappear into the darkness. "Do you know anything of his story?"

"Nothing," Graham admitted. "I suspect Maisy knows some, being as she's been alive for almost forever."

"He doesn't live in the forest, does he?"

"No, that I do know. One of the huts in the workers' village is for single men. He's had a bed there for as long as I've known him. He just … wanders. He's smart enough; does anything you ask of him and you only have to tell him once, unlike others I'm stuck with." Graham turned and reached up to touch her face. "Are you well? Is everything all right? I've not seen you in so long, it seems, and yet I always figure if there's a problem you know how to get in touch with me." He leaned in and kissed her on the nose. "And here you are. I'm not the most hospitable person on the planet and my hut surely isn't fit for social calls," he looked up into the dark night sky, "and this isn't the most suitable time for a young lady to come calling on a young man, so…"

Mena sighed and leaned into his hand that now stroked her hair. Pulling her down beside him, the two of them sat on the front porch steps of Graham's hut, side by side for a long time, simply enjoying being in each other's company. At long last Mena said, "I've missed you, Graham."

"It seems I spend a lot of time going out of my way to just miss you … the windmill … the worker's village … the Great House. This craziness with the distillery construction should calm down in a few more weeks once I'm fully confident that we have the work crews organized and properly placed."

"And then what?" Mena asked quietly.

"Is that why you've come all the way out here this evening, Miss Westwood," Graham asked with a grin, "to ask what my intentions are regarding you?"

"I need to talk with you, Graham. We just never have the time or the privacy to do it. So I've come here determined to have both." The smile slowly slipped from Graham's face. "Come," Mena said pulling him towards his hut, "you can eat your dinner and I'll talk. Hopefully you won't lose your appetite."

If he'd known that she was going to barge right into his hut he would have cleaned it up a bit. At Mena's insistence he sat in his only chair at the table by the light of his only lantern and slowly worked through his meal, while Mena paced about the room's small space wringing her hands. "Just spit it out, Mena," Graham finally growled.

"I've already shared private things about myself that no one knows," Mena began. "You know the most important things about me: my hopes and dreams and passions." She stopped pacing to look at him. "But you don't know some very basic information that with each passing day becomes more important. I honestly didn't withhold it to be secretive or deceitful so much as I wanted to *be forever done with it*. I wanted Barbados to be a fresh start for me."

Graham put down his fork, crossed his arms and leaned back in his chair. "What kind of basic information?"

"Like my full name."

He pushed his plate away. She was right; he'd lost his appetite. "What is your full name?"

Mena took a deep breath and looked into Graham's blue eyes. "My full name is Lady Wilhelmina Constance Westwood Windermere, only daughter of Alexander Malcolm St. James, Marquis of Windermere, Earl of Lindsay, and his wife Lucinda, Marchioness of Windermere, formerly Lady Lucinda Westwood. Lord Gabriel is my half-brother; a product of my father's first marriage."

He stood so quickly that his chair fell backward to the floor. Graham stood with his fists clenched at his side as he stared at the floor processing what she'd just told him. Her father was … the Earl of Lindsay. Her father was … the owner of Windermere plantation. Her father was the man who'd … He looked up at her standing stoically as he wrestled with his thoughts. "Your f-, your father … he …"

Mena's chin jutted out. "Social status means nothing when judging a person, Graham. *I told you that.* Wealth is no guarantee of happiness or integrity."

He started to laugh then; it was either that or cry. The irony of the position he was in once again was so inconceivable that even Graham struggled to comprehend it.

"Graham, I-," Mena stepped forward but he held his hand up to stay her.

"Don't, Mena," he said, when he had time to catch his breath. "Don't start with your worthless platitudes about God's guidance or your ill-informed words of encouragement about my character. If God exists it is only to play twisted jokes on poor bakros such as myself, and if I have a redeeming quality, it's simply that eventually I'll be dead. I may be a foolish man but I'm not an ignorant one; I know my place in this world, and it is most definitely not beside someone such as you." He reached up, put his hat on his head, and headed for the door.

Mena sighed, but surprisingly felt no tears. So that was to be the way of it. She had been here so many times before -

alone with no one to rely on except for herself and God. It was like an old, comfortable shoe that you were glad you'd had the presence of mind not to discard. Just like that, with no real change except the information of her identity, Graham was willing to dismiss everything that had been growing between them.

"You're a coward, Graham Rhyder," she said with absolute conviction. "You're afraid to let yourself be happy, afraid to acknowledge the goodness in this world, and afraid to believe that God might have plans specifically with you in mind. You'd just rather wallow in your own misery, content to collect only the awful around you and ignore all of the good."

He turned, at the doorway to look back at Mena standing proudly in the soft glow of the lantern light. "You're absolutely right, Wilhelmina," he said and walked out the door.

"I don't *need* you, Graham Rhyder," she called out to him as he walked across the porch and down his front stairs, "but I had begun to think it would be so wonderful to *stand beside you*." He did not stop, and in fact felt a sudden compulsion to run.

As I conclude this report on the state of Windermere Plantation for the month of July, 1854, I feel compelled to broach a subject of the most difficult nature. It involves an individual in a senior position of power having taken advantage of individuals in positions of no power (namely children) over a period of at least a decade regarding heinous crimes of a sexual nature. This individual, due to his station, has never had to answer for these crimes. It is my opinion, as an officer of the court, that this situation must be addressed.

Let me impress upon you the seriousness of this crime. In Section 16 of the Offences against the Person Act of 1828 *it is stated that 'every Person convicted of the Crime of Rape shall suffer Death as a Felon'. And while the death penalty for rape was indeed abolished by Section 3 of the* Substitution of Punishments for the Death Act of 1841 *which substituted transportation for life with death, the gravity of the situation is in no way diminished.*

In addition, these facts are important to note should we consider the mounting of a criminal case:
1.   *There is <u>no statute of limitations for serious sexual crimes.</u>*
2.   *Rape is classified as a felony (serious crime).*
3.   *Proof of carnal abuse (rape of a young girl) is significantly easier to prove due to Section 18 of the above cited Act of 1828.*

I plan to speak with the plantation's resident teacher regarding these matters. I believe, with her assistance, we could indeed develop an airtight case which would not only provide some vindication for the wronged parties but appropriate criminal penalty for the perpetrator.

At your earliest convenience, I wish to discuss this with you in greater depth.

Sincerely yours,

Mr. Nelson Topher, Esq.

Yuh runnin' from da station house to jail.

Chapter Twenty-Three

Graham headed for the cliffs. There was nowhere else for him to go; nowhere else he could stand to be. Almost immediately he heard the running of her feet behind him and he trudged on, determined to get as far away from *Wilhelmina Windermere* as he could.

"Mistah Graham!" came the breathless call behind him. "Yuh gots ta come quick! He goin' ta kill him if'n he hasn't done it already! Please Mistah Graham yuh hafta come!!" Turning, Graham saw John Paul standing not ten feet away gasping for breath. "Dahlia tol' me ta fetch yuh as quick as I cud, Mistah Graham."

Cursing under his breath, Graham walked toward John Paul. "Who's going to kill whom? John Paul? What the hell's going on?!"

When Graham reached John Paul the boy immediately grabbed his hand and began to run again, doing his best to drag Graham along with him. "It's Silen' Joe dat's getting' killed! Mistah Wagner caught him wit' Ab'gail an' den started beatin' on him sumpin' fierce firs' wit' his hands an' his feet an' den wit' a shovel. Silen' Joe jus' layin' der takin' it all an' Ab'gail jus' kep

~ 273 ~

screamin' an' screamin' an' screamin'. Dat's wut woke me up at firs' an' made me cum runnin'."

Graham squeezed John Paul's hand and pulled him to a stop. "I'll run ahead. You walk back with Miss Westwood."

"Miss Westwood?" John Paul looked around like Mena was going to appear out of thin air.

"She's in my hut. I'll trust that you'll get her home safely, right John Paul?"

"Yessir, yuh gots dat right."

Graham heard Abigail's shrieks long before the Great House was visible; they were long, drawn out howls from a throat raw from screaming. As he came around the corner at a run he found Dahlia sitting on a crate holding the trembling girl in her arms. "Joe's locked up in da root cellar," she said without preamble. "He needs Maisy ta see to him; he's hurt bad."

Graham looked down at Abigail, whose howls had now quieted down to moans. "Abigail?" he asked.

"I'll see ta her. Jessie Lynn's run to fetch Rachel. If'n Isaac cums too yuh might be needed ta keep him calm."

"Where's Wagner?"

"Inside sippin' his kill dev'l wit Lord Ga'briel." Dahlia made a face. "He's a mite upset hisself. Almos' killin' a man will do dat to yuh." Abigail's howls began at Dahlia's last comment, which made her begin to rock the girl like she was a small baby. "Der, der, chile, Joe's got a thick skin an' an even thicker head. He goin' ta be al'right."

"You tell Isaac that I'm here and I'll get to the bottom of this. *Under no circumstances* is he to go to Joe. You tell him to see to his family."

"I'll tell him dat but mans don' always lis'en ta good advice when der loved ones are involved."

"Mena's on her way; she'll help you reason with Isaac. She's coming with John Paul and should be here any minute. *You make him listen, Dahlia,*" Graham said over his shoulder as he stalked into the kitchen door and headed to the study.

"What happened?" Graham said as he strode into the study. Lord Gabriel and Mr. Wagner were seated in two facing wing chairs sipping rum from crystal tumblers. It was the first time Graham had ever seen Mr. Wagner out of his immaculate formal butler uniform. Sans jacket, he sat in a hastily pulled on shirt which was spattered with blood.

"I don't owe you any explanation, Rhyder, but I'll tell you anyway. I heard cries out in the back of the house and went to investigate. I saw Joe manhandling that new upstairs girl – Abby I think her name is – and she was struggling and crying. I stepped in; ordered him to step away from the girl. He made a threatening move toward me so I hit him. A number of times. I didn't want to risk him rising in anger and attacking me … or the girl … again."

Lord Gabriel raised his glass. "Mr. Wagner is a hero, Mr. Rhyder. That Silent Joe must outweigh him by three stone at least, and is well over six and a half feet tall. I'm not sure I would have had the courage to step in had I been there first."

"Did Abigail say anything? Did she accuse him?"

"The girl did nothing but that ear splitting screech. I was ready to hit her myself to get her to be quiet, but then Dahlia stepped in."

"And Joe? Besides making a "threatening" move? Did he do anything else?"

"Well, everyone knows that the imbecile doesn't speak," Mr. Wagner said with a small smile just before he took another sip of his rum. "No miracles occurred, if that's what you're asking. He didn't utter a word."

"He can remain safely locked in the root cellar tonight. I'll have the authorities summoned from Friendship in the morning to come and take him away," Lord Gabriel stated as he swirled his drink. "Gone are the days when we could mete out our own justice, unfortunately."

Mena suddenly appeared in the door, taking in Lord Gabriel and Mr. Wagner seated sipping their drinks, and then, almost regretfully, Graham. "What's going on?!" she asked to no one in particular.

Lord Gabriel raised his eyebrows. "I thought you'd retired long ago and yet here you are fully dressed from apparently a night out on the town." He glanced meaningful at Graham and had the audacity to give him a smug wink.

Dismissing both of the seated men, Mena turned to Graham. "I'm going to the Freemans'. Dahlia tells me that Rachel has taken Abigail home and that she was … attacked."

"You're not going anywhere unescorted," Graham responded.

"Don't be ridiculous," Mena said, turning and dismissing him as quickly as she'd done the other two. Before Graham could think it through he grabbed her arm to stop her departure. She stopped, looked down at his hand grasping her arm and said coolly, "Remove your hand from my arm, Mr. Rhyder. *Now.*"

"My, my, I never imagined I would get to see one fight in a night, let alone two," Lord Gabriel chuckled with delight.

Slowly, Graham took his hand away, never once breaking eye contact with Mena. "I'll go with you to the Freemans. If Abigail's up to it, I'd like to ask her a few questions."

"Leave the girl alone," Mr. Wagner said with a dismissive wave of his hand. "The facts speak for themselves."

"Facts?" Mena asked looking again between the three men.

"Come along," Graham said with resignation. "I'll fill you in as we walk."

$\mathcal{e}\mathcal{e}\mathcal{e}\mathcal{e}\mathcal{e}\mathcal{e}\mathcal{e}\mathcal{e}\mathcal{e}$

It had taken Graham a few terse sentences to explain to Mena what Dahlia and Mr. Wagner had told him. *Never keep secrets from those you care about.* Sir Russell's words seemed to hammer into Mena's head and heart with each step she took beside Graham on the way to the Freemans'. Because the reality was that there was *one more secret* she had - regarding Mr. Wagner - and she now most assuredly had to tell. Turning to look at Graham's angry, closed expression, she sighed.

"What?" he practically growled at her.

"I have one more secret that I must tell you."

"You're actually betrothed to the Prince of Wales," he groused and despite everything, Mena laughed.

"No, Graham. No one's ever expressed even a vague interest in me ... until you. No worries on that front. Although just before I left, Father *had* informed me that he planned to announce a betrothal between me and one of his cronies. I left before that was official, however."

"He's coming here, you know."

"Correction: *he's here.* In Bridgeton, apparently. According to Mrs. Wagner, he may be here as soon as tomorrow."

"What will you do?"

Mena stopped to stare at Graham. "Whatever do you mean?"

Graham walked a few more steps and then turned impatiently to face her on the path. "Are you worried for your ... safety?" he said haltingly.

"He ...," Mena bit her lip, trying to distance herself from the terror that was just a breath away, "he hasn't ... in years ...," She sighed. "He only likes ... young girls ..." and the old fear swept through her so suddenly that she gasped and closed her eyes. As the sick rose in her throat, she clapped her hand across her mouth and moaned.

Graham had her in his arms before she could draw a fresh breath. He held her until she stopped trembling and then ground out, "I want to *kill him,* Mena. Just how am I supposed to look him in the eye and say, 'Yes, your Lordship' and 'No, your Lordship'?"

The temptation to snuggle into his arms was so great ... but she must not. Mena disentangled herself and stepped back so she could look Graham in the eye. "The same way I said, 'Yes, Father,' and 'No, Father,'" my entire life, Graham," she said in a wooden voice. "It's amazing what you can find the strength to do when you need to." She began to walk down the path again and Graham fell into step. "What I must tell you is something that will require that kind of strength, Graham. You *must* remain calm and in control no matter how you feel. You must *promise me* that you will not behave irrationally when I tell you. Your presence here at Windermere is crucial to the safety and welfare of-,"

"Dear God, what is it?" He stopped again and interrupted her.

Mena turned and said flatly, "Mr. Wagner is the father of Elizabeth's baby. Dahlia so much as implied that he's been ... molesting young women in the Great House for years— including her. Mr. Topher also knows, but is powerless to prove it.

There's no way that Silent Joe hurt Abigail. I'm certain that he was *protecting* or *rescuing* her from Mr. Wagner."

Graham stepped forward and gripped Mena by the shoulders and shook her until her teeth rattled. *"How long have you known this?"*

"Dah-, Dahlia spoke with me the day after the Crop Over Fete! I finally had a chance to speak with her alone about Elizabeth and … you know how she speaks in riddles and sayings … Well, I finally understood what she was telling me, and then she made me realize what Isaac would do if he found out … Or you … And how it would be impossible to prove even if Elizabeth would accuse him, which we know she never would … I felt so incredibly helpless …," In the dimness, she felt tears trickle down her cheeks.

Graham released her and turned away. Ripping his hat off his head, he ran his fingers through his hair in frustration. "So now you know everything I know, Graham," Mena whispered. "That's it. I give all of this … putrid awfulness … to you to do with as you see fit."

He seemed to sag with the weight of it all. "And just what am I supposed to do with all of this now that you've given it to me?"

Mena took a deep breath and forced herself to stand tall. "Nothing if it suits you. Or you're welcome to stand beside me, although just a few hours ago – now that you know *who I really am* – you seemed quite adverse to that in more ways than one. I've spent my entire life on my own, Graham, so don't feel pressured to make a decision one way or another. In one of our first conversations I told you that I was far stronger than I appeared. Why, I even have a battle cry. Would you like to hear it? You may consider it a 'worthless platitude' but it's gotten me this far. *Fear thou not; for I am with thee: be not dismayed; for I am thy*

God: I will strengthen thee; yea, I will help thee; yea, I will uphold thee with the right hand of my righteousness."

Just as she had done once before, Mena stepped towards Graham, invaded his space and looked him right in the eye. "I *refuse* to let the accident of my birth and the evidence of my past define who I am, Graham Rhyder! I will only look towards the future with determination because my Lord has promised me a future and a hope – and I believe in Him. You may walk along beside me *or get out of my way."*

As she turned and walked purposely towards the Freemans' she threw over her shoulder, *"God always sends help. Yuh jus' gots ta know where ta find it."*

"The accommodations on this ... boat ... are abysmal. If we are ever forced to visit this backward island again, I insist that you purchase and outfit a floating mode of transportation which is suitable to the lifestyle to which we are accustomed.

"I hardly thought it was necessary, my dear, for us to go to such drastic measures for a mere three hour jaunt. Here; you always enjoy a nice glass of sherry."

"Which is <u>exactly</u> my point, Alexander. You don't honestly think that this ... boat ... will have anything that qualifies as 'nice' do you? The sherry they serve is probably also used to remove paint. You go ahead and sit there and enjoy your rum while I sit here in abject misery. Why I actually feel physically ill being forced to endure this degradation."

"It's the heat, my dear, you must be careful of it. Remember what we were told; fluids are important in this tropical climate. Why here's Emilia with a nice pitcher of water and fresh squeezed lemons. You so enjoyed that in Bridgeton, I insisted we bring along the makings for our brief trip. I insist you have a glass."

"Oh, all right."

Yuh dead longer dan yuh live.

Chapter Twenty-Four

The arrival of Lord and Lady Windermere the next day was unlike anything that could have anticipated; including Mena. Having endured a sleepless night knowing their arrival was imminent, Mena thought she had anticipated every scenario possible. But having the expected outrider arrive with news of profound illness for her Ladyship (as well as her maidservant, and his Lordship's man) was not one of them.

It was not Mena's place as the plantation's employed teacher to welcome Lord and Lady Windermere personally, nor was it her duty to see to their comfort and care upon arrival. At best she would have stood beside all the other workers for both a formal welcome and inspection, which was one of the many things she had agonized over prior to their arrival. All that flew out the window as the coaches and riders arrived in an uncharacteristic flurry of panic over the state of her ladyship. Mrs. Wagner was at her best ordering and directing servants and seeing to the needs of the plantation's most esteemed guests.

With nowhere left to go, Mena made her way to her room to pace, wring her hands and do her best to calm herself through prayer. A brisk knock on the door interrupted all that.

Opening her door, Mena came face to face with a very concerned Moira Wagner.

"Miss Westwood," Mrs. Wagner said with uncharacteristic deference, "may I come in?"

"Yes, of course." Mena stepped back to allow Mrs. Wagner to enter her room. "How is her Ladyship? Is there anything I can do to help?"

Mrs. Wagner walked into Mena's room and over to her small desk which was neatly arranged with a stack of writing paper, an inkwell, and a quill. "I'm not sure," Mrs. Wagner murmured as she made a miniscule adjustment to the paper stack. "Her Ladyship is in quite a bad way; almost to the point of delirium. She's significantly dehydrated already and is unable to keep even the smallest amount of liquid down. We've sent for the doctor from Friendship although, Dahlia seems quite certain as to what the illness is." She turned to make eye contact with Mena. "It's cholera."

Oh dear God ... Mena swallowed. "Cholera?" Cholera had devastated London the year before she had been born, killing over six thousand people. According to the stories she'd heard, Mother had been so petrified of catching the sickness that she had refused to leave their country estate in Northampton for two full seasons.

"Yes," Mrs. Wagner continued, looking directly at Mena. "Her Ladyship is in quite a bad way and is not at all cognizant. She keeps asking for ... her daughter, Wilhelmina. She *insists* that she's here."

Mena stared at Mrs. Wagner for a moment before she sighed in resignation. "What would you have me say, Mrs. Wagner?"

"Let us start with the truth of your identity."

Straightening to her full height, Mena said clearly and distinctly, "My full name is Lady Wilhelmina Constance Westwood Windermere. I will go to Mother at once since she is aware of my presence here and, even in her delirium, is asking for me." Mena gathered her skirts and made to exit but Mrs. Wagner stopped her with a question.

"*Why?*"

"It would seem," Mena said honestly, "that both of us have spent a significant portion of our lives bemoaning the accidents of our birth, Mrs. Wagner, and trying somehow to escape who we truly are. Unfortunately, as I'm sure you'll agree, it's easier said than done."

"I was only doing my job ... m'lady." That title, reluctantly and painfully delivered, caused Mena to stop once again at the doorway and turn to Mrs. Wagner.

"I did not come here to spy or evaluate, Mrs. Wagner; I came *to teach*. No one seems to believe me when I tell them that. Perhaps I should scream it from the rooftops each morning before I get on with my day. I prefer 'Miss Westwood' if you would. It's who I wish to be. These months here at Windermere have been the happiest and most satisfying of my life. Being 'Lady Wilhelmina' *was never* an identity that I felt comfortable or happy with."

Both Jessie Lynn and Mary Jean were standing in petrified attendance when Mena entered Mother's room, scanning the numerous trunks that she always traveled with. The stench of sickness already hung heavily in the air despite the windows being wide open. "Miss Mena! Don' cum in here. Dis is bad sickness! Terrible bad," Jessie Lynn urged.

Mena turned to them both as she began to roll up the sleeves of her blouse. "You are dismissed. I'll care for her ladyship. Please bring me clean bedding, towels, soap, and a pitcher of fresh water. Then bring these trunks into the adjoining sitting room. Find as many comfortable bed clothes as you can find as I'll need a number of fresh changes for her ladyship. Once that is done, I'll leave soiled clothes and linen in the hallway. I think it's best to burn everything rather than attempting to clean them." She looked pointedly at both young women. "*I insist* that you thoroughly wash your hands whenever you handle these soiled things, do you hear me?"

"Yas miss!"

"You will relay these same instructions to whomever is caring for both Lord Windermere's man – he's called Winston - and her Ladyship's maidservant Emilia." Both young women nodded their assent and were only too happy to assume duties that took them away from the sick room.

Mena walked to Mother's bedside and looked down at her. There had not been one time, in Mena's memory, that Mother had not looked regal and commanding. But not today. She lay in apparent slumber, as pale as the fine linen pillow slip she rested against. Her mouth, slightly slack, had a small stream of vomit trailing out and onto her cheek. Mena took a cloth from a bowl of water, rung it out and wiped her mouth. "Mother? Mother can you hear me? It's Wilhelmina. I'm here to care for you. Can you try to drink some of this nice, cool water? Just a bit to wet your lips. Then I'm going to clean you up."

"W'ilmina?" Mother struggled to open her eyes, her usually carefully arranged make-up and hair in sorry disarray. Mena gently removed some hair pins that had worked themselves loose. Diamond earbobs glinted in the tangle of her hair, and what Mena remembered to be Mother's favorite diamond and pearl necklace moved at her throat as she tried to speak. "My ... dau'ter?"

"Yes Mother. It's me, Wilhelmina. I'm here. You are in Barbados at Windermere. You are very sick. You must rest. Here, try to take just a sip of this." Mena held Mother's head as she trickled a small amount of liquid into her mouth

"Watch that no one -," but a wave of sickness interrupted whatever Mother was about to say. Long moments went by as Mena performed all the necessary duties. Finally, Mena once again lifted Mother's head and tried to trickle a small bit of water between her parched lips. After Mother had taken a small sip she once again tried to speak, clutching Mena's hand with a desperate urgency. "Watch that no one ...," she swallowed, struggling with the dryness that seemed to be consuming her entire body, "takes my jewels ..." she managed before she fell into a restless sleep.

Straightening, Mena collected all the soiled bed clothes and linens, and left them in the hallway. *Oh dear Lord, don't let this sickness spread. Guide me. Help me. Keep us safe.*

Dr. Thomas Franklin arrived late in the afternoon, having been summoned by Isaac at Mrs. Wagner's direction. He was a short, obese man with a grey mustache, bald head, and a well-worn suit that had seen far better days. Whether he was rarely called upon due to the travel distance from Friendship to Windermere or the distinctly strong smell of rum that pervaded him, Mena wasn't sure. After a cursory examination he muttered, "Aye, it's cholera. It's already sweepin' through Bridgt'n, and no doubt will do its damage here now that it's arrived. There's naught I can do. Try to get liquids down her; that's the only hope. If you can't do that, then she'll just dry up."

Mena was stunned by his lack of concern or care. "That's all you have to offer me?"

"What would you have me say, miss?" He gestured towards Mena's mother lying unresponsive in the bed. "Her skin has already lost much of its elasticity and her rapid heart rate is indicative of severe dehydration. Soon, if hydration is unsuccessful, her skin will take on a bluish tinge and ..." He shrugged. "Do all you can to get liquids into her, but if you can't there's naught to be done." Walking over to the fresh bowl of water he'd insisted on being brought up, he began to meticulously wash his hands. "I'm surprised it's started ... like this. Cholera is a poor man's illness; usually starting in the slums. Usually the ... upper classes ... aren't so significantly affected." After drying his hands, he helped himself to a drink from a flask he produced from his coat pocket. "Must have been a result of traveling from Bridgt'n on the packet boat up to Speightstown."

"How ... can we keep it from spreading here at Windermere?"

Wiping his mouth with the back of his hand, he gave Mena another shrug, "It's not contagious. I was stationed with the British Army in India during the cholera outbreak of 1823." He shook his head. "Indians and British soldiers died by the thousands, but many of us who treated them escaped with nary a hiccup. Most believe that it has to do with living in filth and decay, which is why it almost always strikes the poor most harshly." He gestured to the opulent surroundings of the room where they both stood. "What's the saying? Cleanliness is next to godliness? You have little to worry about regarding contracting the disease by caring for Her Ladyship."

Every word the man said was more offensive than the last. "I am concerned for *all* the inhabitants of Windermere, sir. I was not speaking out of fear for myself."

He clapped his hat on his head and took one more swig from his flask before carefully returning it to his pocket, and said, "Well, you can't clean up the darkies; they're held together with filth. As for those here in the Great House, I'd encourage

hand washing and general cleanliness. I saw the bonfire out
back and understand you ordered the burning of contaminated
clothing. That's wise. You could boil dirtied linens too, I
suspect." He had the audacity to chuckle and wink at her.
"Guess you could try boiling the darkies to clean 'em up, but I
don't suspect they'll be much use to you afterwards."

"Get out." Mena felt a rage flood through her the likes
of which she'd never imagined.

"Well, that's not the kind of response I'm due after
traveling over an hour! Besides, I answer to Mrs. Wagner, not
some high and mighty lady's maid. I've been promised a meal as
well as a drink or two before I face my long journey home."

Mena followed Dr. Franklin out into the hall only to
come face to face with Mrs. Wagner. "I've come to inform you,
... Miss Westwood ..., that Lord Windermere has also fallen ill.
I have him in the adjoining bedroom off the sitting room."

"Where is Lord Gabriel?" Mena asked through tight lips.

"I believe he's in the study," Mrs. Wagner said as she
indicated Dr. Franklin should follow her. "Shall I tell Lord
Gabriel that you wish to see him?"

"No," Mena sighed, "I'll go. Oh and Mrs. Wagner," she
called and the housekeeper stopped and turned. "Dr. Franklin
will not be staying. If he wishes, you may provide him with a
pack lunch which he may eat *on* his hour journey back to
Friendship, but *under no circumstances* is he to be given anything
but water to drink. Am I understood?" Dr. Franklin gave an
indignant gasp and turned, expecting Mrs. Wagner to defend
him.

For long moments Mrs. Wagner stood beside the
offended doctor and stared at Mena. Then, to the doctor's
shock, Mrs. Wagner simply said, "Yes, Miss Westwood."

Once Jessie Lynn was assigned to watch over Mother Mena made her way down to the study. She didn't knock and found him lounging in one of the wing chairs. "Gabriel, I need your help."

"Gabriel, is it? I was getting quite used to your deferential use of my title. Is the game over?" He sighed in mock disappointment. "I was so enjoying our little ruse."

"Father is ill, as is his manservant Winston. I'm caring for Mother; I can't possibly care for the two. You're needed."

Gabriel stood. "You expect me to *care* for father? Clean up his … sick?" He shuddered with genuine revulsion and then shook his head. "Enlist one of the darkies to do it."

"The *doctor,*" Mena forced herself to keep derision out of her tone, "says that the illness is not contagious as long as we make efforts to keep ourselves clean."

"Tell that to the hundreds of thousands who have died over the past thirty years all over the world! How can anyone with any intelligence possibly think that cholera is not contagious! I was in America during the last outbreak. Do you know how many thousands it killed? Why even president James Polk succumbed. If I wasn't so worried of contracting the illness as Mother and Father did – on board ship – I'd be gone from this accursed island already!"

"Gabriel, it's your duty-,"

Gabriel rounded on her, fury etched in his features. "Don't you dare talk to me about duty, sister dear. I didn't run away from home and abandon all my responsibilities; *you did.*" Gabriel waved his hand, dismissing her as he went to the sideboard to pour himself a drink. "You see to *your duties* as you see fit, Wilhelmina, and *I'll see to mine.*"

Late in the evening of their second day at Windermere Mena's mother died just as the doctor had described. Drained empty of fluids, she looked like a dried husk of a person. Exhausted and defeated, Mena wandered out into the night. There was no moon, but the stars filled the night sky, reminding Mena of some of Mother's beautiful gems strewn across her black velvet drape. Standing and gazing up into the heavens, Mena allowed herself to grieve over the death of Mother, and the fact that until her very last breath all she was concerned about were her precious jewels.

PREVENTION
OF

CHOLERA

The Island of Barbados requests the attention of all Householders, Owners of Houses inhabited by the Poorer Classes, and the Inhabitants of the Island generally to the following recommendations made by the

Medical Officer of Health,

as affording the best means of

Protection against Cholera, Fever, and other Contagious Diseases

1st. All areas, basements, yards, cellars, kitchens, and other dark and damp places to be forthwith cleansed from dirt and rubbish, and the walls and ceilings covered with a thick coating of Lime Wash. All dirty rooms and staircases to be also thoroughly cleansed and purified.

2nd. All drains, water closets and sinks, to be daily flushed with water, and to be afterwards purified with *Carbolic Acid, Chloride of Lime or Condy's Disinfection Fluid; care being taken also that the traps to the drains and sinks are perfect and in their proper places.

3rd. All dust bins to be regularly emptied at least twice a week, and no animal or vegetable refuse of any kind on any account to be thrown into them. The dust bins should be further purified by the daily use of the Carbolic Acid Powder. (Vegetable and other refuse, if it cannot otherwise be disposed of, may be burned."

4th. All cisterns, bottles or other receptacles for water to be immediately and thoroughly cleansed, and kept well covered. (The water from pumps and wells contain … [8]

Wat' good fuh da sick bettah fuh da well.

Chapter Twenty-Five

Graham stomped his boots on the tiles outside the kitchen. His belly cramped with hunger but it was far past the dinner hour. The last three times he'd missed dinner Dahlia had slid him a plate just the same, but he didn't know how much longer that luck would hold out. Work on the distillery had halted as a result of the cholera. There were barely enough workers available to cope with the necessary business of the plantation during Hard Times, let alone continue construction work. Graham regularly found himself doing all manner of jobs as there was no one well enough to work but him. He and Mena had not spoken since the terrible scene on the way to the Freemans'. Catching only brief glimpses of her, and always from a distance, he did not seek her out nor did she him. He tried to convince himself that he was content with Dahlia's regular reassurances that Mena was well, if not completely exhausted caring for the many on the plantation who had fallen ill.

The battle raged against the cholera at Windermere as in the rest of Barbados, and for almost a full month all wondered who would win. The sickness did show a greater propensity to attack the poor, and besides Mena's mother, the workers' village experienced twelve deaths. There was no time for grief; it seemed as one was claimed in death a new one was claimed by illness. All bodies regardless of age, race or rank were hastily buried, and it seemed as if an endless fire burned with the sole purpose of eradicating any remnants of the sickness.

Graham knew that the sickness was rampant throughout the island because word trickled in from the occasionally brave worker hoping to find work. Heavily populated areas such as the major city of Bridgeton and the busy local port of Mullins Bay were overwhelmed with the scope of the cholera outbreak. Beaches all along the west coast had been claimed as hastily constructed seaside graveyards to deal with the numerous dead. Graham knew that Mena traveled from one sick bed to the next doing her best to win a battle that had seemed hopeless almost from the start.

Mena's father survived, as did his manservant Winston and Mother's maid, Emilia. Recovery left one so incredibly weak it was sometimes a full month until one was sufficiently recovered to resume any kind of normal activity. Silent Joe, cared for by Dahlia, had healed from his beating by Mr. Wagner and remained 'prisoner' in the root cellar, although often Graham saw him sitting quietly just outside the open door whittling a piece of wood or weaving fans and the like. No one, it seemed, had the wherewithal to deal with anything other than surviving the cholera epidemic. Determining Joe's guilt or innocence was left in limbo.

Despite Graham's exhaustion he couldn't fail to notice changes within the Great House. Much to her delight, Dahlia now had Peach and Fancy May as full time assistants. They greeted him tonight with enthusiasm as he dragged his tired, aching body in. Moira Wagner entered just as he was about to beg for a dish, and Graham cursed his timing. She didn't even glance at him but approached Dahlia. "I need to bring up His Lordship's tray."

"Yas yuh do, Missus Wagner. It's over der by da sideboard. I gots a hearty beef soup taday, but don' let His Lordsh'p eat it too fast. Yuh know wha' happened las' time an' whut a mess yuh were stuck wit'."

"I'm well aware of that, Dahlia. Mr. Wagner will need preparations for His Lordship's nightly bath as well. Has the water been put on to boil?"

"Not yet. Yuh know I gots ta get da main meal up an' finished b'fore I use all da pots ta heat da water. I'll have dat goin' jus' as soon as I can. All should be ready by da time yuh bring da empty tray down as usual."

"All right." Mrs. Wagner disappeared from the kitchen with a loaded food tray and Graham sat there open mouthed with shock as Dahlia, Peach, and Fancy May resumed bustling around the kitchen.

Dahlia eventually noticed his stunned expression and suppressed a tiny grin. "Shut yuh mouth boy unless yuh hopin' ta catch sum flies."

"What did I just see?!" Graham sputtered.

Fancy May and Peach gave him a quick grin but remained silent. "Dat," Dahlia said with relish, "is da new way a tings here at da big house. At least fo' da time bein' until sumbody says different. An' mighty nice it is, too."

"How...? Why...?" Graham sputtered.

Dahlia shrugged and went back to her work at the sink. "Don' rightly know fo' sure. 'Cept Missy Mena ain't da quiet little mouse she used ta be. She says in her nice po-lite voice, 'I tink we need to give soup ta any family dat asks durin' dis crisis,' an' befo' yuh know it we makin' soup fo' every family no questions asked."

As she set a plate in front of Graham piled high with food Dahlia continued. "Or, all of a sudden like, Missy Mena says, 'Let's loosen up da meal times a bit', an' befo' yuh know it I don' have ta make dose fancy-schamcy meals ready at six on da dot no mo'. Instead I jus' have a huge pile o' food ready an' warm for any worker dat needs ta fill his or her belly no matter da time."

Dahlia walked over to the oven and took out three huge pies. "Den Missy Mena says, 'Someone needs to care fo' his Lordsh'p while he an' his man are still recoverin' an' da next ting I know Mr. an' Mrs. Wagner are haulin' food trays, givin' baths, an' cleanin' up sick. Or," Dahlia gave Graham a pointed look, "Missy Mena says to dat Lor' Gabr'l, 'Yuh need to stop dat foolishness wastin' Mister Rhyder's valuable time wit' yuh no-account meetin' ev'ry mornin'", an' b'for yuh know it *yuh* whistlin' a happy tune cause yuh a free man an' Lor' Gabr'l ridin' round da place like a man wit'out a purpose."

"Mena managed all those changes?" Graham said in wonder.

"Dat she did," Dahlia said with tremendous satisfaction. "I don' know how or why she can, but ders a new boss in dis house an' it's a wonderful ting."

"Amen ta dat," said Peach and Fancy May as they grinned and looked heavenward.

Mena. Looking down at his evening meal, Graham was dismayed with the powerful wave of longing for Mena that swept through him. Not that they had ever spent that much time together, but the *hope* of eventually seeing her, talking with her, and spending a few stolen moments with her seemed surprisingly powerful incentive to get out of bed each morning and putting one foot in front of the other.

Much to his dismay, it had taken *the loss of that* to finally make the painful discovery. Over and over in his mind he saw her standing before him, the heat of passion sparking from her green eyes. *I refuse to let the accident of my birth and the evidence of my past define who I am. I will only look towards the future with hope and determination because my Lord has promised me a future and a hope – and I believe Him.*

Shaking his head, Graham shoveled a mouthful into his mouth. How tremendously attractive it was to stand eye to eye with a beautiful woman and realize that her most appealing quality was her inner strength. Graham had no doubt that what Mena determined to do, Mena would accomplish.

Walk along with me or get out of my way.

And much to his dismay, now that he'd gotten out of her way he realized, more than anything, he wanted to be right by her side. How could he not? She was strong, loyal, and loving.

Fiona … would have liked Mena. Fiona … would have said the very same things in the very same way and would have probably added a slap or two. Both women had tried to get him to see; to understand the reality of life. No one was perfect. Everyone had failures. The reality of life was that it was *terribly hard,* but having someone to love and stand beside made it bearable. And the one thing that really mattered was *to keep trying.*

He did Fiona's memory no good by wallowing in his grief and shame. *She had loved him* to her dying breath! Despite his inability to believe that he was worthy, the reality was that she had believed him to be.

And now, here was Mena. No, scratch that. Here was Lady Wilhelmina Westwood Windermere saying, *Walk along with me or get out of my way.* Maybe there was hope for him yet.

Suddenly, Graham saw the reality of his life so incredibly clearly that it took his breath away. He had been privileged to have been loved by not one but *two* amazing women, and it was about damn time he faced that incredible fact. Oh, Mena hadn't said she loved him in so many words, but, dear God in Heaven, actions always spoke louder than words.

He'd just thought *Dear God In Heaven*. How many people did he love or respect who recognized the power and might of God?

"Thou believest thyself to be more powerful than God Almighty?"

"Why, I even have a battle cry. Would you like to hear it? Fear thou not; for I am with thee: be not dismayed; for I am thy God: I will strengthen thee; yea, I will help thee; yea, I will uphold thee with the right hand of my righteousness."

"I gots ta believe in God, Boss. Why else wud I be here doin' dis life? My baby boy isn't in da groun' here. No sir. He dancin' in heaven waitin' for me ta join him.

Just who did Graham think he was to challenge, dismiss, and ridicule their strong, unfailing belief? Hadn't he always been quick to sing the truth of his ignorance? Shouldn't he be sitting up straight and paying attention to anything that *went against* what he claimed to believe?! Lord Russell's words spoken at Fiona's and the babe's graveside came clearly to mind. *Into Your hands we commend to You their spirits, Lord. Hold them close to You, just as You have done with my dear Mary, until I can join them in joyful eternity.*

Standing up from his half-finished plate, Graham said to Dahlia, "Tell Lord Gabriel he's in charge of overseeing the business end of the plantation. I've got something to attend to."

She'd lost track of her days and nights and many times awoke from an exhausted slumber, not knowing where she was or who she was caring for. Though she never succumbed to the sickness, just as Dr. Franklin had predicted, Mena felt drained and dry from the tears she had shed over her many failures to save those she loved and cared for from death. When she closed her eyes, exhausted as she was, she saw all those she had lost in her mind dying a slow agonizing death one after another: Beloved Maisy, tiny little John Paul and Biter Joe, Isaac and Rachel's Rebecca and Abigail … Far too often she rose from one death bed to go and bide her time at another with no end in sight.

As a result of the sickness she had changed yet again.

Well, perhaps the first rumbles of change had happened after her final conversation with Graham. *Walk along with me or get out of my way.* Never had she been so fiercely furious in the moment, like a warrior going into battle. She forced herself each day to remember that feeling and cling to it, for at times she felt … utterly bereft. Mena ached with missing Graham. Even though she knew clearly there was no hope, there was also no doubt in her mind that she loved him. *Why?* She'd asked God that question numerous times in the past weeks. Why had He denied her love and romance in the comfort and appropriateness of London society? Why had He allowed it here in Barbados with a man who could not love himself enough to let him love another? One thing her life in London had taught her was that she would much rather be alone than in a marriage that lacked love. She had willingly accepted that truth, and honestly would have found great happiness and contentment here in Barbados without it. So why had God finally allowed her to find a love that offered her no hope of a future? Why must she have a heart that ached so?

The next change was Mena's inability to bite her tongue, or extend any patience for ignorant fools. At some point perhaps she would examine the irony that it took death and chaos to make her at last relish and appreciate the fact that she was Lady Wilhelmina Windermere, with all the rights and privileges that name offered. With Mother dead, Father completely indisposed, and Gabriel terrified to approach any human being for fear of contracting the illness, Mena by all rights was mistress of Windermere, and wonder of all wonders, she gladly took full advantage of it.

At Mena's direction Dahlia made endless pots of hearty soup which were distributed to any who asked for it; no questions asked. Also available simply for the asking were clean sheets and clothing to encourage those less fortunate to burn rather than attempt to clean soiled linens. If she wasn't so exhausted, she might even smile in remembrance of the night when this change in her had begun. She'd arrived from Maisy's deathbed – she'd died within a day of Mother – only to be told that she was too late for the evening meal. Hungry, exhausted, and heartbroken, something inside Mena had snapped.

"I think, Dahlia, from this moment on we will begin to relax a few of the rules in place here at the Great House," she had said to the cook, as she stood in the kitchen door looking directly into Mrs. Wagner's furious eyes. "From now on, any employee here at Windermere who has seen to his *or her* work may request a meal *at any time*. It need not be fancy; only be nourishing and filling."

Mrs. Wagner's response had been immediate. "In that case, Dahlia, I suspect that you will now be needed around the clock here at the Great House. Your work hours are therefore extended."

"A most difficult thing to ask of you, Dahlia," Mena said smoothly. "So, from now on you will have both Peach and Fancy May working with you *full time,* for *full pay,* and *at your discretion.* Will that be sufficient help for you?" Dahlia, looked with wide, shocked eyes first at the back of Mrs. Wagner's head and then at Mena's calm demeanor. She was barely able to nod her head.

"In addition," Mena continued, now looking only at Mrs. Wagner, "as His Lordship and his man are far too ill to care for themselves I will need someone to see diligently to their needs. This would include feeding, bathing, dressing, and overall caring for them until he and his man are fully recovered." She stared calmly at Mrs. Wagner and waited. The silence grew. And grew. When Mena finally arched her eyebrow (as she had seen Mother do hundreds of times before) Mrs. Wagner crumbled.

"Mr. Wagner and I would be happy to see to their needs," she managed.

"Thank you," Mena felt herself say as regally as a queen. "And please, be polite and respectful to both Dahlia and her helpers when dealing with them since, as you have so astutely pointed out, that we have greatly increased their workload. I'll not have you or Mr. Wagner inconveniencing them in the course of their duties." Mena had waited. Again.

"Yes, Miss Westwood," Mrs. Wagner had choked out.

"Thank you again." Mena had then turned to Dahlia who stood in the kitchen doorway with a look of such shock and awe that every time she thought of it Mena could almost laugh out loud were she not so utterly exhausted. "Now, might there be a bite or two to eat, Dahlia? I'm famished and don't remember when I've last eaten."

"Right away, Miss Westwood!" came Dahlia's quick reply as she disappeared into the kitchen.

As Mena lowered herself tiredly into a dining room chair, she'd met the angry eyes of Mrs. Wagner. Speaking quietly, Mena said, "I ask nothing of you, Mrs. Wagner, but what you are paid to do. I will not shame you unless you put me in the position where I must. I will not overrule you unless I see an injustice I cannot ignore. It was never your work ethic that I found offensive; it was your cruelty. Do we understand each other?"

"Yes, Miss Westwood," Mrs. Wagner said.

"Good. Now if you'll excuse me, I must concentrate on consuming my meal before I collapse with exhaustion. I trust we will not have to have this discussion again." But before Dahlia could return with a plate of food for her, Mena had fallen asleep on her arms at the formal dining table.

Word had spread throughout the plantation faster than the cholera that "Missy Mena" had had a set-to with "Missus Wagner" and won. Everywhere she ventured in her battle with the sickness, Mena was met with appreciative smiles, warm words of encouragement, and often a wink or two of outright delight. It did not escape Mena's notice that were she not truly Lady Wilhelmina Constance Westwood Windermere, none of these changes would have been possible.

That final realization seemed to have brought Mena full circle back to her starting point. Although she *was* different, she would no longer hide who or what she was. Weren't we all called to be thankful in *all things*? Instead of running, she would now embrace *everything* that the Lord had given her to work with and be thankful for it.

Who knoweth whether thou art come to the kingdom for such a time as this?

Look out, world! Lady Wilhelmina Constance Westwood Windermere was on the island.

If you sit down at set of sun
And count the acts that you have done,
And, counting, find
One self-denying deed, one word
That eased the heart of him who heard,
One glance most kind
That fell like sunshine where it went --
Then you may count that day well spent.

But if, through all the livelong day,
You've cheered no heart, by yea or nay --
If, through it all
You've nothing done that you can trace
That brought the sunshine to one face--
No act most small
That helped some soul and nothing cost --
Then count that day as worse than lost. [9]

Yuh dancin' to da music he playin'.

Chapter Twenty-Six

The epidemic of cholera finally began to ease its deadly grip on the island In the blistering high heat of August. When two full days passed with no new cases of cholera, Mena at last began to believe that the worst was indeed over. For the first time in almost five weeks, her thoughts turned back to her Windmill School and the endless possibilities that existed now that she was in a far more commanding position than she had been when she'd first arrived.

And then the summons came from Father.

Four weeks and three days after Lord Windermere arrived at Windermere Plantation, Mena was summoned for the first time to meet with him. For the past two days he had been helped down into the large, spacious study by Mr. Wagner, and there he had begun to see to the business of being the Marquis, owner of Windermere Plantation. There had been a steady stream of people – some familiar and some not - with Mr. Topher having arrived just that morning.

Mena was stunned at how calm she felt as she stood outside the study door. Many times in the night since her father had arrived she had lain awake in her room trying to envision how her life was going to play out. She prayed aloud and silently whenever the opportunity afforded, thanking God for His guidance, asking Him for clear direction, and committing all her plans and her purpose to Him. *Here I am, send me.* As a result she regularly felt a peaceful presence beside her, within her, behind her, above her … She felt purposeful and in control. She knocked purposefully on the study door. "Enter!" she heard Father's voice for the first time in over six months calling to her from within.

"Don't blame me!" Gabriel was shouting at Father as Mena entered. She nodded politely to Mr. Topher who sat amidst his papers and quills. "I had no idea that Rhyder was missing! I can't be expected to just step in and know everything that needs to be done here!"

Graham was missing? "Of course I can blame you, Gabriel," her Father's cultured voice responded. "Whether Rhyder's present or not, *you* were the authority here. Rhyder was needed, but never essential. I find it absolutely stunning that you are having such tremendous difficulty understanding what needs to be done in Rhyder's absence, and have been unable to answer my simple questions thus far. It's off-season! What *is* so difficult? You've been supposedly running the Rhode Island plantation – with far more responsibilities - for how many years now? In addition, you've been here at Windermere for almost three months, have you not? Any variations in process and production should have easily been accounted for *and* easily adapted. You were sent here to be the resident expert overseeing the construction of the new distillery, since you were present when the Rhode Island one was constructed. In addition, you were charged with evaluating the present operation here and bringing the modernization concepts we've been so pleased with back to Rhode Island."

Gabriel fisted his hands and glanced furiously over his shoulder at Mena. "Ask your daughter how essential Rhyder is;

she's spent more time with him than I have, although I doubt they've been discussing plantation business."

Mena kept herself from rolling her eyes. It was a tactic Gabriel had relied on since childhood; redirect any unfavorable attitudes towards the always available scapegoat Mena. All eyes turned to Mena. "Father," she said calmly. "I see that you are in the midst of something. If now is not a good time for us to meet. I could come back at a later time. Perhaps after dinner?"

"Wilhelmina," Father said after a brief glance, "sit down. I'll be with you in a moment." Turning to Gabriel, he said, "The *real* issue here is the fact that you were *absent* from Windermere apparently for days, perhaps weeks, in the midst of the cholera epidemic. When Rhyder's departure was discovered, *no one could locate you.* How is it that your presence here at Windermere is so insignificant that 1) no one missed your presence for apparently *a full week* and 2) knowing you would be gone for an extended time you felt no need to inform *anyone* where you were going? Were it not for Mr. Topher's information regarding this...," he looked down at the papers in front of him, "...Isaac ... currently seeing to all field work for the past ten days, I would never have known that not only was Rhyder *gone* but apparently so were you! Where *have* you been? *What have you been doing with yourself?*"

"I took a few days to go and visit some new acquaintances here on the island." Father gave Gabriel a direct, silent stare. "What with the cholera ... I thought that perhaps ... well, I was concerned about the welfare of ..."

Father sighed. "Who's the woman?"

"Father, I-"

"WHO'S THE WOMAN." Father never yelled but he had a way of stressing a word that made one feel as if he were.

"I've made acquaintances with a Lady Maureen Walcott of Forster Hall Plantation. She's recently widowed with a young child, and I was concerned that perhaps, given the terrible epidemic sweeping the island that-,"

"You are dismissed." Turning to Mr. Topher, Father said, "I will meet with this Isaac. You say he's a darkie?"

"Yes, sir. Mr. Rhyder thought highly enough of him that within months of assuming the job as Manager he made Isaac his foreman. He's an exceptional worker and has been as essential as Mr. Rhyder to the successful seasons we have been having."

"Send for him."

"Yes, sir." Mr. Topher rose and left the study.

Father looked up at Gabriel, who still remained standing silently in front of the desk. "Why are you still here, Gabriel? I dismissed you."

"Father, I-,"

"I'm a cursed man," Father said with a pained expression as he rose and poured himself a glass of rum. "I've got a son with no brains and a daughter with too many." Turning to Gabriel, he said coldly, "Do not make me repeat myself."

Alone in the study with Father, Mena took the time to examine him. The cholera had taken its toll, leaving him thinner than she ever remembered seeing him. She'd gotten her height from both Mother and Father, but her green eyes and her straight brown hair were from him. In the six months since she had last seen him he seemed older, with grey liberally sprinkled throughout his hair.

"You escaped the cholera, I understand."

"Yes." Short, succinct answers were always best when being interviewed by Father.

"Mr. Topher impressed upon me how you cared for your mother as well as many others."

"Yes."

He sipped his drink and stared dispassionately across the desk at her. "I've read all the reports about your ... Windmill School. It seems that you have been moderately successful with this ... endeavor of yours."

"Yes."

"What has happened to Rhyder?"

"I wouldn't know. I was unaware that he had left Windermere until just now."

Father gave one of his patented cold smiles. "Gabriel is an idiot, but he's not completely useless. What *is* your relationship with this Graham Rhyder?"

"We are coworkers."

"Hmmm. You know that when you lie your pulse," he tapped the base of his neck, "right here picks up. Were you a card player it would be called a 'tell'. I always knew when you lied when you were a child."

"I was never a child."

Father shrugged unmoved by her statement. "No, I suppose you weren't. From the moment you were born you always had this way of looking directly at a person with those green eyes of yours. Into his very soul, it seemed. As if you could read his mind, his thoughts, his desires...,"

She must shut him up. "I wish you to remove Mr. and Mrs. Wagner from their positions here at Windermere."

Father looked suitably surprised at this, which told Mena he had as of yet not read Mr. Topher's monthly report. "Why would I do that? The Wagner family has been serving at Windermere for decades."

"I also wish you to exonerate the young man known as Silent Joe from all accusations that were made towards him regarding a young woman named Abigail Freeman."

"Ah yes. I've heard about Ol' Silent Joe taking liberties with a young woman, and how he had to be suitably chastised for his actions. I believe the constable from Friendship was supposed to come and collect him only to be waylaid by the cholera." Father gave Mena a smug smile. "Wilhelmina, we have been here before; you making requests and I explaining to you the reality of things. You are hardly in any position to make demands."

As Father spoke, Mr. Topher returned. "Isaac is in the far west fields supervising the fodder collection and weeding of the irrigation ditches. I took it upon myself to invite him to come and speak with you after the dinner hour, m'lord."

"That will be fine, Mr. Topher. You may leave us now," Father said dismissively.

"Actually," Mena said, so she turned to look at Mr. Topher as he made to leave the room, "I wish to discuss an item of interest in Mr. Topher's July report. It would be prudent for him to remain."

Mr. Topher looked first to Mena and then to Father, uncertain as to whom he should obey. Father frowned. "I have not as of yet had the opportunity to read through Mr. Topher's report, Wilhelmina."

"No problem," Mena said briskly. "The item itself stands alone from the report and is found on the very last page just above Mr. Topher's signature. It should take you no time to read." Since Father made no further instruction for Mr. Topher's departure, but instead began to turn the pages of the report in search of the item Mena had referred to, Mr. Topher hesitantly resumed his seat amidst all of his materials.

Father looked up and frowned at Mr. Topher. "I don't understand."

Mr. Topher started to speak, but Mena glanced quickly at him and began to speak instead. "More accurately, I'm sure you are confused, Father. Mr. Topher names no perpetrator nor does he name any specific victims, although he does well in describing the crime."

"She's quite right, Mr. Topher. Who is the accused? Who is the supposed victim?"

"M'lord, the accused is Mr. Walter Wagner. There are no victims willing to speak against him, however."

Father looked at Mena. "Is this why you wish to have *both* the Wagners dismissed? Over unsubstantiated hearsay evidence?" He shook his head and had the audacity to chuckle. "Wilhelmina, you cannot accuse a person of a crime when *there are no victims*. And that is exactly the situation you have here. The law does not work that way, and Mr. Topher will most assuredly back me up on this. Without *credible* witnesses and *solid* evidence we cannot possibly accuse Mr. Wagner of such a crime. Why, his family's history here at Windermere alone stands as strong evidence *against* such accusations and points strongly in favor of his sterling personal reputation.

"Furthermore, it is Mr. Wagner's *sworn testimony* regarding what he came upon between this Silent Joe and the girl Abigail that bears the strongest evidence. What has the girl said about the attack?"

"Abigail Freeman succumbed to the cholera, m'lord. Prior to her death she refused to speak of the attack to anyone."

"And what is this Joe's defense?"

"He is a mute, m'lord."

Father turned once again to Mena. "Young women ... have a penchant to make up stories, Wilhelmina. You must know that! You're a young woman! They make accusations based on emotions rather than facts; sometimes to save their reputation, sometimes to seek revenge, and sometimes because, quite frankly, they are *not of right mind.*"

Turning to Mr. Topher, Father continued. "Mr. Topher, you have never had children, is that correct?" Hesitantly, Mr. Topher nodded. "Had you lived through that experience with a daughter, you would understand the incredible differences between the female mind and the male. I would caution you in future dealings with women to remember that important fact."

Father stood and poured himself another drink. In a world-weary voice he said, "Once again, Wilhelmina, reality takes precedence over your wishes. The Wagners have been loyal employees and will remain so. As for this silent Joe, the constable from Friendship must be summoned immediately."

Ignoring Father's unsurprising pronouncement, Mena turned to Mr. Topher. "What is your understanding of a *credible witness?*"

Mr. Topher swallowed. "A credible witness would be someone with an appearance of honesty and forthrightness who is competent to give clear solid evidence based on the fact that he or she was actually present and paid sufficient attention. In addition, he or she must be able to adequately express what he or she knows to be the truth."

"And what is your understanding of *solid evidence?*"

"Wilhelmina, enough of this foolishness. Mr. Topher's time is-,"

"That would be," Mr. Topher spoke over Father stunning everyone including himself, "information based on actual facts that preferably can be supported via physical or verbal proof."

"Could evidence be from a doctor or a nurse or a caregiver with a reputation in good standing?"

"Most assuredly," Mr. Topher said.

"Then," Mena said as she stood and faced both men, "as there is no statute of limitations for serious sexual crimes, I would like to accuse my father, Alexander Malcolm St. James, Marquis of Windermere, Earl of Lindsay, of carnal abuse. By my calculations the abuse began when I was of the age of ten and continued on a regular basis through age fifteen. I believe that I qualify as a credible witness as my personal reputation is without blemish. As for evidence, I believe on at least two occasions I was seen by doctors for … injuries sustained. In addition, two of my childhood caregivers are still alive and living on pensions provided by my family for *exceptional services performed*. I believe they would vouch for my … injuries … as well."

Mr. Topher sat amongst the tools of his profession with a look of such utter dismay that Mena worried at one point that he would begin to cry. Father merely took another sip of his rum and began to laugh.

In Polite Society, the home is the basis of morality and a sanctuary free from the corruption of the city. As guardian of the home and family, women are more emotional, dependent, and gentle by nature. This causes women to be more susceptible to disease and illness, including insanity. Proper upper and middle class women should be completely dependent on their husbands and fathers, and their lives should revolve around their role as respectable daughter, housewife, and mother. Little power, control, and independence should be allowed to prevent depression, anxiety, and stress.

Characteristics such as nervousness, eccentricity, and erratic behavior are the earmark of a type of insanity specifically identified as female hysteria. For hysterical women and their families, the asylum offers a convenient and socially acceptable excuse for inappropriate and potentially scandalous behaviour. Rather than being viewed as bad and immoral women, honour and reputation can be maintained by proper diagnosis and commitment to an asylum.

Hanwell is progressive and innovative in its treatments employing the latest technologies, trends, and theories of treatment. At Hanwell, successful surgical procedures have established the facility as a leader in gynaecology. As female reproductive organs are connected to emotional and physical well-being, they are also the cause of mental illness. Combined with the accepted theory that curing the body will indeed cure the mind, treatments for female insanity at the Hanwell are grounded in the belief that removal or correction of the afflicted organ will restore sanity. Gynaecological surgeries, such as hysterectomies, are regular procedures...

Yuh don' set a t'ief to catch a t'ief.

Chapter Twenty-Seven

"Does Mr. Topher know of your time at Hanwell Asylum, Wilhelmina?" Father asked Mena gently and then turned to Mr. Topher. "She was only ten years old but had already begun to exhibit disturbing behaviors which our family doctors could not explain: wetting the bed, refusing to bathe or wear suitable clothes, uncontrollable screaming fits of rage ...

"Both my wife and I were beside ourselves that our only daughter would behave in such an *out of control* and *unacceptable* manner. We decided to take her to the doctors at Hanwell. We told Mena it was just a visit for her to witness some of our philanthropic outreach to the community, but it was actually to have her formally evaluated. I have the reports to this day with our solicitor in England and ... even at that time the doctors were significantly concerned." Father looked at Mena and tapped his chin as if deep in thought. "What was some of the phraseology? Let me see if I can remember ... *Potential danger to herself and others... Unexplainable bursts of rage and emotion ... Female hysteria ...*"

Standing, Father strolled out from behind his desk to stand center stage. "The doctors explained to us that, being female, she was more fragile and sensitive; she needed firm male dominance to make her feel safe and secure. We were encouraged to keep her isolated at home, which we did, and as a result unfortunately, much of her time growing up was spent in bookish pursuits. Her bouts of hysteria continued throughout a significant part of her early adolescence, and the doctors encouraged us to find her a husband as soon as she was of eligible age. But after two unsuccessful seasons, Wilhelmina grew despondent and was unwilling to try a third. She spoke irrationally of "going off to serve God," and violently rejected our attempts to find her a suitable marriage arrangement." Father sighed as if the weight of the world were on his shoulders. "As you can see, Mr. Topher, since she was a child Wilhelmina has had a history of irrational, uncontrollable behavior, been unwilling to listen to sound advice, and consistently refused to acknowledge the responsibilities that her place in society demanded."

Father dropped his voice and said, "I'm sure you are unaware of this, Mr. Topher, but she came here to Barbados *without* our permission or knowledge. We were desperately concerned about her mental and physical well-being - unaware of whether she was alive or dead! Why, the only reason that Lady Windermere and I undertook this perilous journey and traveled all the way to Barbados was to see to our daughter's welfare."

Mena remained standing silently throughout Father's speech; nothing he said was surprising. The threats about Hanwell, the innuendoes about her sanity, and the criticism about failures regarding familial responsibility were the usual songs he sang. Had Mother been present, she would have added to the list her horrible fashion sense, her overall lack of genteel skills, and her inability to be accepted into Polite Society.

She had been only ten years old when Father had taken her to Hanwell *and left her there for two days.* The memories still terrified her as a twenty-four year old woman … Back then she'd been \

a petrified child desperately trying to cope with the shocking, horrifying direction her life had taken with her Father's heinous visits to her in the dark of night. When Father had unceremoniously brought her to Hanwell "to think" she had been beside herself. A nightmarish collection of images remained from that time, with no goodness and no hope. There had been no timeline discussed and no explanation given; just the handing over of his 'disturbed daughter' to the asylum's attendants. When he arrived to retrieve Mena two days later, she had been suitably ... cowed. His message had been thoroughly received: she must always remember that things were not as bad as they seemed, in fact they could be exponentially worse.

But Mena was no longer a terrified ten-year-old child, she was an intelligent, faithful woman. *Who knoweth whether thou art come to the kingdom for such a time as this?* She thought of Rachel, Abigail, Dahlia and the other nameless, faceless women who had suffered under Walter Wagner, and who were far less able to fight the monster. Mena's life had indeed prepared her for such a time as this and God was, as Mr. Topher had said, far greater than her biggest problem.

Smiling his falsely benign smile, Father expected Mena to backtrack and cower like she always had before. She felt her back straighten and her chin thrust out and she took two steps *forward* so that she was almost looking Father eye to eye. Gazing into his startled expression, Mena spoke to Mr. Topher. "I stand by my accusation, Mr. Topher. I am ready to give a full account of the crimes committed. The time for secrets and silence *is finished.* I will be believed ... or I will not ... *but I will speak loudly and clearly* for all to hear. Please call Friendship's constable immediately."

Long moments ensued as Mena and Father stared into each other's green eyes. Finally father sighed and murmured almost to himself, "Well, well; if only my son had the same fortitude. But then I always knew you were the stronger, smarter one. Would that you had been born a man, Wilhelmina," he said with honest regret. "All of our problems would have been solved.

"Very well, I do not wish to *completely* destroy your already questionable reputation, Wilhelmina. The family name need not be dragged through the mud with your outlandish allegations and insane ramblings. As you feel so very strongly about this, I will dismiss the Wagners."

"Immediately. Without references," Mena said instantly.

"Immediately and without references," Father agreed stonily.

"And all charges will be dropped against Silent Joe," Mena pushed.

"Yes, Wilhelmina," Father said with not a little impatience. "I will cede to both of your demands *on one condition.*" Mena stood expectantly, knowing full well what Father would say. It had never occurred to her that Father would not attempt some sort of victory, and as of yet he had none. "You will return to London with me. We cannot have you remain here at Windermere *working* on the property; it's improper … and unseemly."

"No." Her answer was immediate and emphatic.

Father shrugged, breaking eye contact and walking back behind his desk to sit down. "Then you are dismissed." He looked at her smugly and added, "Without references."

In her heart, Mena had known that it would probably come to this. She had only known how to deal with Mrs. Wagner because in some respects it was similar to dealing with Father. Some people were incapable of losing; they always had to have something they could point to as a victory. She nodded in acquiescence. "Dismissal of the Wagners without references and exoneration of Silent Joe in return for my dismissal from Windermere," Mena murmured, "*also* without references."

Father leaned back in his chair. "What are your plans now that you find yourself unemployed?"

"That is none of your concern." Mena turned to Mr. Topher. "Thank you for your assistance in this matter, Mr. Topher. I will collect my things immediately."

Visibly disturbed with the recent events, Mr. Topher looked first at Mena and then at Father. "I would suggest, m'lord, that we summon both the Wagners and Silent Joe immediately. It would only be proper to follow through on all of these decisions considering Miss, Lady Wilhelmina's intended immediate departure."

Mena made a point to sit as if to wait for Father to reject his idea. "Very well," was his frustrated response. "Let us see to this endless tedium."

Silent Joe was the first to arrive, coming hesitantly into the study, eyes wide and uncertain. Mena wondered if he'd ever had the opportunity to be inside the Great House. He relaxed somewhat when he spotted Mena, and she smiled and nodded reassuringly at him. He stood silently and tall in his too-small clothes and bare feet. As she awaited Mr. Toper's return with the Wagners, Mena tried not to think about what would become of Silent Joe and his love of learning with the dissolution of her windmill school. Suddenly she had a thought. Getting up from her chair, she crossed to Father's desk and commandeered a pen, ink, and a piece of paper. "Joe," she said as she approached him, could you write down for me what happened the night with Abigail? Could you tell us *exactly* what you saw?"

Joe looked first at Mena and then at Father sitting stoically at his desk. At last he nodded. Pulling out a chair near the side table, Mena encouraged Joe to sit down, placed all the writing materials next to him, and then joined him at the table.

Walter and Moira Wagner entered the study with Mr. Topher just as Mena sat down. Joe immediately stood at their arrival and looked desperately at Mena who once again smiled and nodded reassuringly, this time with little success. With great trepidation, Joe sat, and at Mena's reassurance laboriously began writing.

"Milord," Walter Wagner said with a bow as Moira executed a curtsy, "how can we be of service?"

Father looked at Mr. Topher. "You handle it," he said dismissively.

Clearing his throat and adjusting his glasses, Mr. Topher said, "Mr. and Mrs. Wagner, the decision has been made to call for your dismissal here at Windermere. As it is still early, you will be given time to get your things in order and then be transported to Friendship at five o'clock. Per Lord Windermere's wishes, neither of you will be given references concerning your past work here at Windermere."

Moira Wagner looked almost as if she was about to faint while Walter Wagner was livid. "I demand to know the reason for our dismissal!"

Mr. Topher hesitated and then looked at Father. Father shrugged and looked at Mena. Mena stood and approached the couple. "The choices that both of you made as to the direction you chose to conduct your lives have finally caught up with you. The female staff here at Windermere will no longer have to live in fear."

Mr. Wagner turned to Silent Joe as he industriously wrote, and then back to look at Father. "You have chosen to take the side of that ignorant nigger? Am I not allowed to defend myself? What evidence convinced you of my guilt?

Have our years of service meant nothing to you, milord? I demand to face the accusers! It is my right!"

"I accuse you," Mena said quietly.

"I have never done you any harm," Mr. Wagner said forcefully. "Why, over the course of your employment I have barely spoken to you."

"Do you deny that you are the father of the child that Elizabeth Freeman carries?" Mena asked.

Walter Wagner let out an explosive laugh. "Most emphatically I do! Is this the accusation she is making? The bitch is desperate to escape the charges regarding theft. Mrs. Wagner caught her red-handed and dismissed her immediately, as was prudent. Thievery among the niggers is a common crime we regularly have to deal with here at the Great House, and must not be tolerated."

"What theft?" Father asked curiously.

"Tell his Lordship, Moira," Mr. Wagner ordered.

"We found in her possessions a silver hairclip that could not possibly belong to the girl," Mrs. Wagner said.

"Why were you searching her possessions?" Mr. Topher inquired.

"Well, after we had dismissed her from the Great Hou-,"

"If you searched her possessions *after* she had been dismissed, then why was she *initially* dismissed?" Mena asked.

Mrs. Wagner glanced at her husband and then back at Mena. "Well, we *suspected* her of theft as a number of things were missing …,"

"Such as?" Mr. Topher asked. "I'm curious because none of this was included in any of your monthly reports."

Mr. Wagner cast a furious glance at his wife. "My wife is
… nowhere near as intelligent as she would have everyone
believe, milord." Moira Wagner's face blushed a furious red at
the blatant insult. "Her capabilities extend only as far as
supervising the darkies on basic household duties; anything else
she does depends purely on what I tell her to do." He smiled
condescendingly at his wife that caused Mena to start with
shock; it was the same smile her father had directed at her
numerous times. *Keep silent. Remember that I am the authority here
and you are nothing.*

"My wife is a … jealous woman. She married … far
above her station … and consequently has always felt as if her
position – as both my wife and as head housekeeper - is tenuous.
Despite *constant* reassurances to the contrary I am continually
faced with-,'

"My pardon for interrupting you, Mr. Wagner, but I am
unable to see how personal problems between you and your wife
figure in to this discussion." Father's voice was both bored and
impatient.

Mr. Wagner bowed. "I understand, milord, and I
appreciate your patience." He stepped away from his wife. "I
have struggled for many years with the truth of my wife's
paternity, which she kept from me until after we were married.
As a result, both her character and intelligence have always been
suspect to me." Mrs. Wagner's gasp of outrage drew everyone's
attention briefly, although Mr. Wagner did not hesitate in his
revelation. "I was unaware that she was of … *mixed race* …
milord, and that her mother is a rather infamous woman of ill
repute in Bridgeton." Mr. Wagner glanced at his wife who stood
frozen with shock, and then back at Father. "She still resides
and practices her trade there."

Mr. Wagner extended both his hands in supplication.
"What was I to do with this painfully shocking discovery,

milord? I could not risk the disgrace of divorce, which would certainly have destroyed my cherished career here at Windermere. For these past years I have done my best to endure; trying to meet my responsibilities as butler while at the same time dealing with the questionable character of my wife and the ignominious specter of her *history.*"

Moira Wagner remained upright as her husband proceeded to destroy every vestige of her reputation. The silence in the room as he paused to draw a breath, aside from the scratching of Joe's pen, was complete. "There have been … accusations … over these past years of my dedicated service to Windermere … of improprieties involving theft, as well as," he glanced at Joe, his meaning clear, "… other *situations.* In each and every instance I have been forced to weigh the issue of truth versus reality. Are the circumstances truly as they appear or are they … my wife's manipulations of the truth?"

Had Mena not spent her entire life watching Father manipulate the truth, she would have felt some pity for poor Walter Wagner. Instead, she looked at Moira Wagner and was shocked to feel some semblance of kinship with the woman. Standing, she said, "Mrs. Wagner, do you have anything to say?"

As if rousing from a dream, Mrs. Wagner looked first at her husband's back and then to Mena. "I never had the gift of being able to twist the truth into some semblance of believability," she said rather absently, "that was always Walter's great skill. I was always too busy merely trying to survive…"

Joe touched Mena's arm at that moment and handed her a piece of paper covered with his childish, albeit legible scrawl. It took her a moment to understand what he had written and then she began to shake with horror.

I see him kil ivy

I keep maree jeen safe

He hert lily

He hert dalya

He hert fancee may

He hert peach

He hert racel

I stop him hert abgale

Joe

Yuh can' hide from a t'ief, but yuh kin hide from a liar.

Chapter Twenty-Eight

As Mena stepped forward to give Mr. Topher Joe's paper, Mr. Wagner turned abruptly toward her. Before anyone had time to think, Joe rushed forward and wrapped his massive arms around Mr. Wagner, holding him tightly.

"Get your filthy, black hands off me!" roared Mr. Wagner as he struggled with little effect. "Remember what happened the last time you dared to touch me!"

In a deep, rich voice Joe said distinctly, "Yuh not hurt da teacha."

"What's the meaning of this?" Father said, while at the same time Mena hastily handed Mr. Topher the paper.

The room was silent except for the sounds of Mr. Wagner's ineffectual struggles as Mr. Topher read what Mena had given him. At last he sighed and walked towards Father. "This changes things, milord, as the constable must be summoned immediately," he said, passing him the paper. "As early as thirty years ago slaves could give evidence in court, and this is clearly evidence."

"What is the lying scum accusing me of?" Mr. Wagner spat out. "Whatever he accuses me of, my wife will defend me! Moira! Speak up!"

Father looked at Mr. Wagner. "What wife?" he asked pointedly. "It would seem that she has left you to face these charges on your own."

Mena also took her leave as Mr. Topher gave directions to Joe and called for further assistance in sending to Friendship for the constable,. She had, unfortunately, packing to do.

"I'm ta tell yuh dat Lord Windermere wants ta talk wit yuh, Missy Me-, a, er," Jessie Lynn stood in Mena's doorway and looked positively frantic as she struggled to determine what exactly she was to call her. The word as to Mena's true identity was out.

"Please continue to call me what you were calling me before, Jessie Lynn. It's what I prefer."

"Yas, miss it's jus' dat now dat I know yuh a lady an' all it jus' don' seem right."

"Well, Dahlia's agreed and so has Mary Jean, so don't you think you could give it a try?"

Jessie Lynn nodded without conviction. "Mistah Topher an' da Lord are waitin' on yuh in da study. Dey been talkin' for hours an da constable jus' lef' wit Mr. Wagner." Jessie Lynn paused for a moment. "Never in mah whole life have I been so happy ta see da back a someone as him. An' Mrs. Wagner bein' gone is jus' icin' on da cake."

Mena looked up from latching her valise. "Is she really gone?"

"Oh yas! She gone an' her room is as empty as a po' man's purse. Elijah said he saw her walkin' down da main road when he was seein' ta da wes' garden dis afta'noon. She had her fancy travel hat on an' was carryin' a bag."

Mena walked toward Jessie Lynn. "Well, let's see what His Lordship wants to say to me."

They were waiting for her. Father stood with his back to the room, gazing out at the front gardens while Mr. Topher sat idly sipping a cup of tea. "Thank you for coming," Mr. Topher said and motioned to the tea pot. "Can I offer you a cup?"

"Yes, thank you," Mena said as she sat down.

"His Lordship and I have had time to discuss the situation here at Windermere and we realize that we are in a significant bind." Mr. Topher gave Mena a very pointed look as if he was trying to communicate something subtly to her. "We were wondering if you were willing to postpone your departure by a few ... weeks."

"Mr. Topher, my departure is only at Father's insistence. You make it sound as if I'm leaving by my own design. Father's stipulation that I leave Windermere was the only way he would agree to my 'demands.'"

"Yes, well, in the light of these most recent events there has been some ... reconsideration ... We realize that Windermere is at a severe disadvantage as the result of the past ... month's events ... with the devastation of the cholera, the disappearance of Mr. Rhyder, and now the dismissal of Mr. & Mrs. Wagner ...,"

"As well as myself," Mena added as she took a sip of her tea.

"Yes, well, Lord Windermere has met with Isaac, who assures him that *for the time being* he is more than confident that he can handle responsibilities in the field until either Mr. Rhyder returns or until a suitable replacement for Mr. Rhyder can be hired. But as Mrs. Wagner was responsible for the house staff and *all accounts* here at Windermere, there is no one who can handle such an enormous responsibility in the interim. We were wondering if you would be willing to assume this job."

Mena looked first at Mr. Topher and then turned to look at Father's still back. She recognized that posture even though she had seen it only on a very few occasions; it was the posture of furious defeat. Still staring at Father's back, Mena said clearly, "Why not ask Gabriel?"

"Gabriel leaves on the first packet boat to Bridgeton to sail back to England," Father said without turning around. "He's needed in London."

Taking another sip from her teacup and then carefully setting it down, Mena stood so she could stand and face Father's back. "No."

That made him turn around. "Why the bloody hell not?" he ground out.

"I will not assume a position where you can, on a whim, send me packing at the first change in your mood or your circumstances. One thing my time here at Windermere has taught me is that distance does not keep you from controlling me; only distance *and severing of ties* will truly accomplish that."

"What," Father began taking steps towards her in fury, "are you going to move into some tiny little hovel in town and begin again with your asinine plan to educate the darkies?"

Mena took two steps forward so that she could see the fine wrinkles around Father's mouth and eyes. She realized she had never seen him this furious, as they stood looking at each other. In the past, his fury caused great terror. He had been so very angry with her when she had begun to act out as a child. After he had begun to … His fury had prompted him to take his ten-year-old daughter to a lunatic asylum *and leave her there.*

After that, Father's fury had been a thing to avoid; to acquiesce to *no matter the horrible costs. I am free,* Mena thought suddenly and clearly. *I am free of this man for the rest of my life. Thank you God for my small inheritance that will see me through to do what you wish me to do. I do not ever need to deal with this man again.* "Yes," Mena finally responded to Father's question, and she was unable to hold back a smile, "that is exactly what I plan to do." And she turned to leave.

"Perhaps," Mr. Topher said just as Mena reached the door, "a business arrangement can be drawn up that would satisfy the both of you…"

꧁꧂꧁꧂꧁꧂꧁꧂꧁꧂

Graham got as close as Friendship, an hour ride from Windermere, and couldn't bring himself to go any further. The hard-won confidence that he had amassed over these past eight weeks seemed to disappear like the early morning mists. What if Mena would not speak to him? What if, in light of eight weeks to consider things, Mena now fully embraced Graham's previously poor opinion of himself and his abilities? What if Mena was *no longer present?* What if she had succumbed to the cholera? No amount of confidence would enable him to stand again at the grave of another woman he loved.

The questions bombarded him with the effectiveness as knife thrusts, leaving him shaking with insecurity. Sitting on Dancer in the center of Friendship, Graham had a pitifully choice of options: there was the general store, the saloon, the blacksmith's shop, the church or he could turn around like the coward he was rapidly becoming and return from whence he came. He sighed, and Dancer pulled on the reins as if to say, "Come on, man, make up your mind."

"We both know where I need to go," Graham said with resignation as he nudged Dancer forward.

"It's a pleasure to make your acquaintance, Mr. Rhyder," Reverend Samuels said. He was a portly gentleman, almost as round as he was tall, with kindly brown eyes and a shock of graying hair that stuck directly out of the top of his head. He looked nothing like a minister when Graham had found him out behind the parsonage. He was knee deep in his garden and singing hymns at the top of his lungs in his stained trousers and billowing white shirt. Now they sat in the shade of the church on a bench. "I'm glad you found me back here, which is one of the reasons I sing. There's only so much sitting one can do inside a church, and then one must go out and make the most of God's beautiful world." He took a sip of water from the pail at his side and then offered the dipper to Graham.

After Graham had quenched his thirst he began rather hesitantly, "I'm the manager at Windermere, but I've been-,"

"Oh you've been away for *weeks*," Reverend Samuels said with a grin. "Everyone is full of curiosity as to what you've been up to. The speculation runs rampant each Sunday." He winked. "I think even a few bets have been cast."

Graham couldn't help but laugh. "Is that so? What are the options?"

Reverend Samuels waved his hand dismissively. "Oh, all manner of things: off to find a long lost love, off to tie on a good long drink, off to work the Panama Canal, and there are some who seem to think you jumped off a cliff or some such craziness."

Graham looked off into the distance. "I suppose any one of those are a viable option, but I'd take the cliff option before the canal option."

Reverend Samuels grinned. "Don't blame you, my boy! Hellish conditions there, I hear; nothing in Barbados is as bad."

"Not true, sir, but you'll have to take my word for that as I'm not interested in providing details."

The preacher nodded and pulled a handkerchief out of his trouser pocket to mop his brow and face. "Rest assured that we all have demons to run from, young man. Come inside. I was just about to sit down to my noon meal and am always appreciative of a bit of conversation." Reverend Samuels stood and disappeared inside without giving Graham an opportunity to accept or reject the offer.

The parsonage was a small living area off the back of the church which Graham would have guessed had been a barn or a shed. Inside was one room that served as kitchen, dining room, bedroom and sitting room. While not opulent by any standard, it was not lost on Graham that in the same amount of space the preacher had managed to make a far more comfortable home than Graham had ever accomplished with his hut. "Plates and cutlery are on the shelf over there," Reverend Samuels said over his shoulder as he removed the lid from a pot on top of the stove, releasing a delicious aroma.

"From the smell, you apparently are a great cook," Graham said as he set the table. "Do you preach as well as you cook?" he joked.

"Well, had you come to one of my sermons you might be able to answer that question yourself, young man." Reverend Samuels softened the rebuke with a smile and a wink. "You'd also know that I'm a widower who enjoys the ministrations of a number of kindly townsfolk who have taken pity on my blatant inability to cook anything edible. In fact, this place used to be the church stable." Setting the steaming pot in the center of the table, he laughed, "I burned down the parsonage two years ago trying to cook myself some rice and beans." Leaning over he whispered delightedly, "You should also know that I'm one of *the* most eligible widowers in town."

They spent a delightful meal laughing and talking about nothing in particular. As they leaned back in their chairs, replete with the widow Pamela Smitton's lamb stew sitting heavily in their bellies, the Reverend finally asked the question Graham had been waiting for. "What can I do for you, Graham? Why have you stopped by to see Friendship's Reverend whom you've worked so to hard avoid me until now?"

"I've come a long way, and now that I'm finally close to my final destination I've begun to doubt myself. Again." He shrugged. "Still."

"The devil likes to toy with us, you know. His only goal in life is to keep us from doing what the Good Lord wants us to do. He just wants us to hesitate, doubt, reconsider, stall and finally stop. Defeat isn't always a massive disaster; it's more often one small decision to not proceed." He sat and studied Graham for a moment. "Might I ask what your 'final destination' is?"

With pride, Graham said, "I need to tell Miss Mena Westwood that I love her and that everything she's been trying to tell me is absolutely right."

"Don't you mean Lady Wilhelmina Constance Westwood Windermere? Mistress of Windermere Plantation?"

Graham looked at the reverend's serious expression and swallowed. "Mistress of Windermere?"

Reverend Samuels nodded. "I don't know how she's managed it but yes; she has been so for the past five or six weeks. Lord Windermere – both father and son – departed a number of weeks ago for London, leaving her as the sole authority there. Aside from your whereabouts it's the biggest piece of gossip in the town and in the surrounding parish. First, a single woman has been put in command of such a large holding, and second, regarding the extraordinary changes that seem to be taking place almost daily."

Graham sat forward. "Extraordinary changes?"

Standing, Reverend Samuels began clearing the table. "Oh, some of it I find just too incredible to repeat! What I know for a fact are that aside from Mistress Windermere, *all* other employees are now native Bajans – all with significant salary increases." He turned and gave Graham a rather apologetic smile. "I understand that your home has been given to the new manager."

"New manager?" Graham repeated.

The reverend nodded. "Yes, Isaac Freeman and his family have already begun building an addition onto it."

"Isaac is the new manager?"

"You've been gone over eight weeks, Graham," Reverend Samuels said gently.

"I know," he swallowed, "I just … I've been …"

"Morning schooling is now mandatory for all children up through age fourteen except during the months of harvest. The children are divided now by age and ability and attend either Mistress Windermere's or Mrs. Topher's classroom-,"

"There are *two* teachers now?"

"Well, Mistress Windermere certainly can't conduct classes for such a large, diverse group of children. I thought it was a rather ingenious decision to make use of both windmills, as the Tophers now reside on the plantation's property-,"

"The Tophers now live at Windermere?"

"Yes, I believe Mr. Topher still sees to his numerous clients throughout the parish and surrounding areas, but they now reside with Mistress Windermere in the Great House. They regularly attend church here on Sundays and Mrs. Topher is extremely pleased with the new arrangements; as apparently Mr. Topher's significant absences were becoming somewhat of a concern now that they are expecting a child."

Graham stood and placed his hat on his head. "I had better go."

"Has your destination changed, Graham?"

Graham closed his eyes. "I, I don't honestly know, Reverend."

"Let me ask you a few things. I'd like to give you a few things to consider regarding your destination. First, are any of these things that you have just heard about Windermere *contrary* to what you would expect from 'your' Miss Mena Westwood, even though she now bears the title of Mistress of Windermere?"

Graham snorted. "Hardly."

"All right. Second, what have you discovered about yourself in these past weeks that made you confident enough to travel within an hour of your 'final destination'?"

Graham turned to look at the kindly preacher and swallowed. It had taken visits to both Nate as well as Sir Russell to reach the point where he could *believe it*. It was a whole other thing to be able to say it out loud. "That I'm forgiven," he said quietly. "That I'm loved. That I have good to offer others. That I would be a better man were I to be given a chance to walk beside Mena."

Reverend Samuel put his hands on his hips. "Do you really think that eight short weeks away is going to change the state of 'your' Miss Mena Westwood's heart, Graham Rhyder?"

When Graham remained silent, the preacher stomped his foot. *"Do you?"*

Graham felt his back straighten and his chin jut out. "No sir."

Nodding his head, Reverend Samuel said, "There is your answer then, young man." As Graham stepped out into the bright sunshine he heard, "And I'll see you at church on Sunday!"

The Rochdale Principles (Established 1844)[11]

1. Voluntary and Open Membership: Cooperative Societies must have open and voluntary membership.

2. Democratic Member Control: Cooperatives must have democratic member control. One member = one vote.

3. Member Economic Participation: Members equitably contribute the capital of their cooperative. Surplus economy (i.e. profits) are managed by the members to develop the cooperative, support other organizations, or returned to the members.

4. Autonomy: Cooperatives must be autonomous and independent. If they enter into partnerships with other organizations it must be on terms that ensure democratic control by their members.

5. Education, Training and Information: Cooperatives must provide education and training to their members.

6. Cooperation among Cooperatives: Cooperatives are autonomous organizations, but they work together to facilitate communication across cooperatives and strengthen the cooperative movement.

7. Concern for the Community: Cooperatives must be responsible partners for their communities. Decisions must benefit the larger community.

No one is perfect until yuh fall in love wit them.

Chapter Twenty-Nine

She didn't have a single place to go to find peace. Not that she was actually complaining, but sometimes a person just needed a place to go to be silent, to commune with God, and to have a few moments to hear her own heartbeat.

Mena had tried Graham's cliff walk, which had not only terrified her, but much to her horror she'd encountered little Mary and Ruth (praying loudly for safety) on her panicked return topside, so that was out. Anyplace in the Great House – whether it was on the top floor where her old room used to be or in the root cellar out back – always guaranteed that *someone* had seen her and could direct others to her. The Windmill School – now a busy two-windmill establishment - was always bustling with people coming and going. Audrey regularly held "reading parties" in which all manner of folk showed up to hear her read "stimulating passages" from her favorite stories. Much to Mena's embarrassment, even the privy was out as on at least three instances lately she'd encountered someone waiting outside to ask her a question.

The workers' village was unthinkable as it had become a site of barely organized chaos. Mena could not have anticipated what the offer of small plots of Windermere land – to work on and eventually own outright over time – had created. Many families had immediately moved out of the village, willing to live in temporary housing, just to be able to say they were *on their own land*. The Windermere Plantation Cooperative that Mr. Topher had introduced and explained to Mena was something people were only just beginning to understand and get excited about, and many of the former huts were slowly being transformed into small businesses. Mr. Topher had established an office in one, refusing Mena's offer of the Great House's study. Silent Joe, no longer silent but still very hesitant to speak much, had established his own business as a jack-of-all-trades fixit man who was also strong enough and tall enough to handle things most other men couldn't. Elizabeth had surprised everyone by refusing to move to Graham's old cabin with the rest of the Freeman family, instead preferring to stay in the old family hut. Rachel had confided to Mena that she suspected that Silent Joe was doing more than just helping Elizabeth renovate the place… Most recently, Mena had heard talk of a general store …

All this was why she had taken to regularly walking out and standing in the middle of a cane field all by herself. It was the only place and time that she could be still and quiet. Mena found that spending time talking and listening to God was essential to the quality of her day. Days that she made the effort, carved out the time, and trudged out to the center of a field were the days that felt focused, purposeful, *possible*. Days that she didn't often left her sleepless with anxiety over what she'd committed herself to.

Father was gone from Barbados, but only as far as London, waiting patiently, confident of her inevitable failure over this "ludicrous venture." If it were just herself at risk Mena would have had little concern, but literally every human being who had committed to Windermere Plantation Cooperative had put his or her life in her hands. She had talked with them before she had agreed, and signed the formal documents with Father.

She had told them about the risks that could destroy them all, and would put them in a situation that was more precarious that they could imagine. *Only one bad year* without a profit, one year when they would be unable to pay Father the agreed upon percentage of profits, and the deal would become null and void. Windermere would revert back to his control, and *every single one of them would be put off the property*. It was the single biggest leap of faith she had ever taken, and it made getting on a ship and traveling to Barbados seem like a vacation.

On bad days Mena felt as if she were balancing on the roof of the Great House with hurricane winds blowing.

Not one person had blinked at the terrible implications of failure. *"Commit yuhr works ta da LORD!²"* someone had shouted from the crowd, and there had been roars of agreement. All they had heard were the fabulous opportunities: for them to own a plot of land outright, to be their own bosses and to shape their own destiny. They refused to be intimidated by the seemingly impossible need to have *twenty-five good years* with exceptional profits. *(Dear God! Please!)* In the twenty-sixth year the deal could not be reverted and the only obligation would be the continual share of the profits. If all went well, in twenty-five years Windermere Plantation would belong to Mena and be half its present size, surrounded on almost all sides by small independently owned farms.

On good days Mena saw only the shining eyes of her friends and co-workers who had never dreamed of being able to claim possession of *anything*, let alone precious farm land.

How could she ask God for *twenty-five years* of profit? What *had* she been thinking? Which was why she was standing in head-high sugar cane trying to calm her head and her heart instead of doing one of the million things that needed to be done. Today had been a bad day, and Father's confident smile and incredulous joy over her agreeing to such a deal ate at her from the inside out. Even with Mr. Topher in residence and Audrey's help at the Windmill School, Mena sometimes felt so incredibly overwhelmed by the responsibility that it almost brought her to her knees with the worry of it all.

Who knoweth whether thou art come to the kingdom for such a time as this?

Maisy's voice whispered to Mena on the wind and rattled through the cane stalks.

Who knoweth whether thou art come to the kingdom for such a time as this?

The question, for Mena, always seemed to demand an answer. Bowing her head, Mena said quietly, "Here I am Lord, send me." She felt tears form and trail quietly down her cheeks.

Usually, standing out here was the only time she let herself miss Graham. Mena could never escape the feeling that God had sent her to Windermere not only to do these wonderful things, but also to learn of true love. She worried endlessly for Graham and prayed for him constantly. *Keep him safe, Lord. Keep him well, Lord. Let him find happiness, Lord. Let him know love again, Lord.* Mena missed everything about him, from his teasing to his conversations to his observations and challenges…

Love is the only thing in the world worth living for.

Mena turned to make her way back to the Great House as she wiped away her tears with the back of her hand. Dahlia would have dinner waiting and Jessie Lynn would have started to heat the water for her nightly bath – one of the few luxuries she had resumed from her 'old' life.

She stopped dead.

There, on the edge of the field sitting astride Dancer was Graham. Too far to see his face clearly, she could still tell that he scanned the field. Part of her wanted to run to him. Another part of her wanted to sit down quickly so that he wouldn't see her.

Why was he here?

In the end she stood frozen as Graham scanned the fields and waited for him to eventually spot her. When he finally did, he stopped dead still and … just sat there looking directly at her.

She felt her back stiffen and her chin jut out, and as much as she wanted to run toward him, her feet remained rooted to the ground. *I'm not coming to you,* Mena made herself say. *You get off that horse and come to me. You left. I stayed. You ran. I fought.*

"I LOVE YOU, MENA WESTWOOD!" Graham suddenly shouted. "I CAME BACK TO TELL YOU THAT." When Mena didn't move or respond, Graham dismounted Dancer and began to make his way through the cane. "YOU WERE RIGHT," she heard him shout, "ABOUT EVERYTHING." Still she stood frozen, suddenly fearful that all of this was just a dream; a figment of her broken heart and hopeful imagination. "I WANT TO WALK BESIDE YOU FOR THE REST OF MY LIFE." And then, more quietly, "If you'll still have me…"

And then there he was in front of her, blue eyes shaded by the ever-present hat. "I hear you gave my job and my hut away," was the first thing he said when he stopped just out of reach of her.

"Say it again," Mena said fiercely. "All of it. *Every single word.*"

He grinned at her, something that she was fairly certain she'd never seen him do. "I love you, Mena Westwood. I came back to tell you that. You were right, about everything." He came one step closer and the cane crackled. "I want to walk beside you for the rest of my life … if you'll have me." He leaned forward and kissed her gently on the cheek and whispered, "Would you do me the greatest honor of becoming my wife?"

Mena stepped forward taking his beloved face in her hands. "Oh, yes," she breathed as she leaned in and kissed him, and then kissed him again. Graham crushed her to him and Mena inhaled the wonderful male scent of him. "You came back to me," she whispered against his neck.

Pulling back, Graham searched her face. "I never left you, Mena, I just had to go and *find myself*. You deserve a *whole man* … not necessarily a perfect one, mind you, but at least a whole one. When I realized that I had been completely wrong about almost everything in my life – except loving you – I had to take some time to get myself together. I'd left pieces of myself all over this damn island, so I made my own little pilgrimage and retrieved them all bit by bit. In the process, I was able to see how right you were; there has been an awful lot of darkness, but there have also been so many wonderful points of light."

As he gathered her into his arms again, he whispered against her hair, "I'm … at peace with things now. I … understand … why faith is so important to you. I … want to … walk beside you for as long as God will let me. I'm a better man with you, Mena."

"And I'm a better woman with you," she said through a voice choked with tears. They took a long time there in the cane to enjoy the ability to hold each other.

As they turned to walk hand in hand back to Dancer, Graham laughed and pointed to the left. "We seem to have an audience," and pulling off his hat, he waved it enthusiastically to the collection of people – adults and children – standing in front of the Windmill School. Grinning, Mena waved, too, and a cheer went up from the collective group. Mena turned to Graham and grinned. "Welcome home, my love. *Welcome home!*"

About The Story

On a business trip with my husband to Barbados in 2013 we spent one late afternoon driving randomly around the island. I was in particularly bad spirits as a terrible cold had interfered with just about every aspect of the trip. As I sat miserably in the passenger seat with my massive pile of tissues, we unwittingly drove  literally to the end of the top of the island. The dirt road just suddenly stopped. As I climbed out of the car (while my husband maneuvered a k-turn) and stood amidst the windswept fields that surrounded me, Windermere Plantation was born. As I climbed back into the car in a decidedly better mood, I said, "I've got a story," to which my husband said delightedly, "Here we go!"

The next day I began my research visiting the lovely St. Nicholas Abbey - a 350-year-old working sugar cane plantation. By departure day my head was already filled with the sounds of sugar cane blowing in the breeze, the smell of raw molasses as it

was being turned into rum, and the whispering ghosts of those long passed who had walked through the halls of St. Nicholas' Great House and wandered its extensive gardens. I didn't think twice about the two old windmills we'd seen until much later.

At the airport, with a bag full of books and pamphlets for my research, I found another book and went to purchase it. The young cashier girl at the shop, noting its title, *Bajan Proverbs* by Margot Blackman, jokingly said something to me which I couldn't understand. Another girl joined her and, giggling, they said it again ever so s-l-o-w-l-y for my untrained ears. *Yuh nevah miss da watah till da well run dry.* They were quoting me a Bajan proverb!

I almost always have my main characters before I begin to write the story, and many authors will tell you, it's often the characters themselves that steer the story. Fascinated with the Red Leg/Bakro history I learned about, I was easily able to incorporate that into Graham's background. (I chose to use "Bakro" versus "Red Leg" when labeling his heritage because from my understanding "Bakro" was more derogatory and consequently fit Graham's personality. "Red Leg" – a label given to the first slaves who arrived from Ireland in their kilts and ended up getting severely sunburned as a result - is often the more common label.) There are still isolated communities of native Bajans with white skin and blue eyes who live in Barbados in abject poverty and have never intermixed.[13] Their quality of life is, if possible, just as dismal if not worse than what it was during Mena's time.[14]

From the start, Mena had secrets even from me and while you might find this odd, I struggled to "figure her out." Not until she sat in the Freeman's home and talked with young Elizabeth about what she had endured at the hands of Father did I come to truly understand the real Mena. She had determined to be a woman who was so rooted in her faith that nothing and no one could deter her from her call. She was a woman who had decided to rise above the horrors of her life and become stronger, rather than let them break her. Making her passionately faithful, she held onto God's promises with every fiber of her being, which forged her into a force to be reckoned with.

Giving her victory over Father in the form of transforming Windermere Plantation into something she would be proud of was the best kind of vindication I could think to give her. While Windermere Plantation was a fictional place, in reality, in 1841 Bajan plantation owner Reynold Alleyne Elcock bequeathed that the laborers on his land should be able to purchase land on his estate. Fourteen years later in 1855 Peter Chapman did the same thing. Because of the generous foresight of these two gentlemen, the first two real free villages of Barbados were established. I saw no reason to not have Mena do the same thing.

The Rochdale Principals are a set of ideals established by the first successful cooperative – the Rochdale Society of Equitable Pioneers in 1844 in England. I was surprised and pleased to find a copy of them in England and on these same principles cooperatives around the world operate to this day.

The Bajan sugar cane industry, in case you're wondering, remained healthy and strong in Barbados up until about 1884, so Mena's "Windermere Plantation Cooperative" should have made their twenty-five year agreement with Father, easily. ☺

Despite the formal emancipation of the slaves in Barbados on August 1, 1838, conditions did not improve. In fact, every resource I read stressed how much worse things became. The Plantocracy, the ruling white elite class on the island, did not acquiesce graciously, but instead made numerous attempts to prevent any loss of their believed rights, privileges, and profits. When I have Mena acknowledge that "Some people were incapable of losing; they always had to have something they could point to as a victory," I was thinking of the endless attempts to thwart any progress for the working class for *decades* after emancipation.

There was a terrible cholera epidemic in Barbados in 1854 in which over 20,000 people died. At the time, Bridgetown, Barbados had the distinction of being the most unsanitary town in the West Indies; once the crisis was over the Board of Health was dismissed and a new one was appointed. Tourists who travel to Barbados and stay at the Cobblers Cove Hotel, the Lemington Villa, the Camelot Suites, or St. Peter's Bay Condos should know that these were the actual sites of the graveyards used to hastily bury the many who perished. One author wrote of his memories as a child of seeing skulls and bones unearthed on the beach after particularly rough seas.[15]

Hanwell Pauper and Lunatic Asylum, built in West London, opened amidst much fanfare in 1831 with twenty-four male patients and eighteen female patients. By 1841 there was a staff of 90 looking after 1,302 patients.[16] While it had impressive results in its pioneering work, such as "therapeutic employment" with its own carpentry, bakery and brewery along with many other services, it also adhered to the concept of 'female hysteria.'

In 1859, it was claimed that a quarter of all women suffered from this affliction, which manifested itself in the form of faintness, nervousness, insomnia, fluid retention, heaviness in the abdomen, muscle spasms, shortness of breath, irritability, loss of appetite for food,[17] nervous, eccentric, erratic behavior,[18] choking, loss of speech, vertigo, knee problems, headaches, heartburn, pulse irregularities, and even death.[19] Horribly, one of the believed causes of this upper class women's affliction was a "wandering womb" (Hippocrates conceived of it). It was the belief that the uterus could move freely within a woman's body causing lunacy. One of the primary cures for this affliction by the 1800s was a hysterectomy. In the stifling confines of the Victorian Age, commitment to an asylum offered "hysterical women and their families … a convenient and socially acceptable remedy for inappropriate, and potentially scandalous behavior."[20]

One of my favorite scenes in the book is when Mena shouts at Graham, "You're a coward, Graham Rhyder! You're afraid to let yourself be happy, afraid to acknowledge the goodness in this world, and afraid to believe that God might have plans specifically with you in mind. You'd just rather wallow in your own misery, content to collect only the awful around you and ignore all of the good." It is a personal prayer that I, too, could be that strong in my understanding of what God wants for me in my life, that despite abject heartbreak I could stand tall and confident. Mena's only concession is when she says, "I don't *need* you, Graham Rhyder, but I had begun to think it would be so wonderful to *stand beside you*." Truly she is a woman worth admiring, no?

I had Graham say at one point, "*All I know besides drinking is sugar cane. Was born in the midst of it. Grew up working it. Was finely educated thanks to it. For a short time before the bottle claimed me, I made a living for a while as a result of it. Lately, I've enjoyed the drunk I could gain from the rum produced by it.*" It seemed perfectly appropriate to me that I would have him declare his love for Mena in the midst of a field of sugar cane, too.

Towards the end (around Chapter Twenty-Seven) I began looking for a suitable image for the book's cover. I needed something with windmills but also something with a tropical island theme. Stumbling on Jill Tattersall's wonderful painting, *Cows at the Old Windmill,* I sat at my computer and just smiled. Here it was! The perfect picture! My mind went back to the first moments when the story came to me and the two very vocal cows that were not particularly happy about our presence! On a prayer, I emailed Jill asking permission to use her painting and was delighted to be able to come to a financial agreement with her. I shared my delight over all this with my supportive Bible study group and one generous, loving, sister-in-Christ (who demanded to remain anonymous) insisted on giving me the full dollar amount I needed to meet my financial agreement with Jill Tattersall. When I think of this friend, Luke 6:38 comes to mind: *Give, and you will receive. Your gift will return to you in full—pressed down, shaken together to make room for more, running over, and poured into your lap. The amount you give will determine the amount you get back.*

Finally, all scripture you find throughout this story are precious verses to me, so I made them precious to Mena. I hope that God's Word plays a vital role in your life for comfort, inspiration, guidance, and assurance.

I hope you enjoyed Windermere Plantation! Write to me and let me know!

Sue McGeown

susanmcgeown@faithinspiredbooks.com

Story Timeline

		Historical Facts	Fictional Story Events
	1605	Captain of a British ship, the *Olive Blossom*, claimed the island for James I	
	1620	First slaves arrive on the island with the first white settlers.	
	1627	Called "Tobacco Island", Barbados was settled by the English.	
	1628	"Young gentlemen" arrive, build houses and fortifications and plant tobacco. They recruited indentured servants in England, Wales, Scotland and Ireland.	
	1636	First Irish indentured servants from Kinsale, Ireland – 120 total. Sold for approximately £7 per head.	
	1637	Sugar introduced to Barbados by a Dutchman. Originally grown for animal fodder and to make a sweet drink for the locals.	
	1650	Black slave population 5680	
	1649	Cromwell invades Ireland	
	1652	"The ethnic cleansing of Ireland" begins on 24 August 1652. In the brief period between 1652 and 1659, tens of thousands of men, women and children were transported to British colonies in Antigua, Montserrat, Barbados, and other locations throughout the Caribbean Islands.[21]	
	1701	By 1701, out of the roughly 25,000 slaves present on the island's plantations, about 21,700 of them were of European descent.[22]	
	1748	The term "Red Legs" is first mentioned in 1798.	

1780		*Walter Wagner's great grandfather hired to be butler to the Marquis St. James, Lord St. James' father.*
1805		*Bridget Rhyder born as a slave onto Forster Hall Plantation*
1807	Abolition of slave trade in Barbados	
1816	Slave Rebellion on Barbados: April 14th Sunday	
1816	92% of slave population on Barbadoes was creole	*Bridget Rhyder (15) catches the eye of Lord Phillip Walcott, owner of Forster Hall Plantation*
1820		*Graham Rhyder born to Bridget Rhyder.*
1823	William Shrewsbury, a Methodist minister on Barbados, had his chapel destroyed by angry whites for teaching slave children to read and write.	
1824	Barbados Assembly Consolidated Slave Law: the way in which slaves are governed: • Can own property • Can give evidence in courts in all case • Reduction in manumission fees	
1825	"The lower whites of the island are without exception the most degraded, worthless, hopeless race I have ever met with in my life. They are more pressing subjects for legislation than the slaves."[23]	

1826	Consolidates Slave Law revised & approved by Secretary for the Colonies William Huskisson • Slaves can be flogged, • Whites could be prosecuted for killing slaves • Right of slave owners to imprison slaves for unlimited periods • Prohibition of slave gatherings after dark and holding social functions without a legal permit	
1829		*Mena Westwood Born*
1830		
1831	Political rights given to Jews, free coloured and free blacks.	*Graham Rhyder (11) taken in by Lord Phillip Walcott as bastard son and educated*
1832	In 1832 Cholera reached London and the United Kingdom (where more than 55,000 people died) and Paris. In London, the disease claimed 6,536 victims and came to be known as "King Cholera".[24]	
1833	Barbados Board of Health established.	
1833	May: Emancipation Bill introduced to the House of Commons by E.G. Stanley (Lord Derby), Secretary Of State for Colonies	
1834	August 1: Emancipation Act: all slaves, black and coloured under the age of 6 years, would be totally and unconditional emancipated; furthermore, all slaves over the age of 6 years were also freed, but under the stipulation that they were to serve their former owners as apprentices for the period of 12 years (later changed to 4 years). Wages would not be paid to apprentices except for additional work conducted in their free time.	

	Masters were to carry on providing material subsistence for apprentices.	
1835	Barbados exports 17,234 tons of sugar	
1836	Unlawful to apprentice children or for parents to offer their children as apprentices.	
1838	August 1st Emancipation • 83,000 blacks • 12,000 coloureds • 15,000 whites	
1838	Barbados sugar export increases to 23,679 tons Only ONE of the 297 major sugar plantations was owned by a non-white, namely Ellis Castle. (480 acres)	
1939		*Graham Rhyder's (19) schooling finished.* *Bridget Rhyder (34) dies.*
1841	There is one steam factory mill on Barbados. Steam produced between 12 to 18 % more sugar than the traditional windmills.	
1841	Despite the reluctance, occasional land would come up for sale. Particularly, in 1841, Reynold Alleyne Elcock bequeathed that the labourers on his land should be able to purchase land on his estate. Fourteen years later, Peter Chapman followed suit, and these two men assisted in the creation of some of the first free villages in Barbados.[25]	
1843	June 6, Samuel Jackman Prescod, the illegitimate son of a free-coloured woman and a white planter was elected by black, coloured and white voters in Bridgetown to the Assembly as their representative, the first man of known black ancestry to sit in the House.	*Graham Rhyder marries Fiona*
1845	The imperial education grant, issued	

	in 1834, was terminated.	
1846	Pressed by Governor Grey and the radical coloured activist, Samuel Prescod, planters reluctantly voted to supply £750 for the education of the "poor" for three years. It was considered a meager, if not insulting, amount. Planters supported religious instruction for blacks as part of their renewed campaign to 'improve their morality and character, and to create a docile labour force'.	
1847		*Graham Rhyder's wife, Fiona Rhyder dies.*
1848	Barbados exports 659,073 lbs. of sugar. A two-year cholera outbreak began in England and Wales in 1848, and claimed 52,000 lives	
1849	In 1849, a second major cholera outbreak occurred in Paris. In London, it was the worst outbreak in the city's history, claiming 14,137 lives, over twice as many as the 1832 outbreak. In 1849, cholera claimed 5,308 lives in the major port city of Liverpool, England, an embarkation point for immigrants to North America, and 1,834 in Hull, England.[It is believed more than 150,000 Americans died during the two pandemics between 1832 and 1849.	*Graham taken home by Friend Nathaniel and resides with him for 6 months.* *Graham Rhyder hired as manager of Windermere.*
1850	Barbados exports 831,534 lbs. of sugar. Many black Bajans leave, to help build the Panama Canal between 1850 and 1914.[26]	
1851	Barbados Public Health Act addressed matters of sanitation.	*Steam engine, at Graham Rhyder's encouragement is purchased and replaces windmill power at Windermere.*
1852	Barbados exports 951,726 lbs. of	

	sugar.	
1853	Public Health Act begins to use preventive measures regarding sanitation.	*December: Mena arrives at Windermere Plantation (Age 23) (Graham 33)*
1854	20,000 die from cholera in Barbados. Bridgetown was reported to be the most unsanitary town in the West Indies: water was polluted, open cesspools and canals were used to remove sewage from households, gutters were clogged and stinking, filth lay about even major thoroughfares.	
1854	Barbados exports 945,849 lbs. of sugar.	
1856	Public health Act – Bridgetown divided into 7 districts, 2 medical officers for each district, General hospital put under control of the central government, basics of health included in school curricula, planters recognized that centralized public health was vital	
1856	Barbados exports 971,028 lbs. of sugar.	
1858	Barbados exports 1,468,449 lbs. of sugar.	
1859	Twelve steam factories exist on Barbados for processing sugar.	
1878	4,982 freeholders of land.	
1884	Sugar crisis – prices plummet from a high of 19 in 1883 to a low of 9.3 in 1897	

Bibliography

Books

Bajan Proverbs, By Margo Blackman, Published in Montreal, Canada 1982, ISBN 0-9699 572-0-3

Natural Rebels: A Social History of Enslaved Black Women in Barbados, By Hilary Beckles, Rutgers University Press, New Brunswick, NJ, 1989, ISBN 0-8135-1510-6

A History of Barbados From Amerindian Settlement to Nation-State, By Hilary Beckles, Cambridge University Press, New York, 1990, ISBN 0-521 35879 5

A True and Exact History of the Island of Barbados, By Richard Ligon, Hackett Publishing Company, Inc., Indianapolis, IN, 2011 (originally published 1657), ISBN 978-1-60384-620-2

English Women's Clothing in the Nineteenth Century, By C. Willett Cunnington, Published by Dover Publications, Inc., New York, 1990, ISBN 0-486-26323-1

To Hell or Barbados: The Ethnic Cleansing of Ireland, By Sean O'Callaghan, Brandon Publishing Company, London, 2000, ISBN 978-0863222870

The Unappropriated People: Freedmen in the Slave Society of Barbados, By Jerome S. Handler, Johns Hopkins University Press, 1974, ISBN 0-8018-1565-7

Slavery & Theology: Writings of Seven Quaker Reformers 1800-1870, edited by Hugh Barbour, 1985, Library of Congress #: 85-070109

The Bridge Barbados, By Patrick Roach, printed in Barbados by Coles Printery Limited, Wildey, St. Michael

Testimony of an Irish Slave Girl, By Kate McCafferty, Penguin Books, 2002, ISBN 0-14-200183X

Articles/Websites

"Red Legs": Class and Color Contradictions in Barbados, Peter Simmons, Ministry of Education, Bridgeton, Barbados: 1982.

Some Aspects of Work Organization on Sugar Plantations in Barbados, By Jerome Handler, Southern Illinois University, Source: *Ethnology,* Vol. 4, No. 1 (January. 1965), pp. 16-38, Published by University of Pittsburgh, 6/19/2009
http://www.jeromehandler.org/wp-content/uploads/2009/07/WorkOrg-65.pdf

A Bajan Tour Girl Exploring Barbados, "White Slavery & Servitude in Barbados", May 15, 2010,
http://abajantourgirlexploringbarbados.blogspot.com/2010/05/white-slavery-and-servitude-in-barbados.html

Migration to, from & within the British Isles: EXODUS Movement of the People, "Indentured Servants to the West Indies, http://www.exodus2013.co.uk/tag/barbados/

Natural History Museum, Seeds of Trade, The Agriculture of Sugar Cane, http://www.nhm.ac.uk/nature-online/life/plants-fungi/seeds-of-trade/page.dsml?section=regions&region_ID=7&page=agriculture&ref=sugar_cane

Barbados Historical Time Line, 1913 Barbados Plantations Owners Names, http://www.creolelinks.com/barbados-time-line.html

BBC History, "Slavery & Economy in Barbados", by Dr. Karl Watson,
http://www.bbc.co.uk/history/british/empire_seapower/barbados_01.shtml

Tangled Roots, "Barbadosed: Africans & Irish in Barbados",
http://www.yale.edu/glc/tangledroots/Barbadosed.htm

"Antigua: How a Sugar Plantation Works" http://areyn-history.blogspot.com/2008/03/antigua-how-sugar-plantations-work.html

"Betty's Hope, Antigua: A Tour of a Colonial Sugar Plantation
http://www.rootsweb.ancestry.com/~atgwgw/bettyshope/betty.html

"The Hysterical Female"
http://www.lib.uwo.ca/archives/virtualexhibits/londonasylum/hysteria.html

"Hanwell Pauper and Lunatic Asylum"
http://en.wikipedia.org/wiki/Hanwell_Asylum

About The Author

Susan McGeown is a wife, mother, daughter, sister, friend, aunt, uncle (don't ask), teacher, author … but, most importantly, a "woman after God's own heart." Always working on a new book, she writes historical novels (including *Rosamund's Bower*, 2008 RCRW's Golden Rose winner in the category of 'Novel with Romantic Elements'), contemporary fiction novels, and nonfiction Bible studies.

She's been a teacher, a conference leader, a public speaker, a children's minister, a deacon, an elder, a vacation Bible school coordinator, a preschool director, and a Bible study leader yet writing stories is just about the best way she can imagine spending her time.

Living in Bridgewater, New Jersey, with her husband of over twenty years and their three children, each of Sue's stories champions those emotions nearest and dearest to her: faith, joy, hope and love.

Philippians 1:20-21 *I earnestly expect and hope that I will in no way be ashamed but will have sufficient courage so that now, as always, Christ will be exalted in my life. For me, to live is Christ and to die is gain.*

Footnotes

1 Esther 4:14, King James Version
2 2 Timothy 1:7, King James Version
3 Romans 8:28, King James Version
4 Isaiah 41:10, King James Version
5 Esther 4:14, King James Version
6 An Analysis of the Law of England, by William Blackstone, first published by Clarendon Press in 1756.
7 "Joy to the World" written by Isaac Watts, an English hymn writer, based on Psalm 98 in the Bible. The song was first published in 1719 in Watts' collection; *The Psalms of David: Imitated in the language of the New Testament, and applied to the Christian state and worship.* The hymn was written intending to glorify Christ's triumphant return at the end of the end rather than celebrating His first coming. The music that was adapted and arranged to Watts' lyrics by Lowell Mason in 1839 were from an older melody which was then believed to have originated from Handel.
8 This is a modification of a preventative Cholera poster put out by the Parish of St. Marylebone (London) in 1854 found at:
https://wcclibraries.wordpress.com/2011/07/26/cholera-london%E2%80%99s-solution-to-a-medical-mystery/
9 Count That Day Lost by George Eliot
http://famouspoetsandpoems.com/poets/george_eliot/poems/3448
MARY ANN EVANS was born at Griff House, England, near Nuneaton, November 22, 1820. Upon reaching womanhood, she married the eminent English author, George H. Lewes. By his suggestion, she commenced to write fiction. Her literary name was George Eliot, and by that name we shall know her in the world of letters. She died in London, December 22, 1880.

10 I could not find any actual 19th century writings which specifically addressed the concept of "Female Hysteria" in the manner I wished to present it for this section of the book. Female Hysteria was a diagnosis given to many 19th century women who failed to fit the "acceptable model" of what a "proper woman" should be. So I altered the current day article "The Hysterical Female"
http://www.lib.uwo.ca/archives/virtualexhibits/londonasylum/hysteria.html
to fit my purposes as a written description that might be used by the actual Hanwell Pauper and Lunatic Asylum in West London. "Hanwell Pauper and Lunatic Asylum" http://en.wikipedia.org/wiki/Hanwell_Asylum In no way have I compromised the intent of the article regarding this diagnosis.
11 http://cultivate.coop/wiki/Rochdale_Principles
12 Proverbs 16:3, King James Version
13 http://www.yale.edu/glc/tangledroots/Barbadosed.htm

[14] https://barbadosfreepress.wordpress.com/2009/12/28/irish-times-most-barbados-red-legs-have-bad-or-no-teeth-many-blind-without-limbs/

[15] http://mullinsbay.blogspot.com/2008/08/cholera-epidemic-of-mid-19th-century.html

[16] http://www.mazefind.co.uk/cgi-bin/cms/ohra.pl?content_id=1040001433

[17] http://19thcentury.wordpress.com/2007/12/05/female-hysteria/

[18] http://www.lib.uwo.ca/archives/virtualexhibits/londonasylum/hysteria.html

[19] http://en.wikipedia.org/wiki/Wandering_womb

[20] http://www.lib.uwo.ca/archives/virtualexhibits/londonasylum/hysteria.html

[21] http://www.exodus2013.co.uk/tag/slavery/

[22] http://abajantourgirlexploringbarbados.blogspot.com/2010/05/white-slavery-and-servitude-in-barbados.html

[23] *To Hell or Barbados The Ethnic Cleansing of Ireland*, By Sean O'Callaghan, Brandon Publishing Company, London, 2000, ISBN 978-0863222870, p. 209

[24] http://en.wikipedia.org/wiki/Cholera_outbreaks_and_pandemics#cite_note-5

[25] http://www.totallybarbados.com/barbados/About_Barbados/Local_Information/History/1184.htm

[26] http://www.courses.vcu.edu/ENGsnh/Caribbean/Barbados/history.htm